The Sorcerer's SCOURGE

BROCK E. DESKINS

A huge water elemental, apparently furious at being pulled from its home, lifted the young mage from the ground and prepared to smash her small body against the stone steps of the church.

"Children, you must banish that creature!" Brother Thomas exclaimed to his three young Chosen of Solarian.

Banishing a creature back to its home plane was not something a normal novitiate would be expected to perform. However, this, like Azerick's mage school, was no ordinary seminary. Brother Thomas's students were pushed to learn and excel just as the wizard and martial students were. It would take all three working together and even then, Brother Thomas was extremely concerned.

Shawna, Angela, and Caleb began the complex ritual of banishment, but luckily, Roger was faster. Roger pulled a wet piece of rock salt from his spell pouch and channeled the Source into it. Jumping to his feet, he lunged at the elemental, slammed the hand holding the halite against the water being, and released his spell.

The effect was instantaneous. The water under his hand froze solid and rapidly spread to the creature's base and up toward the arm holding his friend several feet in the air. Roger continued to pour energy into the spell until the giant watery hand holding Ellyssa froze solid. Roger knew he could not hold the powerful creature in stasis for long and prayed that the three Chosen could banish it. Already the ice was melting as the monster's will overcame his magic. Just as he was sure he was going to lose control, the water elemental lost all cohesion and vanished with a splash, dropping Ellyssa painfully onto the wet, muddy, and unyielding ground..

PROLOGUE

(10 YEARS BEFORE ULRIC'S DEATH)

The tavern was bright and cheery as Landrin played his lute and sang for the crowd at the Prancing Pig in the beautiful city of Brightridge. He kept most of his songs joyous and playful, avoiding the heart-rending ballads that made women weep and men think about the hard times. The people certainly needed cheering these days.

The king was dead, but a son that no one even knew existed, Jarvin, ascended the throne and swore to end the long war with Sumara. It was the third night in a row for a packed house as word had gotten around of his lyrical voice, and he was making a small fortune just in tips. He played on top of a table next to the fire that burned in the large stone hearth, painting the nearby surfaces in a wavering orange glow.

He returned the smiles of the fair women in attendance as he strummed his lute and sang a ballad of love found, not a tragedy, which women always liked. He was dressed in maroon trews, a purple silk shirt, a black velvet vest, and a pair of soft, black, doeskin boots. He was a handsome man and he did not feel arrogant or conceited in the least for being aware of that fact. He had wavy, shoulder-length black hair, kept his strong jaw clean-shaven, and stood just under six feet in height. Although people came for the music, his looks played nearly as great a role in his tips as did the lyrical quality of his voice.

As the evening wore on, his tip jar grew full again. He emptied most of the coins into his pack, wetted his throat with some ale, and began another song. The hour was getting late and the crowd started thinning out. Landrin decided that he would play two or three more songs and call it an evening.

A candle mark later, most of the inn's patrons had left, and the serving women started putting the chairs up onto the tables and sweeping up. The innkeeper was wiping down the bar when Landrin approached him for his payment.

"You really brought them in, Landrin," the portly but friendly barman beamed. "I made a tidy profit even after subtracting your wage. I wish I could keep you around for a bit. Have you ever thought about settling down in town? You would have regular work year round without all the hazards on the roads these days."

Thousands of soldiers returning from the war found themselves without work, and many had turned to banditry and slavery as a means to support themselves. Only the foolish or truly brave traveled these days without an armed escort. Even the streets of the prosperous cities like Brightridge and Southport were becoming increasingly dangerous.

"Sorry, Amos, I have the bard's wanderlust as well as his tongue," the musician replied. "I would go stark raving mad if I stayed more than a week in any one town."

"There are a lot of ladies here that wish you would stay," Amos urged, trying to get the bard to change his mind.

"And there are hundreds more in Brelland that wish I would not keep them waiting," Landrin shot back with a sly wink.

"Aye, Brelland and near every city and town in Valeria I'll wager!" Amos joined in with a laugh. "All right then, here you are," the innkeeper said as he handed the bard a pouch of coins. "You stop back at the Prancing Pig the next time you find yourself in Brightridge, and I'll top anything anyone else offers you for your first performance."

"I will, Amos. You have my word," Landrin assured him as he hefted the pouch in his hand a couple of times before tucking it into his pocket. "Take care now. I hope to come back through Brightridge by summer festival."

"The door will be open to you, have no doubt about that. You have a good evening."

Landrin slung his pack and lute case onto his shoulder as he stepped out into the frigid night air. The temperature was below freezing, but fortunately, this area rarely got much snow even in the winter. Landrin considered that a plus as he thought about his trip to

Brelland, the capital of Valeria. He hated traveling through the sleet and snow, and Brelland promised plenty of both if he left at the wrong time. He pulled his heavy cloak tighter against the chill wind and started walking back toward his own inn several blocks away.

A movement caught his eye as he passed by an alleyway. The flickering, oil-fueled street lamp briefly illuminated the fleeting image of a dark shape. He gripped his rapier as he slowed his steps and peered toward the mouth of the darkened alley, watchful for muggers or cutpurses who might mistake him for an easy target. As much as he enjoyed looking and playing the part of a dandy, he was quite competent in using his needle-sharp rapier to deadly effect. In a pinch, he could also call upon a small bit of wizard magic that he learned at his relatively short stay at the Academy in Southport.

He spied the silhouette of what appeared to be a couple having a late evening tryst, perhaps even a prostitute arguing with a customer, although he found it hard to believe that anyone would even try to conduct such business in this bitter cold. More likely, it was a couple from the inn whose blood was running hot from his music and the alcohol, and they had decided to duck out of the light for a quick kiss and nuzzle.

He was about to walk past with little more than a nod and smile of greeting when he heard a whimpering cry escape the woman's lips. The sound made him turn and take a closer look. The lamplight reflected off what Landrin thought may have been a tear streaking down the woman's face. Ever the gallant, the bard was compelled to interrupt and determine if the damsel was indeed in distress.

"Is everything alright? Milady, do you require assistance?" Landrin inquired as he shifted the small load on his back.

"Be gone, young popinjay. This is no concern of yours," a thin voice hissed out from the shadows.

Landrin dropped his pack, set his lute quickly but gently on the ground, and drew his rapier.

"I'm afraid I must insist that you release the woman and let her step out into the light so she can tell me herself if this is my business or not," Landrin challenged the dark figure, feeling more and more uncomfortable with the situation.

"You will find no glory in your heroics tonight. Only your death resides within these shadows if you do not leave immediately," threatened the figure holding the woman.

"We shall see, rogue."

Landrin conjured a bright magical light with his free hand so he could see whom he was fighting and if there was more than one waiting for him in the alley as he stalked forward, rapier up, ready to defend himself.

The man hissed a curse as the bright light fell upon him. He was dressed in dark colors that contrasted sharply with his extraordinarily pale skin. He lunged at the bard with astonishing speed, his long, sharp-nailed fingers extended before him as if he meant to rip out the throat of the nuisance that dared to interrupt his activities.

Although prepared for the attack, Landrin was barely able to bring his slim blade around in a quick slash that cut one of the man's hands deeply across the palm. The bard spun to the side as the man continued his charge. Landrin found it inconceivable that anyone could move so fast. Even a cut across the hand would cause most people to pause, given its depth. However, before his spin even brought him around to face his attacker, he felt a burning slash across his back and the warm trickle of blood as it ran down in several rivulets to pool at the small of his back where his shirt was tucked into his trousers.

"You should have left us alone, warm blood. Now it will be your blood I savor tonight," the dark figure hissed malignly.

Landrin barely had a second to try to figure out exactly what the man meant before he threw himself at the would-be rescuer with that impossible quickness. However, Landrin was no slouch when it came to defending himself and was better prepared for the charge. He brought his rapier down in a wickedly quick jab as he snapped his left arm out straight, trailed his right leg behind, and leaned into the thrust by shifting his weight onto the forward foot to add power to his lunge.

It was a textbook perfect move, but the man managed to dart to the side. The slender blade pierced the flesh and slid between the ribs of the rushing figure well right of the heart at which Landrin had aimed. Although not immediately lethal, it was still a grievous wound that would stop most men in their tracks, or at least make them balk at pressing on. Nevertheless, the man continued his charge, throwing his body against Landrin's extended blade and struck the bard in the chest with his fist.

Landrin flew back and hit the wall heavily as the man grasped the handle of his rapier and pulled it out of his body.

This is not possible! Landrin thought as the man casually tossed the sword aside as if it were no more than an annoyance.

It was then that Landrin realized he was not dealing with a mugger, thief, or even a man for that matter. It was a vampire! The very thought sent ice coursing through his veins. He had heard legends about the powerful and evil creatures, but he had given them scant attention. He dismissed them as old wives' tales and stories used to frighten children.

A scream filled the alley and the bard was unsure whether it was his or if the woman had finally broken whatever spell held her in shock and kept her from fleeing. Landrin gave the woman the credit since he was hardly able to draw a breath much less produce a scream of that magnitude.

"I can tell from the look in your eyes and the smell of fear wafting from your body that you finally realize what is about to kill you this night," the vampire said with a cruel humor in its voice as it stalked toward him once again.

Landrin stood, called upon his wizardly power, and sent three magical bolts of energy into the foul, undead creature. For once, his attack elicited a response other than amusement as the creature let out a hiss of pain and anger. The bard's elation at actually having hurt the vampire was short-lived as the undead abomination hurled himself at him, leaping across the alley with apparent ease and crushing Landrin in his cold, deadly embrace.

Landrin felt the vampire squeeze the air from his lungs while a fiery burst of pain lanced through his neck when the needle-sharp fangs pierced and tore his skin. Helpless, Landrin could only stand against his will as the incredibly strong grip of the vampire held him up while his blood poured down his neck. Landrin felt a certain detachment as the vampire feasted upon the blood pumping from the horrific wound. The light of the distant streetlamp started growing dim as he slowly lost consciousness. Darkness finally took him as his body succumbed to the blood loss.

Eldon preferred the blood of young, attractive women, but this buffoon had interrupted him. He was still annoyed at that, but fortunately, the bard was not a bad substitute. The young popinjay was healthy and his minor control of magic gave his blood a rare flavor as exquisite as a fine wine. He thought about taking the woman back home to drink from another day but realized that she had fled.

He was just moments from finishing off the last of the blood from his latest victim when he heard the rapid stomping of booted feet, the flickering of torches, and the shouts of men coming down the street. The appearance of a few locals did not concern him. He could fight and kill a roomful of average men with little fear of being harmed, but he had a good life here and did not want to attract too much attention by slaughtering a score of men and having their bodies found strewn about the street to be discovered in the morning. Nor would it please his master to reveal himself to the populace until it was time. As it was, his victim's death would likely be attributed to some brutal murder by a desperate hoodlum, surprised in his attempt at robbing or ravishing the woman who had fled and summoned help.

As the sound of footsteps grew near, he decided to flee, his hunger satiated for a few days. He ran down the alley, leapt a full twenty feet up to land on the roof of a two-story building, and disappeared across the rooftops into the night.

The men entered the alley with their torches casting wavering light on the walls, brandishing all manner of weapons from shortswords and a meat cleaver, to several cudgels and a few butcher knives. They peered into the shadows cast by the flickering light of the torches and saw the body of the young, handsome bard lying in the filthy alley. One of the men walked closer, bent down to inspect the body, and looked into the open blue eyes of the dead singer.

"Bloody hell, that's Landrin. He just sang at my inn tonight," Amos quietly announced. "Poor fool decided to be a hero like the ones in his songs and paid dearly for it," Amos said as he closed the bard's eyes.

***

Landrin opened his eyes and initially saw only darkness. Panic gripped him as he tried to raise his hands only to strike something hard just a few inches above his body. His eyes adjusted to the dark and he made out the grain within the wall of wood that was only a few inches in front of his face.

By the gods, they thought I was dead and they buried me. They buried me alive!

Panic gave way to terror as the bard screamed at the top of his lungs. He shouted until his voice became little more than a raspy wheeze, and then started punching at the top of the pine wood box. The fear of being buried alive gave strength to his attack as he repeatedly struck and clawed at the lid of his tomb.

The cracking of the soft wood rewarded his struggles as it gave way under the force of his terror-driven blows. Landrin forced his fingernails into the wood where it had split and tore at it in frenzy. Dirt showered his body as he ripped chunks of wood from the coffin lid.

I'll suffocate under the dirt, he thought, but he was determined to free himself from his grave.

More dark soil ran into the wooden box as he tore through the lid and turned the fissure into a gaping hole. The cascade of dirt covered his face as he destroyed the planks above him. His panic increased as it filled his mouth and nose and covered his eyes.

Finally free of the wooden barrier, he frantically clawed at the dirt as it pressed in all around and above him. Landrin thrust his hands above him and pulled the soil down into the wooden box in his bid to burrow his way to freedom. His struggles seemed to go on for an eternity, and he was sure that whatever air he had stored in his lungs would never last long enough to see him escape his underground prison. Elation filled him as he felt his hand burst out of the soil and grasp at the cool night air above.

Landrin pulled himself out of the terrifying embrace of the engulfing soil and let out the stale air he held in his lungs. Or he would have if he had been holding his breath. He realized that he had no air in his lungs, in fact, he was not breathing at all. He had to have been breathing in order to shout. He drew in a deep lungful of air and let it out. He drew in another, whistled, and hummed as he was normally able to do, but now he actually had to think about it, had to concentrate on performing the action that used to come as naturally as, well, breathing.

The vampire, he thought as he recalled the fight with the evil creature. *It can't be! It's not possible! What can I do? Where can I go? Is there a cure?*

Those and a hundred other questions raced through his mind. He studied his hands. His nails should have been ripped out by his clawing at the coffin and digging his way out of several feet of dirt and stone, but they were sharp and intact. He looked around the graveyard where he had been buried on the outskirts of the city. His eyes pierced the darkness like a dagger through cloth. Everything stood out in stark detail. He stared up at the sky and saw easily tenfold the number of stars that he recalled seeing when he was alive.

When he was alive. He nearly choked on the thought. He became aware of something else—a hunger. A hunger like none he had ever felt before burned in his stomach and in his soul. Or whatever it was that he now possessed. He craved sustenance of some kind and knew the direction in which he could find it. The bard walked back toward the city, drawn by the craving as his mind continued to try to come to terms with this new reality. He knew the gates would be closed and guarded at this time of night, especially since the former king had just recently been assassinated. He sought out the shadows and swiftly crept up to the darkness-shrouded base of the thirty-foot wall surrounding the city.

He dug his fingers into the slim cracks of the tight-fitting stones and lifted himself up. Landrin was amazed at the ease with which he was able to support his own weight as he crawled up the sheer face of the wall. He braced his feet against the stone and felt them find purchase where he should have found none. His feet seemed to cling to the wall with a will all their own.

The bard pulled his hard, sharp fingernails out from between the large cut stones, placed a hand against the wall, and felt it grip the stone just as his feet did. He tried it with the other hand with the same results. He hung ten feet above the ground clinging to the stone like a spider. In his elation at discovering this newfound talent, he almost forgot the horrible price he had paid to attain it. He climbed up the wall, his movements swift and his handholds secure, and perched himself on the top as he surveyed his surroundings. He could smell the scent of the living. It was not just the sweat and filth he smelled, but their blood as well—and he craved it. He knew he would stop at nothing to attain it to feed his hunger.

Landrin knew that even at this late hour, the streets would not be empty. Thieves, prostitutes, and their customers wandered the dark byways and alleys. He dropped to the ground thirty feet below and stalked down the dark lanes in search of his quarry.

It did not take long before he found his first living prey. Several men, sailors from the look of them, staggered down the street toward him, likely returning to their ship after a hard night's drinking and carousing. Landrin decided to let them pass unmolested. He felt certain that he could kill them all, but that would make far too much noise and attract too much attention. He was not entirely certain of his power yet. It could be fatal to overestimate his strength and abilities. He laughed aloud at the thought after remembering to draw a breath.

His laughter caught the attention of a prostitute standing under an oil-fueled streetlamp. She shot him a smile and batted her painted eyelids at him. Fortunately, in the darkness she could not see the dirt that still clung to his clothes and hair.

"Looking for a good time, handsome stranger?" the woman of the night asked flirtatiously.

"Indeed. You might say I am starved for some companionship," Landrin said, chuckling at his little jest.

The former bard walked over to the woman and asserted his will upon her.

"Come. Follow me, My Lady," he gently commanded as he guided her by the elbow to the unlit alley across the street.

He looked into her blank stare as the pulsating artery in her neck drew his eyes. Landrin could see and smell the blood flowing just under the skin. He leaned forward as he tilted her head back, his lips brushing the perfumed, tender flesh that his sharp fangs would rend apart like tissue paper.

"No!" he shouted, shoving the woman away from him. "Go! Run away as fast as you can!" *I cannot do this! I will not do to others as was done to me. I will not make another vampire and I will not take a life like an animal!*

He dropped to his knees and prayed to Solarian, god of light, that he would never take a life just to feed his wicked desire. He would never create another vampire. He would never allow himself to become the instrument of ultimate evil or spread the disease that was their existence.

"What have we here? It looks like a pretty little bird got out of its cage," a voice sneered at him through the opening of the alley. "I hope you didn't give that whore all your coin before she ran off. What are you doing down there? Did she stick ya for your coin instead of you sticking her?" he laughed as he pulled out a knife and advanced toward his target.

"Leave me alone if you value your life," Landrin advised, not even looking up at the man who threatened him.

"You're not in a good position to be makin' threats, boyo. Now give me all of your coin, jewelry, and anything else you have of value. Those look like good boots. I'll take those too."

"I said go away," Landrin hissed as he sprang to his feet with a speed and grace that surprised the mugger.

"You shouldn't have made this hard, boyo, but I guess I'm going to have to kill you for it now," he said as he lunged forward, thrusting the knife deep into Landrin's chest.

"You're too late. Someone else already beat you to it," the vampire said as he reached out and grabbed the man by the throat.

He bent the man's head to the side and opened up his neck with a slice from a razor-sharp fingernail. He placed his mouth over the pumping gore and drank hungrily until it slowed to a trickle then stopped completely. The man struggled briefly and futilely against his iron grip. The man pulled the knife out of Landrin's chest and tried to stab him again, but he lost the strength to drive the blade home.

Satiated, Landrin released his hold and let the dead body crumple to the ground. The realization of what he had just done filled him with horror, and he dropped to his knees, nearly retching the entire contents of his stomach back out onto the ground.

I had to kill him! He attacked me, and he was an evil man and deserved to die. I did not bite into him, so he should not rise again, he thought as he tried to rationalize what he had done.

Landrin decided he could live with it. He chuckled again at the unintended joke. *I will have to drink human blood from time to time in order to survive, but I do not have to murder people to get it.*

He tried to appease his guilt with this seemingly rational argument, but knew he was only fooling himself. He could not live this way. He would not live this way. He would find another way. He had to. Landrin also knew that he had to find someone. He did not know whom, but he knew he needed to seek them out, wherever they were. Some unknown sense pointed him in the direction that he must go to find them, and he knew they were not far off. Across the city perhaps, no farther. He followed the direction in which his instinct compelled him to go, and set off in search of whoever waited for him.

Landrin stuck close to the shadows of the street as he stalked across the city, pulled by some unknown force to some unknown place. Traveling in the darkest shadows seemed to comfort him like a warm blanket on a cold night. And it was a cold night, but he felt no discomfort nor did his breath fog the air when he chose to take one. A large, mangy cur darted out of an alley and growled at him only to tuck its tail between its legs and run when Landrin glared at it. He could smell the fear and urine the beast left behind in its flight.

His movements were swift, and although he had crossed half the city, he did not feel the slightest bit of fatigue. Being undead certainly had its advantages.

No! he shouted at himself. *I must not take pleasure in this form or I will be lost to the madness and evil that it represents. I must keep control or I will lose myself and everything I ever was!*

He knew he was getting near his destination and began to wonder what fate awaited him. He was in the wealthier merchant district now and soon found himself standing at the gates of a large manor. Landrin looked up and down the street to ensure no one was around to observe him before he leapt the ten-foot wrought-iron gate with ease. He landed on the other side of the gate without a sound, and keeping to the shadows once again, crept toward the impressive house.

The mansion was a three-story brick and stucco affair with an elaborate balcony wrapping around the entire second and third floor. Once again, he tensed his legs beneath him and sprang high up into the air to land with a cat's grace upon the second-floor balcony. He located an unlocked, glass-paned double door and slipped silently inside.

Whatever force had led him to this mansion was now throbbing almost painfully inside his skull. He knew he was close to whatever it was he was supposed to find here. He opened the door to the vacant bedroom that he had entered from the balcony and stepped into a grand hallway. As he turned toward the direction of the urging, an incredibly powerful hand seized him by the throat and shoved him back hard into the wall.

"You have chosen the wrong house to rob tonight, little thief," a familiar voice hissed into his ear.

Landrin reacted instantly, knocking the hand away from his throat, and delivering a powerful punch into the man's chest, driving him back several steps. The blow would have nearly killed a normal man, but the owner of the manor was far from ordinary as recognition blossomed on both men's faces.

"You!" Landrin cried out in shock and rage.

"Well, if it isn't the gallant hero," the vampire laughed mockingly.

Landrin charged at the vampire who had replaced his life with this abominated undead substitution.

"What have you done to me?" the enraged bard demanded as he lunged at the vile creature that had cursed him to an eternity as an undead monster.

As fast as Landrin's new body was, his speed and power were no match for that of the elder vampire. The older creature easily sidestepped his attack and sent him reeling with a blow to his side. Plaster cracked and crumbled to the tile floor of the hall when Landrin's body struck the wall.

Landrin was amazed and terrified at the speed and power with which this other vampire moved, but he refused to submit or run from him. This *thing* took away his life and cursed him with something far worse than death. The least he could get from this battle would be a proper death. Landrin picked himself up off the floor and prepared for another assault. He charged forward, bent on enacting his revenge on this foul creature or achieving his own end.

"Stop," the elder vampire softly commanded.

Despite his burning rage and overwhelming desire for revenge, that simple, single word arrested Landrin's charge. All he could do was stand there as he dropped his hands to his sides in supplication.

"Interesting," the vampire mused. "I guess that warm-blooded rabble interrupted me prematurely. I really had no interest in creating another lesser servant, especially a male. I have one already I can hardly tolerate. Now I must decide if I wish to destroy you or keep you."

The vampire slowly circled the mind-bound bard. "What do you think I should do? Go ahead. You may answer."

Landrin gritted his teeth in impotent fury. "Kill me. Do it quickly because if you give me even the slightest chance, I will kill you."

Landrin watched the vampire's face twist with indignation at the temerity of the fledgling, and for a moment Landrin thought he would get his wish. Then the vampire looked away as if listening to someone speak. The creature nodded and returned his attention to his captive.

"No, I think I shall keep you with me. My master thinks your minor grasp of magic may be improved upon and you can be of use to his plans."

"No! Kill me or I will destroy you, I swear it!"

"Not likely. I created you. Therefore, I control you utterly until I choose to release you. You will do precisely what I say when I say it, or even think it. If you do not…"

Landrin dropped to the floor, writhing in agony. He felt as if every nerve in his body were on fire.

"My name is Eldon VonTrellin, but you will refer to me as master. Now, pick yourself up. You will find suitable clothing in the bedroom you just came through. Consider it yours, but know you must retire to the catacombs beneath the house before the sun comes up. Now, go."

Landrin regained his feet and processed what Eldon had just told him. He could throw himself out into the street and let Solarian's cleansing rays purge him of this affliction. Perhaps then he would find his peace in death and join his god in the afterlife.

The vampire spoke even as he thought this. "You shall not cast yourself away. My master has plans for you, plans that are years in the making. However, that is but a blink of the eye for such as us. Go now and do not entertain such foolish thoughts again."

Landrin wanted to deny this monster. He wanted to disobey him and tear open the heavy curtains of the bedroom the instant the sun broke the horizon, but all he could do was say, "Yes, master," and do precisely as he was told.

CHAPTER 1

Azerick and Rusty stood nervously outside the great double doors, knowing that on the other side lay at least two hundred people just waiting for the sorcerer to appear. Azerick gripped his staff firmly in his hand, reassured by its presence despite knowing it would be useless against what faced him in the chamber beyond.

"It's all right, Az," Rusty reassured his best friend. "I have your back."

The sorcerer swallowed hard, took a deep breath, and pushed through the doors. The assault was instantaneous. His entire body shook under the massive sonic onslaught that struck him with the force of a strong wind. Azerick felt defenseless. Despite being surrounded on all sides, it was the figure awaiting him at the far end of the massive vaulted chamber that nearly dropped him to his knees.

Lady Miranda looked so stunning dressed in dozens of layers of white and light blue silk and lace that Azerick could no longer even hear the horns that blasted throughout the cathedral. His legs seemed to carry him forward of their own volition, almost floating above the golden carpet in a semi-dream state. The golden rays of the sun streaming through the majestic stained-glass window of Solarian's temple bathed his bride-to-be in an aura of angelic radiance.

Azerick was amazed at the number of people in attendance. Every bench was packed to capacity. Even King Jarvin sat firmly wedged between his wife, Duchess Mellina, and Prelate Howarth, the residing lord of Brightridge. The ranking nobility would not be so tightly seated had Azerick not insisted that half the cathedral be reserved for the men, women, and children who worked and studied at his school. This, of course, was not well received by the nobles, which pleased Azerick immensely.

The young groom looked up at the enormous stained-glass window set high in the wall of the steepled ceiling and spied a human form just on the other side, peering in. Azerick's first response was alarm, certain that some assassin was set to kill him, or worse yet, Miranda, to make him suffer for some pain he had caused someone. His eyes adjusted to the bright surface and recognized Wolf's grubby face peering through one of the clear panes. The wildling caught Azerick's gaze, flashed a bright smile, and gave him a thumbs-up through the window.

Azerick could not contain the laugh that came out as a strangled snort. His face reddened as everyone paused to look at him as if he had gone mad. Embarrassed, the sorcerer mouthed *sorry* to Miranda and the priest and begged him to continue.

Bishop Edmonton droned on about the purity and sanctity of marriage for what seemed an eternity before finally getting to the part Azerick had been waiting for—the end. And it was none too soon. Azerick felt as though his legs were going to give out if he had to stand here any longer.

"Do you, Lord Azerick Giles, Magus, Savior of North Haven, and Defender of the Crown take Lady Miranda Covaire, First Daughter of North Haven, to be your wife to love, honor, and defend unto death?"

Azerick wanted to say something sharp and witty, but one look at Miranda's brilliant eyes and joyous face stole away everything but the profound love he had for her.

"I do," he simply but wholeheartedly replied.

"And do you, Lady Miranda Covaire, First Daughter of North Haven, take Lord Azerick Giles to be your husband to love, honor, and cherish unto death?"

Miranda looked up into Azerick's nervous but adoring face and replied, "I do—until he aggravates me and I crack his thick skull with a mace."

Miranda smiled broadly as Azerick and the bishop gave her a shocked look while several in attendance, particularly those familiar with the sorcerer's contrary nature, gave her jest a polite chuckle.

The priest cleared his throat and continued. "Then by the power vested in me, as witnessed by the people, and consecrated under the glow of Solarian's holy radiance, I pronounce you married."

Azerick's heart raced as he leaned in and kissed his bride. Miranda returned his kiss with equal love and passion and the pair held each other in a tight embrace for several long moments. The couple was so lost in each other's arms that the loud cheering and clapping, mostly from Azerick's side of the chapel, did not even register with them until they finally untwined themselves from their shared embrace.

Flower petals rained down upon the newlyweds as they exited the cathedral and made their way to the luxurious open coach. Peck stood grinning from ear to ear in his fine suit as Azerick and Miranda approached. The palace had an official coach driver for such special events, but Azerick once again insisted on having his personal coachman drive them despite Peck being only twelve years old.

Azerick thought everyone in the city must have been crowding into the cathedral, but that assumption proved false as the carriage took a long and meandering ride through the city on their way to the castle for the reception. The castle was less than a mile from the cathedral, but due to the twisting parade route, it took nearly an hour at the sedate pace they traveled.

People lined the streets block after block, just waiting to catch a glimpse of the newlyweds. Loud cheers rang out as the coach, headed by a mounted contingent of castle guards dressed in their ceremonial armor, reached each new turn. They finally arrived at the steps of the castle where the chamberlain was waiting to hustle the pair into the grand ballroom.

More horns blared to announce Azerick and Miranda's arrival. The myriad conversations ceased as the guests of honor entered the room, a room nearly as equally divided as the cathedral had been. Azerick noticed that his people were largely on one side of the room. They mostly gathered around the table that held the banquet, while the elites gathered amongst themselves, several eyeing the feast table as if they expected to have to lay siege to it if they wanted to partake in the bounty.

Azerick could not help the grim sort of smile that crept onto his face as he watched the nobles shy away from the common people as if they carried some sort of disease, or as if they thought being poor might rub off onto them. Azerick returned his focus to himself and his wife as he noticed someone addressing him.

"Magus Azerick, it is good to finally meet you in person," King Jarvin was saying.

Azerick took Jarvin in with a glance. His brown hair had a strong hint of auburn, most notable in his close-cropped beard, he had a strong build to him, and he stood several inches taller than Azerick did. Everything about his countenance spoke of his regal bearing and good breeding. Azerick disliked him immediately.

On his arm was a woman he assumed to be his wife. She was a handsome woman but not beautiful like Miranda, or even her mother, Mellina. There was a powerful spark of intelligence in her eyes that held the look of someone who would not tolerate nonsense, but not in a haughty or pretentious sort of way. She almost reminded him of his own mother, particularly after they had lost their home. The stress of her husband's tumultuous claim to the throne was telling in the lines around her eyes. Azerick found her far more to his liking.

Miranda gave her king a deep curtsy. "Your Majesty, I am so glad you and the queen could attend the wedding. I know you must be so very busy."

Azerick gave Jarvin a nod and a minuscule bow after Miranda elbowed him in the ribs. Jarvin merely quirked an eyebrow and grinned at Azerick's lack of recognition for his status, which raised Azerick's opinion of him just a little.

"Miranda, you have grown into such a lovely young woman since I last saw you."

"Thank you, Your Majesty."

"Please, this is your home. Call me Jarvin."

Miranda turned and addressed Queen Annette. "You look lovely today, Your Majesty."

"Oh please. I have three children and look like I have birthed half a dozen. If it were not for this corset keeping all of my bits together, I would be spilling out onto the floor," Annette scoffed. "But it is kind of you to say so."

"I would pull you away for some girl talk, but I absolutely dread leaving my husband alone. He has an unerring ability to get himself into trouble."

"I am not that bad!" Azerick protested.

Miranda looked at Azerick. "Shall I regale our guests with some of your exploits? Shall I explain why Lord Effrin practically knocked down a server trying to escape the room when you walked in?"

"I would rather you did not," Azerick replied, but he was unable to suppress a smile as he recalled turning the lord into a donkey-like creature for being rude. That had been well over a year ago, but the man still appeared to be traumatized from the event.

Jarvin came to Azerick's rescue. "That is quite all right, Miranda. I just wanted the chance to meet Azerick face to face. I had expected to see him when I bestowed the accolade of Defender of the Crown upon him. I assume the invitation was lost in transit."

"I received it," Azerick replied. "It was very nice paper and it was much appreciated."

Miranda was aghast. One did not ignore a summons from the king.

"How could you just ignore something like that? I never saw it. What did you do with it?" Miranda demanded to know.

"Like I said, it was very good paper," Azerick answered, looking askance.

"I don't understand..." Miranda started to say then gasped.

To his credit, Jarvin laughed loudly and even Annette let a smile creep to her lips. Nearly everyone in the room turned to look at the unexpected outburst before returning to their own conversations.

"It is quite all right, Miranda. I would like to do the same thing with half the documents that come across my desk. Perhaps I should decree that any papers submitted to me be of similar quality so as not to chafe His Royal Highness."

"Miranda," Annette invited as she took hold of the other woman's hand, "I think this is the perfect time for us to go have our girl talk, seeing as how men are incapable of speaking without being crude."

"An excellent idea, Annette," Miranda responded then glared at Azerick. "You better behave yourself!"

Azerick returned her glared warning with a look of innocence. "As I always do."

"You better do a lot better than that or it is going to be one cold nuptials night," she threatened, then poked him hard with a finger.

The women left the two men alone to endure several moments of awkward pause. Of course, it was Jarvin who finally broke the silence.

"When Maude brought back word to me about how you destroyed the armor, I was unsure how to respond."

"Perhaps with a simple thank you and maybe a nice cake," Azerick replied with a shrug.

"Do you enjoy being contrary to everyone, or just the nobility?"

Azerick let out a deep breath. "I apologize, Your Majesty. I have had few positive encounters with the nobility. After losing my parents, living in the streets dodging killers and slavers, having my school laid to siege, and saving your throne from the aspirations of such men, well, it is hard to be completely objective."

"It is quite all right. I actually find your lack of pretension refreshing. It is most distressing wondering if the man who is smiling at you is about to plunge a dagger into your back the instant you turn around."

"Speaking of plunging daggers, how sits His Chafed Royal Highness upon his throne now that Ulric is gone?"

"As precarious as ever, I think. The overt actions of Ulric have been squashed, largely thanks to you, but I am certain there are still rats gathering in the shadows. I lost a powerful ally when William was killed. Mellina is the only trusted friend I have left. As if I did not have enough trouble from the living, I am continuing to get more reports of the dead crawling out of their graves and terrorizing the populace. Have you seen such a thing up here?" Jarvin asked.

Azerick shook his head. "I did run afoul of a large group of creatures a few years ago, but that was nearer Brightridge. I have neither seen nor heard of anything since. Is it truly becoming a problem?"

"I am afraid so. It is mostly small groups easily dispatched by militia or townsfolk, but the reports are increasing. My advisor, Bishop Caalendor, has sent out several units of Solarian's Light to consecrate the tombs and graveyards closest to human populations, and only a few battles have been of any significance. I fear that may change, however. I am sure you have noticed the exceedingly long winters."

"I have. It is early summer and the snows just broke a few weeks ago up here. Already the winds feel as though they are getting colder."

Jarvin nodded. "Ill tidings indeed. Let us talk of happier things on such a wonderful day. I snuck away and took a ride up to that school of yours this morning. It is quite impressive. I am glad to see so much good done for the less fortunate citizens."

"Well, someone certainly needed to do something."

Jarvin let out a sigh. "Azerick, I know you probably think that as king, I can simply snap my fingers and have done whatever I wish. But if I could do that, I would be twice the wizard you are."

"Actually I'm not a wizard at all, I am a sorcerer."

Jarvin looked quizzically at Azerick. "I don't understand the difference."

"That's all right. It seems to me that no one else does either."

"Perhaps you can explain it to me."

Azerick let out a small laugh. "Maybe once someone explains it to me, but I will do my best. A sorcerer and wizard are both thirsty. Each has an empty glass. A wizard takes a bucket to a well, fills the bucket, and then pours it into his glass. The sorcerer simply forces his will upon the well and the water comes to him. A poor metaphor, but the best one I have."

"It certainly sounds like a sorcerer has a great deal more power."

"Both have their advantages, but generally speaking, yes."

"I will not keep you from your beautiful bride any longer. If I don't let some of these other people fawn over me soon, they might have a fit of apoplexy," Jarvin said with a look of exasperation, then waded into a knot of nobles hovering just on the other side of an imaginary border created by Azerick's glare.

Azerick found Miranda talking to a group of commoners by the refreshment table and slipped his arm into hers.

"Miss me?" Azerick asked, leaning down and kissing her neck.

Miranda smiled coyly. "I did not hear anyone call for the guards. I assume you behaved yourself?"

"I can behave when I want to. I am just lucky Jarvin is not as big a fool as I expected."

"I told you that, but you did not want to listen."

"Well I can hardly be blamed for that," Azerick insisted.

Miranda turned and looked at him. "Why, because you think all noblemen are arrogant swine?"

Azerick shrugged. "It is not as though you are the best judge of character."

"What do you mean by that?" his wife demanded.

"Well, you foolishly married me, didn't you?" Azerick answered with a wry smile.

"You are lucky I am also terrible at listening to people, because they all said the same thing."

"Everyone?"

"Near enough."

Azerick and Miranda spent the next two hours mingling. The nobility accepted Azerick more now that he was one of them and had the ear of not only the duchess but possibly the king as well. Word had also gotten around that Azerick had a great deal of wealth, and the one thing rich men liked to do was look for investors so they could make more money. With a great deal of elbowing from Miranda, Azerick was able to fake a polite smile and decline all of their offers.

King Jarvin stood upon a raised dais and called for everyone's attention. The crowd pressed in and quieted down, eager to hear what their king had to say.

"Lord Azerick Giles, would you please attend me on the dais?" Jarvin called out, making eye contact with the sorcerer.

Azerick was unsure of what was happening, but he was certain he was not going to like it. The sea of people parted as he approached with Miranda by his side. Miranda stopped at the foot of the dais while Azerick took three steps up to stand a single step below the king.

"Most of you know what the magus has done here in North Haven, not just in its defense, but for the common good of all its citizens," Jarvin addressed the crowd. "What most of you may not know is the extremes he went to, and the great harm he placed himself in to protect those close to him, and perhaps by sheer coincidence, saved the kingdom from civil unrest and possibly my very life. He has shown himself to be a man of contrary but noble character. He has shown that he is a man of morals with a powerful sense of duty. The only thing he has not shown is himself at his own awards ceremony!"

Jarvin let the laughter die down before continuing. "Since I could not properly reward him for his services in Brelland, I have decided to do it here. Lord Azerick Giles, for your bravery and duty to the crown and the kingdom, I bestow on you this statuette and the title of Defender of the Crown. From this day on, you shall be known as a friend to the crown."

A functionary brought forth a polished wood box with ornate engravings covering the lid and sides. Jarvin took the box from the bearer, opened the lid, and presented its contents to Azerick.

Azerick looked at the small statue inside as if it were a dead bird. The statuette was of a knight with his sword raised and shield held to ward off a blow. On the shield was Jarvin's coat of arms with a crown hovering over it. With a gesture from the king, Azerick picked the figure up out of the box. It must have been solid gold, because even though it was only six inches tall, it weighed several pounds.

Azerick could only nod in recognition, thinking what an incredible waste of wealth the thing represented. He gently put it back in the box and the bearer stepped away. Jarvin cleared his throat and prepared to address the crowd once more.

"Now, Lord Giles, there is the small matter of the oath of allegiance you must take," Jarvin informed the sorcerer with an abashed grin.

"I must?" Azerick asked without a trace of humor.

Behind him, Miranda cringed. Depending on his mood, if someone told Azerick he must breathe, he would hold his breath until he passed out. Miranda stepped next to Azerick, took his hand, and looked pleadingly into his eyes. Azerick returned her look and gave Jarvin a small nod.

"Very well then," Jarvin continued. "Please repeat after me. I, Lord Azerick Giles…"

Azerick repeated the oath as Jarvin seemed to drone on. With his ability to ramble with endless redundancy, Azerick thought the king could make a good priest. His attention returned as it appeared they were nearing the end.

"And do solemnly swear to support and defend the crown of Valeria," Jarvin finished.

"And do solemnly swear to support and defend the *kingdom* of Valeria," Azerick returned.

Jarvin opened his mouth as if to correct the new lord then closed it. "That is the best I am going to get, isn't it?"

Azerick slowly inclined his head to the king and felt Miranda squeeze his hand even harder.

Jarvin paused as the assembled crowd held their collective breaths. "Then I shall take what I can get," he declared with a smile.

Everyone, especially Miranda, let out the breath they had all been holding. No one had ever altered the oath before an assembled crowd. Most took it and simply discarded it if it did not fit their true intent, as Ulric and several others had done. There were a few rare historical accounts of a nobleman refusing outright. Those people were promptly stripped of title and lands, and on some occasions imprisoned or executed.

Although Duchess Mellina had bestowed a lordship upon Azerick for his defense of North Haven, that title was predominantly ceremonial outside the region she controlled. Now Azerick was officially a lord of the realm with all of the rights and responsibilities it carried.

The king then motioned for Azerick to kneel, which he did after an uncomfortable moment's hesitation. Then Jarvin held out the back of his hand for Azerick to kiss his signet ring to seal his oath. Miranda was sure this was the end of Azerick's tolerance and tried to brace herself for the chaos that was sure to ensue.

Azerick looked at Jarvin's hand as if he were holding a snake. This was too much. It was bad enough the man forced him into an oath that made him feel as though he were chewing glass when he spoke the words, but to expect him to kneel and place his lips upon his bauble was beyond unbearable. It was an attempt to disgrace Azerick's dignity.

How dare this insufferable man think he has the right or the power to lord over you? Klaraxis seethed in rage. *He is a weak man on a weak throne! Destroy him where he stands and you shall be king!*

Shut up, demon, Azerick ordered Klaraxis. *You play with my emotions at risk of your suffering.*

Azerick felt Miranda's presence once again as she knelt beside him and beseeched him with her eyes. He gave his beautiful bride a smile and knew then that nothing was more important than she was. No sacrifice was too great to give for her love—even his own pride. He lightly gripped the king's hand with his own, and with a touch as light as a feather, brushed his lips across the ring.

The tension that had been building amongst the assembled guests evaporated like a puddle under the desert sun. Some even laughed as they spoke of the near disaster they had almost just witnessed. Azerick stood, helped Miranda to her feet, and hugged her tightly.

Jarvin laid a hand on Azerick's shoulder and led him off the dais and slightly apart from the crowd. Fearful Azerick might say something unspeakable, Miranda kept a tight grip on his other arm. She could feel the tenseness in her husband's body that spoke of an ill mood the unexpected ceremony had put him in.

Jarvin turned to the sorcerer and replaced his friendly smile with a look of utter seriousness. "Azerick, I hope you appreciate the leniency I have regarded you in taking your oath."

"And I hope you appreciate the fact I made one at all."

"Azerick, please!" Miranda begged.

Jarvin held up a hand. "No, Lady Miranda. Azerick and I must come to terms and fully recognize where we stand. Lord Giles, I have bestowed a lordship and title upon you. Along with those come certain conditions that all of my lords have had to agree to."

"How has that been working out for you lately?" Azerick practically snapped back.

Jarvin's face colored and he fought to maintain a civil tone. "Failure to make or meet those requirements can have dire consequences. I would have been fully within my right to take every copper and every inch of land you own had I not accepted your improvised oath."

Every hair on Miranda's body seemed to stand on end when Azerick replied. "Why don't you go pay Ulric's grave a visit and ask him what happens when someone tries to take what is mine?"

"I have given you an enormous amount of vocal freedom for what you have done for me, the kingdom, and its people. But when you make threats, you have exceeded that latitude!"

"I am not threatening you, Your Majesty. I merely point out examples that I hope serve as a warning to foolish men. As of yet, I do not count you amongst them. Let us both pray I never do."

The king stood with his jaw clenching and unclenching for several long moments. Then the flush slowly drained from his face and his flesh returned to a more natural hue. He let out the breath he had been holding for at least the past minute.

"Why is it that one of the men I probably trust most in my kingdom dislikes me so much?"

"Your Majesty, Jarvin, I do not dislike you. I do not think you fully understand what I have gone through and the sacrifices I have made largely because of men of a certain station. It has created certain—demons—you might say. Some of those demons have come home to roost, and it makes me act much more harshly than some might deserve," Azerick explained by way of an apology.

Jarvin extended his hand to Azerick. "I had best find my wife. It is a long journey back to Brelland, especially seeing as I must travel to Southport and give that city some much-needed face time. I let Ulric out of my sight for too long. I shall not make the same mistake with his cousin."

Azerick clasped the king's hand. "I too have had about as much celebrating as I can stand for one day."

Azerick sent a page to have Peck bring the carriage around then led Miranda through the palace halls and outside.

"Azerick, why are we taking the coach?" Miranda asked as they stepped out into the light of the summer sun.

"It is a rather long walk, especially in your wedding finery," Azerick replied as he helped Miranda and the many folds of her wedding gown into the carriage.

"Do you mean to go back to the school?"

"Of course," Azerick replied as if it were an obvious and forgone conclusion. "Where else would I live?"

"I thought we would live here in the castle. It is where I must perform all of my duties."

"And the school is where I must perform mine. I am sure you can look pretty there just as well as you do here."

"Is that what you think I do all day, stand around and look pretty? I will have you know I attend court with Mother, advise her, and deal with a number of things that must be addressed for the duchy to run properly!" Miranda declared, scandalized.

"I am sure your mother is quite capable of running the duchy and making decisions without you, just as I am certain it will not be terribly inconvenient to schedule matters of importance in a manner in which to accommodate you. The school is my home. Besides, I can walk the grounds there without the overwhelming desire to strangle nearly half the people I pass."

Miranda knew he was right but impishly crossed her arms and faked a pout. "What if I do not want to live in your drafty tower?"

"You are certainly within your right to stay at the castle, but you might find it every bit as drafty without your clothes," Azerick replied.

Miranda looked at Azerick in shock. "What do you mean without my clothes? Where are my clothes?"

Azerick smiled mischievously. "I had them all crated and moved into the tower this morning."

"You boxed and moved all my clothes?" Miranda asked in feigned outrage.

"Well, not all of them. I gave most of them away to the poor. Honestly, you have enough clothes to outfit an army."

Miranda laughed loudly. "Perhaps if someone lays siege to us again we should do precisely that! Can you imagine the effect it would have on an invading army to see their foes charge them in my ball gowns and finery?"

"If it makes you feel any better, I have a wedding present for you. Hold out your hand."

Miranda smiled brightly and held out a cupped hand into which Azerick dropped a small object. Miranda's smile shifted to a look of puzzlement.

"It's a ring. A man's ring. Why are you giving me a man's ring? Is it yours?" Miranda asked. "It looks too big to fit you."

"No, it is not mine. It was Jarvin's."

Miranda gasped loudly and looked at Azerick incredulously. "You stole the king's ring? How could you?"

Azerick shrugged. "Apparently with quite a bit of skill. Kiss his ring indeed. He is lucky I did not tell him to kiss my—"

"Azerick Giles, how dare you steal from the king?" Miranda demanded indignantly. "I am beyond shocked at your behavior and audacity. He is supposed to be a friend! You cannot steal the king's ring!"

"I have rather empirical evidence to the contrary. I do not understand why you are so upset. It is not as though I stole his signet ring. That would be treason. Besides, I thought you would be happy to know that I maintain a skill set I can use if this whole 'wealthy lord' thing does not work out. Now you know that no matter what happens, I will always be able to take care of you."

Miranda laughed and punched Azerick in the shoulder. Peck expertly guided the coach up the long road to the orphans' academy. Despite its name, not all of the students were orphans or homeless. Over the past year, the school had grown into something resembling a small town. Like the Academy in Southport, the orphans' academy now hosted a general education section for any child not able to pay for private tutoring as well as those for magic studies and martial training. Azerick had tried to change the name to the people's academy, but the name simply would not stick.

Most students were housed on the grounds, as the five-mile walk was too far to go every day. Several children piled into a few wagons that did make the daily trek, but most stayed in the dorms and went home on the weekends. Those who had homes. There were now over seven hundred students, but only about three hundred were permanent residents who counted the school as their home.

The forest to the south was now nearly a mile away. The trees had been cleared and the ground plowed to help sustain the population of the school. It still was not enough by itself, but Wolf had absolutely forbidden any further clearing, particularly to the east. How he had assumed ownership of what was included in the deed to Azerick was unclear, but the fact was undeniable.

The most notable addition was the second tower, just recently completed. It stood two stories higher than the original five-story tower and was half again as wide. A hall stretched fifty feet and connected the two towers at the base and fourth floors. Azerick had thought most of the work around the school would be long over with by now, but workers still pored over several areas as the need for more dorms, expanded walls, and classrooms continued to grow with the increasing population.

Peck was still the head groom but now had five assistants to help him tend the one hundred horses housed in the greatly expanded stables. The fact that he was in charge of people up to thrice his age might appear odd to most people at first glance, but Peck showed that he deserved the position with his tireless effort and natural ability working with the animals.

Peck pulled the coach up to the front of the new tower and Azerick helped Miranda descend the steps. She looked up at the new tower and marveled at its stucco-covered stone exterior and large glass windows.

"Oh, you finished the new tower!" Miranda exclaimed in joyous surprise.

"I thought transitioning from the grand palace of North Haven to a drafty old tower might be hard on someone of your *sensitivity*, so I thought I would make it as comfortable as I could," Azerick replied facetiously.

Miranda showed how sensitive she was by punching Azerick in the shoulder hard enough to make him step back. "You better watch your tone, mister. You are still in trouble for stealing the king's ring. Now, show me to my new home."

Azerick led Miranda up the steps then scooped her into his arms. She squealed in surprise and delight as Azerick whisked her across the threshold, making the doors open before him with a tiny streamer of magic.

Miranda wriggled out of Azerick's grasp as she looked in wonder at the ground floor. The main hall of the old tower was lovely with its chandeliers, beautiful furniture, tapestries, and carpets. The new tower was palatial. Marble sheathed every surface. Five chandeliers glittering with strings of polished crystals brilliantly illuminated the huge room with what Miranda assumed were magical orbs of light.

Everything in the room, from the furniture to the tapestries and paintings, reminded her of the most beautiful rooms in the castle, only everything here was brand new. Not a speck of dust marred a single object or surface.

"Azerick, it is amazing. It's like you took the best of the palace and put it in the tower!"

"I thought about that, but it was easier to just build a new one on a smaller scale. Moving something as large as the castle inside an area this small involves a great deal of specialized magic," Azerick replied.

"Could you do that, move the entire castle inside the tower?"

Azerick thought a moment then answered. "I suppose it is possible. Aggie would be the best person to ask about that. I am sure she could move Captain Brague's quarters into one of the privies. I will ask her tomorrow."

"Don't you dare! *General* Brague is a hero in his own right. You should respect him more."

"I do respect him. I just do not like him. Now, enough talk, my wife. Allow me to show you to our room. We have the entire third floor to ourselves in a suite of rooms that includes a study, solar, dining nook, and of course—the bedroom."

"Oh, lead the way, Lord Giles, Savior of North Haven, Defender of the Crown, and stealer of the king's jewelry," Miranda commanded seductively.

CHAPTER 2

Landrin sat at his desk engrossed in the book set before him. Since his turning nearly a dozen years ago, he had re-established his pursuit of magic. No longer needing to sleep, he had learned a great deal in that relatively short time. He knew that if there were a cure or at least a way to break the dominion Eldon held over him, it would be through magic.

He sensed Jacinth enter the room but refused to acknowledge her presence. Eldon liked to surround himself with beautiful things and Jacinth was no exception. Her fair skin and brilliant copper hair would spark desire in any man, but her grey eyes held nothing but power-hungry malevolence.

"What are you doing, Landrin? Studying your little book of spells again?" Jacinth asked derisively. "Maybe you are learning a new song to sing for us? I do love it when Eldon makes you sing."

The vampiress walked slowly around Landrin, pressed herself against his back, and traced his jaw with her index finger. "Maybe you are not studying at all. Are you praying again? Why do you pray to a god who has ignored you every day for the past decade? Do you think he will reward your vigilance? Do you think he will ever show mercy to our kind? He despises you, my pretty bard. He laughs at your devotion just as Eldon does."

Without warning, Landrin lashed out with a snarl. Jacinth leapt away with astounding speed and agility, clinging to the wall near the high ceiling, hissing in outrage. Landrin shaped the Source with a thought, ready to incinerate her, but was unable to release the spell.

Jacinth laughed at his impotent gesture. "You cannot use your magic against us, fool. Eldon has forbidden it, as you well know."

"What do you want, Jacinth?" Landrin asked as he let the gathered magic ebb away.

"Eldon commands your presence in the parlor."

Landrin left the sound of Jacinth's mocking laughter behind him as he walked dutifully down the richly appointed hall toward the parlor. As usual, Filip seemed to be waiting for him before he was halfway there. Filip had been a play actor and was destined for fame until he caught Eldon's eye. The elder vampire thought he would be a good addition to his family and would help break the daily tedium by performing with Jacinth, Celina, and Karla for his amusement.

It had seemed a good idea, but Eldon became bored of him, and the three women ensured that he would never be favored above them. Then Eldon had brought Landrin in, and now he found himself lower in station than someone who, by rights of age, should be beneath him. It could be argued that Landrin had become Eldon's favorite amongst them all, and that made the entire atmosphere of the mansion rife with jealousy.

Filip leaned against the wall, all black silk and white lace. He pushed himself off the wall and fell into step next to Landrin. "I see the favorite has been summoned once again. Mind if I tag along?"

"I don't care half a whit what you do, Filip," Landrin replied, not even trying to hide the contempt he held for his fellow vampire.

"So what do you think he wants this time? Shall he have you sing him a song? Maybe you can dazzle him with your little magic tricks."

Landrin knew Filip was trying to provoke a fight, but he refused to rise to the bait. "I do not know, nor do I care. Whatever I do, I do against my will."

"Why must you be so dour? Why not embrace this gift? It is not as though you gave up wealth, fame, and women with your little tavern trilling. I should be the angry one. I was set to be the greatest actor in the kingdom. I was to play for the king in the spring before Eldon made me. Women walked for miles just to see me perform. Many of them even came after the show was over. Now I am tossed aside every time Eldon finds a new pet," Filip complained.

"I am sure your victims rest easier in their graves knowing how you suffer so."

"You mock me now, but soon you will be cast aside for something new as well."

"A pity that would be," Landrin replied sardonically.

The pair entered the parlor where Celina and Karla doted upon Eldon, buffing his nails and brushing his hair. Karla was beautiful, as were they all, with hair like spun gold. Celina was equally beautiful, but with hair as black as a moonless night. All three looked at the two men as they entered. The women cast hateful glares, but only Eldon spoke.

"Filip, why are you here? I did not summon you," Eldon said crossly.

Filip bowed obsequiously and replied, "I assumed it was a mere oversight that you forgot me, Eldon."

"You presume too often and always too much. However, I suppose this concerns you too, so you may as well stay. There is a grand ball being held at the castle, and through my connections I have gotten us all invitations to attend."

With ever-perfect timing, Jacinth strode through the doors and exclaimed, "A ball! How delightful! What is the occasion for such a rare treat?"

"It seems the king will be stopping by on his way home to Brelland after having toured the other three duchies, likely in some feeble attempt to reinforce his rather shaky rule. We are going to ensure such bolstering does not happen."

"It sounds like we are going to get to be bad," Celina crooned.

Eldon softly brushed her cheek with the back of his hand. "We are going to be more than bad. We are going to be horrific. Our master's plans are nearly coming to a head. This is the perfect opportunity to destabilize the warm-bloods even further just before he makes his decisive strike."

Landrin listened to Eldon's plans in horror. The bard maintained his existence, due to Eldon's command not to take his own life, by drinking the blood of humans, but without participating in the kill. He thought that perhaps Eldon found his squeamishness amusing. However, tonight would be a slaughter and one Eldon would not allow him to miss.

Eldon smiled at Filip. "It looks like you finally get to perform for the king, Filip."

Landrin left the others to laugh and talk about the mayhem they would cause tonight. He felt the need to be alone and sought out one of the least used rooms in the mansion. There he prayed to Solarian for the strength to resist his master and somehow prevent the tragedy that was soon to unfold. As usual, he felt no signs of his prayers having been heard despite his hours of entreaties to his god.

Landrin felt sick as it came time to attend the ball. He donned the costume he found lying on his bed when he returned to his room. One of Eldon's non-vampiric minions must have delivered it while he was praying for some kind of miracle that he knew would never come. There were several of them in the mansion, cooking, cleaning, and doing chores. Even after ten years in the house, Landrin did not know even one of them by name, nor did he care to. They were drones, slaves with even less free will then he had.

The costume consisted of white tights and a gold doublet over a white silk shirt. A cord held a gold mask with the face of a lark in place. He found the others already gathered in the parlor. Filip was dressed in a veritable rainbow of bright colors and wore a silver performer's mask. Eldon preferred an outfit of simple black, a scarlet vest, and a red demon mask.

As distasteful as the demon mask was, the women's costumes troubled him far more. Jacinth, Karla, and Celina wore heavy black hooded robes and faceless white masks. They were the three sisters of fate. The symbolism was not lost on him. The fate in store for the people at the party was too horrible to contemplate.

"Ah, just in time, Landrin. Let us all proceed to the party," Eldon commanded, then led the grisly group to the awaiting coach.

The ringing of the horses' steel shoes upon the cobblestones sounded like the pealing of funeral bells to Landrin's ears. He searched his mind for a way to work past Eldon's compulsion and prevent the massacre that was going to happen tonight. Eldon sensed his inner battle and smiled at his futile efforts to thwart his will. By the time the coach pulled up to the mansion belonging to the host of the gala, Landrin had given up and simply rode the waves in the sea of despair that washed over him, and tried not to drown.

Eldon stepped out of the coach and addressed his driver. "You may return to the manor. We shan't need the coach to return home."

The driver gave Eldon a nod of recognition with his soulless eyes, flicked the reins, and disappeared into the night. The three sisters giggled and practically leapt about with barely controlled excitement at what was to come. Landrin trailed the group morosely, lost in his own despondency.

A liveried man at the top of the steps examined their invitations before ushering them inside. Eldon chose to be fashionably late, so there was already a respectable crowd milling about in a sea of fanciful outfits and masks. The masked vampires spread out amongst the crowd. Landrin found a nook and tried to look as inconspicuous as possible as his growing anxiety gnawed at his soul.

Rumors flew from gossiping mouths like bees around a nest that the prelate and king would be making an appearance. A game formed of who could spot the notable guests first. Lords and ladies continued to trickle in over the next hour. Both the king and prelate were easy to spot, although Landrin did not know precisely when they had arrived.

"You seem to be rather thoughtful, My Lord," a woman sidled up to him and said.

Landrin started at the unexpected company but calmed himself before replying. "I fear I have had a great deal to ponder today, My Lady."

"Ah, I thought perhaps you were busy playing *spot the king* with the other sycophants so that you might get a chance to curry favor."

"Hardly much of a sport."

"Really? Do you think you have spied them then?" she asked.

"Indeed I have," Landrin replied. "The one in orange and wearing the gold mask in the shape of a sun is obviously the prelate."

The woman followed Landrin's eyes and saw the man amongst a small knot of people. "Oh yes, I see now. Then the man in blue and purple must be the king."

"That is what they wish us to believe, but the king is in the drab green and brown next to him," Landrin corrected her.

"You seem awfully sure of yourself. How do you know this?"

"The crows always circle where the food is," Landrin explained cryptically.

The woman looked at the four men dressed in black, each wearing the mask of a raven, and each undoubtedly a member of the famous Blackguard. "You have a very keen eye, My Lord. Are you a magistrate or some such?"

"Hardly, My Lady. Just perceptive."

"Call me a sycophant, but I suppose I must go and say hello," the woman said, starting to leave.

Landrin grabbed the woman by the wrist and gently pulled her back. "You should depart this place, My Lady."

The woman ripped her arm from Landrin's grasp. "Leave, you say? Are you offering me a better night's entertainment than the ball, milord?"

"As much as I wish I could leave, I cannot. But you should not stay," Landrin tried to explain past his compulsion.

"I imagine my boredom will compel me to leave soon, but unless something better comes along, not just yet. Good evening, milord," the woman said in farewell.

"Prelate Howarth, Lord Henrick," Jarvin said to the two men next to him, "I appreciate the invitation, but I fear I am beyond exhausted from my traveling and shall retire for the evening so that I and my retinue can get an early start as we make our way home to Brelland."

"Of course, Your Majesty. I completely understand. I am very grateful that you took the time to stop in at my ball, and I am sure the gesture is equally appreciated by my guests," the man in deep blue and purple answered with a small bow.

"Allow me to escort you back to the castle, Your Majesty," Prelate Howarth offered.

"I am sure my Blackguard can see me back. No need to cut short your pleasure on my account."

"It is no problem, Your Highness. I am afraid the only crowds I enjoy are when they are in neat, orderly rows within my church," the prelate insisted with a small laugh.

The king and prelate left with Jarvin's Blackguard in tow as quietly and unobtrusively as they had arrived. The only one who seemed to note their departure was a handsome man hidden behind the mask of a lark.

Lady Sharleen went in search of a mirror to check that the mask she wore had not smudged her makeup for when they would all reveal themselves near the end of the festivities. She rounded the corner of the dim hallway and came upon a couple embracing in a shadowy doorway.

"Oh, I beg pardon!" Sharleen cried in surprise.

The man dressed in black with a crimson vest pulled his face away from the woman's neck and looked at her with a smile. A scream of unbridled horror tore from Sharleen's throat as the woman slumped to the ground with blood pouring out of the gruesome wound in her neck.

The terrified woman turned and ran back toward the ballroom as a second shrill scream preceded her down the hall. She burst into the crowded ballroom, trying to form words as everyone stared at her, trying to figure out what had made that awful noise. Her mouth opened and closed several times, and then she seemed to float a foot off the floor. A sickening crack echoed across the silent grand hall just before Eldon hurled the woman's body into the crowd.

"Time to start the real party!" Eldon shouted, his face covered in blood, flashing his fangs with a hiss.

It took a full two seconds for the shock of what was happening to register in the minds of the mortals. The ballroom erupted in shrieks of terror as the men and women scrambled for the exits. Most people headed for the entrance from where they had entered only to find Filip and Jacinth blocking their egress.

The two vampires cast aside their masks and tore into the mass of living flesh with their fangs and unnaturally sharp claws. It was chaos as the terrified mob tried to backpedal against those shoving them from behind. Many of the men wore slender swords more for decoration than defense, but brought them out anyway.

One man managed to slip his blade between the press of bodies and stabbed Filip deep in his chest near his right shoulder. With a hiss born more of anger than injury, Filip grabbed the wrist attached to the offending, weapon-bearing hand and snapped it with contemptuous ease. He then pulled the man close and tore out his throat with his fangs before flinging him aside and tearing into a woman who could do nothing but scream until his claws silenced her forever.

Seeing only death in that direction, the horrified crowd shifted like a school of fish and made for the glass doors that emptied into the gardens, only to find Karla and Celina waiting and blocking their escape. The two vampiresses tore into the crowd with gales of sadistic laughter, reveling in the smell of blood and fear permeating the room.

Landrin could only watch the slaughter unfold as he battled his own nature. The smell of blood spiked an almost irresistible desire to feed and take part in the carnage. A body slammed into him and someone clung to the front of his doublet. He looked down and saw the woman he had tried to warn away looking up at him.

"Please help me!" she begged, her eyes wide in terror.

Landrin started to shake his head helplessly, but with a force of will, he grabbed her by the arm and pulled her toward a servant's door obscured in a shallow alcove. Several people saw Landrin open the near-hidden passage and piled in behind him in hopes of escaping the nightmare come alive.

Landrin led his small group through narrow passages that eventually emptied into a large kitchen. He did not know whether to yell at the frightened staff to run or if they would be safer staying where they were. Seeing the terrified look on the faces of the nobles, most chose to run despite being oblivious as to the cause of the screams coming from the ballroom.

Landrin picked passages at random, guessing where a door might lead them outside. His efforts were finally rewarded as they burst out of a small side door into an herb garden. An ornate, wrought-iron fence with a small gate leading to the streets lay a dozen yards away. Just before the group reached the gate, Eldon seemed to drop out of the black sky and landed in front of Landrin, blocking their escape.

"Delivering me a treat personally are you, Landrin?" the elder vampire asked mockingly.

Eldon grabbed the woman's free hand, pulled her close, and buried his fangs into her neck. Landrin could only watch helplessly as her eyes looked to him beseechingly until they closed, never to open again. The other men and women screamed in horror and retreated in different directions. Some ran alongside the outside of the mansion while others fled back inside the way they had come.

Eldon casually dropped the woman's lifeless body to the ground. "Come, it is time to return home."

Landrin looked at the dead woman for a moment then followed his master home.

Having received a magical summons from Prelate Howarth, Paladin Samone and her arm of Solarian's Light rode through the night and arrived in Brightridge the morning after the terrible attack. Prelate Howarth personally led her and her companions into the cold underground chamber of the temple where the victims of last night's attack lay.

Several men were already in the room when they arrived. Numerous bodies lay upon stone slabs, although most were simply laid out on the floor. Nearly all bore evident wounds, but a few had suffered crushed skulls that were only obvious after a closer examination.

"Prelate," a man dressed in the livery of the city watch, bearing the insignia of captain, addressed the de facto city leader. "I told Chief Inspector Collin there was no need to trouble you or the Church. My guardsmen and I can handle this."

The captain of the guard was a slightly portly man and short with a bandy-legged stance as though accustomed to the saddle. Samone doubted he had ever ridden a horse in his life and was more likely to be found astride a barstool given the veiny redness of his bulbous nose.

"And I have spent the better part of the evening trying to convince Captain Bertrand that this is no simple attack by desperate men, and is far more than he and his men are prepared to deal with, hence my coming to see you last night, Prelate," Collin replied, which elicited a sour glare from the Watch captain.

"I am a little sketchy on the details," the prelate said. "Please explain them once more for myself and the Solarian's Light."

Captain Bertrand took a step forward, cutting off the inspector. "A group of men snuck into Lord Henrick's mansion and attacked the assembled nobles. It is my theory that Lord Henrick ran afoul of a powerful and audacious criminal element. This was obviously an act of retribution of some kind, seeing as how it appears that nothing was stolen nor any of the wealthy attendees robbed of coin or valuables."

The chief inspector let out a breath of forced patience. He was a thin man and not much taller than the squat captain, but he held himself like a man of cunning and confidence. He pulled out a sheaf of papers with notes neatly written with a charcoal stylus.

"Shortly after King Jarvin and the prelate left Lord Henrick's estate, two men and three women attacked the partygoers with their bare hands. Several witnesses attest to the fact that the attackers moved with inhuman speed and strength. A few claim to have seen one or two of them stabbed through the chest with a sword or dagger without any discernible harm."

"Hysterical nonsense, obviously," Captain Bertrand scoffed.

"As you can see, the victims show wounds that look as though they have been mauled by bears or enormous cats." The inspector shuffled through his notes. "There may have been three men involved, not just the two."

"How is that, Inspector?" Samone asked.

"A few witnesses state they were led outside by a man in a gold mask stylized in the image of a lark. He first appeared to be leading them to safety, but just as they reached a side gate, one of the assailants dropped out of nowhere, called him by name, and then killed the woman he seemed to be with," Collin explained.

"Did any of them recall the name he used?"

Collin looked under the top page of his notes and answered. "There are a few variances but the most likely is Landrin."

Samone asked, "Do any of you know anyone named Landrin?"

Captain Bertrand spoke up. "It's not a common name but not unheard of. A city the size of Brightridge is bound to have a dozen or two men by that name."

Samone and the cleric, Brother Charles, began inspecting the bodies, making particularly close inspection of what appeared to be bite wounds. Samone looked at the mass of bodies and turned back to the inspector.

"Are these all of the victims?"

"Yes, twenty-six of the wealthiest, most influential citizens in Brightridge," he answered in disgust.

"It has to be vampires. What do you think, Charles?" the paladin asked the cleric.

"I would say there is little doubt."

"I do not know much about such things," Collin said, "but that was my guess, considering the reports I have been hearing. That is why I asked the prelate to contact you."

Samone nodded. "Very good thinking, Inspector. There are too many bodies and the attack was far too conspicuous to have been a simple feeding. You say the king was there, Prelate?"

"Yes. He was weary so I escorted him to the castle early."

"Is he still in the city?"

The acting duke shook his head. "No. He wished to return to Brelland as soon as possible, and I felt no reason to inform him of what transpired. He and his people departed early this morning. Paladin Samone, have you encountered this level of undead in your recent duties?"

"No, Prelate. Nearly all of the undead we have discovered have been relatively weak and mindless. The worst have been a few shades or specters, but nothing as powerful as vampires."

The prelate looked crestfallen at the implication. "Then it is safe to assume the situation is getting worse."

"I fear that is so, Prelate."

"I will need to inform Bishop Caalendor. Paladin Samone, I need you and your people to find these murderous abominations and destroy them."

Samone ducked her head. "Solarian's will be done."

CHAPTER 3

Azerick was busy in the large, underground laboratory he had constructed under the new tower. It was by far the most spacious room, but only one of several subterranean chambers and passages running beneath the two towers and several of the surrounding buildings. He was just fitting the shoulder guard of the steel golem in place when he heard the shouting.

Thinking he may need to intervene, Azerick stopped what he was doing and went to investigate. He had barely reached the top of the stairs when Agnes, his head cook, confronted him.

"Master Azerick," the older woman practically shrieked, "you must do something about that gluttonous beast!"

"Is Sandy filching hams again?" Azerick asked.

Agnes waved a hand dismissively. "The dragon I can tolerate. At least she has manners. I mean that disgusting demon child, Wolf! They are in the meat cellar again."

Azerick went into the kitchen, conjured a light, and headed down the creaky wooden steps. He found the source of Agnes's distress sprawled out on the stone floor of the chilly room. Sandy lay on her side with the end of a large ham bone sticking out of her mouth. Wolf was on his back clutching a half-eaten sausage in one hand and his stomach in the other.

"Oh, I think I'm going to be sick," Wolf moaned.

"I told you I could eat more," Sandy said heavily after spitting the bone out of her mouth.

Wolf glared at the dragon. "You barely ate three times as much as me and you weigh five times what I do. That means I ate more."

"The bet was raw volume, not by scale in accordance with each other's mass, so you lose. Next time, don't make such foolish wagers."

"What do you two think you are doing?" Azerick demanded, trying to sound cross but failing to hide the laughter in his voice.

"Eating contest," the half-elf and dragon said in unison.

"It looks like you two have eaten an entire week's food in a single sitting."

"I ate a week's worth. Wolf maybe had two, three days' worth— tops," Sandy answered in a moan.

"You're huge. It wasn't a fair contest," Wolf groaned.

"Not fair is the motto of the loser." Sandy fixed an eye on Wolf. "Loser."

Wolf threw his half-eaten sausage at the small dragon and laughed as it bounced off her head.

"People all over the kingdom are hungry right now and you two are wasting food," Azerick lectured. "Now, get out of here and do not ever have another eating contest unless you hunt down your own food."

"You can count on that. I probably won't be able to eat for—hours," Wolf said as he and Sandy rolled to their feet and started up the stairs.

"Sandy," Azerick called up to the departing dragon, "you need to exercise more. You are getting fat."

Sandy's mouth dropped open in indignation. "I am not getting fat! That is muscle. We sand dragons are naturally stocky and strongly built."

"Well, your stomach muscle is nearly scraping the steps," Azerick pointed out.

Wolf started laughing so hard he let out an enormous belch, which made him laugh even harder.

"Laugh all you want. Not all of us can be skinny little elves, something for which I am eternally grateful. Uh oh."

Wolf wiped the laughter-induced tears from his face. "What?"

"I'm stuck in the doorway," Sandy replied sheepishly. "Stop laughing! Obviously the moisture of the cellar caused the wood frame to expand!"

"Yeah right! And maybe the moisture caused your belly to expand too!" Wolf barked out in uncontrollable hilarity.

"Shut up and give me a push!" Sandy demanded.

Still shaking with laughter, Wolf put his back against the dragon's wide rump and pushed with his legs. Sandy wriggled from side to side trying to squeeze through but only wedged herself more firmly.

"Stop holding your breath!" Wolf ordered.

Sandy let out the pent-up air in her lungs and released a belch several times the volume of Wolf's. It worked and Sandy popped through the door and into the kitchen.

"See, I'm not fat. It was just gas from all that food," Sandy said.

"I'm just glad it came out in a burp or you might have blasted me down the stairs!" Wolf said, then roared with laughter once again.

Sandy gasped. "Dragons do not—do that!"

Azerick listened to the pair laughing and arguing across the grounds as they left the tower and headed toward the woods, likely to sleep off their overindulgence. All he could do was shake his head and wonder if life had been less complicated when he was just battling demons and fighting armies.

"I swear, those two get into more trouble than every child in this place," Agnes told Azerick as he emerged from the cellar.

"They are quite a pair. Speaking of troublesome children, I have hardly seen my apprentice in a couple days."

Ellyssa and Roger were in her room, examining the results of her latest work. Numerous runes and sigils scrawled in different colored chalk adorned nearly every surface of the large wardrobe.

"Is this amazing or what?" Ellyssa asked her best friend.

"It is interesting," Roger replied uncertainly. "Are you sure it will work?"

Ellyssa scoffed. "Of course it will work! It's simple. I applied the same runes on the inside of the wardrobe in our applied magic class. All I have to do is activate them, step inside, and pop out of the one in class. No more walking these stupid stairs. It is genius."

"Where did you learn how to do this?"

"You know that big book Azerick is always looking at and told me to stay away from?"

"Yeah," Roger said slowly with a mounting feeling of dread.

"In there."

"Ellyssa, there is a reason he does not want you reading that book."

"Yeah, because it has all kinds of great stuff in it."

"No," Roger said in exasperation, "because it is full of magic way beyond our level and is really dangerous! You are messing with transdimensional magic here!"

Ellyssa snorted and dismissed his worrying with a wave of her hand. "This is nothing more than a fixed version of the gate spell Azerick uses all the time—sort of. It's no big deal."

"Azerick is also probably one of the most powerful spellcasters in the kingdom!"

"I really doubt that. I'm sure Allister and Aggie know a lot more."

"Well, he's probably one of the scariest," Roger amended as he studied a rune more closely. "Are you sure this one is right?"

Ellyssa looked at the rune in question. "Of course it is. That's the sigil for the astral plane. It's what makes the whole thing work."

"I don't know. I'm pretty sure these squiggly lines are supposed be vertical for the astral plane, not horizontal."

"Nonsense. I copied exactly right out of the book. Do you know what your problem is? You follow the rules too much. You are too afraid to try anything new. You stick your nose in your book and recite what the pages show you over and over," Ellyssa told him.

"It's called practice. It's called being responsible and safe!"

"It's called being boring and predictable. Now watch this!"

Ellyssa pulled power from the Source and fed it into the runes scrawled onto the wardrobe, and the chalk-drawn sigils glowed in response. Ellyssa grabbed the handle of the closet and looked haughtily at her best friend.

"See, it was easy. To the applied magic class!" Ellyssa proclaimed grandly, then tugged open the door.

Thousands of gallons of water poured out of the closet as if a dam had burst. The raging torrent of water slammed into her and Roger then swept them out of the bedroom door and down the stairs. The conjured river hammered their young bodies against the unyielding stone walls at every turn. They wondered through their fear-filled minds if they were going to drown or be bashed to death first.

Grick had just come up the stairs of the basement rooms after a boring night of catching rats. The keep was practically rat-free now and Grick thought it was probably a good idea to pick up a hobby as his night duties were becoming exceedingly dull. He was standing in the center of the grand hall when he heard the screams and what sounded like someone emptying a giant washtub down the stairs. His yellow eyes went round as he saw the wall of water rushing down the stairs, carrying along the master's rotten apprentice and the boy with half his foot missing.

Without pausing to think, Grick lunged for the front doors and wrenched them open just as the flood of water hit him in the back and carried him, the two children, and several pieces of furniture outside. Still the water kept coming, pushing them down the avenues and between buildings—when they were lucky—and slamming them painfully into the sides of them when they were not.

The water flooded Ken's forges and quenched the fires used to heat the metal. It poured into Peck's stables and made a sodden mess of the stalls and the straw that covered their floors. Thankfully, Ellyssa had drawn the runes in chalk and the force of the water washed them away, returning the wardrobe to an ordinary closet, and depositing them on the steps of the newly built stone church.

Grick coughed out a lungful of water and glared at the young wizard. "Oh yeah, the woods fairy gonna come for you tonight, for sure. Make you into the ugliest, smelliest goblin ever."

Ellyssa looked at Roger as she expelled the last bit of water from her lungs. "I think you may have been right about that rune."

"You think?" Roger shouted at her.

Brother Thomas and several of his novitiates stepped out of the door of the church to see what had made such a ruckus. He looked down at the two soaked children and the goblin at the bottom of the steps and shook his head in disapproval.

"Ellyssa, what have you done?"

"Why does everyone always assume it was me anytime something weird happens around here?" the girl asked indignantly. "I'm not the one that brings home dragons or runs around with wolves and steals food! I'm not the one that had an assassin following them who then got stabbed by a goblin who skulks around at night killing rats! But anytime something catches fire or floods the tower it's all like, 'Ellyssa, what have you done?' I swear, the next eclipse that happens everyone is going to say 'Ellyssa, what have you done', because apparently I'm responsible for everything up to and including celestial orbits!"

Brother Thomas patiently let the girl vent before speaking again. "Are you responsible for this?"

Ellyssa chewed her lip for several moments before responding. "There are a lot of factors involved, many of which could cast a wide net of blame. I think we should just focus on the fact that no one was hurt and be grateful."

"Ellyssa!" the young priest shouted at her.

"Fine, it was my fault! Are you happy?" Ellyssa shouted back then screamed as something lifted her up off the ground and into the air.

A huge water elemental, apparently furious at being pulled from its home, lifted the young mage from the ground and prepared to smash her small body against the stone steps of the church.

"Children, you must banish that creature!" Brother Thomas exclaimed to his three young Chosen of Solarian.

Banishing a creature back to its home plane was not something a normal novitiate would be expected to perform. However, this, like Azerick's mage school, was no ordinary seminary. Brother Thomas's students were pushed to learn and excel just as the wizard and martial students were. It would take all three working together and even then, Brother Thomas was extremely concerned.

Shawna, Angela, and Caleb began the complex ritual of banishment, but luckily, Roger was faster. Roger pulled a wet piece of rock salt from his spell pouch and channeled the Source into it. Jumping to his feet, he lunged at the elemental, slammed the hand holding the halite against the water being, and released his spell.

The effect was instantaneous. The water under his hand froze solid and rapidly spread to the creature's base and up toward the arm holding his friend several feet in the air. Roger continued to pour energy into the spell until the giant watery hand holding Ellyssa froze solid. Roger knew he could not hold the powerful creature in stasis for long and prayed that the three Chosen could banish it. Already the ice was melting as the monster's will overcame his magic. Just as he was sure he was going to lose control, the water elemental lost all cohesion and vanished with a splash, dropping Ellyssa painfully onto the wet, muddy, and unyielding ground.

"You did it!" Brother Thomas cried out, hugging his three Chosen.

"You were saying something about no one getting hurt?" Roger panted from the exertion of his spell.

"You almost froze me to death!" Ellyssa accused, shivering heavily.

"Yeah…you're welcome."

"What is going on out here?" Azerick demanded as he, Rusty, and Allister ran up to them. "Is everyone all right?"

"Everyone seems fine," Brother Thomas answered. "It seems that Ellyssa managed to conjure a water elemental. Fortunately, young Roger was able to slow it long enough for us to banish it. I assume that is where all of this water came from as well."

Azerick glared down at the girl he considered his adopted daughter, who was now looking extremely miserable sitting in a puddle near his feet. "What did you do?"

"I tried to make a permanent gate from my closet to the classroom," she answered dolefully.

If she expected pity, she would find none here. "Do you realize what you have done?"

"I mixed up the astral rune with the water rune?" Ellyssa replied with a tiny smile in hopes of defusing Azerick's anger.

It did not work. "You could have hurt or even killed someone! You have probably destroyed your room, ruined the main hall, and from what I can see from the steam, destroyed Ken's workshop! Whatever gave you the idea you could make something so complex and so dangerous? Where did you find out how to do it?"

"In the big book you keep downstairs in your laboratory," Ellyssa squeaked out.

"I should have known better. I should have warded it or locked it up. I forbade you to read that book just for this reason!"

"You're right!" Ellyssa shouted back, tired of everyone verbally assaulting her. "You should have known I would read it the moment you told me not to, so this is your fault too!"

Azerick's fury was at a boil as he and his apprentice glared at each other. "You are grounded for two months. You will not leave the tower except to go to class, and that only after you have cleaned out the stables, done whatever Ken needs you to do to fix his forges, mopped out the downstairs, and done whatever else it takes to make this disaster look like it never happened."

"Two months! That's not fair! I'll miss summer festival!"

"You want to know about fair? Go visit the nine graves of the children that died defending this keep and ask about fair! Imagine more gravestones belonging to the people you will inevitably kill from your foolish recklessness! What if Colleen had been downstairs with the twins and gotten swept away? It was only dumb luck, again, that prevented exactly that from happening this time."

Azerick turned to Roger. "You were with her?"

Roger nodded. "Yes, sir."

"Then you are grounded for one month and will help with everything I have told Ellyssa to do."

"Azerick, it's not Roger's fault! He tried to tell me not to, but I did it anyway!" Ellyssa said, trying to come to her friend's defense.

"You're right. It is not his fault. Just like it is not the fault of most victims who get hurt from someone else's selfish actions. You have shown me time and again that punishing you does little good. Maybe if someone close to you suffers for your actions you might actually learn something. Now, go start on the hall."

Ellyssa jumped to her feet and ran to the tower in tears as Roger followed more slowly. Azerick looked at the crowd that had gathered.

"I am sorry, everyone. I will do what I can to make sure something like this does not happen again."

Azerick was so furious he did not know what to do, so he simply began walking. Rusty fell into step beside him and waited until they were near the outside wall before speaking.

"You do know this is partly your fault, don't you?"

Azerick came to a stop and turned on his friend. "How is this in any way my fault?"

"I warned you before you took off and picked a fight with the Black Tower that it was dangerous and irresponsible to shift all focus to applied magic and neglect magical history, particularly the part dealing with ethics. This is exactly what I feared would happen. I am just surprised it took this long and it only involved one student."

"This is not about the curriculum! Ellyssa has always been stubborn and reckless."

Rusty began ticking off his fingers. "Powerful for her age, willful, reckless, does what she wants despite practical wisdom or the advice of her closest friends. Now, who does that remind you of?"

"This is different! I did what I thought best given some extreme circumstances. I was trying to protect the school and these children. She was trying to figure out a way to avoid stairs!" Azerick defended his actions.

"She's eleven! You were twenty when you turned a nobleman into a donkey for being rude when you could have easily just shut the door in his face!"

"He was not hurt. It was a temporary spell."

"And you were certain of that when you cast it?"

Azerick paused and thought back to that day. He had practically grabbed a scroll at random since it was not a spell he actually knew. Transmogrification was not an area he delved into much.

"Reasonably," he replied. "Fine. Return to teaching the ethical use of magic. Make it a fundamental part of the history lesson."

"Thank you," Rusty replied a bit haughtily.

"I really hate you sometimes. Do you know that?"

Rusty smiled. "Because you know I am right?"

"It certainly does not help."

CHAPTER 4

Samone pored over a stack of papers. "Say what you want about the Watch captain's intuition, but his record-keeping skills are spot on."

"I find that those with the least imagination are often highly organized," Brother Charles responded. "Given his complete lack of theoretical flexibility, it is no surprise his orderliness borders on the obsessive."

Griff looked up from his own pile of papers. "Way too many big words, Chuck. How about dumbing it down for the kid over there?"

"I understood every word of that, Mr. Griff," Kyle replied sharply.

"What it means, Griff, is that the watchman is a twit, but a very orderly one," Samone explained, despite knowing that Griff understood exactly what the cleric said.

"Orderly or not, I still don't see how looking at all these murder reports is going to help us find the vampires," Griff said in frustration.

"Separate the ones with questionable causes of death. Bar brawls, spousal murders, and normal killings, we don't care about," Samone replied.

"And how is that going to help? We already know there are vampires here."

"But we don't know how long they have been here or if they even live in the city. These reports will show whether or not the attack on the party was an isolated event or if it is a larger example of longer-term predation. At least that might let us know if we are wasting our time searching the city."

Griff grunted in response. "Great, we might be able to narrow it down to the largest city in Valeria."

Kyle broke his usual silence and spoke up. "Actually, Samone, I have been thinking on that and may have an idea."

"Put you in a dress, troll you up and down the streets at night, and see what bites?" Griff asked.

"No," the wizard replied.

"Well, I can't do it; I have a beard, Chuck is too ugly; and I think Samone was born wearing her armor."

"What was your idea, Kyle?" Samone asked, coming to the young man's rescue.

Kyle cleared his throat. "I was thinking that with the detail with which Captain Bertrand has written these reports, it is possible to pin each suspicious killing on a map. I do not know a great deal about vampires, but I imagine they would avoid killing close to where they live. The area surrounding their lair is likely to be free of such murders."

"Kyle, you are brilliant!" Samone exclaimed.

Kyle's face turned red at the lovely paladin's praise. "Well, I don't know about brilliant. It just seems logical to me."

All heads turned as Chief Inspector Collin walked into the room he let the holy order use to formulate their plans.

"Chief Inspector, good to see you. What's the word on this Landrin person?" Samone asked.

Inspector Collin took off his hat as he entered, tucked it under an arm, and pulled out a sheet of parchment. "I found seventeen men by the name of Landrin. Two are out at sea, three on caravans, and two are old enough to be my grandfather. An innkeeper spoke of a bard that played in his establishment once by that name, but a mugger killed him some ten years or so ago. Of the ones remaining, most had solid alibis, and those who did not did not appear to be vampires, as far as I could tell. I did make them all step out into the sun and none burned, if that is a reasonable test. I admit no great knowledge of such things."

"I can think of few if any that are better, Inspector. Do you have a good map of the city? Kyle had a fantastic idea and I would like to put it into action," Samone said.

"I have several in my office. I will get one immediately."

About an hour later, the inspector and the Solarian's Light were studying a large map tacked down onto a sheet of cork with several dozen pins sticking out of it.

"Anyone see a pattern?" Samone asked the group.

Collin shook his head. "Not really. It is not surprising that the vast majority are in the poorer districts to the west and south."

"If we assume these few in the north and east are part of the circle, we have a hub just here where there are no murders whatsoever," Kyle pointed out.

"Great, right in the middle of one of the wealthiest districts," Griff grumbled. "How many doors do you think we can kick down before we get thrown in the dungeons? My bet is about two if we do it really fast."

Samone looked at her big friend. "I guess that means we will just have to conduct our investigation tactfully."

Griff curled his lip at the idea. "I hate tactful."

The group of Solarian's Light spent the rest of the day knocking on doors and speaking with the residents of the wealthy district. They met little resistance to their intrusion as nearly all had heard of or experienced firsthand that night of terror and were eager to help. They had visited at least two dozen stately homes and decided this would be the last one they would investigate before they retired for the night and renewed their search in the morning.

Samone rapped loudly on the door with a gauntleted fist and waited several minutes before someone opened it. An older man in formal livery looked at them inquisitively from just beyond the threshold.

"Good evening to you Mr...." Samone greeted the man and inquired of his name.

"Claudius, mistress," the man supplied. "Was there something I could do for you?"

"We are investigating an attack that occurred the other night at a ball. May we come in?"

Claudius hesitated before opening the door wider and gesturing for the group to enter. They passed through the foyer and into a large parlor.

"I am afraid with the master and missus away I am not allowed to take you beyond the outer parlor. It is just myself and a few servants staying in the house at this time."

"Where did the lord of the house go, if I may ask?" Samone inquired.

"He and the lady went to Brelland last week. We do not expect them to return for at least two more weeks."

Samone used one of her more subtle holy powers to detect the presence of undead or beings of evil intent but sensed nothing. She looked at Charles who gave her a small shake of his head.

"Sorry to have disturbed you, Claudius," Samone said, then turned to leave.

The haunting melody of a viola resonated through the mansion. Samone stopped and cocked an ear.

"That is one of the servants," Claudius supplied. "He enjoys the viola when he is not working and the master is away. Something about the acoustics of the house when no one is here."

"He is very good. What is that tune called?" Samone asked.

Claudius listened a moment and replied, "I believe it is *The Nightingale and the Lark*."

Samone nodded. "It's lovely. Good evening once again, Claudius."

The party sat at a table in one of the nicer inns of the district. Each sipped at their preferred drink while waiting for their meal. Nearby, a minstrel played a mandolin and sang for the crowd.

"This is getting us nowhere," Samone complained. "We haven't searched half the homes on the list and too many of the occupants fled after the attack for fear that someone is targeting the nobles."

"We will get an early start on the morrow. If it turns up nothing, we will formulate a new plan," Charles said in his baritone voice.

Samone turned to the singer and asked, "Do you know *The Nightingale and the Lark*?"

"A classic, milady, and a fine choice," the bard returned with a smile, then began to play.

Despite being played on a mandolin, the song translated to the instrument well and Samone found herself humming along as the food was served. The serving woman set the plates before the crew then set a package wrapped in a sheet of cloth next to Samone.

"What is this?" the paladin asked, looking at the parcel.

"A gentleman asked me to give it to you. He said he thought you might be looking for it," the woman answered.

"What man?"

The serving woman looked around. "He seems to be gone now. I don't know who he was. I didn't recognize him."

"What did he look like?" Samone asked.

"It was hard to tell. He wore a hooded cloak, but from what I could see, he was quite handsome. I am sure he will be calling on you again," the woman said with a knowing smile.

Samone slowly removed the cloth from the object and stared.

"What is it, girl?" Griff asked.

"It's a mask of some sort," Samone replied.

Charles leaned over for a better look. "It looks like some kind of bird."

"A lark!" Samone cried out.

"What's the matter? You don't like larks?" Griff asked at her sudden agitation.

"Inspector Collin said the man the vampire addressed wore the mask of a lark. This must be his!"

"Why would he give it to us? Is he taunting us?" Kyle asked.

Samone shook her head. "I think he wants us to find him."

"Why would he want us to find him if he is involved in murder and vampires?" Griff asked.

Samone ignored Griff and spun back to the minstrel. "You, play *The Nightingale and the Lark* again."

"Milady, I just played it. Surely, there is another song you wish to hear? I know dozens of them."

"I wasn't paying attention before, so please play it again!" Samone demanded impatiently.

The bard bent to his lute and began strumming out the tune and singing the song once again.

The nightingale sang alone in the park
When a beautiful tune touched her heart
She flitted and fluttered from tree to tree

Until she found the trilling lark
The two birds sang in harmony
Always together upon their tree
One morn the nightingale was alone
The lark was locked away in a nobleman's home
The lark swore never again would he sing
Until the day that he could be free

"He's the lark!" Samone shouted, receiving several stares from the other patrons.

"Who's the lark?" Griff asked.

"Landrin! If he is part of this, he is an unwilling participant and wants to be found."

"Then why not simply come to us? If he can get out and deliver a mask, why not just leave and inform the guard, or the Church?" Kyle inquired of the group.

Brother Charles answered his question. "Vampires are capable of some very powerful compulsion magic. It is likely that he cannot. This Landrin must either have a very strong will, or he found a loophole in the vampire's orders about revealing their existence."

"What do we do now? We know who, but do we know where?"

"Yes, we do," Samone replied. "That last house we visited, I heard *The Nightingale and the Lark* being played. It must have been Landrin trying to give us a clue."

Charles looked at Samone. "You do realize that if he has been turned, we will have to destroy him as well."

Samone nodded. "I imagine he knows that as well and does not care. If he has enough volition to betray his master, he has enough humanity to prefer death to this undead existence he lives in now."

"We'll need to hit them in the daylight, and even then, it is a risky endeavor. Going into that house at night would be suicide," Griff pointed out.

"Agreed," Samone concurred. "We will prepare tonight and investigate further in the morning."

Samone and Brother Charles spent much of the remaining twilight communing with Solarian. Kyle prepared his spells that were best suited for what was almost certainly going to be close quarters combat in confined spaces. Griff honed his blades to a razor's edge while keeping cadence with his strokes by repeating prayers. Knowing what they faced tomorrow, the group got as much sleep as they could before rising early the next day.

"There are at least five, maybe six, vampires in that place," Griff remarked as they left the inn and marched toward the manor. "Think we should grab a couple dozen city watch to take with us?"

Samone shook her head. "This requires Solarian's holy strength to deal with it. The vampires would slaughter the Watch and gain strength from feeding on their bodies. They would be worse than just being in the way."

"And you still want to just go up and knock on the door?"

"We have little in the way of real evidence to support our theory of involvement. We must take a subtle approach until we are sure. We should know shortly whether this is our house or not," Samone explained.

She did not really need to go over what they had discussed last night, nor did Griff need to hear it again. Talking simply helped calm their nerves and kept them focused on what they could control. Soon enough, even if everything went to plan, there would be little in the way of control as the two opposing forces fought for the right to exist.

Just as before, there was no one guarding the decorative gates, so they pushed through and knocked on the door. A minute later, the door partially opened and Claudius's face appeared in the crack.

"I'm sorry. I thought I explained that the master would not return for at least two weeks."

"That is what you said, but we believe the master is at home now and we will speak with him," Samone informed the man authoritatively.

Sweat beaded on the man's balding forehead. "No, I am sorry, but you are mistaken. There is no one here. If you please, I have duties to attend to."

Samone used her armored foot to keep Claudius from closing the door. "Then perhaps we could speak with the lark?"

Claudius surrendered his pretense and ran back into the house. Samone kicked the door wide and shouted to the cleric.

"Charles!"

Brother Charles rattled off a quick incantation and Claudius froze midstride in the middle of the room just beyond the foyer. Samone secured the man's hands behind his back and tied his ankles together with strips of stout leather. Kyle stood close to Samone while Griff and Charles spread out and scanned the room.

"I don't suppose you think he'll tell us where they're hiding?" Griff asked as he studied the obvious passages leading from the room.

Samone answered as she tugged the cords tight. "Doubtful. He is in thrall of whoever commands here and will not reveal anything. It is unlikely the creatures are above ground with the sun out. We need to find the way down to wherever they hide during the day. It is almost certainly hidden behind a wall panel or secret doorway."

It took nearly an hour of searching before they finally located the hidden doorway that led under the mansion. Stone stairs delved into a dark, cavernous room at least thirty feet below the house. Samone uttered a word and her shield lit up like the lens of a lighthouse.

Charles and Kyle also created magical light, but none could pierce the unnatural blackness for more than a few yards in any direction. It was almost as if a thick black fog absorbed the light, particularly near the stone surfaces. They could see several yards down the passage, yet the ceiling and where the wall met the floor refused to allow the light to penetrate and held onto its shadows like a mother protecting her child.

"By Solarian's Light," Samone exhaled. "They must have been here for years creating and enspelling these passages. They appear to go on forever."

Charles's deep voice rumbled down the dank passageway. "I think these were likely the old aqueducts and storm drains the city used before the sewers were built. They probably bricked up several of the passages where the newer sewers connected, and claimed these halls for their own. They could well span several miles beneath the city."

As they stepped further into the tunnel, a woman's laughter echoed up the passage. "Go home, creatures of light. You will find only death within the darkness."

"We come to send you back to the earth where you belong, abomination!" Charles roared back.

More laughter responded to his threat. "The world belongs to us, breather, or soon will. Go back to your world of light and enjoy the last few weeks of life you have left."

No one bothered to reply to the threat this time. No words would end this battle, so the squad of Solarian's Light delved further into the darkness to put an end to the contemptuous voice with steel and fire.

A dark form flitted across the passageway several yards ahead of Samone, mocking the living with its laughter as it sped past. Another form darted across to their rear, cackling gleefully as it toyed with the humans. Kyle leapt to the side and launched a massive fireball after the fleeing form, but only scorched the stone wall at the end of the corridor and a few of Griff's whiskers as it streaked by.

"Easy there, Sparky," Griff warned with a small laugh.

The wizard's failed assault brought forth a gale of fresh laughter as the vampire's voice echoed throughout the labyrinthine maze. Onward the party pressed, alert to the slightest sound or movement. Even at this level of heightened vigilance, the first real attack caught them completely by surprise.

Celina darted in, flashing a dagger at Griff's throat with astonishing speed. The big warrior barely had time to raise his own blade and deflect it away from his throat, but he still received a deep cut along his left cheek. Brother Charles reacted instantly and called out to his god.

"By the light of Solarian, I rebuke you, abomination!" he shouted as he held out his amber holy symbol.

The golden orb flared in a brilliant light that managed to erase even the pervasive shadows from all around them. Celina screeched in pain and rage as the light washed over her. Kyle sent several fiery bolts from his fingertips into the vile vampiress as she reeled from the hateful radiance. She leapt straight up into the air, clung to the ceiling like a spider, and scuttled away, vanishing almost as quickly as she had appeared. The powerful light winked out and only the cloying scent of burnt hair and flesh remained to give witness to the attack.

"I smell your blood, breather. I can taste it on my blade," Celina mocked from somewhere down the dank passage.

"All I can smell is your cooked hide," Griff shouted back.

"Your wizard will pay for that effrontery, I promise you!" the vampiress raged, no longer amused.

"Are you all right, Griff?" Samone called back.

"Yeah, the little minx just scratched me."

"They're getting bold, so let's be careful," Samone cautioned.

Griff gave a short laugh. "Yeah, because I was so overconfident before."

Black passages continued to branch off every few yards. Between bouts of the vampires' laughter, the silence was so pervasive the warriors could hear their own hearts pounding in their chest.

A form darted past to their front and rear just as before. Kyle held his spell this time and the others readied themselves, anticipating another attack. Hidden in the darkness of the ceiling, directly above Kyle, Karla silently extended her legs and lowered her upper body until she hung upside down, perpendicular with the floor. Her dagger flashed out with incredible speed and power, slicing deeply into the wizard's throat.

Kyle crumpled to the floor almost instantly, gagging on the blood that ran down his throat. The bright red spray was lost in the darkness of the passageway. Charles dropped to his knees with a prayer of healing on his lips, but Celina and Jacinth flew into the group, short blades and claws flashing.

Griff interposed himself between Celina and the cleric, catching the blade aimed for Charles's neck. The man and vampires fended off each other's strikes in a flurry of steel, claws, and fangs. Jacinth's claws made three long rents in Griff's chain mail. The fighter managed to cut the undead woman deep in the side, but the wound failed to slow her down.

Celina also leapt for the cleric and bore her talon-like nails through his leather and chain armor. Charles responded by slinging holy water from a clay vial each of them carried on their belt in a wide arc. Celina and Jacinth hissed in rage and pain as the holy water burned them as if it were acid. Samone smashed her shield into Celina's ruined faced and prepared to take her head off with her sword as Jacinth leapt away and retreated into the darkness.

Some sixth sense alerted the paladin to a new threat just above her. Samone thrust straight up with her holy sword and stabbed Karla through the chest as the vampiress prepared to attack her from above just as she had done with Kyle. The vampire lost her magical grip on the ceiling and fell heavily downward.

"Griff!" Samone shouted as she guided the vampire away and to the floor with her sword.

Griff turned and swung his sword without hesitation, striking Karla's head from her shoulders. Charles turned back to Kyle, but it was clear that it was too late to save the young wizard. He used another vial of holy water on the vampire's severed neck, ensuring that the creature would never rise again.

"Kyle?" Samone asked as she looked down at the motionless body.

Charles simply shook his head in reply.

A click, instinct, and a lot of luck were the only things that saved Samone's life. The paladin raised her shield and just barely managed to deflect the heavy crossbow bolt Filip shot at her. The bolt glanced off the shield at the same time as Celina and Jacinth renewed their attack. Samone turned to her two remaining comrades to shout a warning, but she lost her voice as she spied the crossbow bolt intended for her sticking out of Charles's neck.

Landrin watched the cleric fall to the ground as Filip, Celina, and Jacinth threw themselves back into the fray. The compulsion Eldon held over him would not allow him to fight directly against the other vampires, but he thought he might be able to aid the remaining two humans enough to give them a chance.

He cast a simple spell that created an icy stretch between Celina and the big man named Griff. Caught by surprise, Celina's feet slipped out from under her and she landed hard on her back while she continued to slide toward the man with both his swords raised and ready to strike. One blade flashed down and pierced her through the chest. The other went into her open, screaming mouth and out the back of her neck. Griff pulled a vial of holy water from his belt, jammed it into her mouth, pulled out his blade, and kicked her in the jaw.

The clay shattered under the force of his kick, forcing its contents down Celina's throat. The holy water burned down her gullet and nearly hollowed out her skull in seconds. She spent the last few moments of her undeath writhing in agony. Griff had no time to revel in his victory as Jacinth scampered along the wall and leapt for him, cursing and slashing furiously with knife and nails.

Landrin turned toward Filip who had dropped his crossbow and was sprinting down the passageway with astonishing speed. He cast another minor spell and some of the stone blocks comprising the floor rose up a few inches. Filip caught a foot on one and sailed headfirst toward the paladin. Samone braced herself for the impact and caught the flying Filip with her shield, much as she had done with the quarrel he had shot at her.

The force of the impact knocked the woman back several steps, but she recovered and charged back at the vampire as he swiftly jumped to his feet. With a shout to her god, Samone caused her sword and shield to burst into an eye-searing brilliance. Filip raised his hand to ward his abused eyes as Landrin looked away and Jacinth hissed and fled the painful luminescence.

Samone shouted once again as she brought her holy sword down in a powerful arc, severing Filip's upraised arm and cleaving his skull in twain clear down to where the head joined the neck. The paladin wrenched her blade free and spun to see how Griff was faring. She relaxed slightly when she saw the big man standing with no enemy in sight.

"Griff, how are you?" she asked warily, knowing there was at least one more vampire out there hiding in the darkness.

"Not so good, babe," Griff wheezed, then turned and fell toward Samone.

Dropping her shield, but maintaining her grip on her sword, Samone grabbed Griff and guided his bulk to the floor. It was there, in the light cast by her enchanted shield, that she saw the handle of the knife sticking out of Griff's chest.

"Hold on, Griff! I got you!" Samone cried out, then called upon Solarian's aid once more.

Her free hand glowed with healing power. As she lowered it toward Griff's wound, pain flared through her back and a sword blade erupted from her chest. Despite the horrible wound, Samone dove forward, tucked into a roll, and sprang back up, sword held ready despite her rapidly failing strength.

Eldon stood a few feet away, smiling triumphantly with his bloody blade gripped loosely in his hand. He flicked his blade invitingly at the paladin who was barely able to keep on her feet much less defend herself.

Landrin sprang out of the dark corridor, slammed Samone into the wall, and pressed himself against her. As he leaned into her, he grabbed her sword in one hand and pulled a vial of holy water from her belt with the other.

"Trust me, my nightingale," he whispered into her ear.

Eldon approached from behind. "Finally, Landrin! I had almost given up hope on you. Kill her for me. I give her to you."

Landrin pulled his head back just far enough to look the paladin in the eyes then glanced back at Eldon. Samone feebly raised her hand and called upon Solarian's deliverance. Her holy symbol blazed brightly in her hand, catching Eldon unprepared. The elder vampire reeled back and Landrin lunged, smashing the vial of holy water against his master's face as the holy aura weakened Eldon's control over him for just a moment.

Both vampires cried out in pain when the holy water splashed upon them. Landrin ignored the burning and brought Samone's blade around in a whistling arc, striking Eldon's head from his shoulders before dropping the sword to the ground as the hilt burned his hand as badly as the holy water had.

Past the blazing pain in his hands, Landrin felt his mind clear as Eldon's compulsion died along with him. Jacinth felt it as well and stepped out of the shadows, a dagger held before her defensively.

"We're free now, Landrin," she said. "Let us feed on the woman and make our own way. You know I have always had strong feelings for you."

Landrin looked at his ravaged hands then up at Jacinth.

"I have always had strong feelings for you as well," he replied as she smiled and stepped closer, "hatred, loathing, and disgust being just a few of them."

Landrin spoke arcane words of power and released a jet of flame at Jacinth, catching and engulfing her completely. She screamed in agony as Landrin stepped after her while she rolled and flailed around in an attempt to smother the fire, but Landrin continued to pour power into the spell until Jacinth was nothing more than a pile of ash with a few bones poking out of it.

He turned back to the paladin still huddling against the wall. "Are you going to be all right?"

Samone managed a nod. "I think so. I was able to heal the injury some. What about you?"

Landrin looked at his hands. The skin on both of them was blistered, blackened, and raw. The pain was unimaginably intense, yet he relished such a human sensation.

"Charred but I should recover."

"You are very lucky. Solarian must still look upon you with a small amount of favor. Touching my sword like that should have destroyed you almost immediately," Samone informed him. "Perhaps that is why you never went fully over."

Landrin nodded as he thought about her words. "I have prayed every day since Eldon turned me. I had thought Solarian had abandoned me. Perhaps I just needed to be tested."

"He tests us all." Samone looked at Eldon's body. "He said he had almost given up on you. Have you never killed before?"

Landrin thought back to the night he crawled out of his grave. "Once, the first night I awoke, but he was no innocent. He thought to rob me, to kill me. It still fills me with dread. Ever since then, I have only had what the others brought back. Eldon made me drink their blood. At least now, I can do as I choose. I can choose how to feed or if I wish to exist at all. I will have to think and pray upon it."

"I am sworn to destroy your kind," Samone told him.

"I know, and as you well should. There is no place in this world for our kind. We can do nothing but bring pain. Such things should not exist."

"I lost my dearest friends tonight, but we all gladly give our lives to our service. If not for you, we would have all died and failed in our mission. I will allow you to go this one time. Leave the city forever. The next time we meet, I will destroy you."

Landrin nodded his understanding. "I need a few days to prepare. Perhaps if Solarian has not truly abandoned me, he will give me guidance. Maybe I have fulfilled my role. If such is the case, I might remain here and let you put me to rest."

Samone stood on unsteady legs. "You have three days. I must return with help to recover my comrades. Do not let me see you again, or I will destroy you."

Samone recovered her sword and shield, and walked shakily down the dark passage toward the life-giving light above.

CHAPTER 5

Ellyssa and Roger crouched upon the drop cloth as they painted the wall of the main hall where the water had marred it. Ellyssa had spent a good portion of the previous morning hanging and beating the water out of all the carpets. Today, she and Roger had to shovel out the filthy water from the stables.

"It's not fair you got in trouble," Ellyssa told Roger for probably the hundredth time in the last two days. "I did it, not you. I'm sorry you got in trouble. Azerick should not punish you for what I did."

Roger was tired of hearing Ellyssa's attempts at relieving her guilt. He stuck his brush in the paint and turned on her.

"You still don't get it, do you?" he said in frustration. "Other than not beating you with a stick, he did exactly what he should have done! You do whatever you please without thinking about what might happen to someone else. Until you learn that your actions can hurt others, you are going to keep on doing what you want. You play with magic as if it were a toy. You have no respect for it or what it can do."

Ellyssa's face turned red and her heart raced. Blood pounded in her temples as her anger boiled over.

"I don't know what magic can do? I've been studying magic longer than you, and I can kick your butt any day of the week!" she shouted defensively.

"You really think you know more than me?" Roger asked. He took several paces back and coaxed the Source into his body as he pulled a few hairs from his head and a piece of string from a pouch. "Let's see what you know. Go on, come at me."

Ellyssa tore at the Source like a furious swordsman yanking his blade from its scabbard to hew down a foe. Grabbing a component from her own pouch, she shaped the swirling, angry torrent of energy into a spell of significant power. She was so furious that she did not consider what would happen if Roger did not shield himself quickly or strongly enough to block the power of her spell. At this moment, all she wanted to do was show him she was right.

Roger smirked at the girl's typical overreaction and sent a tiny bit of power through the string and hair in his hand. The brush he had thrust into the bucket of paint flew up and slapped Ellyssa in the face. Blinded, Ellyssa lost focus on her spell as she tried to wipe the paint from her eyes. Another trickle of power and the canvas cloth she stood on leapt up and engulfed her. She looked like a butterfly with just her head emerging from her cocoon.

Roger walked up to her as she glared and fumed over her ignominious defeat. "Being stronger does not mean being more knowledgeable or better."

Roger grabbed his brush and bucket of paint, gave Ellyssa a small push, and went upstairs to work alone. Ellyssa screeched and flailed about on the floor as she wormed her way out of the canvas. Once free, she leapt to her feet, cleared her eyes, and was about to stalk up the stairs for a rematch when she saw Azerick looking at her from the top of the basement steps.

She opened her mouth but closed it without a sound when Azerick simply shook his head in disappointment and disappeared back down the stairs. All anger left her in that moment. She could handle his anger and even Roger's victory, but the look of disappointment in Azerick's eyes was too much. She slumped down with fresh tears washing twin clean streaks through the paint on her face, and returned to painting the wall.

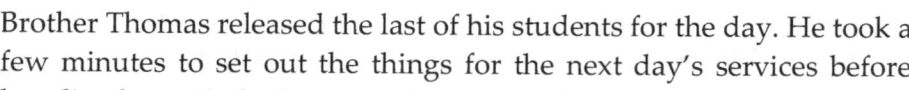

Brother Thomas released the last of his students for the day. He took a few minutes to set out the things for the next day's services before kneeling beneath the big stained-glass window for evening prayers.

He thought about his novitiates, particularly his three Chosen. He still could not believe his luck having three Chosen in his church, especially considering he was barely out of seminary himself. He should have sent at least the three Chosen to seminary in Brightridge long ago, but there had been so much going on with the attack and building the new church.

He sighed as he realized much of that was simply an excuse to keep them with him a while longer. He enjoyed teaching the children, and being amongst the Chosen made him feel a little closer to Solarian. As Thomas knelt and prayed for Solarian's forgiveness for his selfishness, he felt the warm glow of the sun wash over his back as it streamed through the stylized window set in the lower portion of the steepled roof.

It took only a moment for him to realize this was wrong. Every church of Solarian was built with the golden window facing east to capture the first rays of the morning sun. It was nearly evening and the sun was just setting behind the solid stone wall of his church.

Thomas's body quivered in fear, excitement, adoration, and a mix of almost every emotion a human being could experience. Unless the church had caught fire, there were only two possible explanations. Either someone was playing a terrible trick on him, or he was being graced with the presence of his god.

"You may look upon me, my faithful servant," an impossibly powerful and kind voice said to him.

Thomas had to take several deep breaths before he mustered the strength to accept the invitation. When he finally marshaled the courage to look up, he nearly threw himself onto the floor in prostration. Standing before him was the sun itself, if it had taken on the form of a man in resplendent plate armor. He could barely make out the form through its blazing glory.

"Be at ease, Thomas," Solarian said kindly. "We have much to discuss."

The amazed priest could only nod his understanding.

"You have done very well. You have fulfilled the task I set you and more. However, there is another boon I would ask of you."

"Command me, My Lord," Thomas managed to gasp out.

"I sent you a dream to come to North Haven and build a church and you did. I sent you three Chosen to care for and teach, and you did. Three children who knew almost nothing of me, I set above nearly all others, yet never did you ask why; never did you question why three homeless children were Chosen and not you."

"Such things are not for me to question, Your Luminescence. I swore to follow and obey, not to question," Brother Thomas answered dutifully.

Solarian gave a deep chuckle. "Yet so many have questioned. There is a great darkness spreading over the land. An evil beyond imagining is coming, and those that follow the light must be prepared. Now is your time to rise to the occasion."

"I have felt the foulness in the air and heard of the undead that are rising, My Lord. Command me and I shall do your bidding."

"The abominations are but the twilight preceding the darkness, my son. A greater evil exists, an evil that has bided its time for over a millennium, and it approaches. It is an evil so great it threatens even the gods. However, it is not the time to discuss such things. For now, we must contend with what is at hand before we deal with what comes tomorrow."

"I am yours to command, My Lord."

"I shall lift you above all others for your heart is pure and true to my teachings. Keep your Chosen close to you. Teach them and guide them in the pure truth of my word. You must be my light against the coming darkness, Thomas."

Thomas's mind reeled at Solarian's words. What could he mean? How could he, the most junior of priests, teach three young Chosen and stand for Solarian above far greater men in the Church? Such a thing would certainly put him at odds with some of the more senior of their order.

"Glorious One, I am awed by your faith in me, but I am just a junior priest. How can I do what you ask of me above so many more deserving?"

"Thomas, I had my Chosen long before any man built a church in my name or assumed a title to set himself above others. Trust in me and trust in yourself. I will not fail you just as I know you will never let yourself fail me. Accept my gift and let the light shine upon you so that you may become a beacon for all those that need shelter from the darkness."

The warmth Thomas had felt earlier now felt like a fire, not the blistering pain flames brought, but a cleansing light that suffused his body and soul. It felt as though he were a physical extension of his god, and he could not fathom how incomplete the life he enjoyed just a moment ago felt in comparison. His soul felt like a bird released from the cage in which it had been born. Having never flown, Thomas could never have guessed at the feeling, or that such a fundamental part of him had been missing. He could only kneel and weep at the sensation. He missed supper and did not even notice. So lost in this moment of wondrous bliss, Thomas did not realize the hour until it was so dark inside that the only light came from the stars shining through the great window. As wondrous as Solarian's blessing was, he could not shake the feeling of dread that this attention heralded.

CHAPTER 6

With the help of some members of the Church, Samone retrieved the bodies of her fallen comrades and commenced consecrating the warrens beneath the mansion. This gave Landrin very little time to gather his things and leave the city. He was in his room, collecting a few precious books and scrolls when a brilliant glow washed over him. The light hit him with a physical force and dropped him to his knees. Had he been alive, it may have felt glorious. However, in his current condition it was nearly unbearable.

"Have you come to put an end to me, Solarian?" Landrin asked through gritted teeth.

The light faded and a rich voice full of regret responded. "I wish that I could, Landrin. No one deserves this curse, particularly one as faithful as you."

Landrin's shoulders slumped. "If you will not cure me or release me unto death, why come to me now?"

"For ten years, you have prayed daily for release. For ten years, you have denied and fought your dark nature, and for ten years, I have watched you and listened to your prayers. We gods move slowly, in your eyes, but I had to take your measure and now I have it. Events of cataclysmic proportions are even now approaching. I need you as you are to aid those who shall fight to prevent it from unfolding."

"What must I do? What is coming?"

"First shall come a blight upon the land that will cast this world into perpetual darkness. However, it is but a prelude to a far more sinister threat that, if left unchecked, shall crush this world beneath its heel. All those capable of wielding magic shall be purged, the gods shall be cast out and destroyed, and those who perish shall consider themselves amongst the fortunate. For those few who survive, it shall mean the end of free will and any semblance of a life worth living," the god of light told his dark follower.

Landrin could almost detect a trace of fear in the god's voice. What could be so terrible and so powerful as to concern a god, much less threaten to destroy it? What could he possibly do that Solarian himself could not do simply by wishing it so?

"I sense your doubts, Landrin. All creatures must obey the laws of their very nature, even the gods. A time will come when we too will join more directly in the battle that comes, but today is not our time."

"What will you have of me, My Lord?"

"For this world to have a chance, the people must be strong. To be strong, they must be united. King Jarvin is the one to unite the kingdom under his stalwart leadership, but he is not yet ready. Like a sword needing tempering, he must first face the hammer and fire of the forge without breaking. Forces are set against him, many within my own church. My followers' faith in their god is strong, but they must learn to have faith in their mortal leader as well. Such a division of faith and loyalty weakens the land and gives strength to our enemies. You shall aid Jarvin and those loyal to him."

Landrin nodded his understanding despite the fact that much of what Solarian was saying was beyond him. "How can I aid the king, especially as I am now?"

"You feel the pull of the evil that lives far to the north. It is the creature your master called master. Soon, Jarvin will speak with a council of lords for governorship of a small but vital town known as End's Run. You shall present yourself to him for the position."

"How can I do that? How can I make my claim and convince him to cede such a thing to me?" Landrin asked.

A rolled vellum scroll appeared in Solarian's glowing hand, and he presented it to the man kneeling before him. Landrin gently took the scroll his god offered, unrolled it, and gaped in surprise.

"It is my father's writ of lordship handed down from his grandfather's grandfather!" Landrin exclaimed in surprise.

"You have all the written authority you require. It is up to you to convince the king that you are worthy. You shall also present him with a gift."

A fanciful wardrobe stood empty against the far side of the room. The crown molding and doors were stylized with the images of what could only be the northern forests. Enormous stags, bears, and other carved creatures inhabiting the forest scenes were rendered in amazing detail. With a wave of Solarian's luminous hand, numerous sigils flared briefly before seemingly sinking into the wood like beads of water on a cloth.

"What does it do?"

"You shall know when the time comes," came Solarian's cryptic reply.

"The paladin, Samone," Landrin said, but could not finish his sentence.

"I have welcomed her faithful friends into my kingdom. Her part is yet unfinished."

"Will we meet again?"

"Undoubtedly. But do not expect a joyous reunion," Solarian cautioned him.

"She said she would kill me, for what I am, if we ever met again."

"Nothing is ever certain. Even fates shift with the cosmic currents."

"So you say, but you speak of things that have not happened yet as though they are inevitable. Did you see me turned? Did you make it happen so that I would be here now doing what you wish to be done?" Landrin asked, unable to cover the strained resentment in his quavering voice.

"The gods can see and follow lines of fate, but we are forbidden from altering them. However, we can put pieces into play to make the best use of them. It is difficult, but I try to understand how you feel about being part of something so much greater than yourself. It feels as though your life is little more than that of a doll in the hands of a child. I share that feeling, Landrin. There are even greater forces than us gods, and we must play our part as well, often without fully understanding these things. It is especially difficult when one does not like to believe there are things greater or more powerful than they are."

"I will do what you command, My Lord, but I do not fully understand," Landrin replied.

"Sometimes, simply keeping faith is more important than understanding."

Landrin looked up and found himself alone in the room once more. It took several minutes to blink away the dazzling blotches of light still floating about before his eyes. At first glance, everything appeared the same as it had and Landrin almost thought he had imagined the encounter. Then he noticed the scroll in his hand and saw another on the small table near the bed. He crossed the room, read the scroll, and tucked them both away. He had a great many things to do this night and little time in which to do them.

Jarvin rubbed his temples as the assembled lords batted around the same argument once again. It had been going on for the better part of an hour without making an inch of progress.

"As much as you all try to deny it," Jarvin tried once more, "the fact remains that End's Run is a hold of the kingdom and needs a lord to administer it. There is potential for a great amount of gold to be made for whoever takes control as well as for the crown."

"Aye, there's also even better potential to get a knife in the back," Lord Abernathy replied with a laugh.

"I do not understand why you are so set on expanding the kingdom when you can barely control the one you have," the elderly lord Malcolm croaked. "And what of this undead menace? I have had to hire gangs of swordsmen to patrol every one of my towns before the common rabble all demand to move into my keep! What are you doing about that?"

"I have soldiers and members of the Church dealing with the situation. That is not the issue at hand, at least not one that can be resolved tonight. If you are so concerned about coin, this venture could double your coffers in just a few years!" Jarvin shouted in frustration.

Lord Whitfield cleared his throat. "Your Majesty, it is just that with the current political climate, few are willing to invest in new ventures, particularly those that pose a significant personal risk and the extreme discomfort of displacement. I would be willing to assume authority of End's Run and manage its governance through an intermediary of my choosing."

"Do you hide behind your wife's skirts when a man looks at you aggressively as well, Markus?" Lord Aderly called out mockingly.

Lord Whitfield's face flushed in embarrassment and anger. "I do not see you trekking up to that godless, frozen wasteland to take direct lordship over those lawless savages!"

"Gentlemen!" Jarvin pleaded, standing up. "Despite Lord Aderly's crassness, he is correct. I must have a true lord to govern with the full authority of the crown. A proxy simply will not do. End's Run already boasts over four thousand citizens who went seeking their fortune. Yet only about half actually reside within the town proper. The others are spread out amongst various camps and settlements. I need someone to create a centralized, stable government."

"Then task the Ice Queen. Her duchy is the closest to End's Run, other than Brelland, and she openly supports you," Lord Langdon suggested snidely.

Jarvin's face clouded at the man's words, and it took considerable effort to control his voice. "She openly supports me while you do what? Openly contest me, or is it more covert?"

The man did not even have the decency to look insulted. He simply smiled and shrugged. It was a testament to Jarvin's self-control, or foolishness, that he paused to think before charging across the table and hewing him down on the spot. Thankfully, there came an interruption before he could decide.

The large doors to the dining hall opened and Jarvin's seneschal stepped in. "Pardon the intrusion, Your Majesty, but there is a Lord Landrin Bailey seeking an audience. He insists it pertains directly to the matter at hand."

"Show him in then."

Landrin practically strutted down the deep blue carpet running up the center of the room. He had done a little acting in his time and he put his meager skills to maximum effect. Upon nearing King Jarvin, he swept the felt, broad-brimmed black hat off his head and bent down into a showman's bow.

"Your Majesty, it is an honor to meet you. I give you my humblest appreciation for granting me this audience."

Jarvin smiled at the man's foppishness and hoped he was not about to waste his time. "As you can see, Lord Bailey, we are in the midst of a serious discussion of state. What is it you wished to see me about?"

Landrin stood up from his bow, straightened his black silk vest, and addressed the king. "I received word that you sought a man to govern End's Run. I could not help but overhear as I waited outside the door, that you are unable to find a man of sufficient courage or fortitude to do so, and wish to offer my services."

An angry muttering filled the room as the assembled lords tried to determine if they had just been insulted.

Lord Aderly leaned forward and demanded clarification. "Are you inferring that we are weak or are cowards, Lord Bailey?"

"Of course not. I *implied* it as politely as I could. You inferred it. Unfortunately there are so very few adjectives I can use in your regard that you would find pleasing."

Lord Aderly jumped from his chair and grabbed the hilt of his sword while the other lords shouted their outrage. "You are lucky we are in the king's hall, or I would demand satisfaction of you here and now, you petulant cur!"

Landrin smiled at the furious lords. "You demand satisfaction in what way, by crossing steel or do you mean in a more amorous manner? Personally, I doubt you have the courage for either one."

Jarvin could tell Lord Aderly wanted desperately to pull his blade, but the confident, almost taunting way the young upstart fingered the hilt of his rapier stayed his hand. This meeting was getting more hostile by the moment, and Jarvin knew he needed to set these men at ease before they all stormed out.

"Let us all maintain our composure and cease these unnecessary and unproductive insults to one another's character. Lord Bailey, you offered to take lordship of End's Run. I assume you can produce a writ of title to show you are who and what you claim?" Jarvin asked.

Landrin produced the scroll Solarian had given him. Jarvin read the scroll and frowned. "Not precisely the credentials I had hoped for, Lord Bailey."

Lord Malcolm seemed to wake up and shook a finger at Landrin. "Now I recall that name! Are you Edwin Bailey's get?"

Landrin gave the venerable lord a single nod. "He was my grandfather, sir."

"Bah! A third son of a landless noble! That title is worth less than the vellum it's printed on."

"And this task is precisely the thing for a man of courage and intellect to raise his family name once again," Landrin replied.

Jarvin rolled the writ back up and returned it. "I agree, Landrin. As none of my other lords or their heirs are willing to step up to the challenge, I have little recourse but to accept your offer. My Lords, if there are no further matters of business to attend to, I bid you good evening. Landrin, please follow me to my study, and we can discuss your duties in more detail."

Jarvin led Landrin through a small door set in the far end of the dining hall. The two men negotiated a series of narrow corridors until one opened up into a wider, much grander hallway, which led to the king's favorite study. A fire was already blazing in the large hearth, heating the room to a comfortable level, not that the cold affected Landrin.

Landrin declined Jarvin's invitation for a drink, but the king poured one for himself, motioned for the former bard to sit, and took a seat behind a large desk. The king removed a piece of parchment from a drawer and began scribbling what Landrin assumed was his name and credentials upon it. After sanding and blotting the fresh ink, Jarvin handed the document to Landrin.

"That writ proclaims you the lawful laird of End's Run and details your authority and responsibilities. Given the remote location of the township, you will be operating with a significant amount of autonomy, which is why I had hoped to convince one of my more senior lords to take on the responsibility."

"Begging Your Highness's pardon, but given what I have seen and heard of your lords of late, selecting any of them would not likely have been an improvement. I might be young and landless, but I hope to prove that my loyalty lies with the crown."

Landrin watched Jarvin's face lose some of its regal stoicism. "Indeed. These days I look for a dagger concealed in every palm. I oft wonder if it would not be better to abdicate and allow another to take my place."

"I would tell you that would be a mistake. Both men and darker things tear the land apart. Valeria needs a strong and just ruler, and no man is better suited in ability or temperament than you, Your Majesty. I believe the time will come when all will see what the common people see in you."

"Thank you, Landrin. It is rare to hear kind words directed at me these days. Even a king needs some affirmation from time to time," Jarvin replied sincerely, smiling gratefully at Landrin's words.

"I brought you more than kind words, Your Majesty. I bring a gift from my former home in Brightridge and wish to give it to you as a token of my appreciation for this opportunity. I left it secured to a wagon with your people, if you would care to send a detail with a trundle to retrieve it."

Jarvin's interest was piqued and he sent a runner to fetch the item. The two men then returned to discussing Landrin's duties.

"How soon will you be able to leave?" Jarvin asked. "I have a contingent of one hundred soldiers who have volunteered for the initial garrison, and they have been ready to march for weeks."

"A hundred soldiers?" Landrin asked in surprise. "I thought this land already settled and claimed. Am I to wrest it from some barbarian hands?"

Jarvin chuckled then grew serious. "No, my father established permanent claim to End's Run and its territory shortly before he was killed. He actually traded steel for it from the barbarian chief that claimed that portion as his holding. The barbarians have since moved farther north and do not dispute the region. A few miners and trappers occasionally wander far enough north to touch upon the barbarian's southernmost border, but the trespassers are soon shown the door and escorted back across the border. We call them barbarians, but I have found them quite reasonable as long as they are treated with respect.

"It is our own people that require me to send soldiers. Make no mistake, Landrin. This is a harsh land and largely ungoverned for the fifteen years it has existed. Although a good amount of raw gold and other resources makes its way south, it is largely unregulated and untaxed. There is some form of leadership, from what I understand, but it is more of a gang or warlord leadership and no friend to the crown. It is my hope that with a hundred well-armed soldiers, you will at least be able to establish a foothold from which you can appraise this man's strength, recruit locals, and toss his carcass to the wolves. When that is done, you will need to establish a presence in the numerous logging and mining camps so that the raw materials can be evaluated for tax and ensure that the king's law is properly abided by."

Landrin pondered this information a moment. He could not wait for the soldiers. He planned to leave tonight and could travel far faster than the soldiers could even if they were mounted. Landrin had no doubt killing this warlord, or whatever he was, would not pose much of a challenge. The trick would be doing it without exposing his true nature, and getting his men to follow him instead.

"Your Majesty, I have a small bit of magic at my disposal and can make the trip to End's Run significantly faster if I am not reduced to the speed of a contingent of soldiers and their baggage. I think I could do more if I go ahead of them, scout out the situation, and see what I can expect in the way of local support."

Jarvin rubbed his chin and thought. "I think I see your point. You will need gold for this."

"It would make my job significantly easier."

"Of course I am sending a chest of gold to pay the soldiers' wages and cover the cost involved with establishing everything you will need. As much as I like you on first meeting, I am hesitant handing over the sum you require with nothing more than your word. Even if you do not simply run off with my small fortune, going there alone might mean you and my gold become the property of this brigand."

"I understand your concerns, Highness. Let me assure you, I am highly capable of taking care of myself. How much gold are you sending with the soldiers?" Landrin inquired.

"Ten thousand crowns."

Landrin nodded as he made some quick calculations. "Give me two thousand to use as—incentives—in hiring and possibly turning some men to my side. I have enough of my own coin to take care of most of my personal needs. With luck, the town will be under my control by the time the soldiers arrive."

Landrin had been able to find a small bit of wealth inside the house that belonged to Eldon, but it was not great. Fortunately, his living requirements were equally as meager.

Jarvin considered Landrin's proposal for a moment then nodded. "All right. I shall have my treasurer draw the two thousand crowns from the chest and send the rest with Lieutenant Oliver. He is the ranking man in the contingent. I am placing a great deal of trust in a man I just met, Landrin."

"Then trust me one more time, Highness," Landrin said earnestly. "Find men whose loyalty is unquestionable and keep them very close to you and your family."

Jarvin leaned back in surprise at the intensity of Landrin's warning. "Do you know of a direct threat?"

"No, Majesty, but I do hear a great deal. I believe there are significant threats drawing ever closer and you need to be vigilant. Keep those guards who you know will give their lives for you and your family close at hand."

Landrin laced these last words with a small bit of his vampiric compulsion. He hated to use such a thing on the king and he used it ever so slightly, but he needed Jarvin to take his warning very seriously.

"I will see to the castle guard rosters personally. Thank you for your concern."

There was a knock on the door and one of Jarvin's servants announced that they had brought Landrin's gift. Four men wheeled the wardrobe in on a trundle at the king's behest. Jarvin stood upon seeing it and crossed the room for a closer inspection. He set his drink on a small table next to the wardrobe and marveled at the craftsmanship.

"This is magnificent work," Jarvin lauded him as he ran an experienced hand across the wood and traced the stylized carvings. He even leaned in close and sniffed deeply at the wood. "Do you know how old it is?"

"I do not, milord."

"It is at least two hundred years old, but I would not be surprised if it was three. Did you know I was a carpenter and quite the cabinetmaker before ascending the throne?"

"I had heard something of the sort, Highness."

"I was quite good, you know, but I would have been hard-pressed to match this level of artisanship." Jarvin stopped his inspection and looked pensive. "I miss those days more often than not. The very same people that praised me for my furnishings now curse me as their king. People can be such fickle creatures."

"I hope you will keep this nearby as well, Highness."

"I certainly will. It will look splendid in the children's room, I think."

Another figure entered the room just then and captured the king's attention.

"Pardon the interruption, Your Majesty," Bishop Caalendor begged, "but I have received significant news from Brightridge. Forgive me, Majesty, I was unaware you had a guest."

"That is quite all right. This is Lord Bailey. He has graciously accepted the lairdship of End's Run," Jarvin explained to his senior advisor. "Landrin, this is one of my advisors, Bishop Caalendor."

The cleric looked suspiciously at the young man and Landrin could tell that the bishop was examining him with more than just his eyes. He fed a bit more power into the ward that helped prevent men like the bishop, with just such ability, from seeing his true nature. Invisible fingers gently probed at his ward then with more determination.

The bishop approached Landrin with his hand outstretched. "It is a pleasure to make your acquaintance, Lord Bailey."

If Landrin had a functioning heart, it would have been racing right now. Any physical contact would make his mystical disguise useless. Thinking quickly, Landrin swung his arm around as if to shake hands, caught the half-filled glass Jarvin had set next to the wardrobe, and knocked it from the table upon which it rested.

With amazing quickness, Landrin grabbed for the falling glass and fumbled with it for just a moment, sloshing the drink it contained all over his hands before it found the floor and shattered.

"I beg pardon, Your Majesty!" Landrin exclaimed, feigning embarrassment as he knelt and made to pick up the pieces.

Jarvin ushered him up from the floor. "Leave that, Landrin. I will get a servant to attend to it."

"Pardon me again, Highness. It has been some time since my family has had servants to deal with such tasks. I beg your pardon as well, Your Grace," he said, turning to the bishop while displaying his wine-covered hands.

Bishop Caalendor pursed his lips in thought. "I am not familiar with House Bailey, and I pride myself on knowing all the noble families of station that might be granted such a land grant."

"My house fell significantly over the past couple generations. It appeared that few if any of the more notable houses were willing to take advantage of such an opportunity, so I begged the king for the chance to perhaps return some measure of prestige to the family name."

"I see," the senior cleric replied dubiously but refrained from further questioning.

"It appears the bishop has urgent news for you, Your Majesty. I would like to start out first thing in the morning. If you could have someone escort me to the treasurer, I will procure the stipend and make to depart at first light."

Landrin had no intention of waiting for the sun, and would likely be huddled in a cave or buried deep in a snowdrift before the first light peeked over the horizon in its attempt to burn him to nothing more than ash.

"Of course."

Jarvin called for a lesser functionary to escort Landrin to the treasurer and for a servant to take care of the spill. Landrin bid both the king and the bishop good evening and gratefully removed himself from the presence of the suspicious cleric.

Once they were alone, Bishop Caalendor addressed Jarvin. "An unusual man this Lord Bailey. How did you come to meet him?"

"He had heard of my request and petitioned me for the position. As every other lord decided to fight me on the issue, I decided to give it to him."

"A bit young, don't you think? Youth is often brash and may not consider what a daunting task this could be."

Jarvin smiled as he replayed the young man's abrupt entrance into the dining hall and his pointed wit in dealing with the elder nobles. "I think a bit of brashness may be just the key to making this a successful venture. Now, you said you had news from Brightridge. Has that terrible matter been dealt with?"

"It has, Your Majesty. Prelate Howarth reports that a unit of Solarian's Light entered the manor of Eldon VonTrellin. Upon inspection, the unit discovered VonTrellin and four others cursed with vampirism and put them to rest. Several surviving witnesses from the ball confirmed sketches of the vampires to be the ones responsible for the atrocity."

The king looked grim at the news but nodded appreciatively. "It is good to hear such a nest was exterminated. I would like to personally congratulate and reward those that destroyed the vile creatures."

"Unfortunately, the unit sustained heavy casualties. Only Paladin Samone survived of the four that went in."

Jarvin's face fell at the dire news. "That is indeed unfortunate. Do any of the fallen have family I could present a posthumous medal to? I still wish to show Paladin Samone my gratitude as well."

"The Church is usually the only close family a member of Solarian's Light maintains. There was a young magus attached to the unit who might have family to appreciate such a gesture. I will find out for you. As for Paladin Samone, it appears she has taken a leave of absence despite requests to stay and rest for a time."

"A leave of absence? Do we know where she was going or why she left?" Jarvin asked.

The bishop shook his head. "The message I received mentioned that she spoke of a greater and darker evil. Prelate Howarth thinks she may have ridden off in search of it. Perhaps she wishes to avenge her fallen comrades."

"For everyone's sake, let us pray she is wrong. If there is a greater evil out there than a house of vampires, it would bode quite ill for us all."

"I shall look into it further. With your permission, I would like to send your pet adventurers north to investigate. They have had little with which to occupy their time since failing in their last mission," Caalendor said.

"Yes, if there is more trouble stirring, best we find its source."

CHAPTER 7

Landrin rode his mount at full gallop mile after mile without slowing. Such a pace would have killed any other horse—any living one that is. It had been disgustingly easy for him to find a recently dead horse and raise it to an unnatural existence that was so similar to his own.

Even if the soldiers who were to follow him north left in the morning, it would take them nearly a month to catch up with him. They would be lucky to make twenty miles a day in these snows, especially through the narrow and rarely used pass in the Northern Range that divided Valeria and the wild northern lands. Landrin expected to make it in little more than three nights.

By the second night of travel, hunger gnawed at his belly until he could no longer ignore its grumblings. He dismounted after spying tracks and was able to run down an elk with his unnatural speed and endurance. If the blood of a human was a fine vintage to a vampire's palate, the blood of an animal was like drinking from a warm mud puddle. It would sustain him, but it would leave him desiring better.

His hunt had cost him time and it was not until late on the evening of his fourth night of travel that he arrived in End's Run. He released his mount back to its natural state of death just outside the town and walked the last mile until he reached the outer wall of the settlement.

The wall, as with every structure in the town, was constructed of sturdy logs, the smallest of which measured two feet across. They were all more or less uniformly cut to a height of about fifteen feet and carved into a point. Had anyone bothered to man the gates, it would have presented a formidable obstacle for anyone lacking scaling ladders, siege equipment, or vastly superior numbers. As it was, the gates stood open and unguarded and Landrin strode through without contest.

Despite the late hour, there was no shortage of people carousing the muddy, slushy streets. Some men appeared to be simply loitering while others looked for potential victims to rob. Prostitutes openly plied their trade while others were simply staggering home from a night of heavy drinking. Landrin followed the sound of loud music and drunken revelry until he located the primary drinking hole of the town.

The tavern was enormous, but it was still packed to capacity. A smoky haze filled the air from the large central fireplace as well as the dozens of cheap tallow candles spread about the room in wall sconces high enough up the wall to prevent being accidentally tipped. The fireplace was an impressive affair. Set in the middle of the room, it looked like a large stone well with a metal hood hovering above it attached to a brick chimney.

On the far side of the enormous common room, a group of men was using what appeared to be a dwarf as some sort of ball or puck to knock down several bottles stacked at the end of a wooden chute covered with a light coating of sand. On further inspection, Landrin saw that it was not a dwarf but a half-man.

Half-men were humans born with a condition that prevented them from growing to a normal size and which often left them disfigured in some sort of way. Most half-men did not live past infancy as the deformity was usually discovered early in life and the parents killed them as abominations. Landrin saw that this half-man was indeed misshapen, with his left arm and leg noticeably shorter than the opposite appendages.

There was no way Landrin was going to be able to capture the attentions of this group with words, so he called upon the Source and directed it to the fire blazing away in the center of the room. The cheery fire erupted into a blazing inferno, lightly scorching those sitting along its stone outer ring. Landrin poured more energy into the conflagration as those nearby leapt away in fright.

He let the flames return to normal as he strode forward, pulled out the writ, and read the proclamation in a loud voice. *"To all peoples of End's Run, be it known that Lord Landrin Bailey,* that's me, *is hereby appointed laird of said township with all the rights and responsibilities of a lord of Valeria.* It goes on, but you all get the point, and I do not wish to interrupt your festivities any longer than I must. *Signed on this date by Jarvin Ollander, King of Valeria.*"

Several men detached themselves from the crowd and stepped forward. One of the men looked back as if counting his followers before returning his gaze to Landrin. Landrin noted that he had a gold pin in the shape of a skull impaled on an upward thrusting sword. Most of the other men who appeared to be part of his group had the same insignia in silver clasped somewhere on their shirts.

"You have come to the wrong place, little lordling. End's Run belongs to me, not the king. Always has and it always will. I'll be sure to pen a letter stating as much when I return your corpse to him."

"And you are?" Landrin inquired although he had a good idea already.

"Finnegan, and I control End's Run," the man explained with false politeness.

Landrin returned Finnegan's smile with equal sincerity. "Mr. Finnegan, the likelihood of you defeating me is only slightly less probable than your ability to actually form a letter, much less string enough of them together to write a coherent sentence. There is a contingent of the king's men following not far behind me. If you leave now, you could escape with most of your ill-gotten gains and live a comfortable life wherever you wish—except here of course. If you insist on staying, I will personally hang your corpse in whatever passes as a town square as a reminder that the king's law does indeed extend to End's Run and will henceforth be enforced."

Finnegan shook his head without losing his smile. "You shoulda brought 'em with you, lordling. Now I'm gonna spill your guts, and when that contingent does arrive, they're gonna find End's Run one hard nut to crack."

The warlord pulled two enormous hunting knives from his belt and strode toward the young nobleman menacingly. It all happened so fast no one even saw the strike. Landrin stood impassively until Finnegan was less than two paces away and drawing back one of the big knives in preparation of a lunge. There was a blur of movement and Landrin's rapier appeared to materialize out of the back of the bandit leader's neck.

Landrin pulled the blade out, whipped it swiftly to the side to fling the blood off it, and let Finnegan's body crumple to the floor. The entire bar was silent and stood motionless for several long seconds as their alcohol-addled brains processed what had just happened.

Finnegan's men surged forward like a stampede of cattle. Landrin ducked a number of clumsy swings, darted between several men, and left three corpses in his wake. He spun around as he passed through, blocking several sword and knife thrusts as well as dodging multiple kicks.

Given the sheer number of blades thrust at him, even Landrin's inhuman speed could not deflect or evade them all. It mattered little, however, as nothing short of a magical or holy weapon could cause him permanent or debilitating harm, unless one of them managed to cut off his head. He stifled a wince as a knife found its way into his lower back and a sword cut a shallow trough in his thigh.

Landrin spun and neatly slit the throat of the man who had stabbed him in the back, then grabbed the wrist of the sword-wielder and kicked him in the stomach hard enough to launch him ten feet and take down two of his friends standing behind him. Most of the men who joined the fight simply for the sport of it backed out once they realized how incredibly lethal this lord was. Of the few who remained, almost all wore the silver skull pin.

In little more than a minute, Landrin faced only three men who now looked very reluctant to press their attack. The vampire heard the whirring of a hurled blade as it cut through the air on its path to pierce the back of his neck or split his skull. Faster than the eye could track, he picked a component out of a pocket, spun toward the hurled missile, and cast a spell. The small hand axe came to an abrupt halt and hovered just three feet from his face. Landrin poured magical energy into his spell and the axe went from cold grey to orange then to white before melting into slag that sizzled and popped as the rivulets of molten steel rained down onto the filthy floor.

The man who hurled the axe could only look on while his face blanched ghostly white as he realized that this was no mere lordling. The man commanded powerful magic, and given how he fought, may very well be a demon of some kind.

"You look like a man of rank within your little organization," Landrin stated as he took in the man's weaponry and appearance.

The man was visibly sweating, and he swallowed deeply so that he could force his words past the enormous lump in his throat. "Wh-who are you?"

"I'm sorry, I thought I had introduced myself earlier. Perhaps you are hard of hearing or simply supremely forgetful. I am the laird of End's Run and the man appointed to enforce the king's law!" Landrin loudly declared, not just for the sake of the man he faced but also for everyone in the tavern. "What is your name?"

"Donnigan—milord."

"You have three options, Donnigan. You can continue fighting me and die. You and your people can grab what few belongings you can carry and disappear forever." Landrin paused for effect. "Or you can work for me for an honest wage doing largely what you have been doing except within the boundaries of the law."

Donnigan did not need to think long. He was a man of limited skills and imagination, but he was not stupid. When you chose a life like the one he had, leadership often changed hands, and for now, those hands belonged to this young, deadly lord.

"Aye, I'll follow you, milord. Pay is pay as far as I'm concerned," Donnigan declared, vigorously nodding his head.

"Excellent. Until Lieutenant Oliver arrives with the king's soldiers, you will be in charge of my local militia, and no, you are not being conscripted into the army. Throw your pin into the fire. Any man I see wearing one after tonight I will personally execute." Landrin turned back to the men who still stood several paces away, loosely holding their weapons. "What about you three? The same options stand for you as well."

The trio looked at each other for a moment then stepped forward and cast their pins into the fire.

"Your first duty is to inform the remaining members of your band of the same three conditions. Remember, you are no longer thugs. You are what passes for the lawful authority here, and you will conduct yourselves as such. There will be no thievery or taking of liberties. Any man that wishes to join and receive steady pay only needs find me, and I shall enter his name in the rolls."

Landrin opened the pack he had set on the floor next to the fireplace and gave each of the four men their initial pay. Several more men came forward and requested to become part of his constabulary. He entered their names onto a piece of parchment and gave them the same instructions as Donnigan and the other men. As the tavern got over the excitement and no one else came forward to sign up for the militia, Landrin found the half-man counting out a few copper coins.

"You, half-man."

"Milord?" the little man responded nervously.

"Is this what you do for coin, let men toss you around for sport?"

"At times. Other times I do little dances, tumble, or whatever will get me enough to eat," he responded.

"What is your name?" Landrin asked.

"Willard, milord, but most folks just call me Fetch because I often run errands and fetch things for them."

"Do you care for the name?"

Fetch shrugged his shoulders. "It's as good as any, I suppose."

"I require a valet, one that knows the importance of discretion and whose loyalty is without question. Would you be that man?"

"A chance at living with some dignity? Aye, I'll be that man. You can kill half the damn town and I won't say a word. Not that many would notice or call it a loss if you did," Fetch replied with a disgusted look at the tavern patrons.

"You will likely not need to keep such gruesome secrets as that, but it is good to know you would be willing to do so. You seem like a clever fellow. How is it you came to be here and debasing yourself for a beggar's wage?"

Fetch regaled Landrin with his tale as he followed him out of the noisy, smoky tavern and into the frigid night air.

"I came up during the early rush after folks learned there was gold practically lining the stream banks and growing out of the ground like carrots, or so the rumors said. Nearly died making the trip. The gold was a lot harder to get to than the rumors said, but I still found a good stake and was doing pretty well for myself. About a year later, some of the brigands started organizing, and I lost my claim and all the gold I had pulled out of it. I couldn't defend myself from most anyone, so I did what I had to do. There was no way I could make the trip south, so I started doing odd jobs, and mostly what you saw in there, to survive."

Landrin and Fetch continued to talk as they walked to the northern edge of town, exited another unguarded gate, and then started up the slope of a hill. To Fetch's credit, they had traveled nearly half a mile before he asked where they were headed.

"There is a bluff at the top of this hill where I plan to set up my new home," Landrin answered.

"You plan on building a cabin tonight? There are rooms to be had in town, you know."

Landrin smiled at the short man. "I have a spell that will aid in the construction of our new home. It was a gift from a friend."

"I saw that bit of magic you cast in the tavern. Scary stuff that. Is that how you moved so fast?"

"Something like that," Landrin replied.

"Do you have one that will make me taller, or at least make my limbs the same length?"

"I do not. Forgive me; I did not think how difficult this climb might be for you. Do you need to rest?"

"We stopping right up there?" Fetch asked, pointing to a plateau just a hundred yards farther up the slope.

"Yes."

Fetch took a deep breath. "I'll make it."

The unlikely pair reached the level area a few minutes later. Landrin let Fetch catch his breath before putting him back to work. He pulled four fist-sized gems out of his pack and handed two of them to Fetch.

"Walk out exactly two hundred feet. When you are in the correct spot, the gem will glow. Place it on the ground, turn ninety degrees to the west, walk another three hundred feet, and do the same thing."

Fetch nodded and began pacing off the length while Landrin took his stone and did the same. The first stone he placed near to where he was standing and then paced off three hundred feet, walking in ever-widening circles until the stone glowed, then he set it down. He pulled a fifth stone out of his pack and went in search of the exact center of the rectangle created by the four cornerstones.

Fetch placed his second glowing gem on the ground just after Landrin found the correct spot for the center stone. Landrin motioned for Fetch to join him outside the pattern. He then pulled out the scroll Solarian had left on the table for him and began to read. The gemstones flared even brighter and illuminated the nightscape like the rising of a miniature sun. It was all Landrin could do to keep his eyes open enough to continue reading.

The ground inside and around the pattern shook and buckled. The earth began rising and the sharp ridge of a roof burst from beneath the soil and snow, like the dorsal fin of some gigantic fish. The dirt and gravel sloughed away as it rose, revealing the slate tiles beneath. The roof continued its ascent higher and higher, revealing thick stone walls. High up the eastern wall, the stained-glass Eye of Solarian practically glowed with an inner light.

"Whoa," Fetch muttered in wonder, then looked at Landrin. "And you can't make my legs a foot longer?"

Landrin looked from the structure that resembled some cross between mansion and cathedral replete with surrounding wall to the half-man.

"It was a gift," he said simply.

Fetch shrugged as if it did not matter much. "What now, Master Landrin?"

"We go inside and await the coming darkness."

Fetch grunted. "Seems pretty dark now, but you're the boss."

CHAPTER 8

Maude entered Bishop Caalendor's private chambers. The high-ranking cleric sat behind a desk covered in thick tomes, scrolls, and pieces of parchment upon which it appeared he had been taking copious notes. The slightly portly cleric looked up as the warrior woman entered.

"Ah, Ms. Ballister. Thank you for answering my summons so quickly. There is a matter of some urgency I require you and your comrades to address."

"I had expected to be released from this indentureship upon completing the king's mission. Why are we still being held here in servitude?" Maude asked in a just-less-than-demanding tone.

The bishop gave Maude a humorless smile. "Ms. Ballister, the king required you to retrieve Dundalor's armor or acquire an artifact of similar power. You failed to do either of those things. The fact that you played a small part in keeping it from the hands of his enemies grants you a marginal success at best. Considering the fact that your service is in effect a stay of punishment for acts of criminal behavior, several of which warrant execution, I would consider myself rather fortunate were I you."

Maude could argue the point, but the truth was he was right. It was not as though they were prisoners either. She and her motley band had been allowed to go out on a few personal expeditions over the relatively peaceful past year or so.

"Fine, what is it you require of us?" Maude asked dejectedly.

"As I am sure you are aware, there have been some very troubling reports of undead activity throughout much of the land over the past few years. The Church has detected an ominous amassing of power far to the north. We believe the relatively minor uprising has been used to keep our attention focused here in the southern regions. Effectively, I am a bit embarrassed to say. I need you and your band to travel to End's Run as swiftly as possible, discover the source of this magical coalescence, and destroy it."

Maude cast the high cleric a dubious look. "Doesn't the Church have an order to deal with exactly this sort of thing? Why send a bunch of misfits, as you have so often referred to us, to deal with what sounds like a seriously powerful threat?"

"The nearest and most capable band of Solarian's Light has recently suffered significant losses. The others are spread thin across the kingdom putting down and preventing further uprisings. It is true that I have likened your band to fools and even worse. However, they say the gods smile upon children and fools. Let us pray they continue to do so."

"With such a vote of confidence, how could we fail?" Maude replied acerbically.

"I certainly pray you do succeed. Failure could mean disaster for this kingdom and beyond."

"The north is a big place. How are we going to find whatever or whoever it is that is causing all the trouble?"

Bishop Caalendor looked pensive for a moment then answered. "Just over a week ago, there was a slaughter at a masquerade ball in Brightridge. A disturbing number of vampires murdered over two dozen of the city's elite. A unit of Solarian's Light destroyed them, but one survived and she declared the nest of the creatures eradicated. A few days later, a young lord by the name of Landrin Bailey called upon the king. Jarvin gave him lairdship of End's Run. That was a week ago. Now we discover a dark power coming from the north that appears to be behind this undead infestation. A coincidence? Perhaps, but we cannot discount it. I met the young lord for a moment before he departed, and I did not like what I sensed. There was nothing I could put a finger on, but I cannot shake the feeling."

"You think he is a vampire, perhaps from the massacre?"

"I recently received the full report of that night. One witness stated that one of the vampires addressed a man by name. Do you care to hazard a guess as to that name?"

Maude let out a deep breath. "Landrin."

"Precisely. If he is truly a vampire, I should have been able to sense it straight away. There is a chance he was able to mask himself from my detection. Regardless, you must pass through End's Run on this mission, so that is where I suggest you begin your investigation."

"Is that all, Your Grace?" Maude asked, ready to depart the opulent but confining walls of the castle.

The cleric appeared to be weighing something heavily in his mind then spoke. "The only survivor, the one that declared all of the vampires destroyed, was Paladin Samone. She has been missing since shortly after the cleansing of the vampires' manor. I have reason to believe she rode north, likely to avenge her comrades. Please watch for her. She could be an invaluable ally and will need your aid as well."

"Do you have any idea what it is we are looking for, other than this Landrin character?"

"I do not, nor do I believe Lord Bailey is the source. I do not know for certain if he is involved or even what I suspect him to be. If he is, then you should have little trouble extracting information from him to point you in the proper direction. If he is not, then your wizard or Chosen should be able to detect the magical emanations from End's Run better than I can from here. I wish I could give you more information and more help, for I truly wish for you to succeed in this mission. Failure could be catastrophic for us all. I must ensure the Church is prepared for whatever may come should you fail. Do not think I am being idle while you and your people risk your lives. I shall be working most diligently to cleanse this kingdom, and at no small risk to myself."

Maude listened to the cleric's words and believed he was sincere and not sending them off on another fool's errand. "We should be able to leave first thing in the morning."

Despite Maude's assurance to Bishop Caalendor, she went in search of her crew with a deep sense of trepidation. Malek was certainly engaged in some form of debauchery; it would take half the day to get Tarth to comprehend what she was even telling him; and the rest of the day would be wasted listening to Borik rant and rave about facing undead and all of the related hardships traveling north would cause: the snow would be too deep for dwarf legs, his beard would freeze solid and strangle him, and there would be no way to keep his beer from freezing into a useless block of ice, which was great when the heat was sweltering, but utterly miserable when it was cold enough to freeze your blood in your veins. His complaints would be endless.

Deep within the fortress made of ice, stone, and bone, Zagrat toiled away in his laboratory creating his monstrous ragmen. The hobgoblin shaman had sought sanctuary in his master's lair after those wretched humans drove him out of his home and they and those accursed elves destroyed so many of his wonderful creations.

Varnath had been furious with his underling's failure and the loss of so many ragmen. He had inflicted so much pain upon his miserable servant after that fiasco. Zagrat shuddered as he thought back to those first few days of unending punishment. He was certain Varnath would kill him, and before his tortures were through, he even begged the lich lord to do so.

After that, Varnath relented and put Zagrat back to work creating his beloved ragmen. The lich refused to allow the shaman to indulge in his pet projects like the Hati creation. Zagrat desperately wanted to show Varnath how superior such a creature as she had been and make more, but the lich demanded he focus on creating as many of the lesser ragmen brutes as he could.

Later, when his master's plan had succeeded, he would show Varnath how valuable the Hati construct was by capturing several hundred strong yet petite women and turning them into a flying army. With the right strength-enhancing spells, he supposed older children would work just as well, possibly even better. Children were less likely to kill themselves as he was certain Hati had.

Zagrat felt the overwhelming cold wash over his flesh before he heard the lich speak as he finished his latest ragman. He hated the fact that he still flinched and tensed up in his master's presence even a year after his brutal punishment. His knees trembled and his heart raced as he turned and looked upon Varnath's desiccated form before averting his eyes.

"You have finished another one, I see," the lich's hollow whisper came.

"Yes, master. I continue to work tirelessly for you, as always," Zagrat replied obsequiously.

Varnath gave the shaman a skeptical look. "How many ragmen do I have now?"

"Nearly a thousand, master," Zagrat replied proudly.

"*Nearly* a thousand. You do not work tirelessly enough. I need more, shaman."

Of course he needed more! He always demanded more. If Zagrat could make him ten thousand ragmen tomorrow, he would insist it was not enough and demand more! Would his work never be appreciated?

"Forgive me, master. I work all through the day and much of the night, pausing only to eat and sleep but a few hours."

"Hmm, you have a point, Zagrat. I failed to consider the limits of your living body. Never let it be said I am incapable of seeing and acknowledging my mistakes, dear Zagrat."

"Of course not, master. You are far too wise to do such a thing."

Varnath smiled at his underling. "Nor let it be said I am incapable of correcting them."

Zagrat looked up fearfully at the lich's words, but there was nothing he could do. The lich moved surprisingly fast and palmed the shaman's large head with his skeletal hand. Zagrat desperately wanted to flee or at least cry out, but the lich's terrifying presence and foul magic held him as immobile and silent as a statue. The hobgoblin's ochre flesh turned grey and shriveled as Varnath drank in his life force, twisted it into a parody of its former self, and infused it back into his corpse. The process took only a few minutes, and when the lich released his grasp, Zagrat stood emotionless and unblinking before his master.

"We have but a few weeks before conditions are optimal for me to enact my plans. I would rather not wait another hundred years for a second chance because you failed to provide what I need. You will do nothing except make your ragmen. I will tell you where you can find the nearest humans for your subjects. We shall not need to be discreet any longer. Have your ragmen capture as many as they can. Capture entire villages if it is possible, and kill any they cannot. All shall be used in the final battle."

"Yes, master," Zagrat answered tonelessly.

CHAPTER 9

Azerick sat at his workbench within his laboratory, rubbing his throbbing temples with his fingers as he stared into a bowl of pure elemental water. He looked up at the sound of the door opening.

Allister walked in, a frown further creasing his wrinkled visage. "What are you up to, lad?"

Azerick shook his head and sighed. "Looking for...something. Damned if I know what it is though."

Allister's bushy eyebrows rose. "It wouldn't happen to be the foulness in the air, or Source to be more specific, would it?"

"You feel it too then?"

The old archmage nodded. "It's been building for a while now, if my guess is right, but only recently has it demanded attention."

"I think I felt it a couple of years ago," Azerick said. "Right around the same time I left the dwarves and ran into a group of undead. I didn't pay much attention to it at the time. I guess I was a little distracted by other things."

Allister chuckled. "Things like building a school and stopping an invasion can take up a good portion of one's attention. Is that what you're doing then, trying to scry out its source?"

Azerick nodded. "Try is an overstatement. Scrying was never one of my skills, and this is like trying to see smoke through heavy fog. Care to give it a try?"

Allister shook his head. "I'd not have much more luck than you I'd wager. However, if anyone could do it, it would be Aggie."

Azerick slapped a palm against his forehead. "Why didn't I think of that?"

"Because you aren't used to having others around who might be more skilled than you, and you're too accustomed to doing everything by yourself."

Azerick quirked an eyebrow. "You sound like Miranda."

"She was always a sharp one. Come, let's go find that old crone and see if she can do something around here other than drive me half mad."

Azerick grinned at the old mage. "You better not let her hear you say that."

Allister scowled at him. "Why do you think I warded myself before I said it? And if you tell her, I'll turn you into a squirrel."

Azerick chuckled as he followed the wizard up the stairs to the tower's main floor. They continued to climb until they reached the library where Aggie spent most of the day when she was not teaching a class on advanced magic. Ellyssa and Roger sat at a table, their faces buried in whatever books Aggie had assigned them to read as part of their additional tutoring.

Aggie looked up from the book she was reading and smiled and their appearance. "Look what the cat dragged in, a hunk and a skunk."

Allister elbowed Azerick. "Hear that? She thinks I'm a hunk."

"A hunk of moldy cheese maybe," Aggie replied with a snort.

Ellyssa and Roger pressed their hands against their mouths to stifle the chortles that erupted from their lips.

"What brings you two to visit my humble abode?" Aggie asked.

Allister's face lost its jovialness. "There's a dark undercurrent in the source. I assume you've felt it."

Aggie also turned serious and nodded. "Been building for a while now if I don't miss my guess. I haven't heard anything from the Academy, not that I'm on their need to know list since I've thrown my lot in with you malcontents, so I guess it's up to us to find out what's going on."

"That's what we were thinking as well," Azerick said. "I've been trying to scry out its source for most of the day with nothing more than a headache to show for my troubles."

"You wasted half the day trying cobble together a cabinet when you have a master carpenter right upstairs." Aggie snorted and jerked her thumb toward Allister. "You're almost as hard-headed as this one."

"That's pretty much what I told him," Allister replied.

Azerick looked at the old mage. "Actually, what you said was—"

The archmage slammed the butt of his staff onto Azerick's foot, eliciting a yelp of pain from the sorcerer. "I told him if anyone could scry this out it was you."

Aggie pursed her lips and narrowed her eyes. "Uh-huh... You bring any elemental water with you?"

Azerick produced a flask from a pocket and Aggie found a silver dish to pour its contents into. She leaned over the shallow bowl and stared deeply into the liquid.

"Whatever it is, it doesn't want to be found," Aggie said after more than a minute.

"You can't break through?" Azerick asked.

Aggie puffed through her lips. "If I can't get past someone's Scrying wards I'll eat my knickers. Heck, I'll eat that old goat's knickers."

Allister gave her a wink. "Joke's on you. I don't wear the things, but it'll be fun having you try."

"Don't make me throw up in my Scrying bowl. I'm having a hard enough time as it is," Aggie snarled, but the quirking at the corners of her mouth hinted her agitation was feigned.

"Got you now, you stubborn bastard," she growled several minutes later.

A desiccated face turned to look right at her. The red, glowing orbs set in its sockets flared with surprise and fury before it hissed a word and waved a skeletal hand. The water in Aggie's bowl exploded into her face.

She looked up, water dripping from her soaked hair. "Well, I found him. I think it was a him anyway. I guess *it* would be acceptable."

"What is it?" Azerick asked.

Aggie shook her head. "I only saw it for an instant, but something evil and very powerful."

"Do you know where it is?" Allister asked.

"Far to the north, best I can tell," Aggie replied.

Allister ran his fingers through his long beard. "Zeb spoke of that shaman creating those ragmen. Could that be it?"

Azerick nodded. "The monster who mutilated that northerner girl."

Aggie shook her head. "No, this was no hobgoblin. It was a necromancer. Possibly a lich."

"The shaman's master?" Allister said.

"Possibly," Aggie said.

Allister turned is head toward Azerick. "Does this mean you're off on another adventure?"

Azerick thought a moment before shaking his head. "Whatever it is, it doesn't appear to be an imminent threat to me or this school. The Academy and the church have people to deal with things liked this. I have better things to do, and I'm tired of racing off to who knows where to battle who knows what. I never signed up to play hero for all the damned world. Let someone else do it for once. I'm too damned tired. Let's just keep an eye on it for now. We can intervene if it appears to become a greater threat."

Allister nodded. "I suppose you're right, lad." He looked down at Aggie and grinned. "Speaking of tired, when I said you were a washed up old wizard, I didn't mean it quite so literally."

Aggie looked up at him and matched his grin. "Whoever that was certainly did something you haven't been able to do for at least the past forty years."

Allister raised his eyebrows. "Bust your Scrying?"

Aggie narrowed her eyes and wiped the water from her brow. "Get me wet."

The archmage's face burned scarlet, and Azerick gave the two a scandalous look.

"I don't get it," Ellyssa said.

Azerick hastened over to their table and ushered her and Roger toward the stairs as if the books had suddenly caught fire.

"What?" Ellyssa asked, looking up at Azerick and back toward the old wizards. "Is it because of the water?"

Azerick bobbed his head as he pushed the two students out of the room. "Yep, that's it exactly."

Maude and her crew crouched in the shadows cast by the low-hanging branches of an enormous evergreen tree and studied the unusual structure standing a few hundred feet away. It looked more like a church or cathedral than a mansion. A low stone wall surrounded it with a wrought-iron gate set in the end facing the main doors leading in.

Bishop Caalendor had given Maude a writ allowing them the use of the Blackguard's network of mounts. Despite the fact that the network that ran to End's Run was poorly supplied, they still made the journey a week ahead of the guard contingent that had left Brightridge days before they had.

The adventurers had spent the remaining day of their arrival talking to the locals about Lord Bailey. Everyone had at least heard of him and many had even seen him, but never during the day. He did speak regularly with his local law enforcers inside his manor at all hours, but never outside of it when the sun was up.

Several people spoke of his use of magic and of how the manor had simply appeared on the hilltop above town the morning after his arrival. They related his use of magic and incredible speed when he had fought the leader of the men who collected taxes and enforced their own laws in the area.

The people generally considered things much improved in the two weeks since he had taken control despite several men having been hanged in the town center for violating the king's law. Some mentioned that a few others had simply disappeared. Thugs no longer shook down storeowners for protection money, prospectors were not being chased off their claims, and the taxes being paid to the king were less than what the warlord had been taking. The banditry was far from eliminated in such a short amount of time, but victims now had a place of recourse, and Landrin swiftly sent his enforcers out to deal with the problem.

"So how do we approach this? Go up and knock politely on the door?" Borik asked.

"Given the high likelihood of this man being a vampire, announcing ourselves would be a really bad idea," Malek responded.

Maude nodded her agreement with the cleric. "I concur with Malek. We have daylight on our side and could simply walk in without fear of ambush."

"I don't know," Borik replied dubiously. "This sure looks an awful lot like what got us in this whole mess in the first place."

"But this time he really is a vampire!" Maude declared. "Bishop Caalendor met the man and practically said so."

"Yeah, and that old bat and half the town of Moronville or whatever it was called were just as certain! And *practically* saying so and coming out and declaring it are about as far apart as a two-foot rope around your neck and a three-foot drop!"

"You're just afraid of vampires," Maude told him dismissively.

"You're darn right I'm afraid of vampires! Vampires, ghouls, liches, ghosts, wraiths, specters, and anything else that don't bleed when you stick a blade in 'em!"

"Ahem," the sound of someone declaring his presence came from behind them.

Maude, Malek, and Borik leapt to their feet, sending a cascade of snow falling all over them when the two humans struck the branches over their heads. All three spun around and looked at the short figure standing a few feet away. Only Borik saw that the man was not a misshapen dwarf but a half-man.

"Damn it, Tarth, you were supposed to be watching for anyone coming up behind us!" Maude shouted at the elf.

"I was, Maudeline," Tarth defended himself. "The little man came around that side of the wall and walked up behind us here."

"The purpose of watching our backs is to warn us before someone sneaks up on us!"

"Oh, my apologies. There is someone here."

Maude ground her teeth in frustration. "It's too late now!"

"There is just no pleasing you sometimes," Tarth replied in a huff.

Maude gave up on the elf and turned to the half-man. "Who are you and what do want?"

"I'm Fetch, and I want to be two feet taller. My master thought you might be cold skulking about in the snow and wishes to know if you would like to come in for tea."

Maude looked from Fetch to the manor and sighed heavily. "Will anything ever go according to plan? Very well, Fetch. Lead the way, but know that if there is any treachery, it's your big head I'm taking first."

"You would earn great credit for such a feat if you had the skill to find my neck," Fetch replied, referring to the fact that his head attached directly to his shoulders without the benefit of that piece of anatomy.

Fetch led the adventurers to the manor with great efficiency despite his odd ambling gait. The tall, ponderous-looking door opened easily for him and he escorted them inside the well-lit and spacious interior.

Maude and the rest of her crew kept a tight grip on their weapons as they entered the manor and scanned for signs of an ambush. The interior was completely open with a set of wide stairs leading to an open balcony that surrounded the entire central chamber, from where several doors led to other rooms. There were similar doors on the ground floor as well.

Chandeliers suspended by stout chains provided much of the light, but the primary source of illumination was the enormous, round, stained-glass window set high in the east wall. All four adventurers recognized the stylized sun as the Eye of Solarian. Such an ornamentation cast great doubt upon the laird of End's Run being a member of the undead. The sun streaming through the Eye of Solarian would turn any such abomination to less than ash in an instant.

"Welcome, travelers," Landrin called out from atop the balcony.

All eyes turned toward the voice as he descended the stairs. Since freeing himself of Eldon's control and receiving Solarian's blessing, Landrin had returned to wearing more colorful clothing, such as he had when he had been a bard. He wore loose red trousers and a silk shirt of orange and gold that bunched up at the shoulders. Although the smile on his face appeared genuine, none of the group relaxed their guard.

"Fetch, would you be so kind as to get the tea? I believe it is ready now."

Fetch gave a small bow and waddled toward the door at the far end of the manor where the kitchen stood.

"I fear you may find my offerings a tad meager. I do not yet employ a full-time cook and Fetch often eats in town," Landrin explained as he approached the wary band.

Not surprisingly, Malek was the first to sense their host's true nature. With a gasp and clipped curse, the cleric held out the gleaming amber orb representing his order's holy symbol and called upon his faith.

"Stay back, you unholy nightmare!" Malek cried out. "By the light of Solarian, I cast away your blackness and return you to your natural state of death!"

The gleaming brilliance radiating off the orb forced Landrin back a step as he shielded his eyes with his raised hand and arm.

"I wish you would not do that, Chosen," Landrin said calmly. "Not only is it rather uncomfortable, it flies in the face of proper manners for one showing such hospitality."

Maude looked uncertainly from Landrin to Malek. "Malek, are you sure he's undead?"

Malek knew that he was not the most capable cleric in his order, but he possessed a strong affinity with Solarian and wielded enough divine power that many of his faith were quite jealous of his connection to Solarian as they considered him something of a disgrace. Whether or not he could destroy something as powerful as a vampire outright was uncertain, but he knew his power should at the very least force the monstrosity to flee.

"I-I am certain..." Malek stammered, not sounding the least bit positive.

"Perhaps if we could all just remain calm a moment, I can explain," Landrin said smoothly.

The light emanating from Malek's holy symbol ebbed until it went completely dim. He looked at it as if betrayed then allowed it to hang loosely around his neck by its stout gold chain, and resumed his two-handed grip on his hammer.

"Do not look sullen, Chosen. Your faith has not betrayed you. I am indeed what you sensed, but not perhaps what you fear. Were I a monster, could I stand beneath Solarian's most holy of icons unscathed?"

"You defame the symbol of Solarian with your magic!" Malek angrily accused.

Landrin shook his head with a smile. "On the contrary, Chosen. I hold this symbol more reverently than even you could possibly imagine. It might be the only place in the entire world I can feel the warmth of the sun without it destroying me. Come, I will show you. I know you have likely performed your morning benedictions, as have

I, but perhaps you would feel more at ease if you joined me in repeating them?"

Without waiting for a response, Landrin turned, walked toward the stained-glass window, and knelt within the glowing beam of light cast by the mid-morning sun.

Malek looked at Maude and said, "Watch him closely," and then folded himself onto his knees next to the vampire.

The two diametrically opposed creatures softly chanted in perfect unison. "Blessed be Solarian whose radiant light shines upon my heart and chases the blackness from the land and my soul. Within his light, I need never fear the darkness, for he shall light my way. Let me carry his light unto the masses so that they shall know the love, warmth, and safety that lie within his holy illumination. All hail Solarian."

Malek looked up into the glorious golden rays of light and trailed a hand through one of the more brilliant beams within which floated a universe of dust motes. He knew it was no mere illusion for he could feel the heat of the sun upon his flesh and the light upon his very soul. He felt Solarian's embrace, strong and comforting in this place.

"How is this possible?" he asked the vampire that knelt enraptured next to him.

Landrin smiled as warmly as the sun coming through the great window. "Despite my transformation, I never lost faith. Solarian rewarded my service and diligence and created this sanctuary for me so that I might continue to serve him and fight the coming darkness."

"Are you Chosen then?"

Landrin laughed so hard tears would be streaming down his face if he were still capable of producing them. It took several long, uncomfortable moments before he could respond to the honest question. He wished he could keep laughing, as it was the first feeling of mirth he had enjoyed in more than ten years.

"Thank you, cleric. It has been so long since I had something about which to laugh. Forgive me. No, I am not Chosen. Solarian is beneficent and generous, but even his compassion has its boundaries. We have an accord. Perhaps one day, should I prove myself worthy, he shall take this unholy existence from me and lift me into his celestial kingdom. But for the nonce, I have his work to do, and I believe part of that is why you are here today."

"So, Malek, are we all right here?" Maude called out.

Malek stood and addressed his friends. "I am confident we are."

"I believe Fetch has been waiting patiently with our tea. Why don't you all strip out of that armor and join me at the table. It looks like he found a bit to eat as well," Landrin said.

The group stacked their armor and weapons into piles near the table then sat as Fetch poured tea and served small plates of bread, cheese, and smoked meat. Landrin partook of none of this and told his guests his condition would not allow him to eat solid food, but he was able to take polite sips of tea.

"So what ultimately brought you all to End's Run and my doorstep?" Landrin inquired once everyone was settled.

As usual, Maude spoke up. "We have been in service to the king for several years now."

"Slavery more like it," Borik scoffed.

"Shut up, dwarf," Maude ordered, then returned to Landrin. "Bishop Caalendor told me of some dark energy or magic gathering to the north, thought it was related to the somewhat recent undead attacks, and ordered us to check into it. He mentioned you might be in league with it or something, and advised us that we should look for more information through you."

Landrin steepled his fingers and smiled. "I had wondered whether or not I had been successful in throwing him off my scent. He is more astute than I had hoped."

"But you do not have anything to do with the undead problem or this gathering of power?" Malek asked doubtfully.

"No, of course not. However, I am aware of it. It is the reason Solarian bade me come to this land, so that I might aid those seeking to destroy it and the one who summons it."

"You know who is doing this?" Maude asked eagerly.

"In a way." Landrin answered. "There is a creature by the name of Varnath. That is all I have been able to discover of his identity. Eldon, the vampire that created me, often referred to him and some great diabolical plan he has been working on for several years. Almost as soon as I destroyed Eldon, Varnath began calling to me with promises of wealth, power, or anything else I wanted. He tries to command me, and although his compulsion is strong, I am able to resist it."

Malek asked, "You don't know what he is though?"

"He could simply be a very powerful necromancer, but I doubt it. I was able to sense some things through his sending to me. I am reasonably certain he is a lich. The strength of his compulsion, magic, and mastery of the necromantic arts I sensed through his limited communications were simply too great to be human. His essence reeked of undeath. Fortunately, his astral or mental projections cannot penetrate my home."

"Great, of all the horrors we have faced, this is the one I really, really do not want to deal with," Borik moaned. "There is just nothing worse than liches, and I don't even know anything about them other than the fact that they are really bad and really dead."

Landrin thought back to his meeting with Solarian but decided not to tell the dwarf that the god of light hinted that there was something far worse than the lich lurking in the shadows. He felt it best to take on kingdom-shattering events one at a time.

Fetch appeared as unobtrusively as he had outside with two men in tow. "Pardon the interruption, Master Landrin, but Mr. Donnigan has urgent news to share with you."

"What is it?" Landrin asked his chief enforcer.

Donnigan inclined his head toward the man next to him. "This here is Edmund. He's a wagon master out of Farrell's Mill to the north and west. He and his men were bringing a load of lumber, iron, and gold to End's Run to be taken south on a later caravan. He says they were attacked about three days north of here."

"Highwayman? Perhaps some of your former associates that declined my offer of employment?"

"No, milord!" the man called Edmund interjected. "Was wolves it was!"

"Wolves?" Landrin asked in surprise.

"Aye, milord! There must'a been a hundred of them darting in and out of the trees, pulling men down, and tearing at them with their teeth!"

"How many men were with the wagon team?"

"Twenty-five, milord. Thirteen drivers and crew and twelve guards," the wagon master answered fretfully.

Landrin pondered what this could mean. It was unheard of for a pack of wolves to attack so many men, especially armed men. Most wolves in these parts knew the scent of steel and the swift death it could bring. However, it was not unheard of for a few men to conspire with bandits to stage a robbery and share the spoils. But what kind of fool would make up a story of a wolf attack?

"Where are the goods and how many men died in the attack?"

"I was able to unhitch the horses. Only seven of us made it out alive, milord. We had to abandon the wagons. Likely everything is still there."

Landrin leaned back and studied the man. His fear appeared genuine and he could detect no deception.

"Edmund, I do not mean to cast aspersions on your character or honesty, but you must understand how difficult it is for me to believe that a pack of wolves attacked a large party of armed men and managed to kill most of them."

Edmund bobbed his head a few times then swallowed hard. "I understand, milord, and I wouldn't believe it neither. But it weren't just wolves. Not just regular wolves anyhow."

Landrin leaned forward and looked at the man intently. "What do you mean it weren't regular wolves?"

Edmund chased the lump back down his throat again before answering. "It was the big one. He was the leader. The men killed the regular wolves when they got a good cut in, but that big one, he just kept killing, no matter how many wounds he took. He'd run off after taking a solid blow then come back just as hale and strong as before. And he was smart! The way he moved and avoided the weapons and attacked only men that was vulnerable just wasn't natural. He looked at me as I jumped onto one of the horses. He looked right in my eyes and I saw hatred. Not the feral viciousness of an animal, but the hatred a man has for another man that done him very wrong."

Donnigan broke his silence at that point. "Milord, I'll take a group of hunters and run down these wolves. With your permission, I'll post a bounty for wolf hides as well. That'll quickly sort this all out."

"Edmund, you may go, but you and the men you rode in with stay in town for the time being."

The wagon master bobbed his head and Fetch showed him the door.

"Let us not act too hastily in eradicating what may or may not be a simple wolf problem, Donnigan."

"Begging your pardon, sir, but you don't really think there are wolves out there that good steel can't put down? I believe what he says about a wolf attack, but this nonsense about a wolf that can't be killed is just the words of a scared man."

"You have been in these parts for a long time, Donnigan, and I bet you have seen some very strange things. There are indeed such creatures as the man described, and I would rather not create more enemies than we already have."

Donnigan looked like he wanted to argue, but chose not to. "If that is what these things are, I'd say them killing over a dozen men kind of makes them enemies."

"Possibly, but let me look into it first. For the time being, I want no wagon trains going through that area. Anyone leaving town especially needs to stay off the route to Farrell's Mill, and inform them of the risks of traveling."

Donnigan knuckled a salute. "You're the boss."

"Every time you think things are about as weird as they can get, something else raises its head, eh?" Borik piped up as Donnigan made his exit.

"It does indeed," Landrin replied.

Maude asked, "Do you really think there is some strange kind of wolf leading this attack?"

"There are creatures that fit that description, but they are very rare and usually go to great lengths to avoid humans and the other intelligent races. If that is what they are, perhaps they felt threatened and reacted violently. If such is the case, I may be able to broker some sort of treaty."

"It sounds like you will be too busy to help us destroy this dead thing causing so much trouble," Maude stated.

"Even were I not, I could not accompany you," Landrin answered. "Right now I am protected by these walls and the distance between me and Varnath. Were I to step into his lair, into the heart of his power, he may well be able to overwhelm me and turn me against you."

"Is there anything you can do to help us?" Malek asked.

"Other than pray for you? Not really. I can tell you that the calling is coming from an area near the Great Barrier Mountains about sixty miles to the northeast. I can show you on a map, but that is going to leave you with about a hundred square miles to search."

"Great, a dead needle in a dead haystack," Borik complained bitterly. "Make that a needle in a hundred-square-mile haystack in the freezing cold!"

"I truly wish I could do more."

"You have done a great deal just by not having to fight you," Maude told him. "Perhaps we will run into Paladin Samone before we leave."

Landrin practically jumped from his chair. "What do you know of Samone?"

Maude was taken aback by his animated response to what she had thought an innocent comment. "The bishop told us he thought this paladin had come north to avenge her friends that some group of vampires killed recently. He told us to keep an eye out for her in hopes we might team up. Having a Light of Solarian on our side would make me feel a lot better. Why, do you know her?"

Landrin sat back down and forced himself to relax. "She helped free me from the control of the vampire who turned me. I saved her life, and in return, she allowed me to depart Brightridge. I was rather taken with her beauty as well as her spirit."

"Have you seen her? Bishop Caalendor was confident she was coming this way," Maude asked.

"I have not, which is probably a good thing. She swore to kill me should we ever meet again. It was not personal."

Landrin found the best map he could, which was not that good considering the wildness of the region. He pointed to his best estimate of the location where the dark magic seemed to be accumulating. Malek said he could keep them going in the right direction with his ability to track the emanations, but finding the source would be like locating the exact center of a blizzard.

Landrin offered to put the adventurers up for the night, but they declined, stating that they already had rooms in town and that was where their traveling supplies were located. He bid them farewell then waited for the sun to go down so that he could address the wolf problem.

"Fetch," Landrin called out for his valet several hours later.

The half-man appeared almost instantly. "Yes, Master Landrin?"

"I must depart this evening. I should not be gone more than three days. Donnigan should be able to handle any technical issues that may arise. If there is anything requiring real intelligence, I leave it in your capable hands."

"I appreciate your confidence, Master Landrin," Fetch replied with a quick bow.

Landrin departed moments later, eschewing the use of a horse, living or otherwise, since he could cover more ground on foot. This was especially true as he crossed the rough, tree-dotted landscape and avoided the roads. This allowed him to travel in a relatively straight path toward the location where Edmund said he and the others had abandoned the wagons.

The wagon master reported that the attack was three days north of End's Run; but that was three days by wagon. Landrin found the wagons and bodies about two hours before sunrise. At first appearance, the scene was just as Edmund had described. A closer inspection confirmed his tale. The wagons were still there and fully loaded with timber, iron ore, and gold ore. The horses that had been unable to break free of their traces showed the greatest signs of predation, some nearly half consumed.

Over a dozen human bodies lay scattered about, most with weapons near at hand. The cause of death was the obvious large bite wounds, although there were signs of smaller wounds, likely the result of scavengers. At least a dozen wolves lay dead amongst the bodies as well. Landrin spent the most time examining these, but none of them were what he was looking for.

Dawn was approaching and Landrin needed to find a dark place to hole up. Fortunately, this region was largely mountainous, and fissures and caves were not uncommon. Landrin, like all vampires, possessed a sort of sixth sense when it came to finding places in which to hide from the sun's deadly light. It took less than an hour for him to find a deep cleft in a rocky outcropping. It was cramped and calling it a cave was akin to calling an icicle a glacier, but it sufficed.

The days were blessedly short this far north even this time of year. Landrin crawled back out of his nook a scant eight hours later and returned to the site of the attack. It did not take him long to locate the tracks left by the wolves. He followed the visual evidence of the animals' path as much as he did their scent. A vampire's sense of smell was nearly as keen as their hearing and sight. Landrin would give all of these heightened powers back if he could be human once more. However, he knew that could never be and focused on following the trail left by the wolves.

Landrin slowed to a jog hours later when his ears picked up the sound of several pairs of feet padding through the snow-covered forest nearby. His keen eyesight spied the dark forms darting in and out of his field of view, but they always kept pace with him. It did not take long before the wolves announced their presence with growls and yips as a warning to the intruder and calls to their own kind.

The vampire slowed to a walk then stopped as the smell of the wolves became prevalent. He knew he was near a den, and moving any closer would initiate an immediate attack. Landrin waited patiently and calmly as first dozens and then scores of wolves warily approached and surrounded him. He had purposefully chosen a shallow depression and let the wolves have high ground so as not to appear as threatening. He only hoped it was enough to buy him a moment to speak with the leader.

Most of the wolves were exactly what they appeared to be — wolves. However, Landrin was able to make out at least a dozen others that were far more than they appeared to be by virtue of their slightly greater size and a distinct difference in their scent. He knew these to be lupin. Lupins were wolves with the ability to transform into human shape. Unlike a werewolf, their wolf form was their natural and preferred state. Lupin only used their human shape when they felt it necessary to interact with humans or the other humanoid races.

A big silver female stepped ahead of the pack and abruptly transformed before Landrin's eyes. Despite knowing what these creatures were, the transformation was still shocking and exciting to behold. In the space the wolf had just been occupying, now stood a nude, middle-aged woman with dark hair shot through with grey.

"I am Luna, den mother to this pack and friend to the others who choose to help us defend our territory," the lupin announced.

Landrin gave the woman a slow bow. "Greetings to you, Den Mother. I am Landrin, laird of the human den called End's Run nearly two days' run to the south."

"You are a perversion of life," Luna declared. "But you do not carry the stink of evil intent as the other abominations do, which is why I have granted you this moment to explain your presence before my pack tears you to pieces."

"I thank you for your indulgence, Den Mother, but I think we both know that it is in both our best interests to listen at this moment and not act rashly. I am not only capable of defending myself due to my nature, but possess powerful magic as well. Violence would be devastating to us both."

The den mother curled her human lip in approximation of a wolf's snarl. "You think you could defeat us all?"

Landrin knew that he could not show weakness and must convey confidence or the pack would not hesitate to attack. He was confident he could battle these creatures and survive, but no one would walk away a winner in such an eventuality.

"I think it would be disastrous for us both. You could force me to flee, but only after I inflicted horrible death on your pack."

"If you do not wish a fight, then why are you here?"

Her tone indicated she already knew why Landrin was here, but she would give nothing away. If Landrin wanted something, he would have to ask for it.

"Your wolves attacked and killed several of my pack. From what I have heard and seen, it may have been the act of an individual enlisting the aid of your wolf allies."

Luna looked upon the vampire unblinkingly as she pondered how best to answer. She finally decided upon forthrightness.

"One of my younger sons acted foolishly, but I will die before I give him to you. The pack will deal with any violation of pack law. I lost one son to the encroachment of the two-legs. I will not lose another for any reason."

Landrin nodded his understanding, but he had to prevent a recurrence and escalation of the violence. It was going to be hard enough as it was to keep hunters and miners from killing every wolf they found once word got around about the attack on the wagons. He was certain everyone in End's Run had already heard about it and would be making a call to arms.

"Why did he lead an attack against the humans, Den Mother?"

"They come into our territory, cut down our trees, dig up the ground, and kill and run off the game. We were all angry and restless, and one decided to act," Luna answered, obviously unhappy about that decision.

"How vast is your territory, Luna? Perhaps I can try to warn my kind away from most of it so this does not happen again."

Luna weighed the words of the vampire carefully. She hated his undead kind even more than she despised the land-defiling humans, but she knew she must protect her pack any way she could. If words could manage that, it would be far preferable to battle; a battle she knew in her heart she and her pack could not sustain. It would not take long for the humans to learn of their weakness, and once they did, they would cut them down like any other animal.

"Our land stretches to those hills there," she answered, pointing with her finger, "to the valley there, and to the river there. Keep your humans out and there will be no more attacks from my kind. Be sure your kind does the same."

There was only one mine in the area that he knew of. He would have to relocate it. It would cause a few grumblings, but concessions needed to be made. The biggest problem was that the only road going to the northern mills and mines cut through the lupin's territory.

"I will close the mine that lies in your range, but we claim land to the north and east that is only accessible by crossing through your territory. May we use our road to travel through it as long as I can get promises of proper conduct from those that use it?"

"I will allow it, but can you guarantee the behavior of all of your people? What happens when they violate the truce?"

"Then you deal with them accordingly, Den Mother, and I promise to do the same. I will warn my people. If they choose to ignore that warning, then they choose to accept the consequences."

"Then so be it, vampire."

Landrin turned to go, but curiosity got the better of him and he turned back. "Luna, you said you lost a son to the two-legged. How did that happen?"

The alpha lupin stared into the distance as the memory brought on a fresh wave of grief. "It was many years ago when our den was far to the north. The two-legged came, wielding cold iron, and drove us away. I decided it best to move the pack instead of fighting. But on the night we fled, one of my sons was left behind. He was always an adventurous one and I could not keep him in the den. I returned for him, but I could not catch his scent. He was too young to hunt and survive on his own. Even after all this time, my heart still cries out for him."

"I am sorry for your loss, Den Mother."

"Life and death are both the way of nature."

Landrin nodded, detecting the allusion to his unnatural state of life. He was a creature that defied them both.

He walked briskly for nearly five miles before his escort of wolves departed. He then broke into a run. A feeling of impending urgency made him push himself. Even so, the distance was too great to make it back to End's Run before the sun rose again. He had only minutes to spare when he located a hole to crawl into, evicting a very unhappy wolverine who chose to sleep elsewhere that day instead of fighting the fearsome creature for its den.

CHAPTER 10

Queen Annette sat in the solar of her apartments embroidering with her handmaiden, Mildred, while her two youngest children played on the floor nearby. Her only daughter, three-year-old Brigitte, stacked wooden blocks while two-year-old Joseph knocked them down. Both children found the activity hilarious, to which their laughter attested.

It was getting late in the evening and Annette wished her husband would conclude his meeting with the Church's hierarchy soon so that he could tuck his two youngest children into bed and read them a story before it got too late. Her eldest son, Miles, was away in Southport attending the Academy. Her only company of late was Mildred, who could go hours without speaking and was a poor conversationalist when she did. A handful of guards tried, and failed, to be unobtrusive as they stood sentinel outside, inside, and all about the several rooms that made up the royal chambers.

The queen started in surprise when Mildred looked up and asked, "Did you hear that, Majesty?"

Annette cocked an ear toward the open door and listened. Above the sound of the children's laughter, she heard the clanging of metal as if someone had dropped an armload of pots and pans. As she listened, she heard the muffled voices of men outside and down the hall.

The queen set her needlework aside, stood up, and stepped into the adjoining room. The clatter of metal and the shouts of men were becoming prevalent and seemed to be drawing nearer. Some of the guards began looking at the door nervously.

"Guardsman, what is happening?"

"I am unsure, Your Majesty," the guard replied. "I will ask one of the men in the hall and find out."

The guard crossed the room, but just as he was about to open the door, the portal burst open. He jumped back, drawing his blade in one smooth motion as several guards, many of them bearing wounds, practically fell through the doorway and into the room. One of the new men turned, slammed the door shut, and dropped the crossbar.

"Guardsman, what is the meaning of this!" Annette demanded while she tried to keep the fear from her voice.

"It is treason, Your Majesty!" one of the men who had burst into the room declared as he backed away from the door.

Before Annette could ask anything further, something heavy slammed into the stout door with enough force to make the crossbar jump in its cradle. All eyes turned toward the door as the men outside began rhythmically pounding on the barrier with some sort of makeshift ram. One of the guardsmen inside stepped away from the others and made to stand guard next to the queen. However, when he turned, Annette saw not the concerned eyes of a man sworn to protect her, but the look of a cold, calculating killer.

The man drew back his sword and thrust. Mildred shoved Annette backwards and interposed herself between the queen and the assassin's blade. Annette watched in horror and let out a shriek when the sword burst out of Mildred's chest. Quiet, doe-eyed Mildred slumped lifelessly to the floor as the traitor pulled back his blade for another strike.

The blow never landed as one of the guards rushed forward and hewed the assassin down with a powerful stroke to his unarmored neck. Two more lay dead amongst the guards inside the room, cut down when they drew steel on their fellows with the intent of finishing the assassin's job. Annette pulled a dagger from a sheath at the dead man's waist and pointed it at her rescuer.

"You, do not leave my side! Can you trust these other men?" she asked, having seen only the one who had so far proved himself loyal.

The guard took only a moment to process the queen's reaction and question before turning to face the other seven men in the room. "I know five of them well, Majesty, and trust them with my life. The other two I know only marginally."

"I can vouch for guardsmen Clemm and Woodred, Highness," another guard told her.

"Very well. Is there another way out of these apartments?"

One of the guards shook his head. "Not to my knowledge, Majesty. I believe there was once a secret passage, but it was sealed for fear of assassins discovering it and using it to get past the guards."

"Then guard the door as best you can, and pray help arrives before they get through," Annette said as she held and tried to comfort her children who were sitting on the floor wailing.

Whoever was outside continued to pound rhythmically on the door. Whatever fighting taking place in the halls of the castle had moved further on as the only sounds that could be heard in the royal chambers were the bashing of the door and the crying of the young prince and princess. Another, more ominous sound soon came from the door as the wood began splitting under the relentless assault. Part of the door cracked and splintered off and a few well-placed kicks completed the destruction.

With the barrier compromised, guards and other men not in uniform, wielding swords and daggers, poured into the room. Annette's few guards launched themselves at the intruders despite being heavily outnumbered. Fortunately, the room's enclosed space worked against the more numerous assassins and prevented their entire number from engaging the defenders all at once.

Annette's guards were still outmanned, but they fought with the determination and knowledge that their deaths were all but certain if they failed in their duty. The guardsmen battled furiously against the men who just yesterday were brothers in arms, but now found themselves on opposing sides of someone else's cause.

Two usurpers fell beneath the desperate blows of the loyalists then one of theirs fell with a thrust through the chest. For every defender who fell, two or three traitors died beneath their blades, but such a battle of attrition would be short-lived as there were always more assassins waiting to take the fallen men's places.

Annette scooped her two children into her arms and fled into the adjoining children's room. She dropped the screaming youngsters onto the bed and made to close the door. She wondered if she had the strength to move the sturdy wardrobe in front of the door since it had no lock or crossbar. As she moved to see if she could shift the bulky piece of furniture, numerous runes flared with an incandescent light.

The doors burst open and a dark shape practically flew into the room from inside the closet. Annette thought it was another assassin and leapt in front of her children with her dagger held before her. The young man who had emerged from the closet scanned the room briefly before turning his attention back to the queen.

"Please do not be alarmed, Your Majesty. My name is Landrin and I am here to help you," Landrin explained.

Annette looked back and forth between the man and wardrobe. "How did you get in here? Have you been in there this whole time?"

"There is no time to explain. Please take your children into the wardrobe. You will find a passage out of here. I have men waiting on the other side to see to your comfort and safety. Where is the king?"

Annette shook her head as she tried to comprehend this strange new development. "In the throne room. He was to meet a delegation from the Church. They will be after him! You must save him!"

"I will, Majesty. Please, flee through the wardrobe. I will return with King Jarvin soon," Landrin instructed, praying he would be able to keep his promise.

Annette grabbed her children and cautiously stepped into the wardrobe. Sure enough, it extended back much deeper than the outside implied. She took several steps toward the soft glow of a light at the far end. It felt as though the wardrobe were spinning. She used her free hand to try to steady herself as she staggered toward the light. She felt strong hands grab her and hold her steady as she stepped out of another wardrobe and tried to shake off her vertigo.

The queen looked up into the eyes of several rough-looking men all bearing weapons. Few wore any armor, so she knew they were not soldiers. She clutched her children even more tightly to her breast, unsure who these men were or their motivations.

"You the queen?" the man holding onto her arm asked gruffly.

Annette forced herself to stand up straight and regain her composure. "I am Queen Annette Ollander. Who might you gentlemen be?"

The man grinned, displaying the gaps created by at least three missing teeth. "I'm not sure there's a gentleman between us, Highness, but I'm Donnigan and nominally in charge of this other scum until the boss gets back. He said to be expecting you and to be on our best behavior."

"Where am I, Mr. Donnigan?" Annette asked, certain that she was somehow no longer in the castle.

"You're in Lord Bailey's house in End's Run," Donnigan answered, grinning even wider in anticipation of the queen's reaction.

How could she possibly be in End's Run? End's Run was hundreds of miles to the north through a steep, narrow, snow-choked pass!

Donnigan spoke again. "If you had known this was an empty hilltop a couple weeks ago you probably wouldn't be so surprised to be here."

"Magic," Annette whispered under her breath.

"Aye. Lord Bailey seems to be full of these little tricks."

Brigitte and Joseph reminded Annette of their presence by crying once more. The queen looked around for somewhere comfortable to sit with them and reassure them they were safe.

"Mr. Donnigan, is there somewhere I can sit with the children?"

"Aye. Fetch will show you to a room Landrin had made up for you. Fetch!" Donnigan called over his shoulder.

A twisted little half-man shouldered his way past the crowd of armed men. "Your Majesty, if you will follow me, I will show you to your room."

Landrin sped through the door toward the sounds of battle as soon as the queen stepped into the wardrobe. Four men were battling furiously against at least twice their number. From the fact that the outnumbered men interposed themselves between the room Annette had been in and the other men, he concluded these were loyal guardsmen and the more numerous combatants were traitors.

He sent a stream of magical orbs slamming into the chests of three of the nearest enemy with his free hand and cut viciously with the sword gripped in his other. Landrin stepped into the place one of Annette's guards left open as he fell to a blow to his thigh. The vampire's incredible speed, strength, and use of magic turned the tide of battle. It took only seconds for Landrin and the remaining guards to hew down most of the attackers, but three ran back through the door, probably in search of help.

"Who are you? Where did you come from?" one of the guards demanded to know, unsure whether to trust this newcomer despite his intervention.

"I am a friend of the king. I do not have time to explain right now. There is a passage inside the large wardrobe in that room. The queen and her children have already fled through it to safety. I suggest you do the same."

The man who appeared to be in charge shook his head. "No, we must go to the king!"

"You are all wounded and exhausted. I will go get the king and can move faster without you. Trust me. He and the queen will need you more once I bring him back. Go. You can continue your service best by staying with the queen, as I am sure you were ordered to do."

The guardsman thought for only a moment, knowing the stranger was right. The king himself had personally appointed him and his men to guard the queen and his heirs. He motioned for his men to grab the wounded and made for the children's room.

Landrin took a moment to study the dead men. Nearly all wore the armor and livery of palace guards and he doubted that very many were fakes. These men had been convinced to turn against their king. He also noted that they each wore a swatch of orange or yellow cloth tied around their left upper arm, obviously as a way to discern friend from foe. Good. That worked for him as well.

He darted out of the room and sprinted down the hall. It did not take long before he heard the clashing of steel and came upon another group of men battling in a hall littered with corpses. Landrin discerned loyalists from usurpers by the colored swatches and lent his steel and magic to the fray. Even outnumbered, the defenders put down the traitorous soldiers thanks to Landrin's aid.

Landrin ordered the men to follow him to the throne room and did not wait for a reply. Glad to have someone seemingly take charge, the men loyal to Jarvin fell in behind him and tried to keep up with the swift vampire. More than once, they lost sight of him only to find him once more standing amongst the recently slain bodies of men, but still they followed without question. He was leading them to their king and that was the only thing that mattered.

Jarvin sat restlessly upon his throne, occasionally glancing at his two advisors standing nearby. Most of his sour looks he directed at Bishop Caalendor, who as one of the leading heads of the Church, would be the one to bear most of the responsibility for the Church delegation keeping him waiting.

"Is there some religious fundamental I am unaware of that requires the Church council to be an hour late to an audience with their king?" Jarvin asked the bishop irritably.

"Forgive me, Your Highness. Given the number and severity of the disturbances about the kingdom of late, it is likely they were held up attending to such matters," the bishop replied.

Jarvin looked at his advisor flatly, trying to decide if the man was being impertinent, but he was unable to tell from his tone. He thought that perhaps his waiting had finally ended as he heard a disturbance from outside the throne room, but it resolved itself into the din of combat.

The king was just about to order one of the guards to check on it and report back when the chamber doors crashed open and a bloody guardsman stumbled through.

"Treason, Your Majesty!" the man shouted to him as he barged into the chamber.

Jarvin stood and was about to question the man when several of the interior guards pulled their blades and approached the dais upon which Jarvin stood. His first thought was that they were moving to protect him, but then one of the men thrust his sword into the back of the man stumbling toward the dais.

Jarvin drew the sword he had made a habit of wearing as the guards continued to advance toward the dais. The king looked at the few doors leading from the throne room, trying to decide which would be the best route of escape and get him back to his rooms where his wife and children were. A feeling of dread raised a chill up his spine as he thought of what might be happening elsewhere in the castle.

Magus Illifan stepped toward the approaching men and began casting. "Caalendor, get the king to safety!"

A ball of fire leapt from his outstretched hands, growing as it sped toward the assassins. The flaming sphere burst violently when it reached its mark, instantly killing half a dozen of the men. He heard the bishop chanting nearby and looked toward him.

"I can take care of this rabble. Get the king out of here," the old magus reiterated as more men began entering the throne room.

"I'm sorry, old friend," the senior cleric said remorsefully.

Flames wrapped themselves around Magus Illifan like a gigantic serpent squeezing its prey. The wizard screamed as the flames constricted about his body and shot to the upper reaches of the high ceiling, engulfing him in a pillar of fire. The wizard's charred body fell and lifelessly rolled down the marble steps.

"You traitorous bastard!" Jarvin screamed in rage, then advanced on the priest with his blade held high.

The bishop stepped away as several men charged the dais, leaping between the cleric and the furious king. The assassins attacked without preamble, and it was all Jarvin could do to keep their slicing and thrusting blades from his body. Adrenalin sped the king's desperate parries, but not for much longer. He was an accomplished swordsman, but there was little he could do against four skilled fighters.

One thrust broke through his defenses and opened a long gash across his left side. Another sliced deeply into the shoulder on the same side. Movement from across the hall caught his eye and he saw several more men enter the throne room, some of them his own Blackguard. Given their lack of haste, Jarvin surmised they were not here to save him.

A third thrust defeated his defenses and pierced deep into the bicep of his sword arm. Jarvin watched the blade slip from his grasp and fall glacially slowly toward the marble floor. He saw in that falling blade the symbolic example of his reign, plummeting in a slow decline like his own inevitable fall. He looked into the eyes of the man who was already delivering the killing stroke.

The world suddenly broke free of the miasma that held time in thrall and raced ahead with wild abandon. A slender blade interposed itself between the death-dealing strike and Jarvin's heart then lashed out and took the lives of the other sword-wielders with a speed that belied belief.

"Your Majesty, we must flee!" Landrin shouted as he grabbed the king by the shoulder and pulled him back.

"Lord Bailey?" Jarvin asked in wonder as he looked upon the young bard.

"Vile creature of the abyss!" Bishop Caalendor shouted in righteous fury. "I know what you are, dark fiend, and I shall not rest until you and all those who consort with you are destroyed! I curse you and all that is unholy in the eyes of Solarian back to the pits of hell from which you were spawned!"

Landrin shielded his eyes and hissed in pain as the priest's holy symbol flared to life with all the power and conviction the man contained. The Blackguard and other soldiers of the coup charged forward as Landrin grabbed the king and fled down the passage whence he had appeared. The loyal soldiers who had been desperately trying to keep pace with the hastening vampire now fell into step with their king.

"We must hurry to the king's chamber!" Landrin ordered. "I have a way to safety there!"

The guards split into a lead and trailing element as they rushed down the body-littered halls toward the king's apartments. Most of the dead belonged to men and women loyal to the king, from guards to servants. Several times, they ran into a group of usurpers and had to fight their way through. Although they lost several loyal men, they were always able to push through, largely because of Landrin's magical ability and his unflagging speed and power.

Every passageway they left behind rang with the shouts and curses of men as they called out the fleeing king's location and gave pursuit. Their pursuers were certain they would run the king to ground along with those foolish enough to aid him. They had all castle exits sealed, including those that were kept a strict secret and known only by the king, his closest advisors, and the captain of the Blackguard.

Landrin practically shoved the king into the wardrobe and ordered every man with him to follow. Several of the guardsmen gave the lord curious looks, but none voiced an argument. The loyal men filed into the big closet and emerged in End's Run a moment later, helped through and guided out of the way by Landrin's enforcers to shake off the disorienting effects of the magical gate.

Landrin followed as the last man jumped into the closet and pulled the doors shut behind him. When he emerged on the far side, he turned toward the opening of his own wardrobe and cast a spell. At its completion, runes flared across the wardrobe still in Brelland and exploded, destroying the closet on that end and killing nearly a dozen traitors who had packed into the room in search of the fleeing king and his loyal guards.

The king was bleeding profusely and was sitting on the floor nearby with his back up against the wall as Fetch tore clean strips of linen from a bedsheet and bound his wounds. Jarvin looked up with pain-filled eyes as Landrin approached.

"You are no man," the king accused. "What are you?"

"I am your friend, Your Majesty. Given your present circumstances, I pray you are not going to do something foolish like be particular. It was men that tried to murder you and your family. Consider that when choosing what you shall base your trust upon."

Jarvin considered the young lord's words and nodded. There would be time for more questions concerning his status and motivations. Right now, there were far greater things to worry about.

"I must get word to North Haven! Caalendor knows who you are and to where you likely whisked me away. Duchess Mellina is the only one I can trust and can get troops here before the bishop can."

"I believe I can get a message to the duchess in time, but why not take you to North Haven instead? Surely North Haven could withstand a siege far better than End's Run."

"North Haven has already been put to siege once recently, and I would not wish that upon them again. Even so, her walls are not yet completed and I would not jeopardize the populace needlessly. I have studied the maps of this region extensively. The southern pass is narrow, steep, and arduous. A smaller force can defend it against a much larger adversary by utilizing the landscape to its advantage.

Supply lines will also be far more difficult to maintain for Caalendor's troops if they come north, while we can stockpile a great deal of meat here in End's Run. Tactically speaking, End's Run provides me with far more advantages than North Haven while risking fewer lives. Of course, that all assumes we can get word to North Haven, and the duchess is willing and able to lend her support."

"Pen your letter, Majesty, and I shall get a raven to carry it," Landrin promised his king.

"Landrin," the king said as his host turned to fulfill his task. "My wife and children?"

"Are safe and are most assuredly eager to see you. Fetch can show you to your rooms. There should be writing supplies there as well."

"Thank you, Lord Bailey. I owe you more than I can ever repay."

"Do not thank me yet, Majesty. We both have far more to face in the coming days."

Landrin turned and left Fetch to look after the king while Donnigan got the nearly two score of guards who had come with him settled. He stepped out into the freezing night air and sent a tendril of magic out into the ether. It took only a few minutes before a raven answered his silent call.

"Forgive me, my feathered friend, but yours shall not be the only life given to this cause in the days to come," Landrin told the black bird as he stopped its heart with another dark thread of magic.

He then used a spell similar to that which created his undead mount and reanimated the bird. Although the raven fluttered its wings and fluffed its feathers, it was not truly alive. It now existed with a cruel façade of life just as Landrin did. Only the raven's would be blessedly short.

Landrin then returned to the king and found him in the rooms he had set aside for him and his family.

"Landrin," the king addressed him as he entered the room, "my eldest son, Miles, is at the Academy. One of the few people that knew of his identity was Caalendor. I must get word to him. I fear his life is in great danger."

"I can prepare another raven, but I would have to send it to someone I know at the Academy, and I have no idea if this person is loyal to you or not. I imagine that Caalendor already has his pieces in place, and if he is moving against your son, any message I send would arrive days too late."

Jarvin's face showed the weight of his sorrow and it was apparent that the king had already considered this. "I must try. For my family's sake, I must try."

"As you wish, Highness. I shall send your missive to the duchess and then prepare another for your son."

Landrin left the king to console his wife and comfort his two young children. After attaching the tiny missive to the raven's leg, he released it outside with instructions to deliver the message to the duchess in North Haven. His work completed for the time being, Landrin began feeling the fatigue of overly stressing his body and not feeding enough. It had been a hectic few days. He had barely returned home from speaking to the lupin when the wardrobe issued a silent warning that the king was in danger.

He went back inside and descended a staircase hidden behind a false panel in the kitchen. The vampire followed the stairs down, where they led to a series of cells. There were twelve cells in all, each with stout steel bars for doors, but only three were occupied. Grabbing a small but very sharp knife and a plain silver goblet from a table at the foot of the stairs, Landrin approached one of the cells.

"Come for your dinner, bloodsucker?" the prisoner asked.

"Have you changed your mind about commuting your sentence?" Landrin asked.

Each of the three men had earned the right to be hanged several times over. All were once part of the former bandit leader's group and had decided to test the new laird's willingness and ability to enforce the king's law. Landrin had given them the choice of life in these cells as a source of sustenance for himself, or being hanged to death in the public square. There had been five of them, but two chose death and Landrin had obliged them.

The man stuck his arm through the bars without another word of complaint. Landrin made a slash across the man's inner forearm and caught the dark blood in the chalice. He handed the man a clean cloth to help staunch the bleeding before draining the blood-filled cup in one large pull. Landrin retired to his own room and thought of the battles that lay ahead.

CHAPTER II

Miranda found Azerick in the large laboratory built beneath the new tower, as he was most often to be found these days. He had been busy attaching and enspelling pieces of steel made by Ken, the blacksmith, to something vaguely resembling a huge iron man. The construct was nearly ten feet tall and almost half as wide at the shoulders. One arm ended not in a hand but a massive sword with a blade four feet long and wider than a man's hand.

"Azerick!" Miranda shouted above the din of his hammering. "Azerick!"

Azerick stopped his banging and climbed down from the ladder he was using to fit the shoulder guard into place. He noted the seriousness on his wife's face as he stepped toward her.

"What is it? Is there something wrong? Is Ellyssa in trouble again? I swear, that girl will be the death of me."

Miranda smiled at the mention of the precocious girl. She reminded her so much of herself at that age, only more destructive.

"Mother just received a missive from the king. Bishop Caalendor has turned traitor and usurped the throne. Jarvin and his family have fled Brelland," Miranda explained fretfully.

"Hmm, I thought that had all been sorted out with Ulric's death." Azerick shrugged and retrieved his hammer. "At least it does not have anything to do with me."

Miranda snatched the hammer from his hand with surprisingly quick reflexes. "It most certainly does! He has asked North Haven to send aid at once to End's Run. He is certain that the bishop is sending soldiers to kill him."

"I still fail to see how that involves me."

Miranda tried to determine if Azerick was being intentionally difficult or if he truly did not understand. "My mother is the duchess of North Haven. I am her daughter and you are my husband. That makes you the future duke of North Haven and a loyal vassal to the king."

"Hmm. Well, if the future king is ever in trouble and the future me is not terribly busy and gives a goblin's odiferous butt about his problems, then perhaps in the future I will see what I can do." Azerick held out his hand. "Hammer, please."

Miranda drew the hammer back as if to strike him with it. "You incredibly obstinate and frustrating man! Do you not recall the oaths you made just weeks ago?"

"I recall someone forcing me to say some words of the sort, but I was more focused on stealing the king's ring at the time. I am fairly certain oaths made under such duress and threats of a lonely wedding night are invalid."

Miranda clenched her jaw in frustration at Azerick's stubbornness. "Do you wish me to go in your stead? Shall your wife fulfill your responsibility for you?"

"I would rather you did not, but I shall not force you to do anything or abstain from anything you have a mind to do. I am not a controlling person. I do however think you are being foolish."

With a roar of anger and frustration, Miranda hurled the hammer at Azerick's head. He laughed as he easily dodged the intentionally poorly aimed projectile and heard it bounce off his steel construct with a loud clang.

"So you are willing to let me ride off to do battle?"

"I will not order you not to. I fail to see that as my right."

"Even if it means putting your child in danger?" Miranda asked, crossing her hands over her stomach.

Azerick felt his knees almost buckle as he took several unsteady steps toward his wife and reached out tentatively for her. "You are with child?"

All of the anger she had been feeling evaporated in an instant and she smiled brightly. "I believe so."

"Why did you not say so in the first place?" Azerick asked.

"Do you think you are the only one capable of being difficult? Now I hope you feel sufficiently embarrassed to do what you know is right."

"It is all the more reason for us both to stay."

Miranda shook her head. "No, Azerick. I will not have our child hearing that his or her father is a man that shirks his duty. It will know you are a man of loyalty and conviction, and I will not allow anyone to have reason to say otherwise. You may not care about Jarvin or anyone else who sits the throne, but whoever rules will have a great influence on the world in which our child grows up. I know Jarvin is a good man and a good king. He will provide a far better kingdom for our children than anyone seeking the throne, and without your help, I do not believe he can win it back."

Azerick weighed her words and knew that she was right. He thought about the convictions and high standards his father had held and knew that he would be sorely disappointed in his son if he were to foreswear his duties.

"I will prepare myself to go the morning after next. I must finish this before I depart," Azerick told Miranda, jerking a thumb at the huge construct behind him.

"What is that thing anyway? You have been working on it for months."

"Protection," Azerick replied.

Miranda folded her arms around her husband and Azerick returned her embrace.

"You had best come back to me and soon," Miranda ordered as she buried her face into Azerick's shoulder.

"The best guarantee is not to go at all."

She pulled back just far enough to look him in the eyes. "You know I could not live with that."

Azerick smiled down at her. "I know, and I could never live with disappointing you or our child."

They held their embrace for several minutes before Azerick insisted that he get back to work so that he could be ready to depart. Miranda told him that her mother, along with the recently promoted General Brague, were working tirelessly to get as many men armed and ready to march as they could in the next two days.

One of the first things the duchess did after Ulric's failed siege was to create a standing army as well as maintain a ready militia. Azerick helped fund the soldiers' pay and the crafting of a large stockpile of weapons. Thanks to Jarvin having ended the war with Sumara a decade ago, there were plenty of able bodies from which to establish North Haven's military.

It was late by the time Azerick completed his golem. The last step involved enchanting a fist-sized gem that acted as the golem's source of power as well as containing its creator's instructions. Azerick secured the gem inside the construct's thick chest cavity before completing the final component. The last piece to be enchanted was a silver necklace with a small pendant in the shape of Azerick's personal sign.

He trudged off to bed and gently slipped beneath the covers so as not to disturb his sleeping wife. His attempts at stealth failed as she rolled over, wrapped her arms around him, and held him tightly. She smiled when he kissed her forehead before he drifted off into what was probably his last good night's sleep for some time to come.

Breakfast began as it usually did, with all of the senior school members sitting around the table discussing the running of the school and other bits of information anyone thought important enough to bring up. Azerick started the conversation once everyone was seated.

"I imagine most of you have heard the grim news out of Brelland?" Azerick asked. "North Haven is sending all of its available resources to aid Jarvin in End's Run and to put him back on the throne. Apparently, I am counted amongst those assets and will be riding out with the army on the morrow."

"Not without me you're not," Allister grumbled as he buttered a biscuit.

Azerick breathed a sigh of relief. "I was hoping you would come, Allister. I was trying to figure out how to ask."

"I think by now you should know asking is unnecessary."

Rusty piped up, "Of course, I am going as well."

As much as Azerick valued Rusty's help and friendship, he was uncomfortable about placing him in the kind of danger they would soon be facing.

"Rusty, I think you should stay here for this one. You have two young children, and I would rather not have that to worry about."

"Well, there is a surprise. Azerick thinks the entire world revolves around him and everything that moves is a result of the wake he leaves in his path," Rusty proclaimed sarcastically.

"Why else would you willingly go to the frozen north to fight for Jarvin?" Azerick asked, feeling a little insulted at Rusty's snide comment.

"I'm duty bound to go to my king's aid."

"How so?"

Rusty put down his forkful of eggs and looked at Azerick as if he were an imbecile. "You might remember my father, Lord George Cossington. It is an inherited title and with it comes the rights and responsibilities it holds. I had to affirm my title and oaths on my sixteenth birthday. Idiot."

"I always knew there was something wrong about you," Azerick poked back. "I just thought it was your terrible grasp of magic."

"You were probably picking up on my terrible ability to choose good friends," Rusty shot back.

Azerick shrugged. "That could be it."

"I think I should go as well," Alex said.

"I don't know, Alex. You are a big part of the martial training, and having one more sword for Jarvin is hardly worth the expense to the school. No offense."

"If it were just about having another fighter I might agree. Brague is a good leader, but North Haven has not had this many soldiers before, and he does not have a strong leadership element practiced in leading large numbers of troops. Of his subordinate officers, I doubt many of them are Academy trained," Alex countered.

"You do make a good point. Besides, we still have Ewen, Jansen, Zeke, and a few other senior fighters well-practiced in the drills and exercises," Azerick agreed.

Jansen, who rarely spoke at the morning meetings, or not at all unless running sword drills, broke in. "I will go north."

It took Azerick a moment to realize who had spoken. "Please tell me you are not some secret lord as well."

"I have taken oaths. I will go north and fight for the king," Jansen answered flatly in a voice that would brook no argument.

"All right then. Is there anyone else we should bring? Ken the blacksmith or Agnes the cook maybe?"

"What about Joshua, Maira, or Umair?" Rusty asked.

The three former Black Tower students had shown themselves to be very capable wizards. Both Joshua and Maira now held the rank of full wizard and were invaluable in teaching the younger students. Even as an adept, Umair showed a level of maturity and responsibility that made him a good teacher for the novices.

Azerick shook his head. "I would not ask that of them. Besides, with me, Rusty, and Allister gone, the school will really need them to cover for our absence."

Aggie spoke past a mouthful of potatoes. "I suppose that leaves old Aggie on babysitting duty again?"

Azerick smiled fondly at the gregarious old wizard. "You are the only one I trust to keep this school together while I am gone, Aggie."

"Ha! I'm about the only one that keeps it together when you're here!"

Azerick shared a laugh along with everyone else at the table with the exception of Jansen who no one had ever heard laugh before. Now that they had taken care of the expedition planning, Azerick felt it important to impose some restrictions while he was gone.

"Given the current state of the realm, I want everyone to avoid leaving the school grounds as much as possible. I definitely do not want any of the students going to North Haven until things are back to normal. Caalendor knows that North Haven and this school support Jarvin, and I do not want to present him with any opportunities to use one of you or the students as leverage against us. I am sure Allister and Aggie have sensed and looked into the strange gathering of magic to the north. If not, I am sure you have heard Brother Thomas mention it in church. I hope to investigate what is happening before I return."

Allister and Aggie nodded as they had both been studying the phenomenon for several weeks now, but a powerful force was blocking any attempt at scrying or divining its intent. Once breakfast was over, they all went their separate ways to prepare or attend to their duties.

Azerick needed to go and find Ellyssa before he began packing his own supplies.

Ellyssa was usually with Roger, Sandy, or Wolf, assuming they were not all together. Roger had mostly forgiven Ellyssa for getting him into trouble, so they might be together, and since Ellyssa was still trying to make it up to him, there was a good chance Roger was in charge of the day's activities. That usually meant the library.

He headed up the stairs and entered the library. Azerick paused when he entered, as he always did, still amazed at how Aggie had transported the entire contents of the Black Tower's store of knowledge and deposited it here. The sorcerer scanned the room and received a few waves from the students who saw him enter, but there was no sign of Ellyssa or Roger.

Azerick decided the next best place to look was the kitchen. If she was with Wolf or Sandy, they almost certainly passed through there. Retreating down the stairs, Azerick stepped into the kitchen, bustling with activity as the staff cleaned up after the morning meal.

It took a moment, but Azerick soon spied Agnes directing the cleanup efforts with brisk efficiency. Threading his way through the busy women, he reached Agnes and narrowly avoided getting a pan of soapy water dumped on him.

"Master Azerick, you are a loose wrench in my cogs," Agnes informed him, not pleased to have an outsider in her kitchen even if he did own it.

"Sorry, Agnes. Have you seen Ellyssa, Wolf, or Sandy?"

"Ellyssa and that boy with the club foot came through earlier and piled up enough food to feed a platoon of lancers. Then I saw them and the fat little dragon walking out toward the north wall. My guess is they were heading out the gate to the east woods to meet up with that thieving little wildling and his hairy friend."

Azerick smiled, knowing that despite Agnes's complaining, she rather enjoyed Wolf's spirited antics. It helped break the tedium of kitchen life. Of course, she would never admit to such a thing even if her life depended on it.

"I will check out there. Thank you, Agnes."

"You can thank me by getting out of the way," Agnes told him.

Azerick promptly obeyed and darted out of the kitchen door leading outside. He navigated the multitude of buildings and eventually found the small sally port set near the northeast corner of the wall. Three boys walking the wall spied his approach and waved. There were never less than ten sentries walking the wall ever since the siege, and often as many as twice that number.

"Hoy, Master Azerick!" one of the young men near the gate called down.

"Good morning, gentlemen," Azerick returned. "Have you seen Ellyssa? She may have come through with Roger and Sandy about an hour ago."

"Yeah, they came through earlier. Is she in trouble again?" the young guardsman asked with a grin.

Azerick was not sure why, but there seemed to be a special tension between many of the martial students and his apprentice. There was always rivalry between the magus and martial students. He had first thought it was simply something at the Academy, but the same thing appeared here almost immediately after both training schools were developed. He was uncertain why so many of the fighters took such enjoyment in seeing his apprentice punished. Knowing her, she had said some unflattering things after being knocked on her backside during her mandatory melee training.

Every magus student had to practice with a weapon, most often the staff, but anything the student chose, for two hours twice a week. Every martial student had to learn magical theory and how best to defend against an enemy wielding magic. Even the Academy did not teach that.

"I am afraid not. Sorry to disappoint you," Azerick answered as he stepped through the small gate.

"You may want to know the passphrase so the next shift lets you back in."

Azerick had a feeling the young guard was toying with him, but asked anyway. "What is the passphrase?"

The young man grinned down and replied, "Steel is real but magic is tragic!"

Azerick smiled as both young men broke into fits of laughter. He left the two boys laughing atop the wall and headed northeast to a spot he knew Wolf and Ellyssa liked to frequent. It took him nearly half an hour of steady walking before he neared the clearing and heard several voices ahead. The talking ceased the instant Azerick stepped out of the trees and into the glade.

A large, flat boulder the size of a respectable dining table held the remnants of their breakfast. Although all eyes turned toward Azerick as soon as he broke from the trees, only Wolf and Ghost looked unsurprised. Nothing seemed to happen in their woods without their knowledge. Ellyssa evinced the strongest reaction as she spun around and practically glared at him.

"We weren't doing anything wrong! We were just talking, and Roger and I will be back before classes start," Ellyssa exclaimed defensively.

Azerick always thought of himself as a master at holding grudges, but Ellyssa's ability to maintain resentment bordered on legendary. Her problem was that she focused on her punishments so much that she completely forgot the reason why she had been reprimanded in the first place.

Azerick tried not to take it personally, but her remark stung. "I am not here to punish you. I have to leave for a while, and I wanted to give you something before I go."

Now it was Ellyssa's turn to feel bad for her waspishness. She would not trade her life or Azerick for anything in the world, but she still thought about her own parents selling her. Despite the necessity and logic she used to try to understand why they did what they had done, it still hurt, and when things went wrong like they did with the wardrobe or the other mistakes she made that got her into trouble, that pain and uncertainty renewed itself.

She wanted to tell Azerick she was sorry. She wanted to tell him she was sorry for snapping at him and that she was sorry for using magic that almost got people hurt and a dozen other things that had gotten her into trouble, but her pride simply would not allow it. It was her pride that enabled her to leave her family and go and live with a stranger without crying, and to face a terrifying ghost without running in fear. Her overwhelming pride was her source of strength when all else seemed to go wrong.

"What is it?" she asked a bit more softly.

Azerick pulled the silver chain and pendant from his pocket and fastened it around her slender neck. He pulled her long blond hair over the chain and smiled down at her.

"It is a wizard mark. It is tied to the golem I have been working on these past months. If you are ever in great danger, and I mean truly life-threatening, simply break the chain and the golem will find you, no matter where you are, and defend you."

"Do you really think I will need it?" Ellyssa asked as she studied the pendant.

"I hope not. But there are things happening in the kingdom, and you or someone else at the school may need it. I pray it does not come to that, but I would rather be prepared. That is also why I have ordered that no students leave the school once I depart."

Ellyssa let the pendant drop and hang against her chest. "I can't go into the city?"

"No. It is a dangerous time right now, and I need everyone to stay together behind the safety of the school walls."

"But Alonzo Janovin is coming to North Haven! He's the greatest bard in the kingdom and I wanted to see him!" Ellyssa complained loudly.

"I'm sorry, but you will have to wait for another time."

"But I haven't been in trouble for weeks! You are here to punish me and I didn't even do anything! I hate this stupid place and I hate you and your stupid punishments!" Ellyssa railed in fury, then ran from the grove.

Azerick sighed at both Ellyssa's anguish at being denied something she had her heart set on and feeling as though he had done something wrong. Perhaps he was being overprotective, but there were troubling things happening on many fronts and he simply could not defend everyone against them all.

Sandy cleared her throat and broke the awkward silence that permeated the grove after Ellyssa's very vocal departure. "Do I have to stay inside too?"

Azerick smiled fondly at the not-so-little dragon. "You are the size of a pony—a pony with very sharp claws and teeth. I think you can take care of yourself. Still, don't go too far."

"Don't expect me to go live in that stone prison," Wolf said with a huff, then crossed his arms in defiance.

"I would have better luck telling Ghost what to do."

The big black wolf responded with a short sneeze that sounded a great deal like a snort of derision.

Azerick sighed and turned back to return to the citadel. He wondered if he could put his and Ellyssa's relationship back on track. She had been so full of wonder and eager when he had first taken her in and started teaching her magic. She still craved the learning, but she seemed steadfast in avoiding the wisdom needed to be responsible. It seemed that she no longer looked upon him with the same awe she once did. Now he was just the disciplinarian who punished her when she misbehaved.

He would need to do something special for her when he got back. He could not directly teach her how to cast magic, but there were many other aspects of magic he could involve her in more. He was so used to isolating himself that he never thought about how she felt when he locked himself in the laboratory for days on end. Once he had reached his ability to improve her use of magic, he had handed her off to Allister. She probably felt some rejection for that. Azerick could not blame her. First, her parents were forced to part with her, and then he became so involved with the school and his own problems that she probably felt abandoned once again.

Azerick realized then that he needed to learn how to give of himself and his time. He was going to be a father soon, an actual father and not just a surrogate parent for an already grown child. That was it then. When he got back, he would make more time for Ellyssa, Miranda, and the baby when it came. He just hoped he could overcome all of his emotional hang-ups to be the husband and father his family needed him to be.

Don't worry. You will always have me to help raise our son properly, Klaraxis's voice invaded his thoughts.

The demon whose soul resided within Azerick had grown very good at lying dormant for days and weeks at a time, coming out only to taunt him or influence his moods and behavior when he was most vulnerable.

Shut up, demon. You will have nothing to do with my family, ever. And what makes you think it is a boy?

Stupid sorcerer. I am already part of your family and our son. I know because I helped create him. Our spirits are joined and inseparable in all things. In all things, human. Never forget that.

I will destroy you and myself before I ever let you anywhere near my family! Azerick raged, then used his will along with Klaraxis's soul name to punish him and drive him deep into the shadows of his mind.

By the time Azerick reached the walls of the keep, he felt better about how he would deal with his family despite the demon's taunting. He had not been gone that long and recognized the same pair of young guardsmen standing above the small postern gate.

"We saw Ellyssa. She didn't look too happy," one said as they both grinned. "I thought she wasn't in trouble?"

"She wasn't and still is not, although she seems to have convinced herself otherwise," Azerick responded, then tried to open the small gate but found it locked. "Can you open the gate?"

"You have to say the passphrase!" the boy called down, hooting in laughter.

"You really need me to say it?"

"You could always go all the way around like Ellyssa did. I got five coppers says you can't get as far as she did and us still hear you cursing!"

Azerick felt bad for Ellyssa, knowing she had already been in a foul mood before dealing with these two practical jokers, but he could not help but smile. Wall duty was as dull as it came, and whatever helped keep them attentive was a good thing. Still, he could not have them think they could so easily manipulate the master of the school. He easily called upon the Source, shaped his gate spell, and stepped through to emerge on the inside of the wall.

"I told you he'd cheat! You owe me a silver sword," James proclaimed loudly, holding out his hand for the coin.

"Damn! That's a week's pay!" the other protested but dug into a pouch tied to his belt.

Azerick called back up to the pair. "Steel is real but magic is tragic."

Alex emerged from a small belvedere built at the corner of the wall. "And that, boys, is a double cheat."

Both young soldiers cursed as they each handed over a silver coin. "How'd you know he'd double cheat?"

"When it comes to wizards or sorcerers, if you give them two choices they will always create a third," their commander educated them.

Azerick knew Alex would let the two earn their coin back through a little extra work, so he did not need to tell him how he felt about the boys gambling, especially with their commander. He reached his room without spotting his erstwhile apprentice and hoped she had gone straight to her class. He found Miranda already packing away several articles of his warmest clothing into a trunk.

"Are you in that big a hurry to get rid of me?" Azerick asked as he snuck up behind his wife and wrapped his arms around her waist.

Miranda stopped what she was doing, leaned back against her husband, and covered his hands with her own. "I want you to be comfortable and safe. It would be terrible if you froze any of your bits off."

"We definitely would not want that, unless you are set on having only the one child."

"I was talking about fingers and toes, you pig," Miranda laughed, twisting in his arms, and playfully punching him in the chest. "Did you give Ellyssa the pendant?"

Azerick released his hold and began picking through the clothing Miranda had laid out on the bed. "I did, but somehow I came off being a tyrant again. I do not understand how to talk to her anymore. Is it normal for children to grow so fast and change so much, or is it just around me?"

"She has been through a lot and seen many things in her short life. Her family sold her, she is learning magic, and she has had to kill men that were trying to kill her. Have you ever asked her how she feels about that day when the soldiers broke through the doors of the tower? Not everyone adapts as well as you, and yet few would call you well adjusted. Some claim you are completely mad."

Azerick nodded and thought about the siege of the school. Ellyssa had used magic to defend herself and others with lethal power. He forgot how incredibly young she was to have had to face such a terrible thing. She was even younger than he had been when he was forced to take his first life. He had not really put much thought into how those events had shaped and changed him.

"I have neglected many things. I plan to do something about that when I return. Hopefully, I can still reach her."

Miranda smiled at him. "She loves you. I am sure she will appreciate some special attention and come around."

"I certainly hope so. If I cannot even prove to be an acceptable guardian, how can I possibly be a decent father?"

"You will be a wonderful father, Azerick. You just need not be afraid to show how much you care. That is your greatest problem. You think too much before you let yourself feel or show those feelings. Showing you love someone is not a weakness."

"She said she hated me," Azerick said sullenly.

"I have told my mother, my father, my maids, and anyone else tasked with keeping me out of trouble that I hated them at one point or another. She does not mean it. She is fighting for her own independence and sense of identity and woe betide anyone that gets in her way."

"You are right, of course. I just wish you could convince my heart of that," Azerick said dejectedly.

"I can always go get that hammer and beat it into you."

"Are you going to get more violent as this pregnancy progresses? If so, I may need to vacation in End's Run for my own safety," Azerick replied.

"You better be back here as swiftly as you can unless you want to see real violence!" Miranda asserted playfully.

"Who is this bard named Alonzo Janovin? Have you heard of him?"

"Of course I have. Everyone has. You would have to live under a rock not to have heard of him. Although, I guess living under a tower works just as well. He is reputed to be the greatest singer and musician to emerge in the last two hundred years. Why do you ask?"

Azerick sighed. "I guess he is coming to North Haven and Ellyssa wanted to go see him. I told her I did not want any of the students to travel outside of the school, and that was when she blew up at me."

"I see. He is putting on a special show for Mother and the city's elite. Perhaps she could go with me. Unless I am grounded too," she teased.

"I would rather you not travel."

"It is five miles away, Azerick. Besides, Mother actually agrees with you about the possible danger, and is sending an escort of palace guardsmen for me."

Azerick thought a moment and shook his head. "No. Ellyssa needs to learn boundaries and to follow the rules. If I let her go with you, it will simply be an example of how to get past those. She is eleven. She will get another chance to hear him sing."

"I suppose you are right. She does lack a certain ability for understanding consequences," Miranda agreed.

Ellyssa listened from the hall just outside the door. *I knew it! Azerick could let me go with Miranda but he wants to punish me! Well, I'm still going to go, and when Alonzo sees me, he will remember me and come back when I am old enough and we'll get married and travel the kingdom. He will sing and play and I will use my magic to create illusions and we'll live happily ever after away from this stupid school and all its rules!*

Ellyssa snuck quietly away before storming to her own room in the old tower to fume over the unfairness of her life. He treated her like a child! Okay, maybe she was *technically* still a child, but she was the best student in the entire school. Okay, *technically* Roger was a better student, but only because he was a teacher's pet and did everything exactly the way they told him to. She was still stronger and she could take care of herself. How much trouble could she get into going to see a bard sing at the palace?

Azerick and Miranda spent the rest of the day together. It was then that he realized how much time he spent alone, preoccupied with his magic and projects. He needed to change that. They spent more hours together that day than they had in the past week. He wished he had seen how neglectful and miserly he had been with his time before having to leave on what would be a week- or month-long expedition, participating in yet another life-threatening battle.

The morning of their departure came far too quickly. Azerick sat astride Horse dressed in warm clothes and a thick wool cloak. Miranda had packed an ice bear cloak replete with hood in his bags, but he would not need that kind of protection from the elements until they reached the western pass.

There was a large crowd gathered to see them all off. Nearby, Simon stood fidgeting next to Teresa. Ewen stood with the bulk of his martial students waiting for the group to depart before herding the young men and women off for their morning drills. Peck fussed with the saddle straps and bridles despite having checked them several times already.

"Are you sure you don't want me to come along to keep the horses, milord?" the small young man asked anxiously. "My men are fine looking after the stables, and you could use a good man to keep your horses and tack in top shape."

"As much of an asset as you would be, Peck, I think I can find someone in Brague's legion to take care of that," Azerick told him. "Have you seen Ellyssa?"

"Not since yesterday," Peck responded. "She was really mad about something and did not talk to me."

Azerick looked grim. He had hoped she had calmed enough to see him and the others off, but apparently, she was still sulking. He would be gone at least a month, probably two, assuming the battle did not drag out. It probably would not since it was unlikely to break down into a siege conflict. Open battles like these were usually resolved in weeks if not days.

The small party headed out toward the northern road where Brague and his army should already be forming up and waiting on them. Allister and Rusty rode to Azerick's side while Jansen followed on his own mount a short distance behind them. Following the quiet warrior were three young men on horseback and another driving an open wagon carrying their clothing, food, and necessities.

Azerick looked back then addressed Alex. "Are those four going with us?"

Alex nodded an affirmative. "They are the oldest and most capable of my students. I felt they were ready to see an actual battle. There is only so much one can learn in a classroom or in training. There was not a great deal of organized open fighting when the school came under attack so this would be a great opportunity to show them large scale tactics."

"I see. Wasn't the battle of North Haven your first real battle as well?"

"It was, but I also had over ten years of training at the Martial Academy where we had far greater numbers and resources in which to practice these kinds of maneuvers as well as greater experience with command and control. This will definitely be a learning time for me too, and one from which all five of us can then bring back techniques to the school and better train the others."

Azerick spotted a familiar bulk in the wagon and turned to Allister. "Is that the tent Magus Bauer and the other two wizards used when they attacked the school?"

The old mage smiled. "Yup. I thought it would be a mite more comfortable than some old field tent."

"Hmm. I will have to show it to Brague so he will have something to think about while he is freezing his self-righteous backside off near a campfire at night," Azerick said with a malicious grin.

Rusty laughed. "I think his anger at the thought of you being comfortable in that portable palace should keep him quite warm!"

The group from the school spotted the army train as they struggled to get organized just outside North Haven's eastern wall. Mounted cavalry headed the long procession while wagons filled with men and pulled by large teams of horses followed. It appeared that there were enough wagons carrying troops that no one would be walking, which should speed their travel considerably. There was still a great deal of shouting and shuffling around as officers and logisticians organized the chaos.

One rider broke free from the convoy and approached at a canter. Azerick identified the man as General Brague, first from the large blue plume adorning the top of his helmet, then from the jingling of tiny bells that rang out thanks to a spell Azerick had cursed him with, and lastly from the undisguised look of hatred plastered on his face as he glared at the young sorcerer.

"Lord Giles, I am rather surprised to see you," the general said, obviously feeling ill over having to use Azerick's title.

Azerick gave the general a confused look. "Were you not informed of my coming?"

"I was. I simply assumed you would not make an appearance until the battle was nearly finished and the field properly littered with corpses," Brague answered with a smirk.

"I do like to stay unpredictable."

The general's smirk twisted to a look of disdain. "You and your party will ride at the rear of the convoy. We are nearly ready to depart so I suggest you make haste."

"Why the rear?" Azerick asked, ignoring Brague's acerbic tone.

"Because I will be riding at the head!" he snapped back.

Azerick could not help but smile at the man's open hostility. He found it comical that anyone could hold a grudge for so long. Particularly one that, when it boiled down to it, was over how Azerick had first saved the man's life along with Miranda's and later the entire city of North Haven; not to mention his actions largely resulted in saving the king as well. At least, it had until all this happened.

"How many men are you bringing, Captain Brague?" Azerick asked, intentionally demoting the recently promoted general.

"Nearly three thousand, and it is General Brague, if you please!"

"I really do not please, but since you brought it up, congratulations on your promotion. I guess my invitation was lost in transit or something," Azerick responded.

Brague smiled. "Oh, it was not lost. I personally delivered it to Lady Miranda's hand. She may have interpreted that I would prefer you not attend."

"I cannot imagine why she would do that."

"It probably had something to do with the fact that I specifically asked in the invitation that you did not attend."

Azerick smiled back at the general. "Such lack of hospitality, and to think I was going to invite you to my tent for tea later, perhaps with a shot of good whiskey to really ward off the cold."

"A good officer does not drink in the field," Brague grumbled.

Azerick arched his eyebrows. "So when should I expect you? How about around the nineteenth hour?"

Brague ground his teeth in indignation. "Get in line! We are about to move out."

"I think you mean 'Get in line, My Lord,'" Azerick informed him haughtily.

Brague whipped his mount around with a loud growl and galloped back to the head of the column.

"This little journey is going to be just a joy," Azerick laughed as he led his group to the rear of the procession.

CHAPTER 12

A gnawing in his belly awoke Miles Jervais, or Miles Ollander, crown prince of Valeria to those who knew him personally. He tried to ignore the angry rumblings, but training had been especially brutal today and it was very insistent. There was no food in his dormitory either. It was against the rules and severely punishable for anyone violating it. So was sneaking to the kitchens in the middle of the night, but since that activity was far less likely to get him caught, it was what he decided to do.

Miles had been a student at the Martial Academy since he was eight years old, and he was now a sixth-year student. If someone caught him, he would receive a demerit and probably be put on additional detail. It was a far less severe punishment than a first or second year would get. It was chilly in the halls of the Academy so he donned a warm set of soft nightclothes and slippers and crept out into the dim halls.

He spied the light of a lantern far down the hall, borne by one of the other students who was on sentry that night. Sentry duty was a two-hour shift and rotated through the entire student body, although the older students got it less often than the younger. Miles had it tomorrow, but it would be another week before he came up on the roster again thanks to the almost overcrowding of the Martial Academy. Unlike the magus side. They did not pull sentry duty over there and would not do so even if they had the numbers. The Magus Academy was almost desolate with entire wings closed off since there were no students to fill them.

Miles, like most martial students, saw wizards as lacking discipline. He darted down a passage and held his breath as a sentry walked by but failed to spot him hidden in the dark recess of the wall. Once the student guard had passed, he crept back out and made for the stairs leading down toward the kitchens. He had to hide from three more of the roving patrols, but he made it to the enormous kitchens without discovery. Now he just needed to find food.

The only light came from the half-moon shining dully through the open window in the far wall. Beyond his ability to make out basic shapes, the darkness left him nearly blind. Miles fumbled about the counters in search of a loaf of bread or smoked meat left out, but so far had only found pots, pans, and a wooden block full of knives.

He gasped and reached out blindly when his hand knocked the block of knives from the countertop. By some miracle, he not only managed to catch the block, but not a single knife fell out to clatter noisily onto the floor. He smiled and breathed a sigh of relief as he gently set the knife block back onto the counter. Only his exceptional training and military bearing kept him from crying out in alarm when a strong hand gripped his shoulder painfully.

Orange brilliance flared from a struck sulfur match then a greater light filled the room as it was touched to an oil lamp. Had his heart not been racing and his mind busy trying to come up with a plausible lie for being in the kitchen at this hour, he may have wondered who would be in the kitchens with something as rare and novel as a sulfur match.

Miles turned to face whoever it was who had apprehended him. He almost smiled in relief when he looked into the face of one of the kinder kitchen staff. Miss Elli had been there about as long as Miles had been attending the school. She was around thirty and was pretty, in a plain sort of way. She seemed intelligent despite being in such a mundane position and had always been nice to Miles in the rare times their paths had crossed.

"Miss Elli, you almost scared me to death!" Miles whispered anxiously.

"Miles, is that you? What are you doing down here at this hour? You know you will get yourself into trouble."

"I was so hungry it woke me up and I could not get back to sleep. I thought I might find a roll or something to settle my stomach so I could get some rest," he explained.

Elli smiled at the young man. "I think I recall wrapping up a loaf of bread and some smoked meat and sticking it in the cupboard today. Let me break you off a bit, but then you get yourself back to bed."

"I will. Thank you miss..."

Miss Elli cut off Miles's expression of gratitude when she yanked him so hard he nearly tumbled past her and onto the floor. A dark blur whisked just past his head as he stumbled across the kitchen and fetched up against a countertop.

"Hey, what was that for?" Miles exclaimed, and then saw the assassins.

Several men clamored into the kitchen with weapons drawn. Miles gaped dumbfounded as Elli yanked a handful of knives out of the kitchen block and hurled them one after another at the dark-garbed intruders. Two of the blades found flesh and the men dropped to the floor and did not stir. Two other men dodged the projectiles and continued to advance.

"Nice bit of throwing, missy, but now you and the little prince are gonna bleed," one of the men snarled as he closed the distance separating him from the kitchen woman and the boy.

He knows who I am! Miles thought frantically.

No one was supposed to know his true identity and that he was at the Academy except his father, his mother, and his father's advisors. How did these men know who he was and why were they trying to kill him? He surmised the why. Obviously, someone who hated his father had sent them to hurt him. Was his father in danger too? What about the rest of his family? He needed to get away, to tell someone, but more men were coming and the only thing between him and certain death was a kitchen woman!

Miles looked around for a weapon and found the knife one of the men had thrown at him lying on the floor. He reached down, scooped it up, and brandished it despite knowing that a fourteen-year-old with a dagger was unlikely to intimidate grown men wielding swords.

The two men charged Miss Elli with their swords, intent on cutting down the minor obstacle in their path. Elli dropped her night-robe to the ground, revealing black scaled armor beneath. She drew two short, wide swords in one smooth motion and met the assassins partway through the kitchen. She blocked the strike of the man on her left with the sword in her right hand and sliced his throat with her left blade. She spun with a liquid grace, casually throwing wide the man's thrust with her right sword and stabbing him in the heart with her left.

She turned to Miles before the second man hit the floor. "Highness, I must get you to safety!"

Miles could only gape like a fish at what he saw. Elli gave his shoulder a hard shake and snapped him out of his shock.

"Miles, you need to listen to me and follow my instructions to the letter and without hesitation. Do you understand?"

Miles swallowed hard and nodded.

"We'll go through the cellar door then out to the stables. I have horses and supplies ready," Elli, no longer a kitchen maid but one of the king's famed Blackguard, informed him.

The woman did not wait for a reply and led Miles into the cellar, holding her lantern and sword in one hand. When they reached the bottom of the stairs, she took them across the musty room where a set of steps led to a pair of doors set near the ceiling. She thrust the lantern into Miles's hands, climbed the steps, and peered out of the doors before throwing them wide and motioning him to follow.

The pair emerged behind the kitchens, near the midden heap from the smell of it, and raced across the yard, sticking to the shadows cast by shrubs and walls as much as possible. Several times, they had to crouch in the shadows as dark forms walked about the grounds. Whether assassins or Academy members, Miles could not say, and Elli was taking no chances.

They finally reached a small stable used exclusively for the staff. Elli ordered Miles to saddle two horses while she shifted several bales of hay and pulled up the floorboards beneath them. From the hole, she pulled two packs and an assortment of weapons and a shirt of mail. The blackguard opened one of the packs and drew out a pair of good boots and a set of plain but sturdy traveling clothes.

These she tossed toward Miles and ordered him to dress while she finished saddling the horses. By the time Miles put on the clothes, boots, and mail shirt, Elli had both horses saddled and bridled for travel.

"Put on that pack and bring me the other," Elli ordered the prince.

Miles did as he was told and handed the woman the full pack then mounted the other horse.

"Highness, forgive my abruptness, but now is not the time to stand on formalities. Something has happened and we must flee this place."

"We should go to the headmaster! He will put the entire Academy on alert!"

Elli shook her head. "These men were sent to kill you, which means someone is moving or already has moved against your father. Right now, we do not know who that is or who are our allies or enemies. The king was worried enough about this exact scenario that he personally tasked me to watch over you and to get you to North Haven if this happened. We can sort it all out once we get there."

"North Haven? Why not Brelland?"

"North Haven has proved its loyalty and Brelland may already have fallen. No one would target you unless something has already happened there," Elli grimly told the Prince.

A multitude of horrible scenarios ran through Miles's brain. "What could have happened?"

Elli shook her head. "We can talk about that later, but right now we need to move!"

Two men must have spotted the light coming out of the stables and burst in with swords drawn. Elli spurred her mount and pulled a small crossbow from beneath her cloak. She let fly the small quarrel and buried it in one man's eye. The other she simply ran down with her mount with Miles following close behind her.

The prince saw that they were not heading for the school gates but toward the trees at the far side of the enormous training grounds. As far as he knew, there was nothing but the outer curtain wall beyond the trees.

"Miss Elli, where are we going?" he called out over the rhythmic thrumming of the horses' pounding hooves.

"There is a small sally port hidden in the wall. We will leave the city that way then head north. If we are separated for any reason, avoid everyone and ride to North Haven. From there you should have little problem getting an audience with Duchess Mellina and she will give you sanctuary."

Everything was happening too fast. Miles was having a hard time understanding what was going on. Was his father dead? What about his mother, brother, and sister? Was he king now? If he was, it was only by title. He would have to raise an army to take back the throne. Did he even want to? He had seen how hard it was on his father and all the suffering it caused. Maybe he would just get on a ship, change his identity, and disappear.

His training took over and he berated himself for his lack of emotional control. He needed to focus on what was happening now and the things he could affect. He would have plenty of time to deal with the other stuff when he reached North Haven.

They had been riding hard for nearly an hour and Miles was beginning to think Elli was going to push their mounts until they died beneath them. With a final look behind them, she finally eased the relentless pace and slowed to a walk.

"There is an official courier station a few miles ahead. We should be able to get fresh mounts there and at the other stations along this route. With luck, we will be having tea with the duchess in two days if we press on without stopping," Elli informed the prince.

Miles nodded. He could do two days without sleep. Operating on little or no sleep was one of the hallmarks of training at the Martial Academy. One of the reasons for the hall duties and other, longer duties that minimized their sleep was so that they would become accustomed to going without.

A shiver crawled across his flesh. It could have been from the mortal danger he was in or simply the cold. Summer never did seem to come fully around this year. The snows lingered well into the spring, and even with summer still a month out from running its allotted course, snow could be seen in some of the higher mountains in the distance.

Elli looked over her shoulder at him. "There are trail rations in your pack. You may have lost your appetite in the excitement, but you should eat. Riding in this chill air will sap your reserves, and it will only get colder as we reach North Haven."

Miles unslung his pack, braced it against the saddle horn, and found the assortment of dried nuts, fruit, and jerky wrapped in cheesecloth. He returned the displaced items and slipped the pack back over his shoulders. Elli was right; he had lost his appetite but he chewed and swallowed the tough fare anyway.

"So my father sent you to watch over me?"

"Yes. He had long begun distrusting many people around him. I don't think anyone knew of my mission except him. To my knowledge, he did not even tell his advisors or anyone in my chain of command."

Chain of command was something Miles was very familiar with, thanks to his Academy training. "How is that? Wouldn't your commander want to know what you were doing and where you were?"

"Your father is a very shrewd man. Do you know anything about Dundalor's armor?" she asked.

"My father was trying to keep someone from getting it. Ulric, as it turned out. His adventurers say it was destroyed."

Elli nodded. "He and his advisors sent a lot of people after it. First, it was the Blackguard. We were his most trusted and capable. But when entire Blackguard contingents began failing to return, he suspected treachery. It was an easy matter to assign me to one of the outgoing units and disappear with them."

"You abandoned your unit?" Miles asked, aghast at such a thing even under these circumstances.

"I was only attached on paper. Once the unit got a few days out, I showed the team leader private orders from the king that stated I was on a separate mission and went my own way. If they returned, so did I. If not, then I was to stay at the Academy. It was good luck and bad that they did not return. It allowed everyone to assume I was dead, so my identity at the Academy was secure."

Miles tried to digest the fact that so many people had died over his father's throne and that it was still happening. How many more would die before the kingdom was settled? Would it ever be?

"Hold up here, Miles. The courier station is just around the bend. Wait behind that thicket until I check it out," Elli ordered.

Miles maneuvered his mount off the road and hid behind the dense stand of slender boles and brambles while Elli rode cautiously forward. She guided her mount toward the shack with a small paddock of horses behind it. A man in plain clothes stepped out as she drew nearer and hailed her.

"Hello there, agent. You need a switch out?" the man asked congenially.

"I need two, actually," Elli replied.

"Tethered? Or is there another rider coming?"

"Another rider, so I'll need two mounts saddled as quickly as you can."

The man gave a small salute and turned toward the paddock. "Alright, shouldn't be but a moment."

Elli scanned the outside of the station and surrounding trees for signs of anything out of the ordinary, but she saw nothing out of place. Maybe it was just the paranoia of dodging assassins, but she could not shake the feeling that something was not right. She walked back toward the corral and attached barn where several saddles, bridles, and bales of hay were stored. Elli found the man saddling the second horse and fitting a bit in its mouth.

"Have you heard any news out of Brelland," she asked.

"Aye. Something about the king being in league with those undead that keep popping up. They say he and some vampire killed that wizard of his and tried to kill the bishop. The bishop ran the two of 'em off and has taken control of Brelland until they decide who to put on the throne. He's marshaled nearly the entire military and a bunch of clerics and set off after Jarvin and that vampire."

"What of Jarvin's family?"

"They say he let the vampire have them as part of the deal for him getting some dark power."

Elli did not believe a word of these rumors. She had met the king and found him to be an open and decent man. Caalendor, on the other hand, seemed like a righteous zealot and often left her feeling uneasy in his presence. She could not afford the time to speculate. She would get thorough intelligence when they reached North Haven.

Just as she stuck her foot in the stirrup to lift herself into the saddle, she chanced a glance behind her. Sticking out from beneath the bales of hay was the tip of a blood-encrusted boot. Elli pushed herself up and over the other side of the saddle. The man's blade struck dully against the leather saddle and rebounded off. Elli dropped beneath the belly of the horse, whipped out her small hand crossbow, and buried its bolt into the man's gut.

He stumbled backwards, clasping a hand over the wound, trying to staunch the bleeding. Elli darted beneath the horse and finished him off with a stab through the heart. Several men burst into the stable with swords drawn. Her throat constricted when she saw that several of them were dressed as fellow Blackguards.

Elli grabbed the reins of the second horse, leapt onto her mount's saddle, and kicked hard into the horse's flanks. The Blackguard mounts were trained for battle and Elli was able to guide the animal with her knees while she slashed down at the men trying to block her way.

The horse trampled two of the men who failed to clear the wide doors of the stable in time while Elli cut deep into the neck and shoulder of another. One of the Blackguard managed to duck her second hasty strike as she darted past and delivered a cut to her leg just below the knee.

The two horses and rider burst from the stables and headed south where the prince waited just around the bend. Elli cut off the road and maneuvered around the thick foliage where she had told Miles to wait for her.

"Get on, quickly!" she ordered as she brought the new mount up close to where he was waiting.

Miles hopped from the back of his horse to the one Elli led without touching the ground. The Blackguard tossed him the reins as soon as he settled into the saddle. He was about to ask why she was so agitated, but then the pounding of hooves from at least a dozen horses rapidly drawing nearer reached his ears.

"Come!" Elli commanded, then turned her mount toward the woods, and kicked it into a gallop.

Miles followed without question as the pair blazed a trail through the forest, cutting onto and off deer paths at a speed that went beyond reckless. Miles was a good rider, but at these speeds through dense woods, it was all he could do to dodge overhanging tree limbs, and he simply trusted the horse to keep its footing as it barreled after Elli and her mount.

The fact that their horses were fresh and the riders significantly lighter than the men giving chase meant Miles and Elli managed to put a fair amount of distance between them and their pursuers. Hour after hour, they galloped through the open trees or along animal trails, slowing just long enough for their mounts to catch their breaths. Surrounded by endless tracts of woods, Miles had no idea where they were or even in what direction they were traveling. He assumed north and perhaps slightly east in an effort to stay away from the roads that ran between Southport, North Haven, and a dozen small villages and hamlets in between.

It was nearing late afternoon by the time Elli began to relax. That changed when the wind brought the baying of hounds and the sounds of horses to their ears. Elli cursed loudly and kicked more speed into her mount. Miles could hear dogs barking and men shouting not just from the west, but from groups to the north and south as well. Their pursuers had gathered in number and formed an open box with which to capture their elusive prey.

"How can there be so many people after us? Did they think they would need this many men just to get me? I thought you said no one knew you were at the Academy?" Miles called out to the woman's back.

"A couple of people knew you were there and probably had multiple plans in place to ensure you did not escape," she answered back. "They knew that if you escaped Southport you would likely flee toward Brelland or North Haven. They probably have every courier station between Southport, North Haven, and Brelland watched."

Despite resting several times, their mounts were exhausted and their speed was rapidly flagging. The baying of the hounds was drawing closer every minute. It would not be long before their pursuers caught up to them. The ground was rising steadily as they approached a long, rocky bluff that ran for what looked like miles in both directions.

Elli reined in her horse and leapt from the saddle. "Our horses are done for. Climb that and make your way toward North Haven. I'll catch up to you."

Miles knew Elli was lying and knew that she knew she was lying. The woman was going to make a last stand to buy him time to get over the escarpment and possibly avoid capture. It was an act of desperation, but the only real chance he had of escaping.

"Just come with me!" Miles cried out. "We can both climb it and run!"

The blackguard shook her head. "They are too close. They can ride around or use ropes to lift the dogs up and over that ledge and run us down. I have to kill those dogs if either of us is going to have a chance. Now go!"

With a tightness deep in his chest, Miles scrambled up the steep hill and began climbing the cliff face. It was not a cliff in the true sense of the word, but a near-vertical rocky ledge about thirty feet high. It was as though the entire hill beneath it had simply dropped thirty feet, leaving the rocky escarpment behind. It was not a great challenge to pick out a path and carefully ascend the stone face.

Sensing that their quarry was near, the dogs rushed forward of their human handlers and bore down upon the woman standing atop the steep incline, ready to match her steel with their fangs. Elli took careful aim at the lead dog with her small crossbow and planted the quarrel deep into the animal's throat. The dog let out a yelp and tumbled down the hill as it snapped at the object that caused it so much pain.

The steepness of the slope slowed the animals enough that she had time to reload and shoot one more of the dogs before pulling her blades free of their scabbards and bracing for the attack. The first dog to reach her got a foot of steel thrust into its chest as a reward for its efforts. She swung her second blade at the next animal, cutting it deeply across its left shoulder. Pulling her blade free from the dead dog, she swung viciously as a third hound lunged, but it managed to dart back out of her reach.

As her focus was distracted by the other animals, the dog she cut in the shoulder charged in and clamped down hard on her left forearm, shaking it so hard she nearly lost her grip on her sword. Elli tightened her hold, knowing that to lose a weapon was to lose her life, and swung her right blade, cutting the dog mauling her arm deep in its neck.

This gave the remaining dog the opening it needed. It charged in and bit down on her right ankle. Whipping its head back and forth, the dog managed to pull the woman's legs out from under her. Sensing her vulnerability, the hound released her leg and tried to clamp its jaws around her throat. Elli managed to intercept those white, slavering fangs with her already wounded left arm. She cried out as the dog's teeth crushed down on the flesh and bone beneath the leather-studded sleeves of her scale armor hauberk.

"Elli!" Miles shouted as he looked down and saw the dog savaging the woman's arm.

Elli locked her muscles in place and thrust her sword, penetrating deep into the dog's side just behind its shoulder. The animal released its grip with a yelp and the swordswoman thrust her blade into the dog a second time, ending its life. She struggled to her feet and looked up at Miles.

"Elli, hurry! You can still climb up!"

The Blackguard looked from the ledge to the men scrambling up the hill and knew there was no time. Even if she managed to climb beyond their reach before they reached the top of the rise, some were sure to have bows or crossbows and could easily pick her off before she could reach the top and clamber over to safety.

"Keep climbing!" Elli shouted at the prince.

Elli thrust the points of her two swords into the soft earth and pulled out several throwing knives strapped across her chest. Her right arm whipped forward, hurling all six blades in rapid succession. Four of the blades found vital organs and stopped the ascent of their targets. One hit a man in the shoulder while the last brushed by and nicked an ear. It was a small victory and Elli pulled her swords from the earth and prepared to meet the men who swarmed up the hillside like huge, angry ants.

CHAPTER 13

The broad fronds of enormous ferns and the stinging branches of trees slapped at Lucas's face as he sprinted through the dense forest. The shouts of the men chasing him echoed through the woods behind him as they rapidly drew nearer. What had been a simple foray into the forest to pick mushrooms and berries had turned into a headlong flight for his life.

The slavers had spotted the boy digging mushrooms deep in the woods over a mile away from the small farming village in which he lived. Normally, their kind did not travel so far inland, but recent activities in the two port cities made it dangerous to ply their trade there for the nonce. Therefore, the more intrepid slavers had begun going inland and picked off any stragglers they came across. Some of the bolder slavers had even taken to raiding solitary farmsteads on rare occasions.

Kalil was not in very good shape and lagged after his two partners. Toman was sure to have the boy trussed up by the time he caught up with them, but he pushed himself through the dense undergrowth as fast as he could. Although he could not see them, Kalil was able to follow the shouts of Toman and Aaron.

Kalil paused a moment to catch his breath as he leaned against a tree. The slaver pulled in several deep breaths and took a swig from the small flask he was never without. Before he could swallow the strong liquor, Kalil felt something like a rope or cord cinch around his throat. Something lifted the man from the ground and his feet kicked futilely at air as the alcohol ran down his windpipe. After just a few seconds, the kicking stopped and Kalil the slaver was no more.

Aaron was only a few strides behind Toman. He could no longer hear Kalil's plodding steps behind him and assumed the man had stopped to rest and drink. Either that or his heart had finally given out after so many years of abusing his body and burst. That was fine with Aaron. It just meant a larger share for him, and the fat Sumaran was never any good for anything other than standing watch and sharing his rum.

A root found his foot and he fell onto his outstretched hands. He hit the ground hard enough to make vocalizing the curse that instantly sprang to mind impossible. Aaron pulled in a deep breath then tried to get back to his feet. The root pulled him back to the ground just as he stood up. Terror infused his body, a scream tore from his throat, and he clawed futilely at the soft earth as the roots dragged him deeper into the woods.

Toman heard a hard thump behind him and assumed Aaron had fallen. He was almost on the boy whose small frame was less adept than his was at forcing its way through the thick ferns and branches that crossed the narrow animal path along which they raced. He then heard Aaron shout, followed by another heavy thump, but this one sounded wet and meaty and the screams fell silent.

The slaver was about to turn back to see what had befallen his comrade when the boy tripped and fell. The kid was quick, but Toman was on him before he could get back to his feet.

"I got ya now, ya little rat," Toman crowed gleefully.

Lucas screamed and tried to scuttle backwards away from the reaching man's hands. Terror gripped him as his eyes looked past the slaver to the brush that seemed to come to life just behind him. A huge arm seemed to sprout from the thick jumble of leaves, limbs, and creeper ivy and an enormous, calloused hand wrapped around the slaver's neck and lifted him from the ground with ease.

The man kicked and clawed futilely and disappeared along with the tree creature back into the shadowy forest. A sharp crack like the snapping of a branch echoed through the woods and then there was silence. Lucas got to his feet and made to run the last few hundred yards to his home. He paused and looked back.

"Thank you, forest spirit," the boy called into the woods, then raced home.

Bron dropped his camouflaging magic, looked at the dead man at his feet, and let out a deep sigh. He would need to burn the corpses, so he dragged it back to where he had left the other two bodies. He tied a length of braided vine around their ankles and dragged them through the woods like a string of freshly caught fish.

It was rare that he had to put down men in his woods, but when he had, he used to give them back to the earth to feed the trees, plants, and insects as nature intended. However, for the past few years, the things that went into the ground often did not stay there. There was an evil in the air, perverting the natural process of life and death.

Although Bron was dragging a combined weight of over five hundred pounds, he trekked effortlessly through the woods with his burden. The few people that had ever seen Bron mistakenly assumed he was an ogre. At eight-feet tall, thickly muscled, and with skin like tree bark, it was an honest mistake. Bron was half-ogre, but about the only thing that stood out as being anything other than one of the brutes was his kind and gentle nature. He took no pleasure in dealing these men their deaths, but he would not allow such unnatural predation within his forest.

As a druid of Ellanee, Bron could travel through the thickest woods almost as easily as a man walked a cobbled road. Ellanee bestowed these woods upon him to watch over and protect. He also stood as a guardian to the creatures that lived within it, and that included the small human settlement to which the boy belonged.

His ears picked up a deep buzzing that grew increasingly louder until it was right in his ear.

"Oh, what did you do?" a shrill voice asked next to his head before buzzing closer to the bodies. "Ew, they smell. Not as bad as you though."

"I bathed today, Trielle," Bron told the wood sprite.

Trielle was a wood sprite Bron had rescued shortly after leaving the human settlement he lived in as a young boy. She had flown into a spider web cast by a gargantuan spider, a species that grew to the size of a house cat. She had damaged one of her four wings trying to escape, so Bron had carried her back to her tree and was nearly pricked to death by a thousand other wood sprites wielding tiny spears.

"Pfft, you could bathe five times a day. You're an ogre, and that stink goes clear to the bone."

"I am only half ogre, in case you have forgotten."

"Yeah, the stinky half. Whatcha kill these guys for? They don't look like they were dead like those others were before you squashed them."

"They were slavers," the druid answered. "They were about to grab one of the human children from the farm settlement."

"Ugh, you should have let them have him. One less dirty human around is always a good thing."

"All creatures have a place in the world. Even humans," Bron told her, repeating the same lecture he had used many times in the past.

"Yeah, they got a place. The bottom of the ocean is a good place. They come in, cut down the trees to make their stupid homes, and plant their food right next to it because they are too lazy to look in the forest for it like everyone else."

"Different does not mean wrong or evil, Trielle."

"Evil schmevil, I'm saying fish food is fish food. You gonna burn 'em?" Trielle asked.

"Of course."

"Yeah, these deaders just don't want to stay dead these days. Speaking of fish food and roasted humans, you have anything to eat? I'm starving!" Trielle asked, jumping between subjects as she often did.

Bron raised one heavy, hairless eyebrow at the wood sprite. "Why don't you go into the woods and find food like everyone else? Or are you too lazy?"

"Who are you calling lazy?" Trielle demanded, then started buzzing wildly around Bron's head, jabbing him with her short spear. "Is that lazy, huh? Take that!"

Her spear had no chance of piercing Bron's thick skin, which was fortunate because wood sprites coated the tips in a rather virulent paralytic poison, but he surrendered nonetheless.

"I have some oat bread and honey in my cave. If you help me cleanse these three, I will share."

"Darn right you will! You still owe me."

"For what? Saving your life?" the druid asked.

"Of course. That privilege incurs a lifelong debt of friendship, and friends share," Trielle explained as if it made perfect sense.

"I do not think you fully understand the concept of what incurs debt and who gets the reward."

"I don't care as long as I get food," the wood sprite dismissed with a snort.

The odd pair reached the open clearing where Bron could safely burn the corpses without fear of starting a forest fire. He began collecting deadfall, made much easier since he started stockpiling it nearby. Trielle actually helped by grabbing armfuls of dry pine needles and tossing the tiny piles of combustibles onto the pyre.

Bron collected the coins, blades, and jewelry of the dead men as payment for his services, and to give him something to trade on the rare occasion he needed something from the humans. Then he tossed the bodies onto the mound of wood and brush and set it aflame with a minor spell.

"All right, let's go eat!" Trielle shouted, flitting rapidly toward the cave Bron called home.

Bron walked at a leisurely pace back toward his cave while Trielle buzzed noisily and impatiently around his head and back and forth along the path. Wood sprites were not known for their patience and Trielle was considered hyperactive and impulsive even by her own kind.

"Hurry up, Big Stinky!" Trielle shouted at him as she buzzed up and down the path, occasionally prodding him in the back of his neck with her spear.

Bron, on the other hand, had the patience of a tree and was just about as immovable. The wood sprite may as well have been yelling at the sun to rise faster so she could begin her day. Bron moved at whatever speed he felt the situation and his mood warranted, and few things, if any, would coax him to do otherwise. However, once in motion, the same held true when it came to slowing or stopping him.

It took nearly half an hour to reach the cave and the first thing Trielle noticed was the massive lump of fur lying directly in front of the door that sealed Bron's home. The wood sprite recognized the lump as Grumph, an enormous dire bear and possibly Bron's best friend. Except for Trielle, because wood sprites were the best friends anyone could have. Even lying down, Grumph's body was so big, only the top portion of the eight-foot door behind him was visible.

Trielle zoomed toward the bear, hovering right next to his ear, and beat her wings as hard as she could, creating a buzzing as loud as a dozen katydids. "Move it, fuzz bucket! You're blocking the food!"

Grumph raised his huge head at the obnoxious noise and let out such a roar that it blew Trielle backwards several feet in the air. The wood sprite recovered and dove toward Grumph's muzzle.

"Take that tone with me again and hibernation will be coming early this year!" Trielle threatened, jabbing at his big black nose with her envenomed spear.

Grumph took a swipe at Trielle with a paw the size of a round shield—a round shield sporting claws nearly half a foot long. Despite his enormous size, the paw swipe moved so fast it was practically a blur. Trielle easily dodged the half-hearted attack.

"Okay, that's it! It's nap time, mister!" Trielle shouted as she ramped up her wingbeats in preparation for a run at the bear's nose.

"Stop it, you two," Bron rumbled. "Grumph, you have to move so I can get inside."

The bear flopped back down and grumbled irritably. Grumph was never in a good mood and Trielle's harassment had made him extremely contrary.

"We're having lunch now, with honey. I know that's why you are lying in front of my door, so if you want any you will have to move."

When you were as big as Grumph, nothing and no one could make you do anything you did not want to do. The only thing you could do was present an option that he preferred over being cranky and obstinate. Fortunately, promises of food, particularly such delicacies as honey, were possibly the greatest incentive there was, and one of the few things Grumph prized over being belligerent. Grumph grumbled noisily as he stood up and shook the dirt, bark, and pine needles from his long fur.

"Hey, watch it, carrion breath!" Trielle shouted as Grumph's shaking pelted her with detritus.

Bron barely had the door cracked before Trielle darted inside and went searching for the promised treat. The inside of the cave was rather homey and not what one would expect to find. The entranceway was fairly short and opened up into a large, cavernous room. Woven mats of reeds and grass covered most of the floor, and a large table made from fallen logs tied together like a raft, and various other pieces of furniture of rough make adorned the interior.

Bron lit several candles he had made himself from either tallow or beeswax, displaying the art adorning the walls, painted directly onto the stone. The druid made paint from extracts from various types of bark and berries. Few would call his work extraordinary, but it did not lack for talent.

Trielle had found the flask of honey and was using her spear in an attempt to pry out the stopper. Bron crossed the room, took the flask from the shelf, and popped out the cork. Trielle retrieved her tiny clay cup and buzzed eagerly as Bron filled it up.

"Oh, gimme, gimme, gimme!" the wood sprite demanded as Bron dribbled the golden delight drop by drop into her cup.

Seeing that Trielle was finally satisfied, Bron then drizzled honey over a large pine cone and gave it to Grumph who was waiting with his head stuck through the cave entrance. He rarely came inside anymore as getting his bulk through the doorway was something of a chore.

Now that he had taken care of his friends, the half-ogre poured himself a bowl of nuts and dried fruit and set out several strips of dried meat. Most druids of Ellanee were strict vegetarians, but this was not in Bron's nature. He did not eat a lot of meat, unlike his ogre heritage, which was nearly entirely carnivorous, but his massive body required it. One of Ellanee's paramount teachings was to accept every living thing as its nature dictated.

The day was drawing to a close. Grumph was outside sleeping off his dinner, Trielle was dozing with her hand over her full stomach, and Bron was reading one of his few books by candlelight and the bit of waning sun streaming through the open door. A change in the energy of the forest caused Bron to look up from his book and focus his attention outward.

"Trielle," Bron called out.

"Hmm?" she answered sleepily from the shelf upon which she was currently perched.

"The crickets."

"No, thank you. I couldn't possibly eat another bite," she responded with a wave.

"They have stopped chirping," Bron explained.

"Good. Noisy little vermin."

Bron was about to explain that it meant something significant, when a large owl flew in through the open door. Birds of prey were probably one of the most feared threats sprites faced and the owl's sudden appearance brought Trielle fully awake and on the defensive. The wood sprite snatched up her spear and buzzed up to the high ceiling so that the owl could not get above her.

"You better watch it, Beaky, or I'll stuff me a new pillow with your feathers!" Trielle shouted, brandishing her spear.

The owl showed little concern for the sprite's threats and hooted softly. Bron listened as the owl "spoke" in soft hoots and whistles. The druid's face took on a look of concern as the owl told its story.

"There are humans in the forest," Bron explained to Trielle.

"I know! That's why I was saying it wouldn't be such a bad thing to let some of them get taken away."

"No," Bron said patiently, "there are others."

"More?" Trielle exclaimed. "This place is really going downhill! Pretty soon you won't be able to swing a squirrel without hitting one!"

"Several men with dogs are chasing a woman and a boy."

"So what?" Trielle asked irritably when she saw that Bron had gathered up his staff and was leaving the cave.

Bron answered back over his shoulder. "They are a threat and do not belong here. Murder resides within the hearts of these men, and murder only strengthens the dark goddess. Such things cannot be allowed in Ellanee's sacred forest."

"All right! Time to kick some big human butt!" Trielle cried out, throwing a lasso made of twine over the unsuspecting owl's neck. "Come on, Beaky, it's time to fly into battle!"

The owl screeched in surprise and indignation as Trielle jumped onto its back, wrapped her legs around its neck, and held onto the twine like a set of reins. Sprites were incredibly swift and nimble flyers, but they were not known for their endurance. Trielle jabbed the large bird with the butt of her spear, goading it into flight. Both creatures let out a shriek as they burst out into the open air.

Bron was not fleet of foot, but he could keep up a jog for days, eating up the miles one unfaltering step at a time. Grumph, ready to punish the source of his rude awakening, loped along after the druid.

CHAPTER 14

The first few men to reach Elli died quickly, and the men racing up the hill toward her had to avoid the bodies as they tumbled back down. Having the high ground gave Elli a decided advantage, despite the slope's awkward footing.

She now beat back the swords of three men while nearly two dozen more climbed toward the summit. She blocked the swords of the men to her right and left with each of her blades and kicked dirt and pine needles into the face of the man in the middle. Blinded, he was unable to parry as she slashed her sword across the man's head, felling him.

Two more parries and a flurry of attacks dropped the other two men in short order, but several more had gained the high ground and forced her into a fighting retreat. Her swings grew desperate as she had to give up her greatest advantage due to the sheer number of men pressing in on her. The steep slope leveled out where she had chosen to make her stand.

Ducking beneath the swings of three swordsmen, she tucked her legs and rolled between a pair of men, thrusting her blades out to the side as she went past, and leapt back to her feet. One blade took a man in the side while the other bit deep into another man's hip. Both men went down but only one was able to regain his feet. Fire erupted from her back as a sword cut through her armor and the flesh beneath. Spinning to face her attacker, she stabbed the man through the heart before he could recover from overreaching himself with the force of his swing.

Elli crossed her swords over her left side without conscious thought, blocking another brutal attack. She forced the blade away with one sword while stabbing out with the other, catching the man just below his leather breastplate. She had no time to witness the full results of her strike as several more blades tried to penetrate her defenses and remove the obstacle that stood between them and the prince.

Elli felt her strength flagging as she bled from at least a dozen wounds, but she refused to relent. Every second she survived was a second Miles was able to put between himself and his assassins. She blocked an overhand chop and kicked the man in his chest with enough force to send him tumbling down the mountain.

Her kick cost her as another attacker barreled into her and knocked her to the ground. Elli prepared to roll in an attempt to avoid the killing blow the man was preparing to deal her, but it never came. Trielle landed on the man's head and stabbed him in the nose with her spear while holding onto the rim of his helmet.

"Ha ha, take that, stinky human!" the sprite squeaked triumphantly.

The man slapped at the spear with one hand and slashed at the sprite with his sword. Trielle darted straight up out of reach with a laugh. Elli rolled back onto her feet, narrowly avoiding the thrusting blade of another attacker. The man who Trielle had stabbed was already looking glassy-eyed and fumbling around drunkenly as the powerful toxin coating her spear took effect.

A sharp pain stabbed into Elli's lower back. She fumbled behind her with her hand and felt the shaft of the arrow sticking out from just below her ribs. Looking past the few attackers near her, she spied half a dozen men drawing back for another shot at her and Miles. Elli launched herself down the hill with a defiant snarl of outrage, intent on killing the archers before they could find their range and pick the prince off the cliff face.

Miles was only a few feet from the top when he looked back at the battle that raged below. Two arrows skipped off the rock very near him as he watched Elli charge down the hill in an almost uncontrolled dash. He could only watch in horror as the arrows slammed into her body and her sprint turned into a tumble.

"No!" Miles shouted as he clamped his tear-filled eyes shut in an attempt to block the horrific image from his mind.

Several more arrows clattered against the rocks next to him, forcing him to open his eyes and renew his ascent. He nearly fell to his death when a huge, hideous face appeared over the rim of the cliff. Only the massive hand clamped around his wrist kept him from falling into open air.

Bron easily lifted the lad up and over the ledge before depositing him onto the safety of the hard ground. Miles scrambled away from the brutish figure like a crab, unable to speak past the lump of fear in his throat.

"Calm yourself. I am not your enemy," Bron told him.

"Elli," Miles said hoarsely with a furtive glance toward the battle.

Bron nodded and stepped toward the ledge despite knowing that it was probably already too late for the woman. Calling up his magic, a thick root crawled out of the ground near his feet. Grasping it in one huge hand while he held his staff in the other, Bron coaxed the root to grow and lower him to the ground below.

There were still over a dozen men converging upon the stony bluff, ready to scale it and continue their pursuit of the boy. All came to an abrupt halt when Bron practically dropped from the sky and stood before them. Three men raised their bows and launched arrows at him. Despite their fear, all three shots struck true, but with little effect. Bron's skin was naturally as tough as boiled leather, but coupled with his magic it was like striking an oak tree. Two of the shafts bounced off harmlessly while the third penetrated just far enough to hang limply down his chest.

"You do not belong here," Bron rumbled. "You chose to bring death, so death has come—for you."

Despite the half-ogre's intimidating size, numbers helped bolster the humans' courage and they cautiously advanced, figuring they could overwhelm this creature despite his size. Then Grumph appeared. The dire bear had followed the bluff along its base and announced his presence with a roar that shook leaves from the trees and made the air tremble.

Their confidence shattered, the humans broke into a headlong sprint down the hillside toward their waiting mounts. With a nod from Bron, Grumph tore after them. Men threw down their weapons and cried out in panic as all three thousand pounds of fur, claws, teeth, and bad attitude bore down upon them.

Grumph simply stomped on the first man he came to, crushing him beneath his awesome weight. The next slowest man received a swat from his massive paw that sent him flying into the lead until his lifeless body rolled to a stop a few dozen yards down the slope. The huge bear pulled another man to the ground and almost casually crushed his head in his powerful jaws.

With the bear seemingly occupied and their horses only a few steps away, the remaining men felt a surge of hope that they may yet escape. Those hopes were dashed as dark forms darted in and out of the trees with howls and yips. The large pack of wolves tore into the remaining men, several of whom they pulled from saddles before they could get their horses moving. Freed of human burden, the horses did not wait around and bolted away with their eyes rolling in fear. The wolves did not pursue them. Their prey this day walked on two legs, not four.

Bron made his way down the hill and examined the human woman's body. Trielle fluttered close by while he checked for signs of life. She was covered in blood, and at least three arrow shafts had snapped off close to her body from her headlong tumble.

"Is she dead?" Trielle asked, almost with a touch of sympathy.

"Very near," Bron answered.

The druid stripped the armor from Elli's body and applied a salve from a clay jar he pulled from the satchel draped around his shoulder. The ointment would prevent infection, slow or stop the bleeding, and hasten healing, but he was unsure if it would be enough.

Bron turned toward the cliff face and watched the human boy as he scrambled down. Concern for the woman he had known for years but just truly met yesterday hastened his descent. In just a few minutes, Miles cautiously approached the creature looming over Elli's body.

"You can come near. I will not harm you," Bron assured the young man.

"Wh-who are you? What are you?" Miles asked.

"My name is Bron. I am a devout of Ellanee, but I assume your question is in regard to my appearance. My mother was human and my father an ogre."

"You are a half-ogre?" Miles asked, having read about the rare possibility.

"Yeah, the ugly, smelly, kid-eating half, so you better watch your step, human!" Trielle snapped.

"Trielle, be nice. This woman obviously meant something to him and he grieves."

"He just better behave or he's gonna go from grieving to bleeding," the sprite warned with a glare and thrust of her spear before zipping up into the trees.

Miles followed Trielle with his eyes then looked back at Bron as he lifted and cradled Elli in his arms. Elli was a slight woman to begin with, but seeing her lying across the half-ogre's arms made her appear small and fragile despite her warrior spirit. Miles was barely able to choke back the sob that lodged in his throat but could not stop the tears.

"Is she alive?"

"Just barely."

"Can you save her?" Miles asked hopefully.

Bron shook his head. "I do not know. I think a Chosen priest would find the prospect daunting."

"You said you were a devout of Ellanee. Isn't that a cleric or healer of some kind?"

"I am a druid. My power lies in nature, not in the power of the gods. Such divine healing as you speak of is not mine to wield. However, I do have skills in healing and herb lore and will do what I can."

"Thank you. My name is Miles, by the way. Thank you for killing those men."

Bron paused before speaking, understanding the boy's attitude. "One should never be thankful of death, unless to end suffering, and never for causing it. Such death is unnatural and is the purview of Sharrellan. Those men chose their course of action, and in protecting this forest and its inhabitants I did what I had to do."

Bron took Miles and Elli south along the bluff for about three miles before it met level ground again. It was another two-mile walk east before they reached Bron's cave. Grumph was nowhere to be seen, but Trielle was already inside helping herself to more honey when Bron entered and laid Elli onto the table.

"Hey, I eat there!" Trielle cried out in indignation.

"She is badly hurt, so stop being rude."

"Oh, I'm sorry. It must be a human or ogre thing, because my people find it rude to bleed all over the table on which someone serves food."

Miles looked from the sprite to the half-ogre who was busy examining and covering Elli's wounds. "She doesn't like humans much, does she?"

"Trielle does not care much for anyone who is not a wood sprite, and even only a few of those can tolerate her for more than a few minutes. It is why she spends so much time with me."

"For which you continually fail to show proper gratitude!" Trielle shouted from her perch in the cupboard. "And for your information, I have hundreds, thousands, of friends! I only come here out of pity. I feel so sorry for you having to wake up so ugly and smelly every morning, I feel almost duty-bound to bring some beauty into your life," Trielle responded haughtily.

Miles watched Trielle repeatedly dip a stick into the flask of honey then lick off the sticky treat. The sprite caught him looking and stuck her tongue out at him. He turned to Bron who was grinding some sort of dried herbs with a mortar and pestle.

"So, is she always like this?"

Bron glanced up at Trielle. "More or less. Stabbing a human with her spear has put her in a good mood."

"How do you put up with it? She is worse than my little sister."

"It is her nature," Bron replied simply. "I am also very patient."

"I think you mean lucky!" Trielle amended.

Miles looked at Elli's battered and fragile body lying upon the table. "Is she going to live?"

Bron sighed. "I think you should prepare yourself to accept the worst."

The tears returned unbidden to Miles's eyes and he wiped them away with his sleeve.

"You care for her," Bron stated. "Who is she?"

Miles actually managed a small laugh. "Until yesterday, she was a kitchen woman at the Academy."

"And today?"

"A person willing to put herself between me and a lot of people that apparently want me dead," Miles answered, his voice quavering. "My father once told me that despite being surrounded by so many people, it was a challenge to find a single friend amongst them."

"Who is your father?" Bron asked.

Miles took a deep breath and wondered if he should tell the truth. True, this creature had come to his rescue, but he hardly knew him or his political allegiances. What if he supported those who wanted him dead and simply did not realize that his father was the king? He decided to trust him, just as he had trusted Elli.

"Jarvin Ollander, King of Valeria."

"I see."

"Does that make us friends or enemies?" Miles asked steadily despite his anxiety.

"I am not sure it makes us either one. Politics do not travel into this part of the forest." Bron sensed more than heard something calling him from outside. "Excuse me, I must go a moment."

Bron left Miles with Elli and followed the soundless summons toward the small spring that trickled near his cave and fed a pool in a grove of willow trees. He felt the presence of Ellanee before he saw her. Pushing the hanging branches of a willow aside, he stepped into the grove and saw her standing near the pool of water. She stood by the water's edge dressed in a simple sea-green gown and glowed with an ethereal light.

"You have done wonders with your grove, Bron," the nature goddess said in a voice that sounded like a song.

"It is my greatest joy, My Lady. To what do I owe the honor of this visit?"

Ellanee smiled warmly at the huge half-ogre. Even the devotees of the four gods usually tripped all over themselves when blessed with the physical manifestation of their god. Nevertheless, Bron was of such stalwart nature, not even facing his goddess could cause him to become flummoxed.

"I come to ask for your help."

"Request infers the possibility of rejection. You need only inform me and it shall be done, My Lady."

Ellanee broke into musical laughter and stepped closer to her devout. "Bron, my dear follower, I do so adore you. Dark tidings are falling across the land. Events are already unfolding and many have a part to play, even the gods. My dearest Solarian has already positioned his pieces, and now it is time for me to do the same."

"I have felt the death that gathers far to the north."

"Indeed, but that is not the darkness of which I speak. What occurs there must be dealt with swiftly, and it is where you must go. However, that is not the true darkness, but only the fire for those who must be tempered to face what is coming," Ellanee told Bron cryptically. "You need to find those that seek to battle that evil, and you must succeed so that others have the chance to face the coming darkness."

"What is this darkness of which you speak if not the abomination of necromancy?"

"Something far more catastrophic and nearly two thousand years in the coming. More I cannot say. You must take the boy to North Haven and then find the adventurers who will face the lich lord. They will require your strength, for only life may defeat death. I shall teach you a way to travel that will allow you to get to where you must go."

The goddess motioned for Bron to kneel then touched him lightly on the head. Bron saw and felt a special connection with the earth and stone that he did not have before. What his goddess showed him was truly remarkable.

"Thank you, My Lady. The woman that protects the boy, can you save her?" Bron asked.

The goddess's face turned sorrowful. "I am sorry, but I cannot. She has fulfilled her destiny, and her spirit has moved on into the grateful arms of my paramour. Even as we speak, she is taking her place beside my beloved Solarian."

"The boy will be sad for her loss."

"The prince shall see far more death and loss in his lifetime. He must be strong, just as his father must learn to be strong if he is to lead his people and have any hope of victory. Take Miles to the duchess in North Haven as swiftly as you can. The fate of the world rests on the success of your mission."

"If I succeed, the world will be saved?"

Ellanee replied apocalyptically, "If you succeed, the world has a small chance. If you fail, then it has none."

With that final warning, Ellanee burst into a thousand motes of light and raced outward in all directions. Bron stood in the grove for a moment after the lights disappeared to ponder the weight of her words.

"Whoa!" Trielle exclaimed from a willow branch just over his shoulder. "Was that Ellanee?"

"It was," Bron answered without looking.

"If she had wings, she would be almost as pretty as me!"

Bron laughed uncharacteristically and walked back to his cave. Miles looked not to have moved since he left. Only the fresh tears carving through the grime on his face showed any difference.

"I think she died," Miles whispered.

"Yes, she did. She died for something she felt worth sacrificing herself for, Miles. Do not ever forget that, and do not ever prove her belief to be a mistake," Bron told the prince.

Miles nodded his understanding. "What do we do now?"

"We shall make her a pyre so that you may bid her farewell, and then we travel to North Haven," Bron answered.

Bron did not take Elli to the spot where he and Trielle usually burned the undead corpses. Instead, he and Miles constructed a pyre near the grove where he had spoken with his goddess. The pyre itself was a bit more elaborate as well. It consisted of stacked logs and limbs several feet high. Miles picked wildflowers and placed them atop Elli's body after they laid her on the low scaffold of timbers.

Bron spoke a prayer, Miles thanked Elli for saving him, and then bid her farewell before touching a brand to the pyre and setting it aflame. Miles felt as though he shed enough tears to extinguish the blaze if he had stood any closer to the flames. Bron finally guided Miles away from the pyre as the flames died down and left nothing but ash behind.

"Try and get some sleep," Bron told the prince. "We will leave in the morning as the sun breaks the horizon."

Bron left Miles to sleep in his bed while he walked down to his grove and sat amongst the willows. Ellanee said he needed to help defeat the lich lord, but that it was only a test for a greater threat to come. What could be a greater aberration to nature than a creature able to summon a legion of undead to wreak havoc on the living? What could be so terrible that even the gods feared for the future? Bron could not shake the feeling that Ellanee and the other gods feared not just for the fate of the kingdom, but their own as well.

Trielle's buzzing interrupted his thoughts as she lit upon his broad shoulder. "Hey, B.S."

"B.S.?"

"Big Stinky," Trielle explained.

"Ah. I thought perhaps you were referring to my name, Bron Sandofen."

"Hardly. I didn't even know your last name. Are you really leaving?"

Bron tilted his head. "Ellanee needs me to do something."

"I heard. It sounds dangerous."

"It does," Bron agreed. "But it is important."

"Come back. Okay?" the sprite said softly next to his ear.

Bron could not help but smile. "Are you going to miss me?"

"Pfft. Hardly! I'm throwing a honey party in your cave when you leave, so you'll need to bring some back with you."

"Well, I will miss you."

Trielle rolled her eyes. "Well duh!" Then she leaned against his neck and repeated softly. "Just come back."

Bron spent the night in his grove and woke Miles early the next morning. They broke their fast with dried nuts and fruit, the remainder of which went into Miles's pack. Miles still had a fair amount of food in the rucksack Elli had packed for him in Southport. Bron checked the contents and declared it sufficient to see them to North Haven.

"Bron, we lost our horses yesterday. It is a long walk to North Haven," Miles pointed out.

"I have secured you a mount," Bron informed him.

As if on cue, an enormous stag stepped nonchalantly from the woods and approached with its large ears forward and alert, but it was not alarmed by their presence.

Miles looked to Bron. "Am I really going to ride that?"

"Indeed. You should have little trouble as we will only be traveling as fast as I can jog."

Bron draped a folded blanket over the stag's back and lifted Miles onto it. The stag was slimmer than a horse but taller. Miles's stomach fluttered uneasily, but he trusted the strange druid and his chosen mount. With a wave to Trielle, Bron took off at a jog and the stag bounded along after him.

It was an odd feeling riding the stag. Its gait was far different from that of a horse even at the relatively slow speed at which they traveled. It was springier but smoother compared to a horse's jarring canter. Miles could not help but smile as he braced his hands against the proud buck's strong neck.

By the end of the first day, Miles was certain they had traveled much farther than they could have on horseback. Bron was not a fast runner, but neither he nor the stag seemed to suffer the effects of fatigue and maintained a strong pace for the entire day and even a few hours after nightfall. Despite years of riding experience, Miles's legs protested greatly when he dismounted, and he nearly fell before he could steady himself. His legs and hips were accustomed to the broad back of a horse, not that of a stag.

It was midway through their third day of traveling that they found themselves on the edge of the forest looking at the walls of North Haven. Bron chose a spot where the forest came nearest the wall as the place to part ways. That left a little over a mile of open ground for Miles to cover on foot. The druid studied the land between him and the city but could not detect any danger. He even sent a hawk to swoop over the area several times, using his magic to see through the bird's eyes.

"You don't want to come with me to see the duchess? I am sure she will be glad that you rescued me," Miles said.

Bron smiled at the naïve young man. "Few if any people are glad to see me. My countenance makes people see a threat to be dealt with, and they often react violently before bothering to ask any questions."

Miles screwed up his face in annoyance. "That is not fair. My father says we need to judge a man by his character and actions and not just the quality of his clothes. I guess that could mean the skin one wears as well."

"It sounds like you have learned some good things from a wise man. Follow his lead, and you too will make a good king one day."

"I don't know if I want to be king after seeing what it has done to my father. He struggles to be fair and just, but so many people still demand more and abuse him to get it."

"Your father just needs to find his strength and have the courage to fight for what he believes in. A king who is too kind can be just as disastrous and ineffectual as a tyrant can be. A good king must hold love and compassion for all his people with one hand while wielding swift and decisive justice in the other."

The young prince looked up at the huge druid. "Do you think my father is even alive to learn to do that? Elli said that if people were after me then something must have already happened to him."

Bron looked down at Miles. "My goddess came to me the day Elli died. She told me your father has some challenges he must face, so it stands to reason that he is still alive and able to fight. This battle will decide whether he can learn to be that kind of king. I believe he can. If he does not, he will fall." The druid looked once more at the distant gates of North Haven. "The way is clear. Go straight for the gate. I will watch over you from here until you get inside."

"Thank you, Bron, for everything."

Bron simply nodded and motioned for Miles to proceed to the gate. He stood and watched as the boy intermittently walked and jogged through the large open field, across the main road, and finally stood before the gates of the city.

Miles found the gates closed to traffic, but a guard stepped through the small postern door nearby and addressed him.

"What is your business in the city? Are you from the school?" the guard asked, making an assumption given the direction from which Miles had approached.

"I came from the Academy in Southport if that is the school to which you are referring," Miles replied, not knowing anything about the orphans' academy on the hill. "I request an audience with Duchess Mellina."

The guardsman laughed as if Miles had just told a joke. "Sorry, kid, but the duchess does not meet with every dust-covered traveler who strides up to the gates, especially with everything that is going on right now. If you truly have business you think requires the duchess's attention, you may file a request with me, I will deliver it to her seneschal, and then it will be decided if your concern merits an audience."

Miles took a deep breath, stood proudly, and in his most regal voice proclaimed, "I am Miles Ollander, crown prince of Valeria, and I demand to be taken to see Duchess Mellina where I shall make an official bid for sanctuary."

The officer of the Watch looked at the proud young man, particularly the strong jaw and piercing blue eyes that were nearly a perfect match of the king's.

"Forgive me, Highness. I did not recognize you. My name is Lieutenant John Cruthers, officer of the watch. It will be my pleasure to escort you to Her Grace," the guard officer said as he bent a knee.

"Thank you, Lieutenant. There is no need for apologies. You are performing your duties admirably. Your assistance is greatly appreciated."

Bron watched as the guard led Miles into the city then turned. "How long have you been watching me?"

"Ghost and I have been following you most of the morning," Wolf answered, his bow gripped in his hand.

"Very impressive. There are very few who could sneak up on me much less follow me for that long without my knowing," Bron praised him.

"Nothing happens in my woods without me knowing. Who are you, and who was the kid?"

Bron smiled at the young half-elf referring to Miles as a kid when they appeared to be about the same age. "My name is Bron. The boy is Miles Ollander, son of your king."

"Pfft. Not my king," Wolf scoffed. "I'm Wolf and this is Ghost."

"It is a pleasure to make your acquaintance, Wolf. Very good to see you, brother," Bron greeted Ghost.

"Brother? I don't see the family resemblance, but I can sure smell it!" Wolf brayed, holding his free hand over his stomach as he laughed.

Of the two creatures being offended, only Ghost looked at the half-elf with reproach.

"You seem nicer than you look. Are you going to be staying long?"

"As much as I would enjoy staying and talking with you both, I am afraid I must be going. I am urgently needed far to the north and have little time in which to get there," Bron answered.

"Too bad you didn't get here a couple days ago. You could have gone with Azerick and the soldiers from the city. They are going north too. I think the king is in trouble again or something. Are you going to go help him too?"

Bron nodded. "We are all in danger, and I believe I will be helping him, but not directly. What I face is a danger to us all. Guard your woods well, Wolf and brother Ghost. Dark times are coming."

Bron turned one hand palm facing downward toward the ground. The soil began undulating then almost boiling around him. He rotated his hand to face upwards and the ground rose up and wrapped itself around him as if creating a sort of cocoon. Bron looked for a moment like some sort of large effigy made of raw earth before the entire form crumbled and fell back to the ground. Only a small mound of churned earth remained where the eight-foot-tall half-ogre had just been standing.

"Now, that is a neat trick!" Wolf exclaimed to his lupine companion.

The earth surrounded Bron, but he flowed through it like water rushing through an underground cavern. He did not fly straight like a bird through the sky, but more like a piece of wood cast out into the rapids of a raging river. The earth spirit was in control, and all he could do was brace himself for the ride until it deposited him where Ellanee needed him to go.

CHAPTER 15

Ellyssa picked out a nice dress but not one too cumbersome, deciding that if she were able to infiltrate the palace to see Alonzo Janovin, she would need to look the part. She chose a satin dress in pale yellow with the minimum amount of fluff and frills as current fashion allowed. She then selected a pair of gold shoes with heels that made her nearly two inches taller, which not only made fashion sense, but helped her look older as well.

Miranda had left earlier in the afternoon, deciding to spend much of the day with her mother, so she was already gone. Allister should be in the library or in his room reading; Rusty and Colleen would be busy with the twins; and Simon and Teresa were likely preparing for bed already. Sneaking out should pose little problem.

Getting to North Haven was another matter altogether. There was no way she was going to walk five miles in a dress with these shoes. She decided she would need a horse, but Peck watched his horses like a miser watched his coin. She would need to use whatever passed for womanly wiles in an eleven-year-old. At least she was dressed for it.

Ellyssa crept down the stairs from her room barefoot, paused at the landing just above the common room, and quietly darted out the front doors. Once outside, she slipped on her golden shoes and stalked across the grounds until she reached the stables. She peeked through the doorway and saw that it appeared empty. Leaving the door wide open, Ellyssa retrieved a saddle and bridle from the tack room, selected a horse she was familiar with, and set the saddle and bridle down outside the stall.

After opening the stall's half-door, Ellyssa picked up the saddle and stepped in. It always made her nervous to be between a thousand pounds of horse flesh and a wall, but the horse was calm and practically ignored her even after several failed attempts to get the saddle onto its back. How Peck managed to do this with such ease despite being several inches shorter than she was, was beyond her. She finally got the saddle situated properly and cinched on tight.

She then slipped the bridle on after coaxing the horse to lower its head with a handful of oats. Ellyssa stepped out of the stall leading the horse by the reins and stopped short when she saw Peck glaring at her.

"What do you think you are doing?" Peck demanded to know.

Ellyssa squared her shoulders. "I am going to the palace to hear Alonzo Janovin sing."

"Azerick said no one is supposed to leave the school. Especially after dark!"

Ellyssa glared back. "Well Azerick is not here, is he?"

"Which is even more reason to do as he says."

"Are you going to tell on me?" Ellyssa challenged.

Peck paused then sighed. "No. But you are not going to take one of my horses. It's one thing to pretend I didn't see you. It's another thing altogether if I actually aid you."

Ellyssa batted her darkened lashes at Peck. "Please, Peck. You wouldn't make me walk all the way there in these shoes, would you? Besides, Miranda is already there and I'll stay with her. She can ground me later, after the show."

Peck had had a sort of crush on Ellyssa from the first time he had seen her at the Golden Glade stables where he used to work, and was helpless to her pleadings. His resolve withered and died beneath those hazel-green eyes.

"All right, but you need to tighten the cinch strap or you're going to get dumped onto the ground before you are halfway there."

"I tightened it as hard as I could," Ellyssa protested.

Peck grabbed the loose end of the strap, ran his fingers lightly along the horse's stomach, and yanked up on the strap sharply.

"No horse likes a saddle so they puff out their stomach and hold their breath to keep it loose. You have to tickle them to make them let out their breath and retighten it," Peck instructed her.

"I did not know horses were that smart," Ellyssa remarked.

"Horses are a lot smarter than people think they are. Just like a lot of people aren't nearly as clever as they think they are."

Ellyssa knew that last remark was directed at her but she ignored it, then leaned in and gave Peck a quick kiss on the cheek. She then climbed into the saddle, her white hosiery allowing her to ride normally, with her dress bunched up around her thighs. She was still young enough to be forgiven the lack of ladylike propriety should anyone take notice.

With a small wave to the deeply blushing stableboy, Ellyssa headed toward the south wall where she could escape through a little-used postern gate. She tried to approach the gate between sentry rounds, but she failed to notice a stationary guard cloaked in the shadows of a crenellation. He stepped out of the concealing shadows just as she neared the gate.

"Who is there?" he asked authoritatively.

Ellyssa cursed under her breath then called up, "It's me, Ellyssa. I need to go into North Haven to meet with Miranda at the palace."

"Then why did you not go with her when she left earlier today?" he challenged.

"Because I didn't, all right? Just let me through."

"Sorry. Orders are no students leave, especially after dark," the guard informed her, not sounding the least bit sorry.

Ellyssa did not have the time or patience to argue. Reaching into a pocket, she pulled out a pinch of sand and cast a spell. The young man on the wall had just enough time to utter a curse before dropping onto the walkway and falling into a deep sleep.

Ellyssa led her horse through the postern door and closed it shut behind her. She walked the horse about a hundred yards before remounting and riding for North Haven. It took only about half an hour to reach the gate where she convinced the guards into letting her pass. It took another thirty minutes to navigate through the town and reach the gates of Mellina's castle.

The guards there let her pass without challenge. There had been a steady stream of well-dressed people pouring in to see the famed bard for the last two hours. They simply assumed Ellyssa was simply a latecomer and the child of one of the many wealthy and influential families in attendance. It was not until she reached the grand castle itself that she ran into trouble.

"Sorry, girl. No one is allowed in without an invitation for the event," one of a pair of stone-faced guards informed her.

Ellyssa was positively furious now. She had already missed the beginning of Alonzo's performance and used magic against one of the other students. There was no way she was going to turn back now.

"Do you know who I am?" Ellyssa asked in her most haughty voice. "I am Ellyssa Jensen, apprentice and ward to Azerick Giles who is married to Miranda, daughter of Duchess Mellina and is the next duke of North Haven! Lady Miranda and the duchess are expecting me, and I am already late!"

The guard on the left side of the doorway looked to the other. "Maybe I should send for Lady Miranda."

The guard on the right shook his head. "The show has already started, and I don't want to be the one to interrupt it. Perhaps it's best if we just let her pass."

Ellyssa looked at the two guards snootily. "Yes, it *would* be best to let me pass."

Both men looked like they wanted to put the girl over their knee and give her a well-needed spanking, but wisely chose to open the door instead. Ellyssa passed with a derisive snort and toss of her hair just as she assumed rich, important women did when they felt insulted by an underling.

Ellyssa knew that she was really racking up the punishment, but it was going to be worth it to hear her future husband sing. It was a shame they would have to wait at least six more years to get married— probably seven if she got into any more trouble tonight. Her grounding would probably be at least that long.

The echoing of her shoes as they slapped against the marble floor preceded her down the long hall. She knew that Alonzo was performing in the main banquet hall; she just needed to find it. Ellyssa was able to navigate the labyrinthine halls after making a few inquiries of some of the castle staff.

Wanting to enter as unobtrusively as possible, Ellyssa slipped in through a side door. The banquet hall was absolutely packed with the wealthiest and most influential people of the city. The young apprentice had felt almost silly when she put on her finest clothes for this event, but looking at the positively ostentatious garb of the women around her, she felt underdressed.

Alonzo was singing in the middle of the room upon a large raised platform amidst a multitude of musical instruments. Most she recognized, but a few were unfamiliar to her. By far the most fascinating was a wooden box on four spindly legs like a dinette table. It sounded akin to a xylophone, but the musician was able to produce the musical notes far more rapidly by pressing the small ivory keys set in the front of it. He called it a harpsichord, and it sounded wonderful.

Alonzo himself was a bit of a disappointment. His hair was thinner and his jaw weaker than the stories portrayed him. His teeth did not quite fit together properly either. Nevertheless, even the rumors failed to give proper credit to his magnificent voice, so Ellyssa forgave his cosmetic flaws, as did most women she guessed.

Ellyssa stood to the back of the room so she could see over the heads of most of the other attendees while partially hiding herself next to a pillar and a large potted plant with broad leaves. From this vantage point, she was able to watch Alonzo, and Miranda who sat upon one of the two thrones atop the dais adjacent to her mother.

It was midway through the show when Ellyssa glanced up at the dais and gasped as she locked eyes with Miranda. The wayward apprentice froze like a rabbit that had just spotted the shadow of a hawk as it passed overhead. Ellyssa prayed Miranda was not really looking at her, or at least did not recognize her. Those hopes were dashed when Miranda motioned toward a guard and, given her pantomiming, appeared to be describing Ellyssa.

The guard beckoned to two others who began quietly working their way toward her from opposite directions. Ellyssa fought down her rising panic, stepped into the waxy fronds of the plant, and tried to think.

She had been studying and practicing illusions in class all week so that is what she employed. Digging into the small gold purse around her waist, she pulled out a bit of wax and began kneading it between her fingers as she cast her spell.

Two of the guards converged right near where she had been standing while the third spoke to the guard standing watch over the nearby door. Both guards standing next to Ellyssa turned toward the dais and shook their heads. Unable to resist, Ellyssa reached up and tickled the nearest guard's ear. He slapped absently at the frond of the plant before he and his partner abandoned their search and returned to their posts. It was all Ellyssa could do not to laugh, which certainly would have ruined the effect of the illusion.

She knew she was doomed from the moment she enspelled that bucket-head on the wall back at the school, but she would be damned if she would suffer the humiliation of being dragged away from the show by guards and returned to the school to face her punishment. If she was going to be punished, she would face it in a dignified manner. After she got what she wanted.

Not being fooled as easily as the guards were, Miranda squashed that bit of amusement when she motioned to a wrinkled old crone Ellyssa had not seen standing to the far back of the dais amidst the thick curtains covering the wall. The duchess had thought it a grand idea to have a wizard of her own after the near-disastrous siege just over a year ago.

The ancient wizard cast a quick spell and began scanning the room with her eyes. When she looked at the two big plants next to the pillar, she had no trouble picking out which was vegetation and which was a troublesome young girl. The wizard, Jennessa, smiled wickedly. Miranda mimicked the expression when the old wizard informed her of the deception, except Miranda was able to show far more teeth.

Ellyssa cursed loudly enough and vilely enough to make several women near her blush. Casting off dignity as an expendable casualty of war, she dropped to her hands and knees, pulled a large leaf from the plant, and crawled toward the side door guarded by the solitary guard.

The man looked from the girl crawling rapidly toward him to the guards converging on his position. Taking a visual cue from one of the approaching guards, he stood ready to grab the girl he assumed to be a party crasher. Ellyssa poured a small bit of magic into the big waxy leaf in her hand and flung it at the guard's head where it stuck tenaciously, covering his entire face.

Taken completely by surprise, the guard stumbled backwards, tearing at the leaf that blinded and threatened to suffocate him. Ellyssa used his distraction to crawl through the door, scramble to her feet, and sprint through the hallway. Her shoes made a terrible racket as they clapped repeatedly against the marble, but not nearly as much as the whistles that began blaring down every passageway.

Whistles! I thought only the Watch used whistles! Ellyssa shouted inwardly.

Ellyssa tried to go back the way she came so that she might retrieve the horse she had borrowed and retreat back toward the school, but between the whistles and her own poor sense of direction, she was becoming hopelessly lost. She raced down one corridor only to find a group of guards running at her from the other end. She braked so hard that she hopped on one leg to keep her balance before making a sharp right turn down another passage. In any other situation, it would have appeared highly comical.

Her lungs burned, her heart pounded in her chest, and it felt as if she had been running for miles. Ellyssa was beginning to wonder if she would ever make it out of these halls when she finally emerged outside through a seldom-used side door. She could still hear the whistles blaring shrilly throughout the grounds until well after she left the castle behind her. Going back for the horse now was out of the question.

Not only is Peck going to be angry with me, now I have to walk all the way back to the school in these stupid shoes! Her thoughts raged, then kicked at a piece of refuse, smudging her stupid, pretty shoes. "Damn it all to the abyss!" she shouted into the night.

Ellyssa kept to the less-used streets, certain that every watchman she saw was on the lookout for her and was just waiting to drag her back to Lady Miranda. Probably in chains, too, just to humiliate her even more. She wondered if maybe that wouldn't be better than walking all the way back in the dark. At least she would have a ride. Her pride dismissed that as a viable option. Bruised feet heal much faster than a bruised ego.

Even her ego began having second thoughts after nearly another hour of walking and realizing she was completely lost. She hugged her arms around herself as she became increasingly nervous. The buildings along the streets seemed to loom over her as if ready to pounce and she began seeing threats in every shadow.

Kayne's artillery had wreaked havoc on dozens of homes and buildings in this area, and several of the street layouts had been changed for tactical purposes making it even more difficult for her to find her way. Ellyssa stepped from a smaller side street to a slightly larger thoroughfare and felt her stomach clench as she found herself accosted by at least three men.

"Well hello there, sweetie. You out for a good time?" one of them called out from a few yards away.

Ellyssa turned sharply to the right and quickened her pace. Two more men stepped out of the shadows and blocked her path.

"Look at that pretty dress," one of the new men remarked. "Could be we can get more in a ransom than the slave markets in Sumara."

Ellyssa's blood froze as her heart hammered in her chest. Slavers! She took off running again, choosing the only route available to her. She darted down a small alleyway to her left. That narrow alley turned into a complete maze created by the walls of shabby homes and businesses. She continued to follow the twists and turns of the alleys that sometimes got so narrow, she had to turn sideways to squeeze through.

She had no idea how many men were now chasing her, but the shouts seemed to be coming from all directions. Until now, she had chosen her path by keeping those voices to her back. Now she did not know what direction was safe. Picking a suitable spot, she decided to try to wait them out. Casting another illusion spell, she squatted down, pressed her back against the filthy wall of the alley, and did a remarkable impression of an old wooden barrel.

She spotted the orange glow of torches and lanterns before she saw the men appear at the end of the alley in which she was hiding. A couple of men walked partway down and called out to another lantern-bearing man coming from the other direction.

"You see anything at that end?"

"Naw. She musta kept running," the lantern bearer called back.

Both men turned away and began walking toward the open end of the alley. Ellyssa began slowly letting out the breath she had been holding. That was when the rat climbed onto her pretty shoe and started crawling up her leg. She shuddered as she felt the rat's tiny claws lift and prick her skin as it moved steadily upward. It was a testament to her focus and willpower that she was able to keep from crying out in revulsion. She had spent almost her entire first year as Azerick's apprentice killing rats with a goblin named Grick. However, hitting a rat with a stick or skewering it with a dart was far different from having one crawling up your leg.

Ellyssa tried to concentrate on keeping quiet and maintaining the focus on her spell. She only needed to keep it together for a few more seconds and then the men would be busy searching elsewhere. She almost made it. Her resolve failed her when the rat reached her shoulder and gave her cheek a lick to see if she was edible.

The young wizard student lost control of far more than her spell. She screamed loudly as she jumped to her feet and began dancing and flailing at her hair in an effort to knock the rat from her shoulder and crush it under the wooden soles of her gold shoes. Every slaver in the area heard her cries and instantly converged on the alley. The men already standing at the ends smiled gleefully as they stalked toward the helpless girl.

What they did not know was that Ellyssa was far from helpless, and now she was furious. First, her grand night of watching the greatest minstrel in the kingdom was cut short, forcing her to walk home in her painful shoes. Then a bunch of filthy, lowlife slavers chased her across half the district and through filth-strewn alleys. Then to top it all off, a rat climbed up her leg and planted a wet kiss on her face!

"You want to chase me?" the furious girl shouted. "Well now you caught me, so here's your reward!"

Ellyssa reached down and grabbed a broken shard of pottery. The spells she had prepared were not geared toward combat but were instead suited for the topics of this week's classes. That still did not mean she was defenseless. Not all magic required precise forms to have an effect.

She pulled from the Source and used its raw energy without bothering to form the weave required to achieve more exact or dramatic effects. Such use of magic was more in line with a hedge wizard and not a true student of the arcane. She let that force build up inside the fired clay shard and then released it all at once, launching the sharp piece of pottery from her hand like a stone from a sling. The shard caught the man approaching from one end of the alley right in the neck. He fell to the ground, clutching his throat and making a strangling sound as he choked on his own blood.

Ellyssa then turned toward the larger group stalking toward her with a little more caution from the other end. Pulling a reagent from her purse, she formed a far more complex spell and fueled it with her anger. A strong wind began blowing down the alley, causing her hair to fly about her face like some fearsome spirit.

The wind began to howl as it strengthened, picking up lighter pieces of grit and debris and blowing it into the faces of the approaching men. The slavers drew short blades with one hand and tried to protect their eyes and face with the other as they continued to slowly advance.

Ellyssa sneered maliciously as she slowly raised her palms face up. Larger pieces of trash consisting of shattered boards, nails, pottery, and refuse rose from the ground and were taken by the wind into the swirling vortex forming in the middle of the alleyway. The slavers could no longer see their prey through that tiny tornado, nor could Ellyssa see them. Nevertheless, the alley was narrow and she did not need to see them. There was no way for them to escape except back the way they came, and she doubted any of them could outrun the wind.

With a small shift in focus, Ellyssa sent the whirling mass of debris toward the men who now realized they were not dealing with just a rich young girl who found herself in the wrong part of town. They turned almost as one and raced fearfully back down the alley with the wizard-made tornado rapidly closing on them.

Pieces of wood and other solid bits of debris smashed into the slavers, breaking bones, cracking skulls, and bludgeoning tender flesh while sharper things like pottery and the occasional piece of glass sliced them like so many knives, all whipped about by winds over a hundred miles per hour.

In such close confines, the spell was devastating. Had the men been able to split apart or had other avenues of escape, most of them would have fled with only a few injuries or none at all. As it was, none of them did. Several unlucky men who had not even been in the alley ran right into the lethal vortex just as it reached the entrance, leaving a mass of dead and badly injured bodies lying still or moaning in pain.

Ellyssa reveled in her handiwork as she turned to escape. She barely had time to process the whirring sound speeding toward her as she turned to leave. The small cudgel smacked her right between the eyes, felling her instantly.

A man stepped confidently out of the shadows near the end of the alley, strode toward Ellyssa, and looked down at her motionless form.

"Sweetheart, you just made me a very wealthy man," the slaver captain told her unconscious body as he easily stuffed her in a large burlap sack and slung her over his shoulder.

CHAPTER 16

The army had been traveling for just over a week now and was halfway to its destination. Partway through the journey, sleigh runners replaced the wagon wheels to allow the conveyances to navigate the deep snow more easily. Azerick and the other spellcasters used their magic to clear the drifts, which prevented the wagons from becoming mired within the powdery terrain.

General Brague had done an admirable job of avoiding Azerick and his party, but he now stood in the waist-deep snow outside their tent. The general knew trying to enter it without permission was futile. He had learned that it was no mere tent but some infernal wizard contraption, and walking in unannounced would simply deposit him in an empty tent bereft of furnishings.

Allister soon appeared at the entrance and held the flap open for the general. Brague stepped inside the vestibule then beyond, where it emptied into a lavish interior fit for a Sumaran king. It was not the appearance of the tent that always drew his attention first, but the warmth. It took only minutes for the multiple layers of wool he wore to become very uncomfortable.

Azerick made his appearance with perfect timing. He strode through another entryway in a robe, scrubbing his hair vigorously with a towel. The sorcerer looked up at General Brague as he entered.

"I tell you, Allister, that bath is so hot I feel like a carrot in a stewpot. Ah, General Brague, I did not realize it was that hour yet," Azerick said, feigning both his surprise and apology.

"Hot bath..." Brague whispered almost deliriously.

The only ablutions he and his men achieved on the march were from a pot of water heated on a camp stove inside a frigid tent.

Azerick arched his eyebrows. "You are welcome to use the bath, General. I am sure your men would understand that leadership has its rewards."

Azerick only offered because he knew the prideful and stubborn man would refuse. They had a similar discussion the first time Brague had entered the opulent tent to discuss the wizards' assistance in clearing the deeper snowdrifts so as to hasten their travel. Azerick smiled as he watched the internal war ripple across the general's face.

"I will endure as my men endure. It is what a man of integrity and leadership does," Brague slowly proclaimed through clenched teeth.

"Well, I'm glad I am not in charge then. So what is it you wish to discuss tonight?"

Brague pulled a map from a large leather tube and rolled it out on the long table occupying the center of the room. He used two silver candlesticks and bowls filled with dates and nuts to hold down the corners.

"We should arrive in End's Run within the week, and I thought it a good time to show you what we have to work with so that you all can best prepare whatever you need in order to provide the greatest benefit to the battle."

The general began identifying key points already marked on the map. "Here is End's Run. About two days to the south, the pass is at its narrowest and steepest. If we can prepare some defensive fortifications at the head of that pass, we can offset what we can assume is our enemy's superiority of numbers."

"How do we know how many soldiers Caalendor is bringing north?" Alex asked. "For all he knows Jarvin rode to North Haven or is simply hiding in End's Run without more than a handful of loyal followers."

Brague shook his head. "It doesn't matter. You can bet a pigeon left North Haven before we were even lined up and headed north. He knows we are going to End's Run. Even if he did not, he would bring every man he could. If he does not find Jarvin in End's Run, the only place for him to go is North Haven. Caalendor's troops would simply march from End's Run to North Haven along the same route from which we are approaching and lay siege to the city if the duchess refused to surrender the king. No matter what Jarvin does, Caalendor knows he has to deal with North Haven's military."

The group around the table nodded their understanding of the situation. There was no way Caalendor was going to come to End's Run with less than enough troops to lay waste to any town or city in which Jarvin might take refuge. Allister studied the map, particularly the pass.

"If there is a large amount of snow on the walls of that pass, we could conceivably cause an avalanche. Timed properly, it could be devastating to the men marching through it," the archmage pointed out.

"I'll leave that up to you all and keep our own men well enough away. If you can cause such an effect, you will have to do it before the first engagement. I will not sacrifice my men needlessly."

Rusty asked, "How long until we reach End's Run?"

Brague did a quick calculation in his head then answered, "A week, maybe five days if we really push ourselves."

"Can you guess at how far ahead that will put us of the bishop's forces?"

"That is a bit harder to figure out. It depends on how hard they marched and how long it took Caalendor to assemble his forces. From what I have heard, the bishop has played this whole thing like a patient chess master. I have to assume he had all of his pieces in place before he made his final gambit. Based on that assumption, that would mean having his army close to Brelland, and knowing he will not want to rest until he captures or kills the king. I think we can expect to reach End's Run one or two weeks ahead of him at best."

"It's not a great lead but enough to allow us to dig in and prepare the battlefield," Alex put in.

"I will leave it to you gentlemen, and Lord Giles, to prepare yourselves. Now I must go see to three wagons with broken runners."

Azerick took the insult without rebuttal and picked at the bowl of nuts while Alex escorted the general out so he could further discuss military tactics.

The army continued to trudge through the deep snows as they pushed relentlessly onward to defend their king. It was precisely six days later that they reached End's Run, exhausted, cold, and thoroughly miserable.

The heavy brigade found the gates closed and several hundred men manning the wooden walls of the town. General Brague, Azerick, Allister, Rusty, and Alex comprised the command staff that was selected to meet with the king and whoever was in charge of End's Run. The gates opened wide enough to permit a man who looked more at home in a stockade than heading a town's defenses to pass through and meet them.

General Brague stepped forward to greet the man. "Good afternoon. I am General Brague, commander of the army of North Haven."

The man spit a gob of tobacco into the snow and replied, "Donnigan, commander of the biggest bunch of scum north of the border and babysitter to about a hundred fifty candy-assed soldiers out of Brelland. I guess you'll be wanting to see the king."

"It would be greatly appreciated."

"Can't put that many men in town all at once. Best have 'em bust camp where they're at. From what I understand, you'll all be heading to the southern pass at first light."

Brague called forth one of his captains and began spewing orders. "Captain, I want you to take the quartermaster and his crew into town, commandeer ever washtub, basin, and kettle big enough for a man to sit in, and set up as many bath tents as you can. Every man will wash before getting one hour in the taverns to enjoy himself. It will be the last chance they will get for some time. Send them in groups of five hundred with strict orders to behave themselves."

"Yes, sir!" the captain barked, saluting sharply before doing an about-face, and stomping off to enact the general's orders.

The command staff allowed Donnigan to lead them through the gates, across the town to where they exited another set of gates to the north, and began following a path cut into the steep hill where a mansion sat overlooking the town.

"Mr. Donnigan," Brague asked as he followed the head of Landrin's enforcers, "have you received any intelligence regarding Caalendor's forces?"

"Yup," Donnigan answered with another glob of black spit ruining the snow. "Scout came back earlier today and said they're about four or five days out, which is why I said y'all probably want to head out at first light."

"Four days!" Brague exclaimed. "How in the six hells did they make that kind of time?"

Donnigan shrugged his big shoulders. "Don't know. All I know is there's near ten thousand of 'em, which looks like they got ya beat by about three to one. Were I in charge, I wouldn't be feeling too good about those odds."

"Ten thousand," Brague whispered. "I never would have thought Caalendor, or anyone else, would be able to field that many men so quickly. He must have been scraping the bottom of the barrel for a long time and hired every sellsword between here and the Sumaran capital."

"Do you think our field advantage is enough to even the odds?" Azerick asked the general.

"Maybe," Brague answered with a look of great unease. "Even if it is, it will be a costly and bloody affair."

Rusty looked to General Brague almost pleadingly. "Surely with three spellcasters on your side we can shift the battle strongly in our favor."

Brague's shoulders almost slumped with resignation. "You can bet he brought at least a few clerics with him. He knows about Lord Giles, his friends, and his allegiance to North Haven and the king."

"Hey, I have not given my allegiance to anyone except my school, my wife, and myself!" Azerick declared vocally.

"It doesn't matter. Intentional or not, you saved Jarvin's crown once and then married his most ardent supporter. He knows you will oppose him, even if only to defend North Haven, so he will certainly use whatever resources are available to counter the threat you pose."

The group broke off discussions as they neared the strange mansion and the doors flew open. King Jarvin Ollander strode forth from the open doorway with a look of great pleasure mixed with the stress of the enormity of what they were all facing.

"Lord Giles, General Brague, and friends, words cannot express my gratitude for your coming so quickly," the king practically gushed as he embraced each man there, with the exception of Donnigan. "I am particularly surprised and pleased to see you, Azerick."

"Well, I did take an oath and all," Azerick replied absently.

Jarvin gave Azerick a conspiratorial wink and asked, "Miranda made you come, didn't she?"

"She certainly did."

Jarvin's warm familiarity took Azerick by surprise. He had half expected the king to be sitting on some makeshift throne, making the very people who were about to risk their lives in his cause stand and wait for the pleasure of his audience. The fact that he had not acted as expected put Azerick in a state of conflict between actually starting to like the man and holding onto his prejudicial hatred of the nobility.

"As I said before, I will take what I can get. Follow me inside where we can discuss tactics. I am afraid we have little time, as I am certain Mr. Donnigan has informed you on the way up."

Jarvin led them inside where numerous maps and figurines were spread out upon a long dining table. Each of them took note of the stained-glass Solarian's Eye set high in the east wall as they entered, bolstering the opinion that the house was as much a mansion as it was a church.

Their host made his appearance at the top of the stairs and descended them as they gathered around the table to study the maps and troop figures.

Now we are finally graced with some acceptable company, Klaraxis practically cooed.

Azerick shifted his sight to take in the aura of the man approaching them. The golden glow of wizardly ability shone quite clearly, but there was another, darker shimmering beneath that confused him. Azerick's heart practically skipped a beat when he finally recognized the tainted pall of undeath the aura represented.

The sorcerer gripped Jarvin by the upper arm and whispered urgently into his ear. "Your Majesty, do you have any idea what that man is?"

Jarvin laid a reassuring hand atop Azerick's. "I do. He is a friend, without whose intervention my family and I would be dead right now. I am certain that if half of the things I have heard about you are true, you can understand that we cannot always choose our fate, but we can choose what we do with it."

The vampire must have had extraordinary hearing because he locked eyes with Azerick as he looked back toward the stairs. Landrin had paused, possibly waiting to see how the newcomers would react, and then resumed his approach when Azerick nodded his understanding.

We should really share lunch with him sometime. I have not had a proper meal since you cursed me to this existence.

You chose your fate when you threw in with those mages in the Black Tower, demon, so shut up! Azerick rebuked Klaraxis, pushing him back further into his mind.

Azerick's vitriolic reaction was not because he felt repulsed by the idea, but because part of him desired exactly what the demon wanted. Of course, that part of him was entirely because of the demon's influence, but their spirits were so intertwined it was impossible to separate them completely. The demon's desires were as real as his own were. He ignored the demon's taunting laughter as Landrin spoke to them.

"Gentlemen," Landrin greeted the assembly of men, "I am Landrin Bailey. Welcome to my home. My manservant, Fetch, shall provide you with anything you need. Please make yourselves at home and partake of anything I have to offer."

Rusty leaned toward Azerick and whispered in his ear, his face paling visibly. "Is that thing what I think it is?"

Azerick twitched his head and made a small motion indicating that it was all right. He glanced at Allister and saw that the old archmage had also made the connection, but he did not appear overly distraught. The three mages would obviously need to discuss the matter in private later.

Jarvin addressed the group but spoke primarily to the senior military man. "Landrin had Mr. Donnigan fetch us any maps he could get his hands on. This is what I have come up with so far. Caalendor's men are coming up the southern pass. If we move out first thing in the morning, that should give us two or three days before we engage them. General, how many men do you have with you?"

General Brague looked almost apologetic when he replied, "Three thousand, Highness."

Jarvin sighed and shook his head. "It is less than I had hoped for, but more than I expected. From what Donnigan's scouts told me, Caalendor is approaching with nearly ten thousand men. How he managed to move that fast is even more perplexing than how he acquired that many to begin with."

"I am no expert on priestly magic," Allister cut in, "but I imagine they have ways of lending strength and influencing the weather to some degree. Particularly if they work in concert."

"I do not know either, magus, but it certainly seems plausible. I had thought to place the bulk of your forces here at the head of the pass," Jarvin said, indicating the position on the map with a few small metal figures. "We keep a reserve element of five hundred men a quarter mile back. What did you bring in the way of cavalry?"

"I am traveling cavalry-heavy with over seven hundred horses. The snow will make most cavalry tactics impossible, particularly an effective charge with lances, but even in general melee, being mounted will provide them with an advantage. All of the horses wear a boot that increases hoof width, much like a reindeer. It's a northern thing so I doubt Caalendor's horses will have them."

"He will still have twice as many horses as us. Do you have any suggestions on how we can neutralize the enemy cavalry?" Jarvin asked openly of the three spellcasters.

Azerick took the lead and said, "We think we can create an avalanche within the pass. The trick will obviously be getting Caalendor to commit his cavalry so that we can trap them beneath it."

"Majesty, do you know who is leading Caalendor's forces? If it is General Haskins, I doubt he will fall for any ruse we might come up with," Brague told the king.

"I would agree. The truth is I do not know who is leading the men. I thought General Haskins and my company commanders to be honorable, loyal, and beyond reproach, but I watched one of my most senior advisors murder Magus Illifan before my eyes, and the captain of my own Blackguard lead the coup. I do not know whom to trust. Forgive me if I say that I pray General Haskins is sitting in a dungeon cell beneath Castle Stonemount at this very minute."

"I hope he is as well, Your Majesty, no matter how uncomfortable that may be for him," Brague concurred. "I would say you have the right of it. These maps are a lot better than what I had to work with on the way up, but most everything is how I planned it out in my head."

Jarvin clapped his hands together. "All right then, gentlemen, if you have any further need of me, you know where to find me. At least Lord Bailey and I can offer you one comfortable night in his manor before we all set out on the morrow."

Azerick cut General Brague off before he could speak. "I know I could certainly use a soft bed and warm bath after living the past two weeks in a tent. It is unfortunate that General Brague will take no succor that is denied his men. The general is a man of such uncommon integrity that he has refused my every offer of magical aid to make his traveling more comfortable. I am certain the good general will not accept the comfort of submersing himself in a hot bath while his men are doing the 'iron pot squat' in a wash tent."

"Is that right, General?" the king asked. "I must say, your dedication to your soldiers is positively admirable. Very few men in your position deny themselves a certain amount of luxury given their station. You are to be commended, General."

"Thank you, Your Majesty," he replied through gritted teeth.

General Brague shot the smiling sorcerer a look that promised great retribution in the future.

Ellyssa awoke with a pain in her head so great she begged to return to unconsciousness. By the vomit-inducing rocking, she knew she either was on a ship or had suffered a severe head injury. She prayed for the latter since being on a ship promised the greatest amount of danger.

She opened her eyes, took in her surroundings, and surmised that she was indeed on a ship. Ellyssa replayed the night's events through her pain-addled mind as she slowly began stitching bits of the memories back together. She remembered the guards chasing her from the castle, getting lost in the city, and then being chased again. Ellyssa recalled the fight in the alley. She thought she had defeated them, but then something hit her in the head and she blacked out.

Slavers! Slavers had been chasing her and now they had caught her, and she was on a ship probably bound for Sumara! Well, she would make them regret taking her! Ellyssa tried to move her hands but found them shackled together. She looked across the cramped cabin and saw a man sitting at a small table watching her. He was dressed in leggings that had possibly once been black but the sun and salt had faded them to a dark grey. He also wore a russet shirt of decent quality. His black beard sported far more hair than his balding head did and his smile reflected a bright gold eyetooth.

"Good. You are awake," the man said. "For a while there I feared I had hit you too hard and ruined the goods."

Ellyssa sat up and glared at the slaver. "You had best let me go if you know what's good for you."

The slaver captain's gold tooth flashed once more. "What's good for me is a chest full of gold, which is precisely what I'll get when I get you to Bakhtaran."

"What you'll get is your own death!" Ellyssa snarled, reaching for the Source.

Despite her hands being shackled, the fool had made the mistake of clasping them in front of her. It was clumsy, but she could still shape a weave into a spell suitable to burn that smile off his greasy face.

Ellyssa's snarl vanished with a gasp when she found the Source completely beyond her grasp. She could sense its existence, but no matter how hard she tried, she was unable to grasp the tiniest thread in which to shape even the most rudimentary spell. Panic almost overwhelmed her as she realized how much she had come to depend on her ability to weave magic. Not being able to touch it was like waking up and finding her legs missing.

"What have you done to me?" she demanded, the fear evident in her voice.

"I wondered if those things would work or not. Those wizards in Bakhtaran promised me they would when they tasked me to bring back some captives able to use magic, but you just never know until you try them out for the first time."

Ellyssa looked down more closely at the manacles clamped around her tiny wrists and saw several runes etched into the surface of the iron. She deduced that the runes must prevent her from being able to access the Source. She slumped back against the cabin wall as she let the despondency of her situation overwhelm her.

NO! she shouted to herself. *Azerick would never let something like this beat him and neither will I!*

"What is your name?" she asked the man watching her, obviously amused at her inner turmoil.

"The name's Captain Jake," he said with a shrug, figuring it could not hurt to tell her. "What's your name, girl?"

"My name is Ellyssa, but that's not the one you should care about. You should be far more concerned with the name of my master, Azerick Giles, since he will be the one that will find and kill you if you do not let me go. What I have seen him do to people that hurt or threaten his family would give you nightmares for the rest of your life."

Captain Jake leaned forward in his chair. "Sweetheart, if he ain't on this boat already, you and he will be somebody else's problem by the time he finds you, and I'll have sailed to some other port at the far reaches of the sea."

Ellyssa sprang from the cot she was on with a snarl of defiance, spit in Jake's face, and tried to claw his eyes out, but managed only to score three red stripes down one of his cheeks.

The slaver grabbed the short chain linking the manacles with one hand, slapped the furious girl across the face with the other, and threw her against the wall to land heavily back onto the cot.

He wiped his face with his hand as his eyes took on a murderous glare. "Girl, I keep you in my cabin because you are more valuable than the rest of the chattel in my hold put together. But you make me regret it, and I'll toss you down there with them. You're too young for most of my men, but not all of them. I only need you alive to get paid. You best remember that!"

Ellyssa hugged her knees and sobbed as Captain Jake stormed out of the cabin. She desperately wanted to be brave like Azerick, but all she could feel was the terror of being helpless and the shame of knowing that it was her own selfish foolishness that had gotten her into this predicament.

She prayed to every god there was that if Azerick came and saved her, she would do what she was told and never misbehave again. She would be polite and study just like Roger did. She would not let her ego try magic that was beyond her. She would be the perfect student, she swore. Yet the ship continued to sail south, undeterred, the gods did not whisk her away, and Azerick did not magically appear to save her and punish her captors.

Captain Jake did not return for several hours. When he did finally come to check on his captive, he found Ellyssa still sitting on the bunk with her knees drawn up to her chin and her arms wrapped around her legs.

"You know, there's no reason to look so glum," Captain Jake told the despondent girl. "I'm selling you to the vila himself where you'll live in a palace and be pampered like a princess. You should know that your future is a damn sight brighter than the rest of the chattel in my hold."

Ellyssa looked up, her face impassive and devoid of emotion. "You should know that your future is the darkest of all. I will escape one day and hunt you down. You will die like the cur you are, unloved and lying in a gutter somewhere."

Jake's face turned scarlet as he crossed the tiny cabin in three brisk strides, grabbed the impertinent child by the chain connecting the shackles, and yanked her from the cot.

"You obviously have too much fire in you, girl!" the slaver snarled. "Maybe scrubbing the decks will help quench it."

The furious captain pulled Ellyssa across the cabin and dragged her out onto the deck of the slave ship. She blinked rapidly as the bright afternoon sun assaulted her gloom-adjusted eyes. Captain Jake forced her onto her hands and knees and then a moment later dropped a bucket of seawater and a stiff brush in front of her. Ellyssa looked at the bucket and brush and glared up at the slaver.

"Stop gawking and start scrubbing, girl."

"I'm a prisoner, not your servant," Ellyssa snapped. "Scrub it yourself."

Jake did not bother responding to the recalcitrant child. He simply glanced behind her and gave a slight nod. Pain flared across Ellyssa's back as the whip laid a line of fire upon her flesh. Ellyssa let out a shriek, scrambled away, and stared back with tear-filled eyes at the man holding the whip. The man was enormous with a thick jaw, a bald head, and almost jet-black skin. Ellyssa knew he hailed from the jungles of Lazuul, but was surprised to see one of his kind since they rarely left their coastal jungle villages.

"This is Sonjay," Captain Jake told her. "We both know I cannot afford to damage you too severely, but if the pain of his whip cannot convince you to work, then perhaps tonight the pain of your hungry belly will. If you do not want to starve the rest of the way to Bakhtaran, I suggest you do what you are told."

Ellyssa did her best to kill both the men with her eyes. When that failed, she angrily snatched up the brush, dipped it into the pail, and began scrubbing. She knew the slaver would not kill her or even harm her severely, but she knew he could make her suffer the entire trip to the Sumaran city. She would do what she was told, if minimally, but one day she would find and kill Captain Jake. The sting of the whip throbbed across her back as she scrubbed and she mentally added Sonjay to the list as well.

The sun beat down with enough intensity that the heat of the welt raised upon her flesh was indistinguishable from the rest of her skin. After only an hour or so, the constant scrubbing raised blisters across her palm and on every finger. Ellyssa refused to weep no matter how hard the tears tried to escape. She may not be able to block the tears from the pain of a beating, but she would not release them to ease the pain of her tortured spirit.

Another bucket clattered beside her, splashing up her arms and soaking her dress. Before she could react, a heavy boot struck her hard in her backside and sent her sprawling into the expanding puddle. She turned and glared up at the black-skinned man, Sonjay. The man returned her glare with mutual hatred.

"Some of those men you killed were Sonjay's friends. Now, you had best get that mess cleaned up before I take my whip to you again."

Ellyssa refused to let the man bait her. "Thank you, but I have plenty of water. I don't need any more."

Sonjay made a deep chuckling sound. "That ain't wash water, girl."

The acrid smell of human waste finally reached her nose and Ellyssa scrambled to her feet and raced for the rail with Sonjay's booming laughter following her the entire way. Ellyssa leaned out over the open sea and vomited violently into the rolling waves. It took the next hour using her brush and fresh seawater to scrub her skin and dress free of the foul waste. She spent the rest of the day wearing a sodden dress while she continued to toil at her labors. This was going to be a long and dreadful voyage. Ellyssa wondered if the worst was yet to come.

CHAPTER 17

Borik had been ranting for the better part of fifteen minutes. It started out as generalized complaining about the cold and being lost, but soon he targeted his ire squarely at Tarth whose job it was to locate the source of the gathering arcane energy and presumably the location of their foe.

Tarth sat near a tree, hovering over a small brazier, inhaling the burning incense it contained. Lost in whatever semi-dream state the fumes put him in, Tarth seemed completely oblivious, or at least immune, to Borik's verbal assault.

"More than two weeks we've been running around this cursed forest, trekking through snow that, for a dwarf, is at an extremely uncomfortable depth! Maybe if you pulled your head out of those fumes that are destroying what little intelligence that feeble elf brain of yours contains, we would stop walking in circles, get to where we're supposed to go, and get on with having our souls sucked out by the granddaddy of the undead!"

"Borik, leave him be," Maude ordered. "I'm sure he's doing the best he can. Malek isn't having any better luck finding the source of this thing than he is."

Borik turned his glare on the big woman. "Malek ain't huffing loopy fumes and impairing an already dysfunctional brain! I've had it!" Borik yelled, kicking over the small brazier and spilling the smoldering incense and glowing coals into the snow with a hiss. "You best pull your head outta wherever it's stuck and start being of some dang-blasted use!" Borik continued shouting, now punctuating his words by poking Tarth in the forehead with a stubby finger.

A thick arrow appeared as if by magic right under his nose, causing him to sneeze violently as the shaft vibrated in the tree trunk next to him and the fletching tickled his nose. The unexpected near-skewering of his thick skull instantly extinguished the dwarf's fired-up temper.

Borik crossed his eyes in an attempt to focus on the arrow then looked at Tarth with his finger still touching the elf's forehead. "That yours?"

Tarth smiled vacantly at the dwarf and the arrow and replied, "It is not mine."

"Remove your filthy finger from that elf or the next one pins your beard to your chest, dwarf!" came a soft but strict command out of the darkness.

Borik snatched his finger back as if burned while Maude and Malek leapt to their feet with weapons drawn and faced the direction from which the order came. A dozen short and slender figures appeared silently out of the darkness from all directions, except the location from where the order was issued, with longbows drawn and pointed at the two humans and the dwarf.

One of the figures strode forward, lowered her hood, and dropped to her knees in an almost supplicating fashion in front of Tarth who was still sitting in the snow, reassembling his brazier. She reached an unsteady hand toward Tarth's face but stopped short of touching it.

"Tarthanalis Moonglow, it is you," the female elf whispered almost reverently.

The other elves dipped to one knee in a show of profound respect.

Tarth smiled and waggled his fingers at the newcomers. "Hello."

"Tarth, where have you been? Lahilonah misses you terribly," the elf kneeling in front of him said.

Tarth's vacant smile slipped a bit as he responded, "I was right here. Now I am going over there. Please excuse me."

Tarth stood up, hugging his arms around his thin body, and strode out of the circle of light cast by their campfire. The elf woman's face dropped in despair, and she stood and faced Maude and the others.

"Are you companions of Tarthanalis?" she asked.

Maude nodded her head. "Yes, for nearly ten years now."

The elf motioned to her comrades and they all lowered their bows. "I am Corana."

"Maude, Borik, and Malek," Maude replied, pointing to the dwarf and the cleric.

"Where did you find him?" Corana asked.

"Several days northeast of Brelland, sitting in a patch of wildflowers in the middle of nowhere, humming a tune, and braiding the blooms into his hair."

Maude could not keep the smile from her face as she recalled that fateful encounter. She, Malek, and Borik were on one of their first treasure hunting forays as a group and came upon the strange elf sitting in a small clearing amongst the blue wildflowers. Maude tried to speak to him, and Malek even cast a spell to determine if he was afflicted in some way when he did not respond.

After a short rest, they had decided to leave the elf where they had found him, but he stood up and followed them like a lost puppy when they set out. He did not say a word for days. He simply followed them when they moved and stopped when they stopped. It was not until a group of hostile orcs set upon them that Tarth showed his magical ability, and an unpredictable one at that. Shortly after that encounter, he began talking, mostly incoherent nonsense.

Maude looked in the direction Tarth had gone. "Corana, you seemed to show Tarth a significant amount of deference. Is that typical when you meet your kind? Tarth seemed a little uncomfortable with it."

"Is he royalty of some kind?" Malek asked.

"Oh, is he rich?" Borik inquired, greedily rubbing his hands together.

Corana paused before answering. "Tarthanalis is special."

"You can sure say that again," Borik grunted, then twirled a finger next to his ear.

"Shut up, dwarf!" both women ordered at once.

Borik fumed but wisely held his tongue as Corana explained. "Tarthanalis Moonglow is one of the greatest heroes in elven history. He is a living legend to our people."

Maude and her crew could only gape in shock at the proclamation.

"Tarth? Our Tarth is a legend?" Maude asked.

"Legendary idiot maybe," Borik rumbled into his beard, which failed to keep his words from reaching the acute ears of the elves.

Corana and the other elves glared at the dwarf once more but did not comment.

"Has he ever spoken of himself or his home?" Corana asked Maude.

"Not once, and I have asked him, but he always drifts off and won't answer."

"I imagine it is hard for him to talk about anything that reminds him of everything he lost and the horrors he endured. I would not inflict our presence on him, knowing how much it must hurt him to see us, if our mission were not so vital. Have you come to destroy the monster that gathers the dark energy for his nefarious scheme?"

"We have, but we can talk about that later. Please, tell me about Tarth. What horrors?" Maude practically pleaded.

Corana peered into the darkness in the direction Tarth had disappeared then spoke softly. "No one knows where Tarthanalis came from. He was found as an infant in the Grove of Heroes in the heart of Everspring, our home. It was nearly a thousand years ago and several hundred years after the Great Rebellion."

"Wait," Maude interjected. "I thought the Rebellion occurred only a thousand years ago?"

Corana gave her a thin smile. "You humans lost a great deal of your history during those first few centuries after the rebellion. We elves struggled to bring peace and unity to the humans, but it was challenging to say the least. After several centuries, we decided we had done all we could for the humans and fled to the far north so that we would not be threatened by the rapid human expansion. We used our magic to create Everspring, a tiny nation like an oasis in the inhospitable frozen north.

"But as the humans continued to spread northward, many of our elders felt that such isolation was not enough. They decided that with the help of the greatest wizard ever known since the banishment of the dragon-elves, they could shift Everspring to a pocket dimension away from all other races."

"Hold on. What are dragon-elves, and Tarth is not only the greatest wizard ever, but nearly a thousand years old?" Maude asked.

"Six dragon-elves were created by mixing the essence of a dragon and an elven mother. The child grew inside a sort of magical cocoon.

The mix of elf and dragon essences created a being capable of unimaginable power. It was the only way to defeat the enemy we all faced."

"You mean the dragons," Malek said.

Corana laughed at the cleric's assertion. "You humans have such short memories, although I suppose it is not your fault. Your task during the Great Rebellion was to battle the dragons. The dragons were merely pawns, the guard dogs, of the true enemy; an enemy even the gods feared."

"Who were they?" Maude asked, her attention fully locked onto the elf and her tale.

"The Scions."

"Who or what are the Scions?"

Corana continued. "The Scions are a race said to be older than the gods. There were five, but the dragon-elves destroyed one during the Rebellion. The shock was so great to the Scions that they agreed to banishment. Eager to end a war that had decimated the population of nearly every sentient race on the planet, the leaders of the three great races agreed."

Maude furrowed her brow. "So what happened to Tarth? He came after they were banished, right?"

"That is so. As I was saying, about three hundred years ago, the elders decided to remove Everspring from this world, and they convinced Tarthanalis, against his objections, to try. The ritual was unlike anything ever attempted since the dragon-elves banished the Scions. The magic used to effect the shift was beyond anything ever dreamt of. Tarthanalis said it was possible but extremely dangerous and fraught with peril. During the shift, something went terribly wrong. A rift appeared and our mages lost control. Instead of shifting to a pocket dimension, they opened a rift to the deepest level of the abyss. A demon lord grasped control of the rift and would not let us close it. Infernal spawn began pouring out of it and slaughtering our people."

Coranas's face took on an almost vacant expression as she thought back to that fateful day. "Tarthanalis knew that the only way to close it was from the inside, and so leapt into that void to save his people. What happened in that rift, we do not know. What we do know is that

Tarthanalis was able to close it, but was lost to us forever. Or so we thought. Ten years later, we found him in the Grove of Heroes just as we had when he was an infant. His body was shattered and savaged almost beyond recognition. Even our greatest healers were unsure if he would survive. It was not until they made his body whole that we understood the real damage. His mind was all but destroyed."

The elf shook herself free of her reverie. "For decades he lay in a semi-conscious state, sometimes screaming about tortures that go beyond my imagination to even conceive. His soulmate, Lahilonah, tended him and rarely left his side through all those years. We thought he might never recover. Then he seemed to improve. He woke but was unable to speak. He slowly began walking, but it was like the walk of someone still sleeping. He would cry out in the night as the nightmares continued to plague him. Quite by accident, we found a mixture of herbs, which when burned and inhaled, seemed to calm him. He sometimes went days without bouts of terror. He began talking, but never about what had happened. Then one day he simply vanished. We think being so close to where it all happened was simply too much for him."

"My poor Tarth," Maude whispered.

Even Borik was silent throughout the retelling. When he spotted Maude looking at him, he turned away.

"Borik, are you crying?" she asked the surly dwarf.

"No! I have a piece of dirt in my eye! A stupid piece of elf dirt," he muttered with a sniff as he stalked away.

Maude turned back to Corana and asked, "Do you think he has just been wandering around all this time?"

"I imagine so. Perhaps he sensed some importance in your group and that is why he attached himself to you. Who can say what is happening inside that mind of his?"

"Hey!" Borik shouted out of the darkness. "Your legend is in a tree trying to talk to a bird!"

Maude and Corana gave into their curiosity and went to see what Borik was talking about. Sure enough, just beyond the orange glow of the fire, sat Tarth next to a large horned owl about fifteen feet up a tree.

"Hoo," the owl hooted softly, seemingly unperturbed by the elf sharing his branch.

"Tarth," the mage replied, pointing to his chest. "Who are you?"

"Hoo," the owl repeated.

"Tarth, and you are?"

"Hoo."

"Look, this conversation has become rather circular. You really must carry on your end of it if we expect it to advance at all," Tarth informed the owl.

"How did he get up there, and how do we get him down?" Maude asked.

Borik began packing a double handful of snow. "I bet I can knock him off his perch with a snowball."

"Don't you dare! Just leave him be. He'll come back down when he's ready."

"Maude, you and your group are searching for the lich, correct?" Corana asked when they all returned to the fire.

"Yes. We have been wandering almost aimlessly for the past week. We know we are close, but we cannot seem to find what Tarth and Malek say is the center."

Corana nodded. "I am afraid my group and I are all rangers, not wizards, but it feels as though there is a powerful spell of disjunction keeping people from finding what we seek much similar to what is cast over Everspring."

"So, do you know how to get past it?" Maude asked hopefully.

Corana gave her a rueful shake of her head. "I am afraid not. We did not discover the convergence of energy until a few months ago ourselves and have been searching ever since. We had been following a hobgoblin shaman that we had thought was the source of the disturbances two years ago, but a group of humans ran him off, and we destroyed a large number of his abominations. After that, we lost the trail. We approached your group hoping that you had discovered a way."

"Then it appears none of us are any closer to finding the source," Malek said. "That is a grave thing, for I sense that whatever is happening is near to reaching its crescendo, and when that happens I fear it may be too late to stop whatever it is."

Everyone: elves, humans, and dwarf, leapt to their feet and drew weapons as a patch of snow at the edge of the camp bulged upward.

The mound continued to rise until it was even taller than Maude was and it took on a vaguely human form. The shape shuddered, sloughing off the snow mixed with the underlying dirt, bark, and pine needles of the forest. An enormous, ugly creature nearly eight feet tall now stood before the group gripping a staff as thick as Maude's arm.

"Perhaps I may be of assistance," Bron said as he shook the last of the snow and detritus from his large body.

"Who are you? Where did you come from?" Maude shouted.

She, like most of the others, was more surprised by the ogre's unexpected arrival than feeling any real threat. The creature was large and obviously powerful, but with three skilled fighters and a dozen elves with longbows trained on its heart, it was unlikely to be much of a danger.

Corana was the first to regain her composure and motioned everyone to lower their weapons. "You are a son of Ellanee, are you not?"

Bron gave the elves a small bow and answered, "I am indeed, sister of the forest. My name is Bron, and I believe we all share a common goal."

"I would never have expected one of your race to be a devout of Ellanee," Corona said.

Bron smiled at the elf. "Despite my appearance, I am only half ogre."

"Yeah, the ugly half," Borik muttered, receiving a hissing rebuke from Maude.

"Druid, you said you may be able to help us?" Corana asked.

"I believe so. You may have noticed the brown needles dotting many of the trees and the decreasing number of animals in the area."

The elves had, but Maude and her crew had not paid any attention to the fact.

Bron continued. "The magical anomaly gathering at the focal point of this confluence absorbs all life. It should be a relatively simple matter for me to find the center by looking for the complete absence of life. There we will find the creature responsible for this."

"Do you know how far?" Maude asked.

"A few days' walk at most. The misdirection spell is stronger the closer we get, but I should be able to reorient by seeking the source of the corruption."

"So this magic is killing everything around it? What is to keep it from killing us?" Maude asked.

"The magic is a subtle leaching of life from the plants and animals and gets stronger the closer we get, but even at its center, I do not think the drain will tax life energies as strong as those that sentient creatures possess very quickly. However, it would be ill-advised to tarry within such an area for long."

"Well, all we need now is a couple unicorns and a dragon to throw in with us and we will officially be the weirdest group ever," Borik said.

"Shut up, Borik" Maude said reflexively.

CHAPTER 18

The voyage seemed to take forever, but when the ship finally arrived at Bakhtaran's port, a fresh wave of dread swept over Ellyssa. On the ship, she was a captive, but soon she would be someone's slave. She had decided to behave herself after Captain Jake's threat, and when she watched the crew unload and herd the other prisoners into cages, she knew she had made the smart choice.

The soon-to-be slaves were all filthy and appeared half-starved. Nearly all had a haunted and defeated look in their eyes, particularly some of the women. Ellyssa shuddered and choked back a sob as she thought of what they may have endured. Captain Jake pushed her toward the gangplank stretching between the ship and the crowded dock. Fear caused her to resist his urging.

"Don't worry, girl, you're not going with them," the ship's captain told her, guessing at her apprehension.

Ellyssa stepped carefully onto the gangplank and crossed over with Captain Jake, who never released his grip from the thick leather belt encircling her waist. Her manacles were clipped to the belt in front while the slaver held a leash attached to an iron ring in the back.

Once beyond the overwhelming stench of the captives, the docks smelled much like those in North Haven. However, once she, Captain Jake, and three of his largest men left the docks behind, that quickly changed. The city was awash with the sights, sounds, and smells of goats, cattle, and some strange animal she had never seen before. A great deal of noise and the scent of strong spices and cooking meat pervaded the streets.

The buildings all seemed to be made of baked clay bricks. Few had windows of glass, most opting for shutters that were thrown open to allow in the breeze. Hawkers shouted at everyone and no one in particular, urging passers-by to purchase their wares. Dogs and children roamed the streets in seemingly equal numbers.

There seemed little logic to those streets either. There were no dedicated avenues until they passed through the poorer neighborhood near the docks and entered a district where painted stucco covered the walls of multi-story homes with fountains and the only green grass visible anywhere inside or outside of the city. These were wide cobbled lanes free of trash, be it discarded rubbish or human. Men and women in bright robes of a thin material casually strolled, rode horses or camels, or were carried upon palanquins down the streets, often surrounded by slave attendants and guards.

Jake led his prize past increasingly opulent mansions until they came to a high brick wall, behind which lay a palace unlike any Ellyssa had ever imagined. The walls were solid white, much like those of North Haven's beautiful castle, but there the similarity ended. Open arches appeared all over the outside leading to balconies ranging from a few square feet to hundreds of feet long. There were more turrets than corners and each was capped not in a conical clay-tiled roof, but with a bulb like a rosebud, which must have been plated in real gold to shine so brilliantly.

Captain Jake must have been known here because they were not stopped until they reached the enormous doors, also covered in a gold veneer. The captain spoke a few words to the guards in a language Ellyssa did not understand and was escorted inside where they were handed off to a pair of interior guards. Ellyssa noted that one of them appeared to be from Valeria, something she saw in several other men and women performing their duties as they strode down the ostentatious marble halls.

The group finally stopped before another set of smaller but much more elaborate doors. The Valerian guard stuck his head inside, said something in the foreign tongue, and then opened the door to permit entrance for the slavers and their captive.

Inside, the opulence of the palace reached its zenith. Marble sheathed every surface and gold inlaid nearly every carving. Enormous glazed planters held trees and plants, many bearing fruit of some kind. At least twenty feet over Ellyssa's head, huge tapestries hung down and constantly wafted back and forth, creating a cooling breeze with the help of a pool and a fountain set in the middle of the floor.

The walkway up to the raised dais created a bridge, splitting the pool in half, where streams of water jetted up into the air on both sides. Women and young boys stood to the sides of the enormous chamber or upon the dais with silver trays laden with fruit, nuts, dates, and pitchers of wine and juice. The boys and young men wore only a short white wrap while the girls wore the same topped with a thin shift.

At least a dozen men and women wore purple and black robes that appeared to be some sort of uniform or symbol of rank. Each of the robed men and women wore a gold choker attached by thin gold chains to matching gold bracelets.

Upon the dais, a large man lay across a lectus, a sort of backless couch, from where he looked down upon his attendants and guests. The man wore gold and white robes and sported black hair and a neatly trimmed beard. He may have once cut a powerful figure, but perhaps the years of luxury had made him edge toward fat. He picked absently at a plate of fruit and sat up as the group approached.

"Captain Jake!" the man cried out enthusiastically. "I see you have made use of my gift to you. Does this mean you have brought me back something wonderful?"

Captain Jake bowed deeply from the waist and replied, "Indeed I have, Vila Mushadan. I found this young magus lost upon the streets of North Haven and thought she would make a great addition to your collection."

"Is she strong?" the vila asked.

"Indeed, Greatness. She killed nearly half a dozen of my men before I was able to subdue her."

"Hmm, so you say, but maybe you say that to get a better price from me." Mushadan turned to one of the purple and black-robed women standing near him. "What do you see?"

The wizard shifted her sight so that she could read Ellyssa's aura. An experienced spellcaster could dampen the effect with a force of will or eliminate it altogether with the right spell, but Ellyssa did not have the ability or know that particular magic.

"She is very strong, Vila. Properly broken and trained, she could be amongst the best of your magi in a few years," the woman responded.

"Do not say such things so loud, Misha. Now Captain Jake knows the girl's value and will desire to make me a pauper!" Vila Mushadan exclaimed with a laugh, obviously not truly concerned with his financial state.

"Forgive me, Greatness."

"So, Captain Jake, now we must decide what she is worth."

The two men began bartering, each defending their bids seemingly as much out of the desire to get the best price as fulfilling a social responsibility. Ellyssa did not know how much a Sumaran golden serpent was worth compared to the Valerian gold crown, but if they were even remotely equal, she could not help but take a small measure of pride in the value these two men placed on her. The captain and the vila finally settled on an almost outrageous sum before another official led the slaver crew away to receive their payment.

"Misha, have the shackles removed," Vila Mushadan commanded once the foreigners left.

The wizard made a slight motion with one hand and one of the lesser mages hastened to obey. The magical shackles opened with a mere touch from the man. Instantly, Ellyssa felt the welcoming touch of the Source return and only her fear and fury kept her from letting out a whoop of joy.

Fingering a few threads plucked from her dress, Ellyssa pulled hard and fast at the Source. Although it took a specific reagent to help shape a spell into the desired effect, almost anything could be used to create the bridge that allowed wizards to access the Source. She also did not have a suitable spell prepared in her mind, but that was not necessary either.

Only spells of a specific effect required repetitious practice to weave safely and properly. Any spellcaster able to access the Source could use the power in its raw form, much as she did in the alley with the shard of pottery, although with significant risks. It was the magical equivalent of the difference between fighting with a rock and a sword forged under the professional hand of a blacksmith.

The ability to wield magic well required three key things: intelligence, creativity, and will. The ability to craft, remember, and reproduce the desired effect of a spell required intelligence and creativity. The raw power of the spell came almost entirely from the will of the caster. It was why her best friend Roger was so much more adept at casting than Ellyssa was. He focused and studied much harder than she did. But when it came to raw power, that innate force of will, she absolutely eclipsed him.

Ellyssa hurled her magic rock at the fat man that thought to make her part of his magical menagerie with all of her considerable might the instant the wizard took off those shackles. Misha and another man in similar robes brought up a magical shield incredibly fast to protect their master. The strength of Ellyssa's attack hit with enough force to make both wizards take an involuntary step backwards and created a thud that was felt by everyone in the room.

The vila surprised her by standing up, laughing, and clapping. "Most excellent! You cost me more than any other slave, but I think I got you cheap!"

Ellyssa dropped to her knees, overburdened by exhaustion and despair. Captain Jake had fed her better than the other slaves on the voyage, but not as much as she was accustomed to. Channeling the Source in its raw form was also far more fatiguing than using the proper reagent and weaving it into a proper spell.

"Misha, it is time to chain our young wizard. I would not want her to try that again. I think perhaps you had best see to her training, personally."

The woman named Misha walked stiffly down the steps of the dais and stood before Ellyssa who was still kneeling from exhaustion. Another figure came forward bearing a cushion upon which rested a solid gold choker and bracelets just as Misha and the other spellcasters wore. Misha spotted the silver chain around Ellyssa's neck and pulled out the silver pendant Azerick had given her.

"This is interesting. Who gave you this, girl? Stand up!" Misha demanded.

Ellyssa swallowed and stood, doing her best to look the woman in the eye and glare defiantly. The woman snapped the chain holding the pendant and studied it.

"What do you have there, Misha?" the vila called down.

"Great One, it seems our little mage is wearing a token with a tracer enchantment."

"How interesting. Do you think we should destroy it, or keep it in hopes of luring another to us?"

"If she is associated with the Academy, it could prove problematic, master," Misha said.

"Quite right. Best destroy it then. If any rescue attempt is not already underway, they are too late to save her now," the vila commanded.

Misha nodded and channeled enough power into the pendant to unravel the ward and then melt the entire charm into a shapeless silver blob. She then clapped the choker and bracelets onto Ellyssa by way of nearly invisible hinges then attached the thin gold chains to each of them.

Ellyssa looked dazedly at the chains and thought she should have little problem snapping them even though they did not restrict her movement in any way. She discovered their true purpose when she tried to reach the Source through her fatigue. Unlike the shackles, she could feel the Source, but her ability to call it to her and form a spell was gone.

"Are you with the Academy?" Misha asked.

Ellyssa remained silent and continued to glare at the wizard. The pendant! If only she had remembered it when the slavers were chasing her in North Haven, but she had been so mad at Azerick she had not listened and had forgotten all about it!

"Enjoy your defiance while you can. Soon it shall be a memory. You will be broken and then I shall train you. I already know you have tried to reach the Source. You cannot unless I allow it. These chains are like the strings of a puppet. You can do nothing except what I direct you to do, just as Vila Mushadan directs us all."

Ellyssa watched the woman slip a gold ring onto her finger and attach another small chain that ran from it to the bracelet she wore. She looked up at the vila on the dais and saw that he wore similar bracelets on both wrists attached to gold rings on each finger by a similar chain. He was the puppet master's puppet master.

"Obey, and you shall live a comfortable life as the highest of His Greatness's slaves. Fail to learn your place and..."

Misha twitched the finger with the ring and chain attached to it and Ellyssa fell to the ground, convulsing in agony as what felt like a thousand needles pierced her body. It felt like the shock spell Roger had used on her once as a prank, only a thousand times stronger.

Ellyssa began to cry. "Please, please don't do that again! I'll behave, I promise."

Misha looked down at the sobbing girl without pity or remorse. "You say it with words but only to avoid more pain. We both know it for the lie it is until you are properly broken." Ellyssa cried out again as the woman sent another round of searing pain shooting through her. "You will call me Chain Mistress. You will speak only when spoken to. You will obey without question or hesitation. You will give your life to the vila. Do you understand?"

Ellyssa's head quivered up and down as she sobbed. "Yes, I understand."

"Apparently you do not."

Another excruciating wave of pain shot through the young girl.

"I understand, Chain Mistress!"

Misha smiled down at the girl. "Not yet, girl, but you are beginning to."

CHAPTER 19

The instant Misha snapped the chain, the golem lying dormant beneath the large tower animated to carry out the instructions of its master. It and the pendant were linked and it knew where it was needed. Well before it reached the end of the long tunnel running from the laboratory and beneath the outer wall, it sensed the charm's destruction. It did not matter. There was another mark, a secret hidden mark, and it knew precisely where it needed to go.

The golem burst through the hidden door and emerged from the ground a hundred yards beyond the northern wall near the base of the mountains. Upon reaching the tree line, it turned south, its long, tireless strides eating up mile after mile.

Wolf cursed bitterly as the rabbit he was about to shoot darted off. He felt the subtle vibration in the ground an instant after the rabbit apparently did and turned toward the source of the disturbance. It was dusk and already dark within the long shadows beneath the canopy of trees. Despite this hindrance, his keen vision picked out the dark form plodding steadily through the forest.

"What is that thing?" the half-elf asked Ghost.

Of course, Ghost did not answer, but his lack of apparent concern told Wolf a great deal. Wolf loped after the strange being and caught up to it in moments. The huge steel construct seemed oblivious to the half-elf and his wolf companion and never altered its pace or direction.

"Hey, you! Where are you going?" Wolf shouted. "Are you the thing that's supposed to go find Ellyssa when she's in trouble?" he asked, remembering what Azerick had said when he had given her the necklace.

The golem did not respond in any way, having no orders to do anything except find the owner of the necklace and defend her with its "life".

Wolf picked up a stick and bounced it off the back of the golem's head. "Hey, I'm talking to you!"

This time he did get the creature's attention. Deciding that the puny flesh creature was attacking it, the golem stopped, turned toward Wolf, and raised the arm that ended in a massive sword.

Wolf held up his hands and backpedaled. "Whoa there, big guy! No need to get upset. I'm just worried about Ellyssa."

Sensing no further hostilities from the small creature, the golem turned back south and resumed its ponderous jog.

"What is that thing?"

Wolf nearly tripped over himself as he spun around to face the voice.

"Dang it, Sandy! You are too big to be sneaking up on people!"

"It's not my fault you weren't paying attention. What is that thing?" she repeated.

"I think it's the thing Azerick was talking about that is supposed to go after Ellyssa if she breaks that necklace he gave her," Wolf explained.

"She has been gone a long time. Should we go tell someone?" Sandy asked.

Wolf thought a moment and replied, "I don't think so. By the time we get back to the school, that thing will be fifty miles from here. Miranda has had half the city looking for her for almost two weeks. Someone will notice a huge metal man missing and can probably follow it with magic. If they can't, they'll need us to follow it and tell them where it ends up."

"All right, but we better catch back up to it. It does not look like it is going to wait for anyone."

Wolf, Sandy, and Ghost broke into a jog and caught up to the construct within minutes and kept pace with it for over two hours before Wolf's considerable stamina began to flag. After following it for half the night, the trio had slowed to the point that they had not caught sight of the golem for more than an hour.

"Sandy, it's no use. I can't keep running like this. You need to let me ride you," Wolf told her in gasping breaths.

Sandy skidded to a halt and looked at the half-elf as if he had grown a second head. "Ride me? Like some common nag? I am a dragon, not a horse to carry some lazy person about because it is convenient!"

Wolf braced his hands on his knees and filled his lungs with air. "I know, but only you and Ghost can keep running forever. I'm too tired, and if it gets too far away even Ghost won't be able to follow it. If that happens, we're going to lose that thing."

Sandy gave in with a curse and allowed Wolf to climb onto her back just in front of her wings and straddle her neck. Wolf was probably her best friend in the world, but even letting him on her back was a powerful blow to her pride. Dragons were not mounts! Unless her other best friend was possibly in mortal danger, then she supposed she could make allowances as long as no one ever talked about it again.

"Heeya, dragon!" Wolf shouted, kicking his heels into Sandy's thick neck.

Sandy twisted her head around, nostrils flaring and eyes narrowed to glare into Wolf's grinning face. "If you ever spur me again, I will find the nearest creek, scrub you clean, and then eat you."

Wolf looked at the peeved dragon sheepishly. "Sorry, I got carried away."

Sandy huffed forcefully then resumed chasing after the golem. Ghost led the way, casting his head back and forth along the trail to keep the construct's scent. It was not terribly hard to follow, as it seemed to keep to a nearly straight line unless the terrain forced it to deviate.

The sun was rising when Sandy realized they were falling behind once again. With the growling of her stomach, it was not hard to figure out why. Even dragons had their limits—especially hungry dragons.

"We have to stop for food," Sandy told Wolf.

"I don't have any food. Can't you go a day without thinking about your stomach?"

"Not when I'm chasing a stupid metal man with a grubby half-elf on my back I can't!" Sandy told him shortly.

Wolf was worried about Ellyssa and did not want to spend the amount of time it would take to track and take down enough game to feed a dragon, but he knew Sandy was right. He slid off the dragon's back with a sigh and started looking around for signs of game. With Ghost's excellent sense of smell, it did not take long.

After nearly an hour of following the tracks left by a small herd of deer, Ghost froze in place, lowered his body to the ground, and perked his wedge-shaped ears forward. Wolf froze and squatted, staring ahead intensely. The half-elf subtly motioned for Sandy to stay put as he and Ghost crept forward and spotted the small herd of deer next to a stream. The buck continually lifted its head from the water in search of predators while the five doe drank.

Wolf slinked silently back to where Sandy was waiting, and mimed six deer and for her to lay in wait here while he and Ghost circled around to the far side. Sandy could move with exceptional stealth for a creature her size, but that skill paled in comparison to the absolute silence of Wolf and Ghost. She was also very fast for short bursts, much like a crocodile. If Wolf spooked the herd and the deer came anywhere near the dragon, a successful kill was all but guaranteed.

Wolf circled the deer from nearly a hundred yards away while Ghost did the same except in the other direction. Even if the animals spooked, being caught between the two predators should flush them toward Sandy. It took Wolf twenty minutes to get to the far side of the herd. He slowly stalked nearer, picking his way through the light underbrush to get a clean shot. His feet seemed to move with a mind of their own, sensing and avoiding any sticks or dry leaves that would alert the nervous animals to his presence.

He stopped when he approached within fifty or sixty yards. Any closer and he risked losing the element of surprise. The buck was already twitching its ears in every direction, sensing that a predator was lurking invisibly nearby. All six deer bolted almost the instant Wolf released his arrow, but for the buck it was already too late. The shaft struck true just behind the animal's left shoulder with enough force to pierce one lung and its heart. It took maybe a dozen bounding leaps before crashing heavily to the forest floor.

Ghost exploded from the cover of the nearby bushes and chased after the fleeing doe, herding them toward Sandy. The deer dashed back along the path until the dragon erupted out of the foliage, uprooting plants and snapping limbs from trees in her haste. The deer broke to their right, but one slipped for just an instant on the loose floor of detritus. That split-second falter was all it took for Sandy to close the few yards separating her and her prey.

She hit the poor animal with the weight of a small horse and the ferocity of a lion. Sinking her long claws into its hide, Sandy pulled the doe to the ground and ended its struggles with a powerful bite to its neck. Ghost padded up and received a hiss of warning from Sandy, for which she promptly apologized.

Lifting the carcass in her jaws, she and Ghost trotted toward the creek where they found Wolf already stringing up his kill by its hind legs using a length of rope and a low tree limb. He used his knife to expertly gut and skin the deer in less than fifteen minutes.

Sandy dug a large fire pit and filled it with fallen branches while Wolf went to work on her kill. In less than an hour, Wolf's buck was roasting on a spit over the flames while he cooked smaller strips of meat from Sandy's kill on makeshift skewers. Wolf and Ghost ate their fill from the doe long before the buck ever finished cooking, but Sandy was far from satisfied. Deciding she had waited long enough, she pulled the entire carcass from the fire, gripped the ends of the spit in both paws, and ate it like a huge piece of corn on the cob.

"I think you have reached a new height in gluttony, Sandy," Wolf said as he watched her bolt down a long strip of flesh.

"I am going through a growth spurt right now, and I need the extra food to have the energy to keep up with that stupid golem," Sandy said pointedly.

"Yeah, you're growing all right. Mostly in the middle," Wolf replied with a grin.

Sandy glared at the half-elf, huffed indignantly, but kept on eating. There were few things, if anything, which could ruin her appetite. When she finally picked off the last strip of meat and sucked out the last bit of marrow from the bones, Sandy tossed away the skewer with a belch.

"So, did you want to start after that metal monster again?" Sandy asked.

Wolf wagged his head as he doodled in the dirt with a stick. "No. We're all tired and it's so far away by now, I don't think it really matters. We'll rest a few hours and then set out first thing in the morning."

Sandy needed no convincing and curled up close enough to the fire to burn almost any other creature. "Sounds good to me."

Morning came with the abruptness of an avalanche. It was on them before they even realized they had fallen asleep. It was far less jolting for Wolf since he had been rising with the sun for years.

"Sandy, wake up."

Sandy grumbled and opened her eyes. The night had turned to a deep blue as the sun approached the eastern horizon.

"Morning already?"

"Yes. I've been thinking."

Sandy groaned, "Great. That phrase always ends in something I don't like."

Wolf ignored her complaining and continued. "We'll never keep up with that thing on foot. It has been maintaining that fast walk for nearly twelve hours while we have sat here. It has probably nearly reached Southport by now, and if it keeps on going south we are going to have to stop to eat and rest again."

Sandy narrowed her eyes, not liking where the conversation was going. "What's your point?"

"We need to fly."

"Unless you suddenly sprout feathers, I don't see that happening."

Wolf amended, "You need to fly."

"Sand dragons do not fly."

"You have wings," Wolf pointed out.

Sandy flexed a wing as she turned and looked at it as if discovering something new. "I do not fly."

"Because you can't or because you won't?"

"Take your pick!"

"Is it because you're too fat to fly?" Wolf needled, knowing that the best way to get the contrary dragon to do something was to poke at her enormous ego.

"I am not fat! Sand dragons are naturally stocky!"

"Do they call you sand dragons because your stomach is nearly *drag-in* in the sand?" Wolf asked as he held his stomach and howled with laughter.

"I am not too fat to fly!"

"Then why won't you?"

"Because I prefer to meet the ground on my own terms. Once one gets in the air, their relationship with the ground becomes rather uncertain!"

"Oh, I see. You're scared."

"I am not scared!"

Wolf waved a hand dismissively. "No, I understand completely. Chickens have wings and they don't fly either. I just didn't realize you were that closely related to a chicken."

"I am not a chicken," Sandy growled slowly.

"Maybe we should call you a chicken dragon. No wait! A sand chicken because all you do is stay on the ground pecking at bugs, or whatever chickens eat," Wolf taunted, then began making clucking noises and moving about like a chicken.

"I am not a chicken!" Sandy roared loud enough to send every bird for a hundred yards flying away in fear.

"Bawk, Bawk, BawwwwK!" Wolf crowed back.

"I'll show you chicken!" Sandy shouted again, then began running.

The dragon took several long strides, leapt as high as she could into the air, and flapped her wings. She made about three full flaps before nosing down hard into the ground, creating a furrow in the dirt with her snout.

Wolf howled with laughter. "You're right! You're not a chicken. Chickens can fly farther and land with much more grace!"

Sandy bellowed in rage, found a steep slope, and charged down its face for extra speed. She poured all of her strength into pumping her wings and felt herself lift off the sloping ground.

"Ha!" she shouted triumphantly just before the ground started rising toward her. "Oh no!"

Sandy struck the ground once again only this time with far more velocity. She nosed down and went into a tumble, all flapping wings and glittering scales, before crashing upside down against a stand of trees. Sandy watched in humiliation as Wolf and Ghost rushed down the hill toward her.

Rolling back onto her feet, she looked at her wing and began shouting. "My wing! I think I broke it!"

"Where? Let me see!" Wolf cried out as he got near.

"No, you stay away from it!"

"Let me see! Maybe I can splint it or something!" Wolf insisted as he grabbed for it.

Sandy lifted the allegedly injured appendage out of his reach. "No! It might be cut and you'll infect it with your filthy hands!"

"It's not cut. Now let me see it, you big faker!" Wolf shouted as he leapt onto her shoulder and grabbed onto the bony edge of the wing.

"Hey! Get off me, you pointy-eared little tick!" Sandy demanded as she tried to shake Wolf off. "You are in my personal space! Now get off me!"

Sandy sent Wolf flying through the air nearly twice as far as her first attempt at flight. Wolf tucked into a roll as he struck the ground and looked at the dragon when he came to a stop.

"I think your wing is all better," he said accusingly.

Sandy looked at her wing then back at Wolf. "I guess it was just twisted a bit. I should still stay off it for at least a few days in case there is some structural weakness I do not yet realize."

"You are such a liar."

"Dragons do not lie! Nor do we take chances where our wings are concerned."

"What if that thing decides to detour to the ocean? How well do you swim?"

Sandy narrowed her eyes. "Sand dragons do not swim."

Wolf grinned evilly and said, "Too fat to swim too? There is an awful lot of things sand dragons don't do. But then I guess with the amount of time involved in eating and sleeping it's pretty hard to diversify your hobbies."

"I am not too fat to swim! Sand dragons are solid muscle and we tend to sink!"

"Uh huh. Whatever you say," Wolf teased.

"At least I have an excuse to avoid water! What's yours?"

"The dirt helps keep bugs away."

"Yeah, well it does a good job of keeping everyone else upwind of you too," Sandy informed him.

"Better suck in your gut, there's a pine cone in the middle of the trail. I wouldn't want you to scratch your belly scales."

"Shut up," Sandy fumed.

"Stop being such a big baby! Ellyssa needs our help and the only way we are going to help her is if you fly us to her! I think you just need a steeper hill. C'mon."

Sandy followed Wolf for about twenty minutes before he found what he was looking for.

"Here it is. This should be perfect for getting you into the air," Wolf declared.

Sandy peered out into the empty space beyond the ground. "This is not a slope, it's a cliff!"

"Even better."

"I'll fall to my death if I jump from this!"

"No, you'll fly or we'll both fall to our death. Now hold still," Wolf ordered as he wrapped his rope around her neck and under her front legs.

Wolf climbed onto Sandy's back once again and pulled the ends of the rope up and around his legs before tying them off. This held his legs tightly against Sandy's back as well as giving him something on which to hold.

"Okay. Get a good run and jump as far as you can when you reach the edge."

"I know how to fly! I don't need some wildling without wings to tell me how to fly!"

"Of course not. You have done such a great job so far," Wolf shot back.

"I know all I need to right up here," Sandy proclaimed, tapping her skull with a claw.

"Yeah, but all this back here is keeping you planted on the ground," Wolf returned, patting her stomach.

"It might be worth letting gravity sort this all out for us just to see you squished," Sandy muttered angrily as she backed away from the ledge.

Sandy took several deep breaths then charged the cliff with a roar of defiance. She coiled her legs and dug her claws into the rock and soil for purchase as she sprang out into open air—and plummeted like a stone.

"Straighten out your wings!" Wolf shouted in terror.

"I'm trying!

Wolf reached back with his hands and pressed down on the wing joints. Sandy's wings locked into place with a satisfying pop of leathery membranes and the two of them shot out across the treetops at a fantastic rate.

"Yahoo!" Wolf cried out ecstatically. "Now, tilt them up and start flapping to get us some lift!"

"Will you stop telling me how to fly?" Sandy demanded, but did so anyway.

Wolf had to hold on as Sandy clumsily beat her wings but managed to put more clearance between them and the ground below. Sandy's egg memories and instincts kicked in and she gained more control with every beat of her enormous leathery wings.

"Can you see Ghost from up here?" Wolf asked as he scanned the distant ground.

"Of course I can. I can practically count the fleas that you probably gave him from here," Sandy called back.

"Who gave whom the fleas is still an open debate, but that's not important right now."

Sandy said, "It looks like he picked up the golem's trail."

The construct had yet to deviate from its southward progression, which made it rather easy to locate. It took over a day, but Sandy and Wolf spotted the golem several hours before Ghost would be able to catch up with it. Sandy was worried they might lose Ghost but Wolf assured her he would return eventually.

Wolf cried out as Sandy banked sharply and began a rapid descent. "What are you doing?"

"Getting something to eat, I'm starving!" Sandy explained.

"After eating nearly two entire deer a day ago?"

"Flying is exhausting work!" Sandy said defensively.

Wolf had no time to pursue the argument as Sandy locked onto a large antelope grazing in an open field. Like an enormous bird of prey, the dragon tucked her wings in, angled her body downward, and dove down with her legs and claws extended. Wolf's belly felt like it was crawling up into his throat before they struck—far too fast. Sandy collided with the antelope and the ground with a bone-jarring impact that propelled Wolf out of his makeshift harness.

He hit with enough force to drive the air from his lungs and prayed there was nothing broken. Wolf shook off his daze and pain and looked around. Just above the tall yellow grass of the plains, he spied Sandy lying in a heap unmoving.

"Sandy! Are you okay?" he shouted, then half-ran half-crawled toward her.

"Ow. Did I get it?"

Wolf staggered over the spot they had struck and looked at the damage. "I'll say. Oh man, you really did a number on that thing."

Sandy pulled herself up and looked over. "Do you think it suffered?"

"I don't think it even knows it's dead yet. Its spirit is still probably trying to munch grass and not understanding why it can't chew it."

Sandy walked over unsteadily and looked at what she had done. "Apparently diving on prey takes some practice. Do you think you can skin it?"

Wolf sighed. "I guess. Half the job is already done."

Sandy had to suffer eating her meal raw since they did not want to take the time to clear a large enough space in the dry grasses to make a fire big enough to cook the entire antelope. Wolf was able to churn up a small area of ground big enough to roast himself a few chunks of meat. He cut up the rest and wrapped them in a large square of soft leather so he could drop them to Ghost.

"It occurs to me that there are no cliffs for me to jump off of," Sandy informed Wolf.

"I guess you'll have to do it the old-fashioned way."

It took several attempts, but with Sandy's recent familiarity and flying practice, she was able to return to the skies. They flew back and found Ghost, who was now only a few miles behind the metal juggernaut. As she swooped down lower to the ground, Wolf dropped the remains of his and Sandy's meal to him.

Wolf leaned forward and wrapped his arms around Sandy's neck as she raced upward, her powerful wings propelling her through the air with each beat.

"Flying might just be the greatest thing in the world ever!" Wolf shouted.

A broad smile crept onto Sandy's scaled face. "Yeah, it is."

CHAPTER 20

Zagrat plodded down the cold, lifeless hall in answer to his master's soundless summons. The shaman had been working tirelessly to create his ragmen army, something in which he had once taken great pride and pleasure. Now, there was simply a cold emptiness that nothing could ever warm or fill.

The lich lord took that pleasure from him when he made him one of his undead minions. He was not entirely without emotion, not like the lesser creatures his master created; nevertheless, the passion, the pleasure, and even the madness that once drove and defined him were but a shadow of their former selves.

"Zagrat," the lich said as his slave entered the vast ritual chamber, "my great plan is nearly complete, but our enemy approaches. Take the ragmen and my minions and destroy them, or at least slow them down."

"You believe I might fail?"

"They are strong, I can feel it, and they have those accursed elves with them. It does not matter. They will be too late to stop me. Even if you fail to stop them, you will weaken them, and then I will deal with them when they arrive—arrive too late to do anything but die. Then they shall become part of my army."

"Yes, Master," Zagrat intoned, leaving Varnath staring into the enormous faceted crystal in the center of the room.

Bron led the party through the snow-shrouded forest using his magic to home in on the greatest absence of life. The disorientation magic that had kept the others from finding the source of the malevolent magic still managed to push him off course, but he recovered his focus and knew they were getting very close.

"Do you have any idea how much farther it is?" Maude asked the druid.

"I believe we should find that which we seek by morning, if we do not stop."

A soft snow had been falling for hours and their breath erupted from their mouths like plumes of smoke. Exposed flesh burned from the cold, and even the parts covered by clothing ached from the bitter air. The sun was setting rapidly, plunging the forest into an orange glow as the last of the waning light reflected off the snow. Bron came to a sudden halt, his body tense, and his senses alert.

"What is it?" Maude asked warily.

"I sense death all around us," the druid replied.

"You think we've reached the source?"

Bron turned his head slowly from side to side. "No, this is different. It is death with intent."

Corana shifted her grip on her bow. "He's right. Something has disturbed the forest here. Something is watching us."

Before Maude could ask what, geysers of snow exploded into the air as dozens of creatures burst from beneath their concealing blanket. Ragmen and creatures long dead rushed headlong at the living, intent on bringing about their deaths and conscripting their corpses into their undead army.

Malek brought out his holy medallion and called forth the purifying light of Solarian. The gold and amber symbol flared with a golden brilliance that chased away both the darkness and the undead anathema, destroying the nearest ones outright.

Corana and her fellow rangers launched their deadly shafts almost as fast as they could pull arrows from the quivers on their backs. Whatever enchantment those arrows held, it reacted violently when they struck a construct. It was almost like touching a flaming brand to a log soaked in lamp oil.

There were far too many of them and they were far too fast for the elves to continue using their bows with impunity. Half of the rangers dropped their bows, pulled swords, and formed a barrier between themselves and the remaining archers. The sword-wielders showed that they were as lethal with blades as they were with bows.

The elves used their swords to intercept the undead and ragmen while those with bows continued to shoot between their comrades engaged in melee. None of them seemed concerned that the gaps through which the archers shot was often barely large enough for the arrow to pass unhindered.

Maude and Borik unlimbered their weapons and formed a defense around Malek as he continued to repel the undead with the magic of his faith. Unfortunately, the holy light that was so repulsive to the undead did little to discourage the ragmen. The big woman and the dwarf soon found themselves hard-pressed under the combined assault of several ragmen until the huge half-ogre stepped into the fray.

Bron brought his thick, bronze-capped staff down upon the back of a rager with the body of a stag and the torso of a barbarian. The sound of the creature's spine shattering echoed through the forest. Another stag-man whipped a massive club at the druid, but Bron ducked the blow and struck back with enough force to double the human torso back upon its stag body, pulverizing its ribs.

Such a blow would have meant instant death to almost any other living creature, but the ragmen were far from natural, and it still managed to make a futile swat with its club at the druid. Bron brought the end of his staff down upon the monstrosity's head, ending its struggles once and for all.

A ragman with the arms of an ice bear slammed into Bron with enough force to knock the big druid to the ground. The rager slashed at Bron with its claw-tipped arms while the druid used his own arms to protect his face, receiving deep gouges in his tough flesh. Bron roared in a rare show of rage, grabbed the creature's wrists in his powerful grip, and rolled, reversing the two foes' position. Now on top, Bron jerked with all his considerable might and tore the arms from the creature like a child pulling the wings off an insect. The rager hissed and spit incoherently, trying to bite the half-ogre until Bron reached down and did the same thing to its head.

No one heard the sharp chanting of the hobgoblin shaman over the din of battle, but his appearance in the fight became apparent. A swarm of magically hardened icicles flew into the mass of living warriors without regard to his monstrous minions. Such piercing damage did little to harm the creatures anyhow, unlike those of normal flesh and blood.

The shaman hurled the shards of ice with enough force to pierce the leather and chain armor of his enemies. Several elves went down and others staggered under the unexpected barrage. What had been an effective defense became precarious as the undead and mutated creatures pressed in.

"Tarth!" Maude shouted as she defended against several foes. "You need to do something about the hobgoblin! We'll take care of these!"

Maude almost groaned in frustration when the elf bent down, scooped up a handful of snow, and casually lobbed the snowball at the hobgoblin. Whether the pitiful attack was by accident or design, Zagrat ignored the idiotic assault as he prepared an even more sinister spell to eliminate these annoying breathers. Then the snowball struck.

Snow cascaded down from the trees as the massive explosion shook loose their frozen shrouds. Zagrat looked up from the crater in which he now found himself, blinking in disbelief as the dislodged snow from the trees threatened to bury him. He stood shakily and climbed out of the bowl in which he stood. Just as he reached the rim of the snow-sided crater, he looked up into the bloodshot eyes of the druid.

"Pitiful druid!" he spat. "Your goddess has no power in this land of death, and soon she and her consort shall have none anywhere!"

"As long as a single plant or animal clings to its right to life, Ellanee shall always be near."

With that declaration, Bron kicked the shaman in the chest, sending him flying back to the bottom of the bowl, cursing Ellanee and her devout. Bron ignored the shaman, reached into a pouch, and flung a handful of seeds down onto the undead hobgoblin. Borrowing from the meager life that remained in the area, Bron fed it into those seeds where they took root in Zagrat's dead flesh and began to grow.

Zagrat screamed despite being beyond the ability to feel true pain as the sprouts grew and took root within him. However, the death pall that hung across the land and within the shaman's body warred with the life Bron fed into those sprouts and they dried and turned brown under the life-leaching effect of the place and its foul magic.

Zagrat's screams turned to laughter. "You see! You cannot stand against my master, and soon all the lands of this kingdom shall be his. Then the entire world!"

Maude's group and the surviving elves finished off the remaining ragmen and undead that had not fled. Maude and Corana stepped up next to Bron and looked down upon the defeated shaman. There was a sudden change in the air and all looked out into the trees as the last few rays of sunshine revealed a wall of fog barreling toward them at an impossible speed.

"What in the abyss is that?" Maude cried in alarm.

Zagrat cackled loudly. "That is your doom! My master's plan is complete! You are too late!"

Bron held an acorn in his upturned palm, gently blew upon it, and watched as it glowed with the cherry glow of a hot ember.

"No battle is ever over as long as there is one who lives to fight," he said, tossing the glowing acorn onto Zagrat's prostrate form.

The desiccated roots and tendrils that sprouted from the shaman's body erupted into flames. Zagrat howled once again and flailed around in the snow trying to smother the flames, but the dead plants burned inside his body and the fire would not die. The hobgoblin finally stilled as the fire continued to consume his corpse.

"What did he mean that his master's plan was complete?" Maude asked. "Did he mean the fog? I don't feel anything, except cold."

Bron studied the pervasive mist. It covered the small valley they were in and he was sure the hills beyond. He could not see much farther than the end of his outstretched staff, but his instincts and magic told him it continued to spread far beyond the northern range.

"I do not know what it portends. Something ominous you can be certain. How fares our band?"

Malek approached and spoke. "I have healed the worst of the injuries. The elves have an ointment that should take care of the lesser wounds. Three of the rangers were beyond my ability to save."

Bron bobbed his head in understanding. "We must press on. I do not know what this fog heralds, but if we do not find and destroy its creator, I fear every soul in the kingdom may be in great jeopardy."

Bron pulled three more of his acorns from a pouch and ignited them with his magic. He then placed one on each of the fallen rangers and let their cleansing fires consume the corpses.

The druid turned to Corana. "I know it is customary to return them to the soil, but I fear the ground here is too tainted. Let the winds carry their ashes to a land teeming with life and the gentle hand of Ellanee."

Corana dipped her head. "You are as kind as you are wise, druid."

The battle between Jarvin's small army and the bishop's superior forces continued to rage on just as it had for the past several days with neither side willing to concede. Their plan to crush Caalendor's cavalry met with remarkable success. A few well-placed illusions brought nearly the entire enemy cavalry charging up the snowy pass only to be buried beneath tons of snow. In the end, over five hundred horses and nearly three times as many men lay entombed beneath the frozen cairn.

After that, Caalendor's clerics did a remarkable job of all but negating Jarvin's magical advantage. The Chosen could not hurl as much in the way of overtly destructive magic as the mages could, but they were quite adept at countering it. The magic they used to stop, deflect, and dissipate the destructive forces used against the men battling on the front lines made Azerick and the other spellcasters feel nearly useless.

That put Jarvin's forces at a significant disadvantage. Only their terrain advantage and the meager defensive bulwarks they had constructed prevented their foes from overrunning their position and forcing a retreat that would quickly become a rout. Although Caalendor suffered a higher body count amongst his own troops, he had the numbers to sustain such losses. Jarvin had already lost nearly a third of his forces, and at least half of those would never rise to fight again.

Azerick, Allister, and Rusty felt the sudden change in the magic flowing through the ether. What had been a slow drift to the north became a torrent that now rushed toward them as if a dam had been holding back all the gathered energy and it had just burst.

All three mages turned to the north and watched as the fog rushed over the tops of the distant mountains and flooded toward them, much like the avalanche they had used to bury Caalendor's soldiers, only it was silent and far larger. Jarvin stood near the mages and turned to see what had caught their attention.

"What in the light is that?" the king asked with his mouth agape.

"Something unpleasant to be certain," Allister grumbled.

The mist washed over them with such speed that several men watching its approach braced themselves and took an involuntary step back, expecting it to hit them with a mass far greater than simple fog. Whatever it was, and despite its speed and thickness, the only physical effect was a sickly chill washing over them.

The battle raging in the pass below nearly came to a standstill. The chaotic shouting of men and the ringing of weapons all but ceased as every warrior on the field stopped and looked at the mist that blasted through the pass and over the mountains beyond. No one could see more than a silhouette beyond a few feet away, and not even that after a few yards.

Men removed from the immediate battle struck torches and lit lamps. Wizards, sorcerer, and clerics conjured brilliant lights to hover overhead. None of it extended the range of vision more than a few extra yards as the fog and light seemed locked in a struggle to destroy each other. All of them waited to see what would happen next, knowing in their hearts that the visual impairment was the least of the cloying fog's effect.

They did not have long to wait. Men fighting near the edge of the battle began shouting in alarm, then in pain and terror. From out of the mist, bodies raised themselves from the snowy ground and began clawing at the soldiers still stunned from the mysterious fog. The nightmare fully revealed itself as all those men and horses buried in the avalanche clawed their way to the surface and threw themselves at the soldiers.

Many of the dead men were still in their saddles as they emerged from the snow and began hacking at the live soldiers with their weapons. Whether the men were previously friend or foe did not matter. Anything that breathed was now the enemy, and they killed without hesitation or remorse. Some were too stunned to move and the undead hewed them down before they could process what was happening. Others tried to run, but there was nowhere to go as the dead littered the battlefield.

Terror gripped the living as they realized the scope of the evil unfolding all around them. Hundreds of wounded men lay in tents, removed from the forward lines of battle. Caalendor may be a usurper, but he and his men still followed the code of battle, both sides allowing the other to collect their dead and wounded. What was meant to be an act of honor and compassion painted the scene for the greatest macabre tragedy yet to come.

The dead lay behind a berm of snow, not a hundred yards from the tents of the wounded. Normally, they would be at least twice as far away and buried. However, the freezing cold made such preparations unnecessary. Now those dead men rose and attacked the nearest and most vulnerable they could find — the wounded.

Azerick heard the screams coming from the medical tents and his blood froze as he gripped his staff tight enough to whiten his knuckles. "Jarvin, get your officers to consolidate the soldiers! We cannot do anything useful right now without killing our own men. Bring the forward line back. I doubt anyone is still interested in killing each other right now. Rusty, Allister, stay by the king and do what you can to keep the undead at bay."

"What are you going to do, boy?" Allister asked nervously.

Azerick turned toward the tents. "I have to help those men."

Jarvin summoned his nearest officers and directed them to pull all of their forces back while Azerick raced up the hill toward the tents. When he arrived, he found two of the tents ablaze. Whether the undead monsters had knocked over a lamp or stove or the men set them on fire intentionally, he did not know. Whatever the reason, it only served to help the wounded men who were desperately fighting for their lives. Those who were able.

Azerick saw some of the worst injured being pulled from tents or back inside by the undead horrors as they tried to crawl away. The ambulatory wounded formed a defense between the two burning tents, hacking at any loathsome creature that came near while trying to protect those who were unable to raise a blade in their own defense.

Scores of undead were converging on the men, mostly from the direction of the dead pit. Several tents were still up between Azerick and the oncoming scourge, but whether or not they still held the living, he did not know, nor did he have the luxury of a choice if they did. This was not a question of how many would live through this scourge. It was a question of any of them surviving at all.

Azerick unleashed hellish flames upon the mass of shambling creatures, incinerating scores of them in an instant. Still they came on. Another massive fireball obliterated as many as a hundred more, but he knew that several times that number still lay within the dead pit and were likely already swarming toward them. Azerick turned toward the sound of his name.

"Lord Giles! Thank Solarian you are here! What can we do?" a soldier asked.

Azerick recognized the man as the officer in charge of the reserve forces. The sorcerer raised a massive curtain of fire practically on top of the leading undead minions. It would not stop them, the passage was too wide, but it would buy them several minutes as the monsters mindlessly searched for a way around.

"Lieutenant, get all these wounded men into wagons and pull them down toward the front line. If you have the room, take with you anything that will burn. Fire and courage will be our greatest defense."

"Yes, sir!"

Azerick turned back toward the dead pits and raised two more flaming walls, extending his fiery barrier to buy the lieutenant and his men more time to take the wounded to safety. He wondered if it would be enough.

The reserve and support units loaded all the wagons they could find with wounded, supplies, and combustibles. There were not enough horses as most had torn the picket line from the ground and fled the instant they got wind of the unnatural creatures stalking toward them. It was left to the healthy soldiers to pull nearly half the large sleighs by hand. Desperation and going downhill provided them all with the necessary means to accomplish their task.

The heart of the battle was bedlam. The fact that so many of the undead had risen in the very midst of the battlefield made it nearly impossible for the men to separate themselves from combat so that they could fall back and form a sound defense.

"How goes it down here?" Azerick asked as he shoved his way through the press of men to reach his friends.

Allister gave the sorcerer a grim look. "It does not look good, son. More of the foul creatures are converging upon us, and every man that falls to them gets back up and we have to put him down again."

"Too bad Caalendor has all the clerics with him. We sure could use some divine intervention on our side," Rusty said bitterly.

Azerick thought a moment. "We have to work together. We need to combine our forces or we are all going to die."

"Good luck with that," Alex quipped. "His people are almost as likely to attack one of ours as one of those monsters."

"Then we will have to convince him," Azerick said resolutely.

Allister raised an eyebrow and looked at the young sorcerer. "You have that look in your eye that says you have an idea."

"I do."

Azerick explained his desperate plan to Allister.

The archmage stroked his beard as he thought. "You know we're shooting blind here."

"I think it is the only way. Once we get him and explain our reasoning, at the very least I think he will agree to a temporary alliance. He is a Chosen of Solarian after all, no matter how misguided his ideas about the legitimacy of Jarvin's reign."

"I hope you're right, son."

Azerick opened a shimmering gate and both men jumped through. They emerged several hundred yards to the south and found scores of men frantically hacking at the tide of unholy creations seeking to spill their blood. Both mages lashed out with their arcane energies at the most hard-pressed groups.

"Break free and flee through the portal!" Azerick shouted at the fighters.

He then opened another rent in the air and jumped through. The two spellcasters repeated the process until they spied the magical lights provided by the clerics. They could not be sure which of the lights belonged to Caalendor, but it was a good guess that it was one near the middle.

No one seemed to notice the two mages who stepped out of the portal right in their midst as they were too intent on driving back the horde of undead, and were largely blinded by the thick vapors. Thanks to the cleric's ability to repulse the monsters, they were able to reduce the number of locations from which the creatures could attack and focus their defenses. However, they also had a greater number of the creatures attacking them due to the numerous casualties they had sustained during the last several days of battle.

It took them only a moment to locate the bishop as he shouted orders to his men and hurled curses at the undead. Azerick casually strolled up behind the cleric and tapped him on the shoulder. Caalendor turned and his eyes narrowed in confusion at the face he did not recognize. Those same eyes went round when Azerick struck him in the gut hard enough to expel every bit of air they held. Before he could fall to the ground, Azerick hoisted him onto his shoulder and turned toward the waiting portal. The bishop was not a small man nor was he anywhere near being thin, but Azerick's demon-enhanced strength had little problem managing the burden.

Unlike their entrance, the assault did not go unnoticed. At least a dozen men and a Chosen advanced upon the two infiltrators. Allister used a strike of raw force and sent the cleric flying backwards while Azerick used the power of his staff to summon a ring of flames to keep the soldiers at bay.

With the gasping priest slung over one shoulder, Azerick and Allister sprinted through the still open gates, slowing just long enough to blast any of the undead monsters that stood between them. The two men with their captive leapt from the last gate and found Jarvin near where they had left him. Azerick carried the bishop over to where the king stood shouting orders, and unceremoniously dropped him to the ground.

Bishop Caalendor struggled to his feet and brushed the snow from his armor. "I should have expected this sort of treachery from you, you and that infernal, soul-damned vampire of yours!"

"You sanctimonious fool!" Jarvin raged back. "Do you not see these things killing my men as well? This is because of you! The Church is supposed to protect us from this sort of thing, but you were too busy worrying about my parentage and failed to do your duty!"

"Lies! You expect me to listen to a man that consorts with the undead? You would gladly slaughter your own men to add to your unholy army!"

Jarvin clenched and unclenched his fists, trying to force a measure of calm upon himself. "I did not know Landrin Bailey's nature until he rescued me and my family from the treachery you set in motion. His actions and character have so far proved significantly more decent and humanitarian than yours have. Listen, Caalendor. What is happening right now is more important than me, you, or our opinions on legitimacy. I do not think any of us will survive this night if we continue to battle each other."

The cleric narrowed his eyes at the exiled king. "What do you have in mind?"

"A temporary alliance. Order your people to fight their way north, my people will battle south, and we will combine our might. My people need your priests to hold the undead at bay. You need my wizards to destroy them."

The bishop's face twisted into a sneer. "I disagree. Those monsters cannot get past my priests, and my men will hack them apart. It may take longer and I may lose more men, but we can prevail. You will be destroyed and I shall be victorious."

Jarvin bit off the scathing reply he was forming when a new outcry sounded all around. Monstrous beasts with the body parts of men and men with the parts of beasts tore into the humans with the same fearlessness and recklessness of the undead, but with far greater fervor. Stag-men leapt completely over the heads of the soldiers and seemed intent upon reaching Jarvin and those near him.

Several of the creatures wielded clubs that they swung about with incredible strength. Blows shattered bones, snapped blades, and sent men flying. Some of the brutes lifted dead or wounded men from their feet and hurled them at the humans or used them as shields or bludgeons against their foes.

Two of the hideous creatures leapt past the thrusting and slashing weapons of Jarvin's men, ignoring the superficial wounds they received in order to strike down the king and spellcasters as their master commanded.

Azerick unleashed his magic at one of the creatures in its human torso at the same instant as Rusty and Allister vented arcane destruction upon the other. The ragman hit by Rusty's flames and Allister's energy strikes died almost instantly, lying in a smoldering heap of twisted limbs and ruined flesh. The monster Azerick attacked dropped to the snow but stubbornly tried to drag itself forward and regain its feet. Alex leapt to the fore, struck off its human head, and ended its struggles.

"What, under the light, are those things?" Bishop Caalendor exclaimed.

"It is the loss of your advantage, Bishop," Azerick replied coldly. "These things are living flesh and blood, and your clerics will be of no more use against them than they would any other mortal creature. We have to join our forces. Do you think this is the only place this is happening?"

"What do you mean?"

"You saw the mist come. You saw it wash over you and you can bet it continued through the pass and over the mountains. How far do you think it went? North Haven, Brelland, Brightridge? It could have traveled all the way to the southern tip of Sumara for all we know, and it is raising these dead everywhere it touches."

"Gods above, could it be?" the priest whispered in fright. "Very well. I will do as you say, but our alliance shall stand only as long as these creatures threaten the realm. There will be a reckoning, Jarvin. You will not sit the throne whilst I draw breath."

"Glad to know we are in agreement," the king responded coldly.

The bishop nodded. "I can commune with my head clergy from here and shall issue the order. I will need only a moment undisturbed."

The bishop bowed his head for several moments then looked up. "It is done. My people are fighting their way here. My colleague told me hundreds of those things struck our lines, targeting those of my order. We lost two Chosen to them before they could effect a new defense."

"Whoever is controlling them knows that your priests pose the greatest obstacle to the undead and likely created these *ragmen*, as a friend of mine called them, to kill them," Azerick surmised.

"Can we stop them all?"

"We have to, or all of Valeria may be lost."

CHAPTER 21

Ellyssa stood in the training pit wearing her black and purple robes just as she had every day for the past two weeks. Misha had furnished her with a spell book and taken her to the training pit to test her abilities and put her through exercises that consisted of launching spells at targets or testing her magical strength against some of the other wizards.

It was not unusual for her training sessions to last twelve hours or more. When she lacked the strength to form even the simplest of spells, Misha would give her a series of mundane tasks. Most of them were mental exercises such as puzzle solving and complex mathematical equations that she said strengthened her mind.

Sometimes she was posed with a series of riddles or simply given orders to complete tedious tasks such as carrying buckets of water across the training pit, emptying them into other buckets, and repeating it for hours on end. Failure to obey or complete any task as quickly as the chain mistress deemed appropriate resulted in excruciating pain.

She hated the thought of being a slave, but it could have been worse. In the beginning, she had resisted any command anyone gave her, but that only resulted in her chain mistress punishing her until she complied. Ellyssa learned that it was far better to swallow her pride and do as she was told. She lived in a nice enough room and ate well when she obeyed. As long as she performed well, her only pain and exhaustion came from the tasks themselves.

She was certain that she only needed to make do until Azerick returned and came to her rescue. Every day, she fantasized about his coming for her. On the days that Misha punished her, he came in blasting holes in the palace walls and struck down Misha and Vila Mushadan. Other times, he simply stepped out of one of his magical gates and whisked her away to the school where she could be with her friends.

Ellyssa missed Roger, Wolf, and Sandy. She knew she aggravated them sometimes, but they were her best friends. She had other friends as well and she missed them all. No one was friends here. The mages rarely talked to each other unless it was about magic, and the other servants and slaves did not talk to the wizards at all unless asked a question or given a command.

Curiosity mingled with dread as Misha strode onto the pit floor pushing a man ahead of her. She cut the cords binding the man's hands together then dropped the knife at his feet.

"What is going on?" Ellyssa asked.

"It is time to raise your training to a new level," Misha replied emotionlessly. "He is going to try to kill you. If he succeeds, he will go free."

"You want me to stop him?"

"I want you to kill him."

Ellyssa had killed before, but that was in defense of her home against soldiers and the slavers trying to capture her. This was different. This was contrived. This man did not want to kill her any more than she wanted to be a prisoner, or so she thought.

"I won't do it!"

"Yes you will. You will kill or you will die. You will do as you are told or you will die."

Ellyssa whipped her head back and forth. "No, you won't let me die. You want me for my power."

Misha folded her arms. "Your power is useless if you will not obey without question and without hesitation. I will break you or I will kill you. You should know that I have never failed to break someone. I was His Greatness's first wizard and I broke nearly all of the others. You will be no different." Misha nodded to the man and the dagger at his feet. "Pick it up and kill her. Succeed and you shall go free and your crimes shall be forgiven."

The man cautiously retrieved the blade from the sand and looked from it to the chain mistress. She gave him a barely perceptible nod and he turned his gaze to the young girl standing a few yards away.

"Sorry, kid," the man said as he advanced on her.

At first, Ellyssa thought the man was apologizing for having to kill an eleven-year-old girl. It took only a moment for her to realize that he was apologizing for her having to kill him. He obviously recognized the robes she wore and knew her to be a wizard. He knew that the vila would sacrifice a hundred commoners like him for the chance to add another mage to his ranks. He likely knew that even a young mage was capable of lethal magic and that Misha would never allow him to kill her even if he got the chance despite what she had said.

As he took several cautious steps toward her, Ellyssa could tell that was not going to keep him from trying. Ellyssa called to the Source and felt the reassurance of its eager reply. She channeled the magic into the air around her just as she had in the alley. A vortex of spinning wind and sand interposed itself between her and the man fighting for his freedom and chance at life—albeit a very small one.

He attempted to shield his nose and eyes from the stinging grit her spell whipped about with enough force to scour away at least a few layers of skin, and sprinted off to the right in hopes of evading the blasting wind and sand. Ellyssa channeled and directed the flow of energy that kept the vortex alive and kept it between herself and her foe. The man tried to bull his way through it, but a shift in the energy sent a gust of wind into him hard enough to knock him to the ground.

"What are you doing, child?" Misha called out. "The more strength you expend in prolonging this battle the weaker you become. Do you want this man, this criminal, to kill you? He has killed others, you know. You avoid killing him out of some misguided sense of morality. Do you think he struggles with that same emotion? I assure you, he does not."

Ellyssa tried to ignore the woman, but she knew she was right. At least the part about wasting her strength. It took far more energy to sustain a spell than it did to call, shape, and release it. This single spell was already fatiguing her, and she knew she could not keep it up much longer. If she held it as long as she could, she would have no strength to cast another. At least, nothing that would kill him.

In that moment, Ellyssa knew Misha had won. She knew she would have to kill this man and it sickened her. She had heard a few bits and pieces of what Azerick had gone through in the hands of the mind reapers, but not until now was she fully able to understand how that had felt, and how it must have affected him.

With tears of anger and sadness in her eyes, Ellyssa dropped the spell. The man sprinted toward her, his knife held low in preparation to strike, but Ellyssa was already channeling the energy for another spell. She raised her hand over and behind her head then flung it forward.

A line of sand formed behind her and launched forward like a whip, but instead of snapping and lashing the man who charged her, it hardened into a long spear of sandstone. The man met the spear at a run at nearly the same instant it solidified and impaled him. The long shaft held him upright as the far end fell and braced against the ground. Then the stone reverted back to sand and he fell face first to the floor.

Misha clapped and crowed with the most enthusiasm Ellyssa had ever seen from the woman. "Well done, child! What an incredibly clever spell. Ordinarily, I would punish you for resisting me, but that was so amusing I think I will simply let you punish yourself with guilt. Do not worry, I will train that annoying trait from you soon enough. I always do."

The chain mistress left Ellyssa alone in her room, the day's training at an end. She wept for what seemed like hours before a servant brought a tray of food to her since she had chosen not to go to dinner. The food was as rich and delectable as always, but what little bit she could force herself to eat tasted like ashes in her mouth. As she picked at a few pieces of fruit and vegetables, the thought of eating meat made her nearly vomit, she thought of Azerick.

She figured he and the army should have reached End's Run at least a week ago. Had the battle already begun? Was it over? Was he already on his way home? It would take about two weeks to return to North Haven. How long would it take him to find out where she was? Would he even be able to since Misha destroyed the pendant? Assuming he could still trace her, it would take nearly three weeks to get here by ship, if he left right away.

Would he bother? She had been nothing but trouble this past year or two. She knew he thought of her much like his own daughter, but Miranda was pregnant now. Soon, he would have a child of his own flesh and blood to worry about. Would he risk himself just for her when he had a real family to care for now?

Of course he would. He loved her. He loved all of them even though he did not like to show it. Maybe he did not know how to show it. Ellyssa could already feel how having to kill someone had affected her. She tried to imagine what it would feel like magnified severalfold. She would have to learn to shut down her emotions, or the pain and sorrow of what she was forced to do would drive her mad. This was what Azerick had worked so hard to protect her and the others from ever having to experience, and she had thrown it back in his face. She had let him down. Maybe it was better if he did not come. Perhaps this was where she belonged.

Self-pity was an exhausting emotion and she finally fell into a sleep filled with nightmares. The gnawing of her belly woke her the next morning, but she found she still had no appetite. She managed to drink a glass of juice and simply waited for Misha to come to get her for the day's training. It was nearly an hour before her chain mistress arrived and took her to the training pit.

"You have skipped two meals. I recommend that you do not allow your despondency to affect your appetite. You will need all the nourishment you can get as your training advances. It is fortunate that today you should not find it nearly as taxing as yesterday."

That was good. Ellyssa had not slept well and had come far short of replacing the energy she had expended killing the prisoner yesterday. It sounded like today was going to be spent practicing forms, or maybe some simple target practice.

Misha deposited her on the pit floor once again then disappeared. Ellyssa's stomach dropped when she emerged a few minutes later with another bound prisoner. She forced the man to his knees then stepped away. This time there was no sign of a knife or any other weapon. She had not even cut the ties binding his wrists.

"We know you will kill to defend yourself. Most anyone will. Now you will learn to kill out of duty. I command you to kill this man."

Ellyssa's mouth gaped open as she tried to form words of protest. This was not a battle, it was an execution. It was pure and simple murder. The difference between defending herself and this was a world apart. This went beyond cruel. It was sadistic, and she knew there would be no coming back. If she did this, she was broken. Misha would have won and she would be lost. Maybe forever.

"No."

"What was that?"

"I said no!" Ellyssa screamed. "I will not murder! You want me to defend the vila, I will. You want me to fight in some battle somewhere, I will. But, I will not murder! Not like this!"

"You still resist. You still disobey. Don't you understand yet? The more you disobey, the more I must punish you and the longer your training will take. You will kill this man today. Tomorrow you will kill another and another until you can do whatever you are told without thought or hesitation."

Misha sent a wave of pain through the link that connected them. Ellyssa instantly fell to the ground, writhing in so much agony that she could not even form a scream. It felt like her blood was on fire and thousands of long needles were piercing her flesh. After what seemed an eternity, the pain stopped and Ellyssa lay gasping for breath upon the ground.

"Kill him."

Ellyssa shook her head in defiance. "Never."

The pain flared once again, and this time Ellyssa did manage a scream. On and on she screamed. She never realized how much air her lungs could hold and for how long she could continue a scream without drawing a breath. Her throat was raw and her lungs burned and demanded air, but still she screamed. When the pain finally stopped, she wept and gasped for breath as her muscles continued to convulse.

The dirt and sand clung to her face, her tears and saliva acting as an adhesive until her body produced more and washed them away. She sobbed so hard that she lost what little food had been in her stomach.

"How long do I have to punish you? How much pain must you endure to assuage your conscience before you kill him? We both know you will kill him. You only force me to hurt you so that when you do, you can feel better about yourself in the end. You can then convince yourself that you had done everything you could to prevent his death. Do you think he cares how you feel about yourself after you kill him? Of course not. So why put yourself through all this nonsense? It serves no purpose."

Ellyssa knew she was right and hated her for it. Hated herself for it. She slowly picked herself up from the ground and stood on shaking legs. She turned and faced the man still on his knees. He began to shake and sob as he beheld the death that stared at him through the young girl's eyes.

"No, please! I have a family. I didn't do anything wrong! Please!"

Ellyssa channeled the Source and raised her hands. "I'm sorry," she whispered.

She could barely call out the words of the spell and form the weave past her own quavering voice and shaking hands. She pulled in her concentration, shut down her emotions as best she could, and struck the man down with a stroke of lightning. The clap of thunder it produced seemed to echo in her ears long after the sound dissipated.

"Very good, child. But you resisted, disobeyed. Worst yet, you apologized." Misha sent a fresh wave of agony through the link. "Never apologize."

Another wizard slave stepped into the pit and whispered something to Misha. Misha ceased Ellyssa's punishment as she listened to the message. The man turned and walked away.

"Stand up and dust yourself off. Something is occurring outside the gates and I wish you to observe with me."

Ellyssa took one last look at the body that lay smoking upon the pit floor. Whatever hope or desire to resist had died with that man in the pit. She did as she was bid and numbly followed the wizard from the pit. Thankfully, Misha sent for a palanquin as Ellyssa was barely able to walk from the pit as they made their way into the city and toward the high wall that surrounded it.

"There it is!" Wolf shouted. "It looks like it's headed to that city."

Sandy twisted her head around and looked at Wolf. "I know. I can see better than you, you know. My tail can see better than you can!"

"Yeah, well it also thinks better than your head!"

"You're pretty mouthy for a creature this high up and does not have wings."

"What's your point?" Wolf demanded.

"My point is that it is a long drop."

"That's a good point. See if you can land behind that dune to the east without killing us."

"Hey! My last few landings were just fine!" Sandy exclaimed.

"I'm not complaining. The deer paste was delicious."

"I crushed one antelope on my first try! Let it go already!"

Sandy veered to the east before they got too close to the city and landed almost gracefully behind a large sand dune. Wolf could just make out the metal behemoth trudging toward the city, certain to gain the attention of the men guarding the walls within the next few minutes. Several people outside the city had already seen the construct and gave it a very wide berth.

"Okay. I seriously doubt they are just going to let that thing stroll into the city. Ghost and I will run up to the gates and duck inside when that thing distracts everyone. I'll find Ellyssa and bring her back here. Can you carry both of us?"

Sandy swung her big head left and right. "No way. I have a hard enough time getting off the ground with just you on my back."

"Hmm. Okay. You carry her to Langdon's Crossing and come back for me. If needs be, you can keep hopping us one at a time back to the school."

"So I basically get to fly to North Haven twice? Hooray for me!" Sandy said sarcastically.

"First of all, you need the exercise. Secondly, it would be like four times. Don't forget, you have to go back each time for the other person as well as fly us both to North Haven. You know, for claiming to be this supersmart dragon, you are really bad at math."

"What would a wild little savage like you know about math?" Sandy demanded to know.

"It's just like our eating contest. You eating fifty pounds of food is like me eating five pounds of food because you weigh ten times more than me! You lost by virtue of our differential mass!"

"That was not the bet! The bet was that I could eat more than you could. Period!"

"It was implied!" Wolf insisted.

"You just cannot let anything go, can you?"

"Sure I can. I let you go and eat yourself round, didn't I?"

"That's it! You think I eat a lot? How about I eat you next?" Sandy said, showing her sharp teeth.

Wolf scoffed, "Yeah, like you would eat someone."

"I have before."

"When have you ever eaten a person?" Wolf demanded to know.

"When those people attacked the school and got into the tower."

"You did not eat anyone, you big liar!"

"I bit a guy and I tasted it so it counts."

Wolf's face twisted in a look of disgust. "How did it taste?"

"It was bad. It was really bad. If any of those stories about dragons eating people are true, I'm almost positive it was to either prove a point or they had lost a bet. There is no way you could acquire a taste for that. People are just gross."

"Okay. I can't let things go, you're fat, and people are gross. None of that gets Ellyssa out. Maybe Ellyssa and I can get a boat in Langdon's Crossing to take us north. Azerick owns like half the ships sailing the ocean. There's bound to be one somewhere close by."

"Fine, but be careful and don't get caught. How are you going to find her anyway?"

Wolf thought for a moment. "I have no idea. Maybe Ghost can get a whiff of her. Besides, she's a wizard. There aren't too many people that could hold her. She might be loose right now running amok in the city. I'm surprised the whole place isn't burned down already. Look at how much damage she causes by accident. Could you imagine what she could do if she was mad?"

"So what do I do?"

"Just hide here in the sand until I get back."

"I can definitely do that," Sandy said, groaning in delight as she sank beneath the sand. "Oh, sand, how I have missed you."

Wolf and Ghost loped across the hot sands until they reached the northeastern corner of the wall. They then kept to the shadow at the base and crept toward the northern gate. Wolf and Ghost reached the gate at almost the same instant as the guards on the inside started pouring out. A dozen men and women thundered out to meet the oncoming juggernaut that was about a half-mile away and closing fast.

Eight horsemen whirled stout ropes over their heads as they approached the golem, hoping to capture the construct intact so that the wizards could study it and possibly gain control over it. It would make a fine prize for His Greatness. The Sumarans were fantastic riders and flung their lassos with a practiced hand.

Two of the corded loops dropped over the golem's thick head, while two captured its right arm and one snagged its left. The others either missed or were fouled by the ones that had landed. The Sumarans tragically underestimated the strength and the speed of the golem. Its movements were neither slow nor ponderous. The golem jerked its right arm inward as the riders backed their horses up to put tension on the ropes. It was a fatal mistake.

The awesome strength of the construct pulled both riders and horses to the ground with contemptuous ease. It lashed out with the arm ending in a massive sword, easily severing the other three ropes. The metal monstrosity charged one of the fallen men and cleaved him in half with a single stroke. Seeing that the construct would not be easily subdued, the wizards launched a flurry of fire, lightning, and strikes of arcane power against it, but the wards Azerick had woven into the creature were strong and it shrugged off the magical attacks with little apparent harm.

The golem charged the other fallen man who was desperately trying to regain his saddle. He had just secured his seating when the golem reached him and swung with a powerful overhand chop. Desperate to avoid the blow, the man leaned back in the saddle while trying to spur his mount into a gallop. He was too slow. By avoiding the blow, the blade whisked by in front of him, narrowly missing his head and cut through saddle, legs, and horse with one fell swipe.

The golem spun toward the wizards and charged with a speed that nearly matched that of the mages' horses for a short distance. Although the horses were slightly faster and able to maintain their speed better than the construct, they would eventually tire and the golem would not. If the mages failed to bring the golem down quickly, it could very well defeat their small party and cause an untold amount of damage before a larger group of wizards could destroy it.

The soldiers loosed arrows at the golem to regain its attention while the wizards spread apart. It was now a game of cat and mouse, cat and mice actually, as the golem chased the harassing humans who used every bit of their skill and luck to avoid the creature's devastating blows.

"Keep it occupied and away from us!" Bheram, one of the mages, shouted to the men as they tried to remain out of reach of the unstoppable killing machine. He then told his fellows, "We must work an unbinding."

The other three mages nodded and began performing the unbinding magic. Azerick's skill and the magic he had used in the golem's construction was formidable. Even working together, the mages struggled to unravel the magical weavings that held the creature together and gave it a semblance of life.

Another guard failed to avoid a charge, and he and his mount fell prey to the merciless and emotionless swinging blade. A loud shrieking of protesting steel rang out across the landscape as the four wizards finally managed to pierce the golem's magical defenses. It shuddered as the wizards pulled at the strands of magic holding it together thread by thread. Another squeal of metal, sounding almost like a cry of pain, rang out as chunks of steel fell to the sand. In another few moments, it was over.

Wolf darted inside the gates, not bothering to watch the battle unfold. It was too far away to see much anyway. He was wondering how he would ever find Ellyssa in a city this crowded and chaotic when he spotted her atop the wall standing next to a woman in matching robes.

"Well, that was easy," he said to Ghost. "Now what?"

As usual, Ghost failed to provide an answer. Wolf doubted he could just walk up and ask for her back. He would need to trail them and rescue her. He decided to watch the pair and follow them to wherever they lived.

It did not take long before Ellyssa and the woman descended the steps connecting the top of the wall with the street below. Wolf watched them both climb into a palanquin, which was then hefted onto the shoulders of four enormous men wearing little more than a wrap around their waists and a huge curved sword.

Their mode of transport made it easy for Wolf and Ghost to follow. Many people gave the odd pair inquisitive looks, but Bakhtaran was a bustling trade city that often brought in all manner of people so no one bothered them. The big wolf's presence also did a fantastic job of keeping away pickpockets and cutpurses.

It was easy for Wolf to keep the palanquin in sight while remaining unobtrusively behind. His worst fears were realized when the conveyance disappeared beyond the walls of the incredibly beautiful palace in the distance. Palaces meant guards and guards meant trouble. Still, Ellyssa was his friend and he had to get her out. First, he needed to get inside.

Wolf scouted around the outside of the substantial wall. The palace grounds occupied a sizable amount of real estate within the city. It was an entire district unto itself. He eventually came upon an aquifer that ran beneath a small arch under the wall. Thick steel bars prevented anyone from simply swimming under. The grate was hinged at the top and a stout crossbar with a formidable lock secured it in place.

The half-elf studied the lock for a moment and pulled out his magnificent black-bladed shortsword. It had cut through the armor of some soldiers as if it were paper; perhaps it would cut through this as well, or at least force the lock open. Wolf slipped the shadowsteel blade between the lock's shackle and the heavy crossbar and slowly began applying pressure to the hilt.

The blade did not slice clean, though, as it had the leather and mail armor, but it did bite deeply. Wolf worked the blade up and down, cutting deeper into both the shackle and the steel crossbar. The shackle was significantly thinner than the crossbar and it gave way first.

Wolf slid the crossbar out of the way, nearly dropping it on his foot as the weight exceeded his ability to manage it. He lifted the heavy grate enough for him and Ghost to slip through into the dark tunnel beyond. It was not very large and there were only a few inches of air between the wall above them and the water.

"Looks like we're swimming. Keep your nose up," he said unnecessarily to Ghost.

The aquifer ran twenty feet under the wall where it continued past another locked steel grate and fed a large fountain within an enormous park or garden. Wolf used his sword to saw through this lock as well, a feat made much more difficult since he had to thrust his arms through the bars and work the makeshift saw from the other side.

That lock soon surrendered to his blade as well, and he and Ghost slipped into the garden and hid amongst the numerous hedges, flower-bearing shrubs, and fruit trees. Wolf decided he had best wait for dark before infiltrating the palace. Evening was not far off, so he plucked several pieces of unusual fruit from a tree, found a soft spot of ground beneath a thick hedge, and took a nap.

A few miles away, Sandy was resting beneath the sands, luxuriating in its warm embrace. She had a sandpit back at the school, but it was not the same. It was a poor substitute for the natural, endless expanse of the sun-heated grains of her homeland. A disturbance made her poke her head up and look toward the city.

She scanned the long wall of the city and the surrounding land but saw nothing more than a few dry shrubs tumbling across the sands, driven by the steady desert wind. Sandy ducked her head back below the surface of the sand and curled back up to go to sleep.

She tried to get back to sleep but something nagged at the back of her mind and would not let her rest. Was Wolf in trouble? Had something gone wrong? No, it was something else. Something closer. The wind. The wind was blowing from the south but the tumbleweeds were coming from the west—the direction of the city.

Sandy thrust her head back above the sand and gasped as the tumbleweeds became six humans wearing purple robes with black sleeves. She darted back below the sand and tried to dig deeper, but some force prevented her from doing so. Despite her efforts to submerge herself further, she felt herself rising to the surface as if lifted by a huge, invisible hand.

When she breached the surface, she felt the hand close tightly around her body. She struggled but was unable to break free. Rising panic sent her blood coursing through her body and pounding in her head. Gathering her draconic power, she called upon the wind and the sand, creating a mighty sandstorm in hopes that it would disrupt the wizards' concentration and binding spell.

The wind answered her call and struck at the wizards and the sand beneath their feet. The savage wind ripped the grains free from gravity's grip and assaulted the wizards with its intensity. However, Sandy had not practiced her inherent magic much and it took only two of the wizards to calm the storm she summoned. The iron grip of magic never relaxed its hold as two of the wizards calmly directed their attention to the magical storm and quelled it with ease.

She lay helpless as she watched a team of horses pulling a large wagon approach. Once the wagon reached them, men used thick ropes to tie down her wings and muzzle her. They then used sturdy chains to secure her legs and the lethal claws tipping each finger and toe.

"I am glad we brought the wagon. There is no way we could carry her back to the palace with our magic," one of the men in robes commented as they magically hoisted her onto the wagon bed.

"She is certainly a fat one," a woman agreed.

Sandy spoke fluent Sumaran and did not appreciate the slander in the least, but the rope tied around her muzzle prevented her from voicing her complaint.

"Even the vila may have a hard time affording to feed this pet!" the first wizard laughed.

Sandy huffed in irritation then let her head slump against the bed of the wagon in despair. This was the second time humans had captured her, and she was certain it was not going to end nearly as well this time.

Ghost nuzzled Wolf awake. Wolf stretched to wakefulness and peered into the early evening gloom. He would rather have waited until the palace was asleep, but that might actually have made it harder. A boy wandering around the halls in the middle of the night with a huge wolf was bound to raise questions. He needed a disguise.

He darted from hedge to hedge, sticking to the shadows as best he could until he finally reached the pristine white palace wall. He and Ghost crept along the outside of the palace until the smell of lye, potash, and soap reached his nose. Following the scent, with Ghost's help, Wolf found a large crofting field practically covered in linens set out to bleach under the sun.

As he suspected, the door near the crofting field led into a washroom where he found hundreds of garments neatly folded and stacked from which to take his pick. Most of the clothing were one-piece white garments that hung from one shoulder and wrapped around the waist. Assuming this was the most common uniform within the palace, Wolf stripped out of his doeskin leather shirt and breeches and spent several minutes figuring out how to wear the strange clothing properly.

Wolf looked down at the piece of clothing and asked Ghost, "Does this look like a really short dress to you?"

Ghost answered the question with his usual cocked-head reply.

"Like you're an expert on cultural fashion," Wolf snapped back. "Your idea of proper dress is deciding what dead animal to roll in, given a particular function."

The laundry room was not far from one of the kitchens, but Wolf, in a rare show of self-control, decided it was more important to find Ellyssa than stopping for a bite to eat. The pair slinked down one marble hallway after another with no clear idea of where to go. The palace was easily twice as large as the castle in North Haven, and it was not as though he could simply shout out Ellyssa's name hoping she answered.

He was almost at the point of deciding to try exactly that when he rounded a corner and ran into a young man in a guard's uniform. Wolf took a step back and reached for the sword belted around his odd, single-sleeved tunic. The man said something in a language Wolf did not understand then repeated it in Valerian.

"Who are you?"

Wolf swallowed visibly and replied, "Wo-Nanarin."

"You are Valerian?" he asked.

Wolf bobbed his head up and down nervously.

"Why are you in the halls, and with a rather large dog?"

"Um, I was told to patrol the halls with Ghost. He is really good at sniffing out trouble."

"He is very unusual looking."

Wolf forced a smile. "Yeah, but don't tell him that. He's very sensitive about his looks."

The guard nodded thoughtfully. "I've never seen you before. Even if I forgot your face, the animal is less easily forgotten."

"We're new. We were both picked up in North Haven. This is the first time we have walked our rounds. Did I do something wrong? Please don't tell on me!"

The guard tapped his chin as he thought. "I suppose not. Carry on then."

Wolf gave an approximation of a salute and hurried away, not letting out the breath he was holding until he was well beyond the next hallway. He leaned against the wall breathing heavily for several minutes until his heart resumed its normal rhythm. Wiping the sweat from his brow, Wolf and Ghost continued their exploration.

His search was proving to be a lesson in frustration. He had not expected to have to comb literally miles of passageways and search hundreds of rooms to find his friend. Ghost went on alert and filled the hallway with a rumbling growl. Wolf sought out a place to hide but groups of people appeared at the ends of the only three directions of escape available.

Four guards stood at the end of each of the passageways with bows and blades drawn. One of the groups had a man wearing the same purple and black robes Wolf had seen Ellyssa wearing. He looked disdainfully down his beak-like nose at the boy and his wolf.

"Take the boy alive. Kill the dog."

Wolf's eyes darted back and forth between Ghost and the guards. "What? No!"

The guards released their bowstrings with a thrum that cut through Wolf's soul. He could practically watch the arrows as they flew toward Ghost. He tried to shout for his friend to run, but even as slow as the arrows appeared to be going, there simply was not enough time.

Ghost yelped and thrashed on the marble floor when the arrows pierced his body. Wolf threw himself onto Ghost, hoping to shield his friend's body with his own, but the damage had already been done. Ghost lay in an expanding pool of his own blood, panting and whimpering for only a few seconds before going silent and still. Wolf unsuccessfully fought back tears as his heart pounded in his chest and his stomach heaved as several guards advanced to pull him off the dead animal and take him prisoner. They paid for disturbing his grief with their lives.

Wolf felt the first man grab him by the upper arm and tug him upward. He sprang to his feet with a savage snarl, ripped the blade from its scabbard, and slashed the man across his middle inflicting a wound so deep it nearly reached his spine. The anguished young man launched himself at the next guard who pulled his sword and tried to intercept the wild swing. Wolf's magical blade cut cleanly through the plain steel and continued on to shear through flesh, bone, and the organs beneath.

There was no attempt at style in Wolf's swordplay. Rage and sorrow directed the blade and pushed him into a near berserker's fury. He wanted to kill the man in the robes and no one was going to get in his way. He looked into the eyes of the guard he had talked to earlier as he sprinted toward the robed figure.

A force like being struck in the chest by a battering ram slammed him backwards and to the floor, pinning him there as if someone had dropped a horse on him. The impact sent the sword flying from his hand and blasted the air from his lungs. He could not even draw breath much less continue the fight.

The familiar guard approached and tied Wolf's hands together with a length of leather.

"Sorry, kid." He looked at a group of fellow guardsmen as he slung Wolf over his shoulder. "Take the carcass out, throw it on the trash heap, and get a servant to clean up the mess."

One of the men grinned and said, "Might make an interesting rug."

Bran let out a weary breath. "Just take it outside. We are not savages."

The guards not tasked with clean-up duty fell in with Bran and the mage as they made their way to the grand audience hall. Bran did not set Wolf down until they reached the foot of the dais and knelt next to the wizard.

"Greatness, we found this boy wandering the halls with a large dog. I believe he was the one we spied upon the back of the dragon," the wizard informed the vila.

"Have we secured the dragon yet?" Mushadan asked.

Misha stood next to the vila's right and answered. "Yes, Greatness, we secured it in one of the training pits just a few moments ago."

Vila Mushadan smiled and clapped once. "Wonderful! Fit her for a collar and give her to the beast master for breaking. We already have the dragon, so why bring me the boy alive?"

The wizard standing next to Wolf pulled back his long black hair and displayed his pointed ears. "I thought you might find him interesting, Eminence."

"Is he an elf?" the vila asked excitedly.

"Half, I believe, but still quite an addition to your collection, Greatness. He was carrying this," the wizard informed the vila, presenting him with the sword.

Mushadan took the weapon, pulled it from the sheath, and examined the blade with great interest.

"Such a wonderful day it is to have gifts brought to me on golden wings. It is as if the gods themselves recognize my importance and reward me. Is it elven, Misha?"

The archmage examined the sword closely. "I do not believe so, Great One. Elves work almost exclusively with arcanum. That is shadowsteel. Dwarves work with both metals, but I do not believe it is their work either, but likely one of the other subterranean races."

"You, boy, where did you get this?" the vila demanded of Wolf.

Wolf looked up defiantly and said, "From the man who's going to kill you."

"Ah, you must be referring to the master of my newest wizard. I look forward to meeting him. I shall have to ensure I am properly prepared to greet him."

"Prepare all you want, fat man. When Azerick finishes mopping up Valeria's army, he is going to kill every one of you."

Andrea, standing nearby holding a pitcher of the vila's finest wine, nearly dropped the carafe when she heard the name of her childhood friend. Could the half-elf be talking about the same person? Azerick had always been determined and resourceful. Could he really have come into such power as to threaten the vila? Even Sumara's king treaded lightly around Mushadan. She would have to speak with the half-elf and talk to Bran.

"Dorran," Mushadan said to the wizard who had brought him the half-elf, "such insolence cannot be tolerated. I will have him as my cupbearer. Take him below and break him. Bring a healer to make him well, and then break him again."

"No!" Ellyssa shouted.

With a twitch of the vila's finger, her shouted protest became cries of agony. Her chain mistress joined her in her pain an instant later.

"You know why I punish you, Misha?"

"I failed to break her, Greatness."

"Work harder, Misha. It is unseemly to have to punish my favorite in front of everyone like this."

"Yes, Eminence. I will redouble my efforts," Misha promised.

Ellyssa sobbed, more for what was going to happen to Wolf and Sandy than the pain Misha promised to inflict upon her. Her friends were going to suffer horribly all because of her. As she watched Wolf being taken away, she wondered where Ghost was.

The two guards struggled to carry the nearly two-hundred-pound wolf outside where they casually flung it onto the midden heap located well behind one of the kitchens. The two complained about having to clean the blood from their uniforms as they retreated into the palace to resume their posts.

Several minutes later, the arrows that the soldiers had not bothered to remove began to twitch and slowly withdrew from the animal as if being pulled out by an unseen hand. One by one, the arrows fell onto the trash heap. Ghost filled his lungs with air then began contorting his body. Within moments, a boy only a couple of years younger than Wolf stood upon unsteady legs, as naked as a newborn.

Ghost looked up into the starry night sky. "Oh, Wolf, what have you gotten us into now?"

CHAPTER 22

The fog stormed across all of Valeria as if pushed onward by a hurricane of unimaginable power. The strange, cloying mist reached Southport and beyond less than three hours after its birth over a thousand miles to the north. Guards and watchmen lit torches along the walls and throughout the city streets, smaller towns closed gates if they had them, and citizens locked their doors. Some of the more predatory amongst them thought it a perfect opportunity to cause mayhem. They were the first to witness the horrors the fog brought with it.

Less than an hour after the fog's appearance, in many cases within minutes, almost every city, town, and hamlet came under the assault of nearly everything that had ever died and was buried in the ground or entombed within crypts. Anything dead that retained a physical body crawled from the earth or clawed its way out of its tomb with a mindless determination to extinguish all life.

The truly horrific nightmares were the shades. Although thankfully far fewer in number, nothing short of a wizard or cleric could hope to combat them. The town's Watch and average citizen were powerless to stop them from absorbing the very life from their victims. No doors or locks could keep them away as they drifted through the towns and cities, leaving a trail of desiccated corpses in their wake.

In towns and cities large enough to have walls, the dead piled against their base and climbed up the backs of their brethren to reach the living who were often fighting off those that clambered from the graveyards and crypts inside.

Brother Thomas was asleep in his room within the church inside the orphans' academy when the mist rolled in. A sudden sense of dread roused him from his slumber. He threw his robes on over his nightclothes, draped his holy pendant around his neck, and hurried to where his three young Chosen shared a room. Solarian had spoken to him nearly three weeks ago, warning him of an impending peril, and he could not shake the feeling that the dire time had now come upon them.

"Children, wake up," he gently called to them.

All three children awoke and rubbed the sleep from their eyes.

"What is it, Brother Thomas?" Shawna, a girl of ten asked.

"Ill tidings, I fear. Dress quickly and prepare yourselves. For what, I am not yet certain, but I suspect an otherworldly foulness is upon us. There is a taint of powerful necromantic magic in the air. I know you are all young, but your faith is strong and this is our purpose. We must all be resolute and not give in to fear."

All three youngsters nodded and grabbed clothes from their wardrobes. Thomas left them, feeling an urgent need to rouse the school. He needed to wake Aggie and the other wizards. Whatever was coming, they would need their formidable power.

It was impossible not to notice the unnaturalness to the thick fog that blinded him the moment he stepped into its cloying embrace. He lost the church and nearly his sense of direction after only a few steps. Even the magical light he conjured did little to illuminate his path. It was as if the light and fog were doing battle and the fog was the stronger of the two.

He had just reached the foot of the steps leading into the old tower, finding it mostly by memorization, when the first deathly scream pierced the fog. The mist was possessed of such tangible density that it even muffled sound. He knew the cry had come from someone walking the top of the wall, but it sounded as if it had come from behind a closed door.

"Alarm!" Thomas shouted at the top of his lungs.

A bell began ringing then abruptly went silent. A short cry that made Thomas's heart lurch punctuated the sudden silence. He raced up the steps and burst into the main floor of the tower shouting an alarm. He ran back out the door as he called upon Solarian's protection. The alarm bell rang once again, and he could hear the entire school stirring and preparing for battle.

Thomas ran for the wall, narrowly avoiding obstacles, from wagons to entire buildings that appeared abruptly out of the gloom. All but blinded by the fog, he followed the screams until he reached the wall. The school walls were only fifteen feet high, and already dozens of zombies and skeletons had gained the top. In a few more minutes, that would change to scores and then hundreds.

The martial students were the first to react. Trained to be combat-ready in minutes, young men, women, and their drill instructors raced to the top of the wall, their feet easily finding the path that hid from their eyes. Dozens of students brandished forked poles, normally used to push over siege ladders, and used them to shove the undead off the wall.

The cleric poured his faith into his light and called upon Solarian's radiance to cast out the undead monsters. Once again, his light warred with the fog, but this time it was the fog that found itself on the losing end. Enhanced with the power of his faith, his light pushed the miasma away for several yards in every direction. Whenever the luminescence touched skeletons, zombies, and wraiths, it returned them to a natural state of death or fled.

Fear coursed through his body, pushed along by his thundering heart as he realized that his abilities were far from sufficient to deal with a threat of this magnitude. The undead avoided his light and dispersed, creating a pocket of relative peace amidst the chaos, but there were hundreds of yards of wall still vulnerable to assault.

Thomas ran back and forth along the wall, holding his luminous medallion high over his head to force back the unending tide of undead trying to sweep over the walls. The presence of his faith repulsed the horde and gave the defenders a moment of respite, but he could not be everywhere as the shouts and screams heartbreakingly reminded him.

A massive explosion rocked the school grounds and a fiery orange glow flared somewhere out in the thick vapors. More blasts and streaks of brilliant light flashed within the mist. Thomas breathed a sigh of relief as the wizards and magus students took the field. Expansive sheets of fire erupted along the base of the wall, clearing away the massed horde of abominations trying to clamber up the side.

Brother Thomas ran down the steps and tried to pierce the mist inside the wall in hopes of finding his young Chosen. He thought his efforts would surely be in vain, but then he spotted three bright patches within the fog that soon became an island of hope within a sea of despair. Over the muffled sounds of battle, he heard their voices, all three singing in perfect harmony a song so warm and full of life that it forced the fog to retreat wherever it reached.

He could see them clearly now, a look of resolute tranquility etched upon their small faces as they walked in an almost hypnotic state, lost in the soulfulness of their song. They then split up, walking to separate sections of the wall, clearing away the miasma with the sound of their voices as if taking a broom to an infestation of cobwebs.

Thomas knew then they would be all right, that they could ride out this unnatural storm. He cast his eyes in the direction of North Haven and prayed that they were not the only ones to do so. He wondered where so many corpses had come from then realized that the hundreds of creatures attacking the school had come from the bodies of the soldiers they had buried after the siege. He shuddered knowing that thousands more had lain in mass graves near to the city, a city that had hundreds of years of history to add to this scourge. All he could do was pray for them all.

Hundreds of miles to the north, the barely settled town of End's Run kept a wary eye toward the battle that raged uncomfortably close to the south. The town had no standing army and the nearest thing to a city watch was the recently created enforcer unit commanded by an unpleasant man named Donnigan.

Unable to find sleep that night, Donnigan was walking the catwalk along the inside of the wooden palisade when the fog crashed down upon the rough town, finding itself the first victims of the lich's depraved plan. It was so dense that the town instantly vanished within its thick haze. Even the torches burning in sconces appeared as little more than an orange glow from more than a few feet away. Donnigan stopped walking, cast an ear outward toward the thick forest beyond the wall, and gripped his weapon tightly.

"Donnigan?" a questioning whisper came from out of the gloom.

"Yeah," he replied without turning his head.

"What in the abyss is going on?"

The enforcer commander shook his head, a useless gesture given the lack of visibility. "Damned if I know. Go wake the men."

"On it."

Donnigan had never been a man comfortable with taking orders, but he prayed for some now. Whatever this was and whatever was happening was far beyond his ken. He wished Lord Bailey was here to tell him what to do, but he had not seen nor heard the laird of End's Run for nearly two days. Landrin seemed to have left everyone to their own devices shortly after that army from North Haven had shown up.

"Light every torch we have and get some fires going where they won't set anything else aflame," he shouted, hoping his men could hear him even though there was no way for them to see him. "I want this place lit up bright enough that the gods above will think we set fire to the whole kingdom!"

He could hear men running about, shouting to each other as they hastened to follow his orders. That was when he spotted the first undead creatures to reach the top of the wooden wall. Despite their numbers, the undead moved with an eerie silence. Donnigan turned and stared directly into the face of one of the men he remembered hanging a few weeks ago on Lord Bailey's order.

His sword leapt from its scabbard and intercepted the arm that came at him in a clumsy but powerful swing. His steel easily severed the limb at the elbow and his backswing liberated the creature's head from its body. Through the fog nearest the torches, he saw more silhouetted forms clambering over the wall and onto the catwalk with the same disturbing silence and malevolent intent.

"Rouse the town!" Donnigan shouted. A man repeated his order by ringing a brass alarm bell.

The bell, while calling the townsmen to arms, also seemed to be the signal for the undead to attack. The men on the walls futilely engaged the vastly more numerous undead, but the horde pushed them from the walls and into the town. Some townsfolk chose to lock their doors, but most men and women poured from their houses with torches and weapons in their hands.

Undead and their living foes battled within the streets, between buildings, and inside the homes. Hundreds, then thousands, of feet churned the already muddy snow into a freezing bog littered with bodies and stained with blood.

The battle for End's Run and the people's very survival raged for hours. Numerous homes and buildings now burned either due to an errant torch, or they were intentionally set aflame to cast light upon the scourge of undead that flowed over the walls and into the town.

The people of End's Run were survivors and developed tactics for dealing with the monsters. One or two people engaged a creature while another speared it in the back and shoved it into the flames of a burning building, wagon, or pile of debris. Still it was not enough. Every man or woman who fell to one of the undead became one as well, and the living were continually being pushed back toward the center of town from all sides.

Donnigan was certain they were all doomed. There were simply too many of them and they replenished their numbers too quickly. Then the howling began. It sounded from several locations outside of the town, but was then picked up by dozens more of its kind. Soon, hundreds of shrill voices answered the call. Dark four-legged shapes began flitting in and out of the pools of light cast by the burning structures, tearing into the pressing mass of undead with a ferocious fervor. Donnigan paused in his hacking, scarcely believing what he saw. Wolves. Hundreds of wolves had come to the rescue of End's Run.

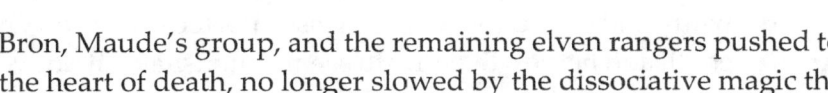

Bron, Maude's group, and the remaining elven rangers pushed toward the heart of death, no longer slowed by the dissociative magic that had previously impeded their progress. No one knew what effect the gathering energy had caused, but it apparently took the spell with it when it was released.

They did not proceed unimpeded, but they easily dispatched the small bands of undead and ragmen that hurled themselves at the party. When they reached what they sought, it was like stepping inside a bubble. The fog ended abruptly and created seemingly solid walls inside of a great sphere of clarity. Ahead of them loomed an ancient fortress, partially carved into the near-black granite of the impossibly high Great Barrier Mountains.

The already frigid air took on a coldness that reached far deeper than their flesh and sapped more than just their body heat. It seemed to suck out every bit of hope or joy and wrapped them in despair.

A few ragmen and lesser undead prowled the grounds and entrances, but the deep clefts and shadows could hide an untold number of horrors—horrors that were likely only to get worse once they delved inside.

"Any chance of sneaking past 'em?" Borik asked in a hushed voice.

"Unlikely," Bron replied, "but it is very unlikely our presence is unknown to the master of this evil place."

"Are you saying we should simply bash our way in and forget stealth?" Maude asked.

"Speed is likely paramount at this point. The time for subtlety is long past."

Maude smiled. "Good."

Getting into the ancient fortress was easy. The ragmen fell instantly to the rangers' arrows and the few undead were lesser abominations that were all but obliterated by Malek's holy rebuke. Finding the lich was going to prove far more difficult. The citadel was enormous inside and covered an area far greater than the outside face had hinted at. To make matters worse, rubble blocked numerous passages and forced the group to backtrack several times.

Neither was the structure abandoned. Abominations of every form leapt from side passages, alcoves, and high ceilings. The individual battles were swiftly ended, but the unending assaults took their toll on the party's strength and nerves. Even Tarth seemed unusually attentive and on edge.

Cobwebs shrouded every corner and doorway, and the bones of animals littered the floors. Dust covered everything in a thick film. Not a single square inch of the citadel had avoided the ravages of time or death.

They found a winding staircase leading upwards toward the top of what constituted the central tower. Since the way down had caved in centuries ago and choked the passage with rubble, the group decided to go up. Upon reaching the top, they found a wide hall continuing deeper into the mountain, much like many of the lower passages and chambers did.

Several rooms branched off from the main hall like leaves on a tree limb. The wooden doors had disintegrated long ago and it took only seconds to see that the rooms were unoccupied. Deep inside the mountain, the hallway ended at a set of bronze doors. They were not terribly ornate nor were they inscribed or adorned with runes or horrific pictures. They did appear to be very sturdy, however.

"What do you think? Blast 'em down?" Borik asked.

"Let's try the handle first," Maude answered.

Maude grabbed the large brass ring set in the door and heaved. The portal swung ponderously outward enough for the party to slip inside. The chamber beyond was enormous. Even Borik and the elves' keen vision could barely make out the far side of the room. The ceiling was nearly lost in shadow.

In the center of the room was a colossal black gem resting on a plinth of obsidian. The onyx jewel was cut into at least a hundred facets, each the size of a small dinner plate. Nightmarish scenes of slaughter unfolded upon each of the facets, played out as though the viewer were right there as it happened. Standing over and nearly hidden behind the gem, gleefully watching the carnage, was a hideous, desiccated creature wearing the rotted garments in which it likely had been buried or entombed.

Varnath looked up and turned his repulsive visage to the intruders who were even now spreading out and readying their attack. "Ah, the heroes have finally arrived. I have enjoyed watching your progress, although not nearly as much as watching my creations slaughter the useless inhabitants of this kingdom. I particularly found Zagrat's destruction highly entertaining. He did tax my patience no end. I had thought that by making him into one of my minions I would find him tolerable. Alas, I was wrong, but he did become far more productive."

Maude shifted her grip on the big two-handed sword she held at the ready. "Stop this madness, monster, and you shall receive a swift death. Your reign of terror ends here!"

Varnath waved a skeletal hand dismissively. "Nonsense. You jumped-up, self-important, would-be heroes and your grand declarations. You read too many stories and listen to too many epic ballads. Valeria will fall in days, and from there I will regroup and do the same to Sumara. First, I shall make you all part of my legion. Elves tend to make rather difficult subjects. Their attachment to nature generally makes them unsuitable for reanimation, but I do so enjoy a challenge. Well, I suppose we must do battle. Unless you wish to surrender. It will be much less painful for you. No? Very well, the pain is the most enjoyable for me anyhow."

The undead lord did not even twitch, but a signal had been sent and inky black shapes slid from the walls and dropped from the ceiling. There were four of the things, each monstrous in appearance, and they looked to be made from shadow, only thicker and more substantial. They glistened with an oily sheen and moved without a sound.

Arrows leapt from the elves' bows. The creatures were not made of the same thing as the ragmen and the enchanted arrows did not destroy them, but they did bite into whatever it was they were made of. The wounds hissed and popped but did not slow them down.

One of the black forms reared up like an enormous bear and swiped at an elf with something that looked more like a tentacle than a paw. The elf leapt backwards with astounding grace while setting another arrow onto his bowstring. Instead of the swing falling short, the tentacle-like arm elongated and struck the elf in the side of the head. The blow sent the ranger tumbling sideways, causing him to lose his bow, and raised a raw, blistering wound across the left side of his face.

Another of the creatures lengthened into something serpentine, and struck like a snake, wrapping around another ranger. She let out a horrible scream as the constricting body of the creature crushed her ribs and its sickly black flesh slowly ate through her armor and skin.

Malek chanted a prayer to imbue a blessing onto the weapons of his allies before brandishing his holy symbol in one hand and his war hammer in the other. A cacophonous boom rocked the chamber as Tarth struck out at one of the creatures with his magic, slamming it with a ball of fire the size of a horse-drawn coach. The inky-black monstrosity sailed across the chamber and slammed against the far wall with a meaty slap.

Maude and Borik turned their attention to the other creatures battling furiously against the elves who were landing solid strikes that at first seemed to do little harm. They continued to hack at one of the creatures until they had apparently inflicted enough damage to catch the thing's attention.

The head of the monster reared up, towering above Maude and the dwarf. Tentacles sprouted from its upper body and slapped at the two fighters. Maude's sword cut deeply, even severing the end of one of the questing limbs as she parried, but that was just a distraction. The other end of the creature spread out around and behind the woman and dwarf. Like a cat flicking its tail, it struck Borik in the side and flung him across the floor. It then wrapped itself around Maude and lifted her into the air.

Maude could hear steel armor protesting and smelled the acidic flesh eating it away as the creature tried to crush her like a tin can. Arrows leapt from the rangers' bows and pierced the monster's hide in half a dozen spots. Malek raised his amulet and a brilliant golden beam shot across the room and seared into the creature's side. It writhed in soundless agony as Malek continued to pour energy into that holy ray of intense light. The fiend flung Maude aside as her eyes watered and her lungs burned from the black, oily smoke that poured off the creature as the ray continued to burn deeper and deeper.

As his creature gave one last shudder before lying still, Varnath realized he needed to take a more active approach. He had thought the cleric was the immediate threat until the power of that unusual elf once again rocked the chamber. He had dismissed the wizard when they had first arrived. Like any magic user of skill, Varnath had looked upon the invisible aura that surrounded all practitioners of magic.

Wizards typically carried a silvery glow showing their affinity with the Source. That color could change depending on the types of magic the caster associated himself with. But when he had looked at the elf, it was like looking into a kaleidoscope of chaotic colors, all shifting and seemingly at war with one another. It was the aura of a complete madman.

Varnath floated to the upper reaches of the dark dome and wove a tangle of black magic. He thrust his cadaverous hand toward the elf, sending out a dozen black tendrils and jerked back as if hooking a fish as they wrapped around Tarth's lean form. The black strands did not retract as Varnath reeled the wizard up into the shadows. They continued to twist around Tarth's body until they completely covered him in a kind of onyx cocoon.

"I shall enjoy dealing with you later," the lich hissed at Tarth as he left him bound and stuck to the ceiling.

Varnath floated down just behind Malek, ready to strike the cleric in the back with an ancient dagger sporting a long, thin, curved blade. Malek sensed the closeness of the evil entity and threw himself forward in a roll, just narrowly missing being skewered. He instantly came to his feet, brandished his holy medallion, and poured every ounce of his faith into it.

Varnath hissed and reeled back, as much from pain as disgust at the radiant light that washed over him. Drawing upon his vile necromantic power, he conjured forth and cloaked himself in pure darkness. Light and dark warred with each other, each struggling to consume the other.

The lich took a step forward, forcing Malek to take a step back as the darkness pressed closer. Varnath continued to approach inch by inch, sending out strands of ebony energy questing for a way past, through, or around the opposing light to reach the human hiding within its luminescence.

Malek felt his back touch a solid surface and could retreat no further. He cast his head left and right, seeking a way to put distance between himself and the evil defiler. In that moment of desperation, Varnath closed the space between them, and Malek looked straight into the glowing red orbs that served as the lich's eyes.

Both opponents could feel the pressure between the two conflicting powers like pushing together the matching poles of two incredibly strong magnets. Malek brought his hammer up in hopes of breaking the stalemate but Varnath was faster. Malek felt the thin knife cut through his armor and pierce his body just below his ribs. The cleric felt himself dying, but not just from the stab wound. He felt the ancient blade sucking out his very life force, his soul, and feeding it to the lich.

Varnath's putrefied mouth turned up in a triumphant grin, and he relished the feeling of the cleric's life energy flowing into him. Out of the hundreds, thousands, of sacrifices he had made, this was the most exhilarating he had every beheld. The world began to dim around

Malek's eyes and he tried one last desperate attempt to stave off his own death as the light of his amulet waned.

A body moving so fast it was nearly a blur struck the lich from the side, launching Varnath halfway across the room. Landrin took a brief second to watch the cleric fall to the floor and cast one last look into Malek's eyes that now stared lifelessly up at the murky dome of the chamber.

Varnath floated back to his feet and glared hatefully at the vampire. "You should have joined me when you had the chance, bard. I would have made you second only to me in the world I am creating. Instead, for your continued defiance, you shall suffer for an eternity!"

Landrin shuddered as the master of the undead asserted his will upon the vampire. With a shout of denial, Landrin broke free of the overwhelming impulse to obey and struck out with his magic. Varnath flew to the side in an attempt to avoid the fireball. He continued to circle, much of his moldy clothing now smoldering and trailing smoke.

The lich looked around the chamber and saw that only two of his nightmarish creatures were still fighting. He knew that it would not be long until that number was cut in half. He saw one of the spawn wrap a thick tendril around the ogre and hurl him bodily across the room to strike heavily against a nearby wall.

At nearly the same instant, the second of his creations lifted the dwarf and flung him against the wall hard enough to topple an open stone sarcophagus down upon him.

"You are strong, vampire, but I am the master of this place. I could crush you like an insect, but I think it will be more fun to watch my newest pet cut you to pieces."

Varnath made a motion with his hand at another sarcophagus standing against the nearby wall. Landrin tried to keep his eyes on it and the lich as the stone lid shifted before falling to the floor with a resounding crash. The former bard nearly dropped the sword clutched in his left hand as he beheld the creature that stepped out.

"Samone, no," Landrin moaned in despair.

The former paladin's face was whiter than the purest alabaster. Her once gleaming armor was black as if fouled from the soot of a fire. Landrin could tell she was not a vampire, but what manner of undead the lich had created from her body, he did not know. He looked into those pale blue eyes and saw the gleam of intelligence and recognition within their unholy depths.

Samone smiled at him. "Hello, Landrin. I told you that next time we met I would destroy you. Of course at the time, it was for a different reason."

"Samone, you must fight him! Reject him! Reject your nature as I have! Solarian will still accept you," Landrin pleaded.

Samone's short black hair undulated as she shook her head. "He will not. I failed him, and this is my eternal damnation." The dark paladin drew a blade as black as her armor. "Now I serve Varnath, and I shall not fail again."

Samone put Landrin in a fighting retreat. Her speed and strength were nearly equal to his, and her armor and seeming willingness to kill him put her at a distinct advantage.

"Samone, I know you can beat him!" Landrin urged as he desperately parried her tireless flurry of attacks.

"I have no will of my own anymore. It too belongs to Varnath." A slight glimmer of her former humanity sparked in her eyes and in her whispered tone. "You must destroy me, Landrin, or I will destroy you and everything in my master's path."

Landrin could see the resolution in her face and hear it in her voice. She knew she could not overcome the lich's domination and was pleading for Landrin to end her, for her sake and the sake of humanity. The former bard lashed out with sword and magic, knowing that there was only one resolution to what they all faced.

Seeing that his newest, and by far greatest, creation had the vampire well in hand, Varnath turned his attention back to the other troublesome breathers who futilely tried to disrupt his grand scheme. The lich found himself face to face with the huge, angry druid. He stared up into the furious eyes of the half-ogre and sneered.

"You are the most ridiculous of all these pathetic mortals. Foolish druid, you are in the heart of death. Ellanee has no place and no power here. Without your goddess, precious plants, and life from which to draw your feeble magic, what are you?"

Bron stared down unflinchingly and responded simply, "Big."

The half-ogre put all of his considerable strength behind his swing and struck the lich with his fencepost-thick staff. Varnath collided with the wall so hard many of his bones shattered, and he bounced nearly half the distance back to the druid's feet. Such physical damage was largely inconsequential, but it rattled the lich to his core.

Varnath seethed with rage as he floated off the floor, trailing splinters of bone, ready to unleash his foulest and most punishing necromancy upon the druid. However, Bron was not yet finished with the creature. The lich was wrong. There was life in this chamber and it fought with every ounce of strength it had. As long as the living fought and persevered, Ellanee was always close at hand.

He listened to her gentle whisperings upon a wind only he could sense. Turning his magic toward his staff, thorny vines sprouted from the wood and pierced his tough flesh. They drank in his life-giving blood as they stretched out toward the lich. Varnath swiped at the green tendrils with his sacrificial dagger, but the shoots writhed and twisted around his wrist and crawled up his arm beneath the tattered remnants of his sleeve.

The lich lord wailed a hideous, blood-curdling shriek as the brambles continued to grow, twisting around his form, and burrowing into the remnants of his flesh. The thorns drank deeply of the druid's blood and pumped its life-giving substance into the cadaverous abomination.

Samone shuddered as her master fell in agony, and failed to parry Landrin's thrust. The vampire's slim blade pierced her armor and the dead heart beneath. Landrin dropped to his knees as he caught Samone and gently lowered her to the ground.

"Landrin," Samone gasped as she shared some of Varnath's pain.

"Forgive me, Samone," Landrin begged. "I never wanted to hurt you."

"There is nothing to forgive unless you do not finish this. Only then shall I curse you for eternity."

"What must I do?"

The fallen paladin turned her head toward the enormous black crystal in the center of the room. "The gem is the heart of his power. It is his phylactery. As long as it is whole, he will always be able to reform his body or simply take another. You must destroy it to kill him and to free me. Take my blade and smash it."

"There must be a way to save you," Landrin said desperately.

"You will save me by destroying Varnath. It is the only way."

Landrin nodded, took the black sword from Samone's hand, and approached the crystal. A short distance away, Varnath renewed his struggles, trying desperately to shed this broken form so that he might take one of the fallen elves' bodies and destroy them all, but the accursed vines and the blood pouring into him held his spirit as firmly as it did his body.

The bard raised the blade over his head in a two-handed grip and whispered, "Fly free, my nightingale."

Landrin smashed the sword down upon the gem, still flashing a hundred different images of the carnage being enacted throughout the kingdom as both crystal and sword shattered into thousands of fragments. The bard felt dozens of sharp slivers stab into his flesh as steel and crystal exploded outward.

Varnath let out a final shriek of anger and anguish before crumpling in a pile of tattered cloth, leathery skin, and broken bones. The last inky abomination slumped to the ground and began spreading out into a pool of sludge. Landrin ran to Samone and cradled her head, praying that she might have returned to her mortal form upon the lich's destruction. His prayers came to naught.

Maude spotted Malek lying still across the chamber and ran to him as Corana and her remaining rangers ran to their injured and fallen. She checked but found no pulse nor signs of breath. She gently stroked his handsome face as she wept and touched the golden amulet that seemed to glow with a faint light.

For a moment, Maude thought the amulet's light was increasing until she realized that the source of the glow came from behind her. She, as did the others, turned and watched the blindingly golden glow resolve into a man wearing plate armor that seemed to be forged from the sun.

Solarian stepped toward Maude and the fallen cleric. Maude stood and withdrew as the god knelt next to his Chosen and laid a hand over the holy symbol. The amulet's glow began intensifying until it nearly matched the nimbus of light surrounding the god's hand. Malek took a deep, shuddering breath and groaned.

"Solarian!" Landrin shouted. "You have another faithful you must return to life!"

Solarian approached and looked down upon the paladin and the vampire that held her.

"I am sorry, Landrin, but I cannot," he said sadly.

"Why not? Why will you save him and not her? Has she not given as much or even more? Haven't I?"

"I did not save Malek. He saved himself by anchoring his spirit into his medallion. I merely helped return it to his body. I cannot restore her any more than I can restore you. Faithful Samone's spirit was lost long ago. It is not mine to return. Take comfort that her soul now resides within my celestial kingdom and is finally at peace."

Maude was furious. "I don't understand you! You stand here telling us what you cannot do. Where were you when we were dying? Why did you not simply crush this thing before he even started all of this? I saw in that thing over there what was happening! How many people died tonight because you chose to sit on your holy arse?"

Solarian held up a hand to stave off Corana and the elves' rebuke of the woman. "You must understand that we gods are bound by rules. Our ability to interfere in the lives and struggles of mortals is limited. We are but the hand that moves the pieces upon a chessboard, not the makers of the game itself."

"So, this is all just a game for the gods to play? Did you ever ask any of us if we wanted to play?" Maude demanded.

"The game was started with the creation of the universe. None were given a choice, not even the gods. Even we are but newcomers to an ancient struggle and are bound by the rules governing the cosmos."

Borik scowled at the god as he finally managed to crawl out from under the heavy stone box. "Rules? How can a god be bound by rules? Why would a god have rules that kept them from doing anything to help those that worship you and rely on you to protect them in the darkest times?"

"Unfortunately, you will very likely see what happens when gods are not bound by rules. Your kind faced them once before and only barely survived. Soon you shall face them again, and this time your prospects are even grimmer."

"And you can't do anything to help us?" Maude asked.

Solarian smiled. "We do everything we can to help you. For if you fail, we fail. We look upon the lines of fate and place our pieces in positions to best defeat the enemy just as we did here and elsewhere. What happened here needed to happen. Just as what happened out there," he pointed in the direction of Valeria, "needed to happen. Thousands died this night so that the rest might have a chance of surviving tomorrow."

"We have to go through more of this crap tomorrow?" Borik asked hotly.

"He was speaking metaphorically, dwarf," Corana snapped. "At least I hope he was."

Solarian inclined his head. "I must return now. You have all done a great thing this night, but the struggle goes on. Stay resolute, work together, and you shall prevail."

Solarian vanished like a snuffed-out candle, leaving the survivors of the battle in the gloom of the cavernous chamber.

Maude stepped over to Landrin and Samone as Malek regained his strength and sat up. "I thought you could not come here?"

Landrin did not take his gaze from Samone's face. "I could not. Not until he was distracted. I spent several days preparing as many defenses against his power as I could. It was not until your people engaged him that I dared attempt a confrontation. Had I come with you, he likely could have seized control of me before we ever reached this place. I am simply another piece in the same game, and I had to choose the best time to be played. Perhaps I chose wrongly."

"Thank you for coming. We may have all failed had you not. Let's take our dead out of this place and put them to rest." Maude looked around then asked, "Anyone seen Tarth?"

Tarth's muffled voice sounded from above them. "I am up here. Please get me down. I fear this cocoon is ruining my clothes!"

"How the heck do we do that?" Borik asked, then turned to Corana. "Think you can shoot him down?"

CHAPTER 23

Azerick picked out a pinprick of light ahead and found Rusty and Allister once again. Just over seven thousand men were gathered in a huge circular mass, the outer ring standing against the undead onslaught. When a man went down or became too fatigued to fight, he was pulled back to the inner ranks and another took his place. Horror after horror unraveled before the eyes of the men as they fought a seemingly unending tide of undead nightmares.

Undead were bound and reanimated with strands of magic much like any other spell, and by inflicting enough damage, those strands were broken and the undead creation destroyed. However, the strange fog seemed to reattach those strands soon after disruption unless they destroyed the host with fire, magic, or hacked it into so many pieces that it was no longer viable. The worst thing to behold was when the reaching and clawing hands of the monstrosities pulled a man out of the defensive circle only for him to reappear minutes later, madly trying to slay his former brethren.

Even Azerick had exhausted his ability to summon and channel the Source and now relied on the sparing use of his staff. Rusty and Allister were both down to a single wand and a few lesser spell-storing magical accoutrements. The priests standing behind the first few ranks of soldiers were exhausted as they poured all of their strength and faith into simply holding back the undead and channeling them into groups that were more manageable for the fighters and mages to destroy.

Despite shifting the men around to give them a rest, Azerick saw the fatigue evident on the soldiers' faces. Some looked grim, some angry, others just resigned to what they saw as their eventual fate, but all of them kept fighting. Even those who were certain they would not live to see another sunrise continued to battle on, because it was what they did; not just as soldiers, but as human beings. They would fight to the end, fight for the right to live just one more minute and then another minute after that and another after that.

Thinking of another sunrise, Azerick was certain that enough hours had passed even in this daytime-deficient land for the sun to rise. He thought there might have been a very slight shift from pitch-blackness to extremely deep grey, but it was hard to tell. The sorcerer stood back from the battle and studied the mist more closely. After several minutes, he concluded that there was a noticeable brightening and thinning to the fog. It looked as though the light from both magical and combustible sources pierced the gloom a bit further. Soon, there was no longer any doubt. The dreadful fog was receding.

Azerick spotted Jansen's dark form appear within the fog. It was not until the man was almost within striking distance that he saw the bright red blood coating his drawn blades.

"Jansen?" Azerick said, his voice taut with caution.

Jansen ducked his head slightly and replied, "Lord Giles."

Azerick's eyes locked onto the bloody swords. "That blood looks a bit fresh to be from any of those creatures."

Jansen looked down as if oblivious to the state of his weapons. "Yeah…no, it's not form them."

"You want to tell me whose it is?"

The enigmatic man met Azerick's gaze. "Had a score to settle. It's settled."

"We have a truce with the usurpers."

"It was blackguard business," Jansen replied, as if that explained everything, and as far as he was concerned, it did.

"The Bishop and his people might take issue with it," Azerick said. "Not to mention I gave my word when we agreed to the truce."

Jansen shook his head. "It won't be an issue with the Bishop. Like I said, it was blackguard business, and not even the King interferes with blackguard business. Is it going to be an issue for you?"

Azerick did not detect a threat in the man's question, but the implication was there. He was exhausted, but he would not back down. "I guess it depends on the nature of the business. You want to tell me what was worth breaking our truce and risking the resumption of hostilities."

Jansen stared unblinking for several uncomfortable seconds before he sighed and spoke. "I was captain of the blackguards when the Rook assassinated Jarvin's father. It was the greatest and most shameful failure of my life. I swore to hunt the Rook down and killed him, and nearly succeeded, as well as nearly died, several times. I left my best man in charge of the blackguard in my absence. Obviously. My trust was poorly placed. He betrayed me and his oath when he sided with Caalendor. I failed to bring down the Rook. I was not going to fail with the betrayer."

"Clearly you didn't."

Jansen looked down at his swords. "I did not."

Azerick cleared his throat. "Let's just hope he stays dead!" he finished with a forced chuckle.

"He will," came Jansen's dry response.

"Well, that was an...illuminating conversation. I guess we both have our own business to attend to. Nice talking to you. We should chat more in the future."

Jansen merely grunted and began cleaning his blades with snow.

The two disparate groups began separating themselves, creating a kind of demarcation line less than a hundred yards wide. Both sides looked ready but had no desire to return to the fight.

Bishop Caalendor trudged to the halfway point of the demarcation line and Jarvin walked out to meet him.

"This night has been exhausting and horrible for both our peoples. I propose a forty-eight-hour truce to deal with our dead and recover. Then we shall finish what was started. I suppose you can flee, but know I will hunt you down no matter where you hide," the bishop promised the deposed king.

Jarvin looked across the blood-painted landscape, took note of the obscene number of fallen men, and could only imagine what had happened this night all across the kingdom. His kingdom.

"I have an alternate proposition."

Caalendor smiled, thinking Jarvin was going to beg for exile. He even considered granting it. Then Jarvin smashed his face with a gauntleted fist. Fresh blood sprayed across the already crimson snow as the bishop crumpled into a heap. Hands flew to weapon hilts on both sides, spears were leveled, and bows drawn back. Jarvin turned and easily picked Rusty out of the front ranks of men and gave him a piercing look. Rusty nodded, and with the last of his strength, cast a simple cantrip upon his king.

Jarvin drew his sword and took several angry steps toward the opposing army. His countenance was so furious, so intimidating, that several of the nearest men took a step back as if the king might actually slay them all single-handedly.

Jarvin came to a stop, thrust his sword into the snow, and shouted, "Enough!"

His voice echoed across the open field and reverberated through the pass, amplified by Rusty's spell. The king stalked back and forth like an angry, predatory hunting cat, glowing with a faint light.

"Enough! Enough fighting and enough dying for the petty desires and twisted ideals of men who care only for themselves!" Jarvin reached down, lifted the severed head of one of the undead by its hair. "Look in my eyes, look at my face and look upon this thing and tell me who the enemy is. Back home, your wives, children, and family may have been fighting and dying while you were up here killing your own kind instead of being at home protecting them! Who is the real enemy?"

The king waved his hand in a circle over his head. "This is what happens when we lose sight of what is important. This has likely been years in the making while those who are supposed to protect us from this kind of evil were too distracted by petty politics to notice! My father was your uncontested king. I am his son and rightful heir. I. AM. YOUR. KING!"

Heads turned as the men looked left and right into the faces of their fellow soldiers. Everything balanced on a knife's edge. It would only take the act of a single man to irrevocably disrupt the precarious situation. That man advanced and drew his sword. The king did not bother stepping toward his own sword sticking out of the snow several paces away as a captain in Caalendor's army approached him. The man spun the sword around, thrust it point first into the snow, knelt, and declared, "My king!"

Jarvin looked down and gave him a single nod then looked intently at the rest of the soldiers watching nearby. Almost as a unit, the assembled army thrust or braced their weapons into the snowy ground, knelt, and declared, "My king!"

Only then did Jarvin retrieve his blade and slam it home in its sheath. "Rise, my people. We have faced a great threat this night, possibly the greatest of our lives, but we prevailed! We prevailed because we fought together! When evil raised its ugly head, we stopped our petty bickering, we stopped worrying about the inconsequential, and we fought together! Now, let us continue to work, and if needs be fight, together so that such vileness can never again gather the power to strike at us as it did this night. Let us tend to our wounded, recover our strength, and then go home and see to our families."

Jarvin spotted General Brague, battered, weary, and missing his helm, and nodded toward Caalendor's unconscious form. "Take that *man* into custody for treason against the crown."

Brague smiled and saluted his king. He turned to his nearest men and ordered them to recover the bishop and put him in shackles.

It took two days to burn all of the dead, undead, and ragmen bodies. Jarvin was unsure what he would face when he returned to Brelland, but with seven thousand men behind him, he was certain it was nothing he could not handle. It would not be a fast trip since they had burned most of the troop wagons during the fight. The few that remained had to be used to carry food, supplies, and wounded men.

Jarvin, his mages, and senior officers were sitting around a table in the command tent discussing the march south to Brelland when a guard showed Donnigan into the tent.

"I truly wish you would reconsider and come with me to Brelland," Jarvin said to Azerick.

"My people and I must return to the school and our own families. I have no idea what has happened, but I have a feeling we are needed."

"I need you," Jarvin insisted. "I could command you as your king, you know."

"You gave a nice speech, Jarvin, but do not let it go to your head," the sorcerer warned, his face devoid of any humor.

Jarvin merely smiled. "Impertinent as ever. Don't get your smallclothes in a twist. I would not dream of forcing you. Ah, Mr. Donnigan, you are just the man I wanted to see."

"Hmm, don't hear that much unless I owe someone money."

"How fares End's Run?" the king asked.

"You mean what's left of it. We burned half of it to the ground fighting those things. Woulda lost everybody maybe if the wolves hadn't showed up."

"Wolves?" Allister asked.

Donnigan grunted. "Yeah. Damnedest thing you ever saw. The whole town was pressed near the center, half the buildings in town on fire, and the wolves found an open gate and started tearing into them things. Hundreds of them, if I were to guess their numbers. Fog lifted and the wolves disappeared with it. I reckon they didn't like the way those dead things smelled and took them as a greater threat than us humans."

Jarvin took a deep breath and asked the question that had been plaguing his mind since the fog appeared. "And my family, Mr. Donnigan?"

"They're fine. First thing I looked in on after the fog cleared. The men I had watching 'em said them things seemed to avoid the manor. Guess Landrin hexed it or something."

"That is good news. And how is Lord Bailey?"

The chief enforcer shrugged his broad shoulders. "Not a clue. He left right after you all. Told me he had something to attend to. I didn't ask what."

"I am sure he had good reason to leave."

Jarvin motioned to a guard who poked his head out of the tent and said something to someone outside. A minute later, another guard ushered Bishop Caalendor into the tent and forced him to sit in a chair. Donnigan's face showed no reaction to the fact that the clergyman looked like horses had stampeded him.

"This was Bishop Caalendor," Jarvin explained. "He is now branded a traitor and stripped of all titles and rights. He has information I need. Unfortunately, I do not have a proper inquisitor on hand and refuse to bring him anywhere near Brelland or any other civilized town within my kingdom."

"You gave me your word of a truce when those monsters struck!" Caalendor protested through split and puffy lips.

Jarvin bent down and pressed his face within inches of the cleric's. "Just as you have done to me for the past ten years—I lied." He turned back to Donnigan. "I need the names of every one of his conspirators. Can you do that?"

Donnigan smiled a very unfriendly smile. "Hell, tell me your favorite song and I'll have him singing them to its tune."

"Excellent. I will give him into your capable hands and notify my quartermaster to send some pigeons with you to message me when you have it."

"What do you want me to do with him after?"

Jarvin stared balefully at the priest for a moment. "Hang him for a traitor."

Donnigan broke character and laughed heartily.

"You find something amusing, Mr. Donnigan?"

The man wiped a tear from his eye and replied, "Sorry, it's just that the gallows Lord Bailey had built were one of the few things that didn't burn." He nudged Caalendor's chair leg with his boot. "Lucky for you, eh? Sorry, folks always told me I had a gallows humor. Guess they were right."

Donnigan had come to see how the king and his army were faring and to deliver news of End's Run and his family. Now that he had done so, he took control of the former bishop and started back on the two-day ride to End's Run.

Jarvin and the remainder of the army marched south to Brelland while Azerick and everyone who accompanied him from the school rode for North Haven. Azerick could not put his finger on it, but an urge to be home pulled at him. He prayed something had not happened to Miranda or the school.

He had so many people to care about now, and for a moment, wondered if the potential for so much pain was worth it. Yes, it was. His doubts were the old him talking. The him who shielded himself in loneliness and solitude. The him who was willing to sacrifice true happiness for emotional security. He had love now and soon he would have a child to raise and spoil. He would not trade a single second of that for his own selfish desire of emotional security.

CHAPTER 24

Ellyssa had been heartbroken to see her two best friends in the hands of these terrible people. They now suffered the same fate as she did, and Ghost was dead because of her. She was so devastated at being the cause of so much suffering that she could not even muster the strength to dread the day's training. Ellyssa plodded mindlessly to the training pit, unable to summon enough self-pity to fear what she would be forced to do today. Considering how she felt right now, Ellyssa doubted that she could manage the appropriate amount of remorse for whomever she was forced to kill.

She knew her training had taken on a new role the instant she stepped into the training pit. Misha was there, as usual, but the wizards Dorran and Bheram accompanied her as well. Ellyssa was uncertain what was about to happen, but she knew it would not bode well for her. She approached Misha and made a slight bow as she had been taught.

"I am ready for my training, Chain Mistress."

The woman gave her a condescending smile. "I seriously doubt that. You have learned how to kill, however reluctantly. We shall work on destroying that annoying conscience you still possess later. Now we shall see what you know about using your gift in a real battle. You will fight the three of us, and we shall gauge your battle prowess."

Ellyssa swallowed hard and failed to keep the trembling from her voice. "Chain Mistress, I cannot hope to defeat you all."

Misha laughed at the absurdity of the girl's comment. "Child, you could not defeat us individually. We will observe your technique and your ability to strike and defend. Go stand over there and begin when you are ready."

Ellyssa trudged through the sandy floor of the training pit, dragging her feet in sullen resignation of the pain and humiliation she was about to receive. All three mages were full wizards and, despite her natural strength in magic, she knew she could not hope to overcome even one of them. Even the youngest amongst them had likely been practicing magic longer than she had been alive. It wasn't fair. It wasn't fair. She kept repeating that in her mind, making herself angrier with each repetition. Ellyssa clung to that anger and fed it. She would use it to power her spell. She knew that she could not beat them, but maybe she could hurt one of them. Bheram looked to be the youngest and likely the weakest of the three.

Ellyssa drew in the Source as she walked toward the spot Misha had indicated. She turned back toward the three wizards and began forming the weave of her spell. Ellyssa pulled so much power from the Source it felt as though her skin were on fire, and it made her hair stand on end. It was a strike of pure force, much like the one she had tried to kill the vila with when she was first brought before him. She shaped the strike in the form of a large cone, broad at its back to act as mass, with a very narrow striking surface to help pierce a magical ward.

Bheram let out a short bark of exclamation when he understood the nature of the spell and that he was its intended target. The Sumaran brought up his strongest ward in the split second it took for the spell to leave the girl's fingers and cross the hundred and fifty feet or so of open ground. Even so, the spell hit him with enough force to send him tumbling backwards. Had Dorran not also brought up a shield, it very likely would have seriously injured him, if not killed him outright.

Ellyssa had little time to revel in her small victory. She had put all her strength into that one spell and could even now feel her legs failing her. Misha paid the two men no mind and lashed out with a similar spell even as the girl began to crumple to the ground. The force of the strike sent Ellyssa flying back several feet and she tumbled in the sand. Before the pain could register in her brain, more strikes rolled her across the arena like a ball being kicked around by children. Ellyssa was certain that just one more blow would send her blissfully into the darkness of unconsciousness, or even death. Misha was not about to let her off so easily.

When Ellyssa was finally able to open her eyes, she saw a pair of feet in front of her face and followed them up with her eyes until she found the chain mistress's scowling visage.

"I do not even know where to begin to explain how stupid you are," Misha snarled. "You faced three opponents and yet you put all your strength into striking just one. You used so much of your energy for that single spell that you were completely unable to defend yourself from a counterattack."

Ellyssa took a shuddering breath and replied, "I wasn't strong enough to beat you all, so I thought I might be able to take at least one of you with me."

"Martyrdom is for morons. A dead wizard slays no foes. I told you before that you were not as strong as any of us. When we face King Yusuf do you think we will have the advantage of numbers? Of course not. That is why we must be smarter! Now, pick yourself up, go to my library, and study. We will try again in a few days, and you had better learn something in that time, or I will make you pray to return to the pain you feel right now."

Ellyssa could not stifle the cry of pain that passed her lips as she struggled to her feet. It took all of her strength and stubborn pride just to walk out of the training pit erect. She refused to show weakness in front of these people, especially Misha. Dorran and Bheram watched the young girl trudge stiffly away and then approached the dour chain mistress.

"Damn that girl can hit hard," Bheram said. "I think she would have killed me had Dorran not added his ward to mine."

Misha spun on the younger wizard and snapped, "And you would have deserved it for being weak and unprepared. We all saw how strong she was from the beginning. Now she just needs to learn how to channel that strength properly."

"You had best hope she breaks before she does, or you may regret that statement," Dorran said, smiling. "She still defies you inside and will kill you the first chance she gets."

"If she did not, I would not be doing my job properly. I have no worries and neither should you. I have never failed to break someone. She will break. In the end, they all break."

It was all Ellyssa could do to keep putting one foot in front of the other. All she wanted to do was curl up on the marble floor and weep. It almost came as a surprise when she looked up and found herself standing in front of Misha's personal library. To call it a library was giving it a lot of credit. The room was entirely devoted to the study of magic. Three bookcases were stuffed with tomes of various sizes, but not one space was wasted on things like poetry or politics. Every book and every scroll served a single purpose—to learn magic and how to use it in battle.

Ellyssa had been in this room before, fetching books and running errands while Misha pored over the texts to find answers for the vila or to increase her own formidable knowledge. Despite having had her hands on many of the books during her service, she had never been allowed to use the books herself. The bookcase on the left was devoted almost entirely to spell books and scrolls detailing the patterns and components of an untold number of spells.

Ellyssa pulled out several books and sat down with them at a small table in the corner of the room. Misha would be back soon, and she wanted very much to be as unobtrusive as any other piece of furniture in the room. Unless the chain mistress came in here looking for her, it was unlikely they would cross paths. Misha's suite of rooms covered more floor space than Azerick's original tower.

Misha told her that she needed to be smarter not stronger, so she scanned page after page looking for spells that could give her an advantage and did not require enormous amounts of power or skill to use. Ellyssa recalled some of the stories Azerick had shared, of how he had defeated opponents stronger than himself by being clever with what he knew. He had bested the headmaster of the Academy, a man who was probably at least as powerful as Misha was. She was under no illusion that she was another Azerick, but that did not mean she could not learn and take lessons from what he had accomplished.

It did not take long for Ellyssa's eyes to ache nearly as much as her body, but she refused to relent to fatigue. Her stubborn determination would not allow her to rest. It was not until late that evening that Misha finally made her inevitable appearance.

"I am pleased to see that you did not return to your room to lick your wounds and wallow in self-pity. Have you eaten?"

"No, Chain Mistress," Ellyssa responded without looking up from the book in front of her.

"Good. I am glad you are taking this seriously. I shall have food brought to you. I want you to be in top form when you show me what you have learned."

True to her word, a servant arrived bearing a tray of food only a few minutes after she departed. Ellyssa was starving, but she knew if she ate too much too quickly it would make her sleepy. She was not ready to end her studies just yet, so Ellyssa picked at the food as she absorbed the knowledge contained within the books spread out before her. Ellyssa finally surrendered to her body's incessant demand for sleep far later than she normally would have. She was used to going to sleep early just to escape the day and pray that the morrow brought her freedom.

Ellyssa rose as early as her body, which protested yesterday's abuse with every movement and inhalation, would allow. She grabbed a tray of finger food from the kitchen and went to Misha's quarters. She did not see the chain mistress that morning and only received a few brief visits in the following days. By the third day of Ellyssa's exhaustive studies, she thought she may have found some spells that she could shape into an effective defense.

She stole out into the training pit after most of the palace had gone to bed. Ellyssa wanted her new skills to come as a surprise. She knew the only way she could hope to break through even one of the elder wizards' wards was if she put everything she had into the spell, and Ellyssa had learned a painful lesson in that regard. She decided she would rely on illusion and transmutation to conceal herself and hopefully confound her foes. It took two more days of study and nights of exhausting practice before Ellyssa felt her skill sufficient enough to have even a marginal chance at success. Misha afforded her one more day of study before telling Ellyssa her time was up.

"I have grown bored waiting for you," the chain mistress said as she entered the room. "If you have not learned anything by now, you likely never will. Meet us in the pit in an hour."

Ellyssa fought to control the butterflies that fluttered madly inside her stomach as she created a few last-minute mental notes and made the long walk to the training pits. Just as it was the last time, Misha, Dorran, and Bheram were all waiting for her by the time she arrived. Bheram especially looked eager for the rematch. Ellyssa was determined to change his mind about that.

She did not bother waiting for instructions and simply paced out across the floor near to the spot of her previous inglorious defeat. The three wizards fanned out, putting twenty or thirty feet of space between them. Ellyssa wondered if they thought she would try to take them all out with an area spell after learning what happened when she focused her strength on just one and ignored the other two. It didn't matter. She doubted that the other wizards expected what she had planned. Any margin of success was going to require all of her skill and more luck than she thought even Azerick possessed, but Ellyssa was determined not to be embarrassed a second time.

Ellyssa took a deep breath to steady her nerves then began casting, furiously moving her hands and fingers to shape the invisible strands of energy into the form of her spell. She saw the other three wizards also forming their own spells. She was certain they were wards. It was the standard practice of every spellcaster since an unshielded body would quickly be destroyed.

The young mage's spell was not very complex, and Ellyssa got it off nearly as quickly as the others were able to effect their wards. A miniature sandstorm erupted in the heart of the training pit, obscuring all vision as the sand that comprised the floor was whipped about by the strong wind brought forth by Ellyssa's spell. It took only a moment for Ellyssa to feel the strands of her spell being plucked apart by Misha and the other two wizards.

In only a few seconds, the sandy tempest subsided and Ellyssa was caught in open ground, obviously going for Bheram once again. Misha smiled as she shaped a ball of ice the size of a small melon and sent it streaking out toward the unprepared girl. The startled young mage raised her arms as if to ward off the missile with her hands. Ellyssa's ward flared as it failed to keep the ice ball from smashing into her body, and it sent her tumbling into a sprawling heap upon the ground.

Not only did Misha's spell shatter the wizard's ward and smash several ribs, it also destroyed the illusion Ellyssa had cast upon poor Bheram, who now lay unmoving just a few yards from where she now stood wearing an illusion of the defeated mage. Both Misha and Dorran stared dumbly at their fallen comrade for a moment, which was enough time for Ellyssa to cast her next spell.

A vaguely humanoid construct made from the material of the pit floor reared up just in front of Dorran, and towered over him. The wizard took an involuntary step backwards and fell into the pit from which the construct was created. The sand man fell atop the prostrate wizard and buried him beneath several feet of sand, dirt, and gravel.

Misha did not pause a second time. The chain mistress frantically waved her arms and sent a swarm of flaming darts streaking out at the young upstart who had just laid waste to two of her more prominent associates. Ellyssa gestured furtively and raised a wall of sand in front of her an instant before the fiery darts would have scorched and shredded her. She could feel the heat through the wall and saw several spots in the surface turn to glass.

Misha watched the wall fall in a shower of sand and glass, but Ellyssa was nowhere to be seen. The child was obviously using another of her clever illusions to conceal herself. The chain mistress was about to show the girl the futility of her tactic by bombarding the entire training ground with a shower of conjured stones when numerous columns of sand erupted all around her, each looking like her angry young charge made of sandstone.

Misha knew that only one of them was the real girl, who obviously thought to confound her and get her to expend precious energy destroying each of the simulacrums while she would likely strike from behind. Misha would teach the young upstart another painful lesson.

The chain mistress gathered in the Source around her then released it in a powerful, expanding ring. Like the rings formed on the surface of water from a cast stone, the energy radiated outward, tore through the constructs in every direction, and blasted Ellyssa to the ground. Misha turned and smiled at the girl who was struggling to regain her feet. Misha practically sashayed over to where Ellyssa had finally given up trying to stand and lay quietly sobbing.

"I must commend you on such clever use of relatively simple spells. The vila will pleased to hear that he made a wise invest..."

The chain mistress never got the chance to finish her gloating as her next step failed to find solid ground where it was supposed to be. Something struck her hard from behind and helped her already falling body to the ground. Ellyssa burst from the sand as if launched from a springboard and landed upon the elder wizard's back, a knife she had stolen from the kitchen held high and ready to plunge into the woman's flesh. Ellyssa never got the chance to drive the blade home as absolute agony flared throughout her body.

Misha threw an elbow behind her as she rolled out from under Ellyssa's spasming body, brutally and needlessly helping the girl off her back and onto the ground. Misha climbed to her feet and looked down at Ellyssa as her body contorted from the hellish pain the chain mistress fed through the gold chains.

"As I was saying, you have done well and pleased me with your cleverness. It is good to know that you have a great deal of potential and are capable of learning swiftly. However, you still resist my control, and I will break you. You had best remember that."

Ellyssa was finally able to look up at Misha when the woman stopped unleashing such unimaginable pain upon her. "If it weren't for these chains, I would have killed you. You had best remember that."

Fire coursed through her body once again as Misha poured out her fury through the chains at the girl's continued impudence. Ellyssa could do nothing, not even scream, until the blackness of unconsciousness thankfully took hold of her. A short distance away, the ground exploded and Dorran clambered out of his impromptu grave looking more annoyed than injured. Bheram on the other hand had yet to show signs of life.

Dorran dusted himself off as he approached and looked down at the girl. "Is she dead?"

Misha gave Ellyssa a disgusted look. "No, but she will soon wish otherwise. I have grown tired of her willfulness. It is time for her to learn her place."

"What about him?" Dorran asked with a glance toward Bheram's body.

As if on cue, Bheram let out a whimper.

It was a cold, boring ride back to the school. Fortunately, the mages' magical tent had survived that hellish night, and without dragging along three thousand soldiers behind them, they made better time. There was little fresh snow, so the trail they had blazed coming in was traversable, but it was still ten days of dreary, unpleasant riding before they spotted North Haven in its secluded seaside valley.

Azerick and his friends were nearly at the gates of the orphans' academy before anyone ran out to greet the kingdom's wayward defenders. Rusty had coined that term, and Azerick promptly told him to shut his big yap before it caught on and the king called on them to solve every problem he faced.

He was as delighted to see Miranda rushing out of the gates as he was sure Rusty was to see Colleen and his two toddlers. He was also surprised that Wolf had not burst from the tree line demanding gifts, and disheartened not to see Ellyssa. Azerick assumed she was still angry. Concern washed away all three amalgamating emotions when he saw the distress plainly written on Miranda's face.

"Azerick," Miranda said in a panicked rush, "something is wrong—something terrible!"

Azerick slid off Horse's back and held Miranda in a tight embrace. "What is it?"

Miranda slung her head from side to side, trying to force her thoughts into an orderly procession. "The school and the city were attacked by dreadful creatures. Several people here at the school died and over a thousand in the city. Mother has received reports from the other major cities and outlying hamlets and they are reporting the same."

Azerick nodded slowly as he took in Miranda's report. He and Allister had suspected much of what she was saying, but the numbers were still staggering. It had been the major topic of conversation on their ride back.

"It happened to us at End's Run as well. We are not certain, but it seems someone was able to put a stop to it. Permanently, we hope."

"There is more." Miranda took a deep, shuddering breath. "Ellyssa is gone, and Wolf and Sandy as well."

"Gone? Gone where?"

Azerick's first instinct was that they had fallen victim to the undead. His heart pounded in his chest knowing that such mindless creatures would never take a live prisoner unless their master had given them very clear instructions to do so.

"Ellyssa snuck out of the school to see Alonzo Janovin, the bard. I spotted her in the crowd and sent guards to bring her to me. I thought she might take it more seriously than if I went to her myself. She ran. We think she ran into the city and was taken."

"Taken by whom?"

Miranda's face twisted in disgust. "Slavers. Aggie tried to find her magically the next morning when she did not return to the school, but was unable to. She said something was blocking her scrying. A couple weeks later, we saw that the construct you made was gone from your laboratory. Aggie was able to follow it with her magic and saw Wolf and Sandy chasing after it. She watched it until it reached a city in Sumara and was destroyed by soldiers and mages. She also saw them capture Sandy. We are certain they took Sandy to the palace and think Ellyssa is there as well. We are not sure about Wolf."

"I see," Azerick said simply.

His face betrayed no emotion as he listened. People who did not know the sorcerer well might assume he was heartless and bereft of concern. Those who knew him well knew that he was simply making a mental tally of the number of souls he would soon be sending to the dark god Sharrellan.

Azerick began stalking toward the school, leaving Horse and his friends to follow in his furious wake. Jansen was close on his heels while Allister tried to dismount without falling in his haste. Azerick strode through the gates like a thunderstorm and pointed a finger at one of the young guards standing nearby.

"You, go fetch Simon and have him meet me in the dining hall."

The guard nodded briskly and ran off to summon the accountant. Azerick stormed into the old tower and shouted for Aggie. The elder wizard appeared on the arm of a much younger man with a close-cropped, salt and pepper beard, and descended the stairs.

"Azerick," Devlin, Azerick's former master, greeted him, "wonderful to see you again. I wish it were under more pleasant circumstances, but I have been enjoying the company of this marvelous woman."

Aggie giggled like a young girl, but Allister found nothing amusing whatsoever. "Have you now?"

Aggie shot the archmage a sour look. "Oh please, he's young enough to be my grandson, with a few greats thrown in. Don't get your beard in a knot or I'll set fire to your eyebrows."

"It is good to see you again, but I am afraid I must be leaving immediately," Azerick replied.

Miranda laid a restraining hand on Azerick's arm. "Azerick, just wait. There is much we need to discuss."

Azerick spun on his wife, his stoic façade vanishing in an instant. "What is there to wait for? My dau—apprentice has been enslaved as well as two very special friends. There is nothing to wait for. Every minute I delay is another minute in the hands of scum doing the gods know what! I will not allow them to suffer as I have."

"Do you think I care any less? I may not know what it is like being in that kind of situation, but I want them safe just as badly as you do. But if you run off without thinking, you might do more harm than good. You are no longer just a sorcerer that can strike out at anyone you think has done you wrong. You are a lord of Valeria, and anything you do you do in the name of the king! Will reigniting a war with Sumara help Ellyssa or anyone else?"

"What would you have me do? Write a letter to the king of Sumara and ask for my people back? What they do is legal down there. Do you think whoever has them will just send them on their way because I say please?"

Devlin cleared his throat. "Actually, in most any other situation it might."

"Azerick, I asked Master Devlin here as Sumara's lawful ambassador. You need to sit down and listen to him," Miranda told her husband, pleading for him to act rationally.

Simon hustled into the room, winded from running from wherever he had been. "M-Master Azerick, you, ah, sent for me?"

"Yes. Let us all go sit in the dining room."

Everyone sat around the long, rectangular table. Azerick called for Agnes to bring them some food and something to drink.

"Devlin, you said a letter would normally get me my people back?"

"As you are a very prominent figure in Valeria, my king would almost certainly demand that the vila of Bakhtaran return your people. He has no desire to resume hostilities any more than your king does. However, Vila Mushadan has been amassing power over the years and has all but declared Bakhtaran an independent state. He defies the king at every opportunity, and we believe that his intent is to seize the throne."

"Why does your king let him do this? Why does he not simply destroy the man?"

"Mushadan has built a very formidable army and his walls could withstand all but a concerted siege of every resource at the king's disposal. Many of the other vilas have taken something of a neutral stance and have resisted aiding the king, unsure of who might be wearing the crown a few years from now. The greatest obstacle is that Mushadan has enslaved numerous wizards. Such a concentration of magical power would make besieging the city nearly impossible."

"These wizards are slaves? How can he hold people with that much power against their will?"

Devlin explained. "He has discovered a way to block a spellcaster from reaching the Source without his explicit permission. He chains the wizards, literally and figuratively, with these devices. He wears a related device upon his person that allows him to control the wizard or sorcerer's power or inflict great pain. This is all our spies have discovered as they are soon found out and executed. We know Mushadan has a spy network within the capital, and it is far more effective than ours is."

"What you are saying is that this is not a problem I can solve by simply blasting my way through it. What do you suggest I do?"

Azerick's former master turned his palms up. "I do not know. You are an unknown entity to him. It is possible you might be able to infiltrate his palace and rescue your people, but with the magic at his disposal it would be beyond challenging."

"No, I will not simply take my friends and leave him be. I have seen what happens when people like him are left alone to work their schemes. I have to punish him—destroy him. You may be right about infiltrating his city." Azerick turned to Simon. "How many ships do I have at hand right now?"

Simon opened the thick book no one ever saw him without and flipped through a few pages. "Oh, ah, nine of sixteen have returned from their summer runs, and, ah, are docked or anchored for, ah, refitting and repairs."

"Simon, have someone send Peck to the city and have him bring Zeb here. Then go to the vault and bring me that speaking stone."

"What are you planning, Azerick?" Devlin asked.

Azerick steepled his fingers and held them under his chin as he calculated numbers and formed his strategy. "Your king cannot get anyone inside Bakhtaran without this Mushadan guy knowing, but he does not have any spies here. If I can get a sizable force inside his city, free all of the mages from bondage, and kill him, I might be able to turn many of his people against him and create an insurrection. Some will certainly continue to follow orders, but if enough are willing to fight for their freedom, they can topple the entire city government."

"Azerick, even if General Brague had not taken the bulk of North Haven's military to aid King Jarvin, you could not ship them to do battle in Sumara without igniting a war, no matter how noble your ideals," Miranda insisted. "Even if Sumara's king secretly applauded your invasion of this renegade state, publicly he would have to denounce you and take action. Remember, you are not just the master of a school, you are the next duke of North Haven."

"I will not go as North Haven's heir. I will go as a master retrieving his apprentice. I will fly no colors of state nor bring anyone bearing the crest of any of Valeria's cities. If I succeed, Sumara's king can claim the attack on the city as his own. If I fail, he can claim it as a strike by mercenaries and bandits."

"But where are you going to get enough people to have the slightest chance of creating this insurrection?" Devlin asked.

"I have a school of two senior archmages, five full wizards and at least a dozen adepts. I have four hundred fighters old enough to choose whether they wish to go and fight for their friends and surrogate family. I employ sixteen ships and over five thousand sailors, dockworkers, and men fully capable of fighting. Most of them were soldiers in the war with Sumara and know how to handle a sword." Simon walked in bearing a small black gem, which he handed to Azerick. "I also have this."

"Is that a speaking stone?" Devlin asked.

"It is, and a man that owes me his life has the other."

Azerick focused his will into the gem and waited. It took a full minute before a tinny voice echoed forth from within its black crystalline form.

"Yes?" a voice asked cautiously.

"General Baneford, do you know who this is?"

"Unfortunately, yes," Baneford's weary voice responded.

"If you are still leading a mercenary company, I have a proposition for you."

"I am. What is it you need?"

"You once told me you wanted your own town where you would be free from the petty dictates of men like Ulric. Are you still looking for one?" Azerick asked the mercenary general.

Baneford paused, apparently in thought. "I have a town, although it is mostly tents and shanties. I could be interested in upgrading. What is it you have in mind?"

"Have you heard of Bakhtaran?"

"Yes," he said, drawing out the word suspiciously.

"What do you think of becoming the new vila?"

"I think you have confirmed what I have long thought, that you are completely insane. I can field nearly fourteen hundred men with a few days preparation. That would still put me at one-fifth the size of Bakhtaran's military might; and that is a best estimate. The odds are more likely half again that. I hear he has a sizable wizard force as well, whereas I have one. As capable as Magus Krendall is, I think even he would last about as long as a soap bubble in a hurricane against odds like that."

"What if you could get your entire force inside the walls and Vila Mushadan was dead before the first man drew steel?"

"That would depend upon the loyalty of the populace, whether they will capitulate, or if we all get crushed in its death throes once you strike the head from the beast."

Azerick explained his plan and described the forces he would bring. Baneford listened as Azerick outlined his intent.

"Assuming you can kill the vila, get word to his people that he is dead, and a large number of them, particularly the wizards, are willing to rise against his rule, then a coup is certainly possible. However, there are numerous holes in your plan. I would imagine there are a fair number of people that would have a far greater claim to his seat than I, and if he or she were to have the support of Bakhtaran's military, they could promptly toss me out onto my backside without so much as a thank you. Even if I was able to claim Bakhtaran, why would the king let me, an outsider and mercenary, keep it? Besides, I risked far too much climbing out from under Ulric's bootheel to willingly put myself beneath another's."

Devlin leaned toward the gem. "General, if Azerick is willing to vouch for your character, I believe I can assist you in working out an agreement between King Yusuf and yourself. Mushadan has not paid a copper in taxes in years. I am certain that if you are willing to give King Yusuf his due, he would sign a compact that would allow you significant autonomy as long as you respected him and his rule."

"And who are you to make such offers?" Baneford asked skeptically.

"I am Magus Devlin Sabaht, official ambassador to Valeria and foreign voice to King Yusuf."

"Devlin, is that really you?" a new voice asked through the stone.

"Krendall, I should have known a scoundrel like you would be mixing company with a band of mercenaries. No offense, General."

"Well, after a particular young sorcerer destroyed the Black Tower and crushed most of the Tower hierarchy in the process, I found myself in need of a new home, and I considered the general to be reasonable company," Krendall explained.

Devlin raised a questioning eyebrow at his former apprentice. Azerick smiled and shrugged.

Baneford spoke to his wizard. "Do you think he has the authority to make a real bid for these claims?"

"He should; he's the king's brother, after all," Krendall replied.

Azerick cast Devlin a questioning look which the master sorcerer returned with a grin and shrug.

"All right, kid. If you can kill the vila, I'll have my people in place to move the instant they get the word of his death. But if this all goes to hell, you can damn well expect to be getting a bill. I'm a mercenary now and I'll get paid one way or another. How much time do I have to get in place? It's not as though I can just march over a thousand men through the gates one sunny afternoon."

"It will take me at least two weeks to get my people to Bakhtaran and put in position. I should be able to get a few thousand right up to the northern gates. If you can hold them open for us, you should have a large enough force to storm the palace and control it long enough for us to convince Mushadan's people that he is dead and that you can offer them a better alternative. At the very least, I should be able to get my people out and retreat back to my ships, and I will pay you in gold."

Baneford did some calculations in his head. "That gives me just under a week to filter my people inside after we reach the city. Shouldn't be too hard. All right, kid, you have a contract."

Azerick ended the communication and slipped the stone into his pocket.

Rusty looked at Azerick. "You have the battle figured out, but how are you going to get to the vila in the first place? And even if you do, Devlin says there's like thirty wizards, some of them full archmages, in there to stomp you flat. Not even you can take that many alone."

Azerick looked at his friend intently. "I will not be alone. I am never alone."

Allister looked at Azerick, his face ashen and grave. "Son, I have seen what that thing can do when you allow it too much control. Think about how much you might have to set it free to take on that many spellcasters. If you let him loose, you might never reel him back in."

"You people do not understand what it is like to be a slave. You have no idea what it is like to have someone else in control of you and your power, to force you to use it in ways that are horrible. I was young, but I was a man when Xornan enslaved me. I was strongly independent and numbed to certain emotional trauma through my experiences. Ellyssa is still a child and has never had to deal with the kind of pain from which I had learned to insulate myself. If this Mushadan is set to use his slaves to become king, she is not sitting around sipping juice and eating cake. He is training her using a device that controls her power and inflicts pain, just as Xornan did to me. Look at what that kind of treatment has done to me. How do you think it is affecting her? I will not leave her, Sandy, and probably Wolf in a place like that. No matter what."

Zeb finally arrived while Azerick and the mages were discussing the best way to use their assets. "Nice to see you back, lad. Your man said you needed to see me and that it was urgent."

"Zeb, have you heard about Ellyssa?"

"Aye. Foul thing that. My people have been asking about every ship they cross, but slavers and those that truck with them are a tight-lipped bunch."

"I am going to go get her. I need you to ask every sailor and every man you know to help me bring her back. I will pay every volunteer, including survivor benefits for the families of those that do not return."

Zeb screwed up his face. "What are ya plannin' ta do, boy, invade the whole of Sumara?"

"Just one city," Azerick answered. "How many men do you think you can get, and how many do we have room for on my ships?"

"Lad, you know most them men wouldn't even ask how high if you told them to jump. They'd just start jumping. Ships to move them is another story. We got nine readily available. Average three hundred men per ship. Any more than that and it starts gettin' real uncomfortable on a trip that far. I say we can move three thousand if we get cozy."

"If you get more volunteers than that, I'll commandeer some warships from North Haven."

"Azerick, I told you, you cannot use any forces belonging to Valeria without risking a war," Miranda reiterated.

"You keep telling me how I am the next duke of North Haven. I never wanted that, but now that I am, I will damn well use it. I will strike the colors and fly my own. I have plenty of my own people to crew them. So unless your mother wants to gainsay me, that is what I will do and more if that is what it takes!"

Miranda knew Azerick would not be dissuaded and if she forced the issue, it would just create a rift in their family. Azerick would do whatever he felt he needed to do to protect those he cared about. Besides, she knew he was right. He needed to use everything he had available if he was to pull off this audacious plan.

"I suppose I'm to stay back and babysit once again," Aggie grumbled.

Azerick turned to the elder wizard. "No, Aggie. I need everyone this time. The school can look after itself for a time. Jarvin will have the attention of any serious troublemakers pointed at Brelland. I need every good person I have, and you are one of my best."

"Now there's that young man I met at the Black Tower who knew how to speak to his elders," Aggie said smiling.

Devlin asked, "Where would you like me? I am yours to command."

"Master Devlin, I do not expect you to put yourself in the middle of this," Azerick said.

"Nonsense. I would not miss this for the world. My brother may not appreciate my involvement, especially if we lose, so we had best win."

"Thank you. Thank you all. Let's go find our volunteers."

CHAPTER 25

A zerick was not surprised at the number of people who stepped forward to risk their lives for him and anyone who belonged to the school. As much as Ellyssa aggravated people with her stubborn hotheadedness, she, Sandy, and even Wolf were all family and everyone at the school looked upon each other as such. So many of the staff and students volunteered, Azerick had to tell most of them that they had to stay behind. Zeb had rounded up nearly three thousand men from North Haven, most but not all of whom worked for Azerick in some fashion. Even with commandeering three of the city's ships, there simply would not have been room for everyone who wanted to go.

The northern seas rolled and churned with the coming of fall. Unlike the previous years, it actually behaved like fall and not early winter. It made for an unpleasant start to their journey aboard the twelve crowded ships, but as they neared Southport and sailed beyond, the ocean calmed considerably. Sped upon winds enhanced by the magicians aboard each ship, the small flotilla raced for Bakhtaran to show that city what happened when anyone threatened the extended family of the orphans' academy.

Almost two weeks after setting sail, the ships practically beached themselves upon the sloping, sandy seabed at low tide less than a day's march from Bakhtaran. It took what remained of the afternoon to shuttle everyone off the ships and onto the shore using the longboats. Once ashore, it took the combined magic of every spellcaster with them to veil their ragtag army under the illusion of several herds of goats, horses, camels, and their nomadic tenders.

The plan was to get all the illusionary critters and people to within a few hundred yards of the gate at about the same time Azerick would be having an audience with Vila Mushadan. He had his speaking stone and would inform General Baneford when he was near so that one of his people could signal those outside the walls.

Eight of the spellcasters were capable of opening magical portals so that they could instantly close the distance to the city. If someone managed to seal the gates on them, they could then open another set of portals and bypass the walls altogether. They dared not get close enough to the city full of wizards to do it in a single casting for fear of being discovered. Even now, the wizards needed to be extremely vigilant in hiding their presence from both magical and mundane detection.

The small army marched south with the setting sun. That would put them within striking distance of the city by early evening the next day. The pace they set was brutal, and by the time they set up their fake nomadic camps, many of them looked back to the cramped confines of the ships with envy.

"We will rest for the night and then I will go in just after sunrise when the gates open for the trader traffic," Azerick informed his core group of leaders.

Even Brother Thomas and his three Chosen came on this mission, knowing that their ability to heal wounds could save many lives. Jansen and Alex led the soldiers while the wizards were largely a force unto themselves. All were full wizards with the exception of Roger and three other adept casters who had proved their capability. Those four would stay very close to the archmages as they all provided protection from the city's wizards and soldiers.

Devlin approached his former student. "Azerick, I think it is a good idea if I enter the city with you. If you do take down Mushadan, my presence could go a long way to ending any violence from the common soldiers. They will recognize me as a legitimate authority and will set down their weapons for me far more quickly than for an outsider."

Azerick listened and bobbed his head in agreement. "Sounds like a good idea. Even with the vila dead, I doubt we could seriously take the city with the forces we have. It is simply too big, too crowded, and too unknown. I know I promised Baneford the chance to become the new vila, but I think we should just flee as soon as I can get my people away."

"You do not look as confident as you did when this started."

The young sorcerer buried his face in his hands and ran them up through his hair as he let out a long sigh. "Even if this goes as well as it possibly can, a lot of people are going to die. I guess I am just getting tired. I am tired of always being at the forefront of every battle and every site of death and mayhem. It has been going on since I was a child. Sometimes, I just want to shout 'why me?'"

"You feel like the world is resting upon your shoulders, and should your resolve fail, you might upset the balance and send it tumbling where it will shatter upon the ground."

Azerick clenched his fists and looked at the sorcerer with intensity. "Yes! It is like it is up to me to solve everyone's problems, and the only solution is built upon the bodies of those I must trod upon to achieve it!"

Azerick felt himself deflate as Devlin leaned back and laughed. "I remember thinking how the world revolved around me when I was young. True, you seem to find yourself in the middle of many desperate situations, but you choose to do so. You choose to come to the aid of others because you are a decent man and you believe in the right for everyone to live with a measure of peace and happiness. You chose to go to the Black Tower, you chose to depose Ulric, you chose to go to the aid of your king, and you are choosing to rescue your family.

"But do not think you are the only one. Many people have come forward to fight for the rights of others long before you were born and many will come after. Do you think your friend Allister or Aggie attained their power without having ever been put to the test? I was in Southport when the fog came. I walked the streets with the wizards from the Academy and the priests from the temples, slaying monster after monster beside them. I saw the streets littered with the bodies of men and women who fought or were dragged from their homes and killed.

"Did you end the fog that raised these abominations? No. Do you think it simply ran its course and expired on its own? I really do not think so. Someone else answered the call and put their life on the line so that the rest of us could go on living. If you decide to leave your people to their fates so that those who follow you are not at risk, and if you do not destroy Mushadan, he will move against my brother. Sumara will be at war with itself, thousands will die in the fighting, and it will not be you who fights for the right of the people to live free. You are a good man, a man of character as well as power, but you are not the be-all and end-all of humanity."

Azerick echoed Devlin's earlier laugh. "Am I really that arrogant and self-centered?"

"Do not blame yourself. It would take a man of godlike awareness not to feel in such a way after facing what you have faced. Just remember that you are not alone in these struggles and, although most of those around you do not have your power, their fight is no less significant than yours."

"Thank you, Master Devlin."

"Remember this as well. Mushadan is a selfish man and will lie and cheat to get what he wants. Do not trust anything he says. Rest now. I do not envy your fight tomorrow."

Azerick nodded his understanding and did his best to follow his mentor's order.

The sun rose early, illuminating the golden sands beneath and the clear sky above the city of Bakhtaran. People were already streaming into the noisy city: walking, riding, herding livestock, or pulling carts laden with goods to sell in Bakhtaran's famous bustling markets.

It was easy for Azerick to don a light robe of local fashion and slip into the city with Devlin. Bakhtaran was akin to a southern mirror of Southport. Both were large cities teeming with activity and a major trading hub of their respective nations. It took over two hours to reach the gates leading to the palace grounds. The elder sorcerer spent the time it took crossing the city to inform Azerick of local customs and what to expect inside the palace.

"I will leave you here and find my own way inside. From there, I shall try to find one of my brother's agents within. I will do my best to be there when you need me, but know that it may be beyond my control."

"I know. Thank you."

Devlin squeezed Azerick's shoulder and melted into the crowd, almost immediately disappearing amongst the throng. Azerick squared his shoulders and walked purposefully toward the gates.

Four burly men stood in front of the gates wearing white, loose-fitting shirts and matching bilious trousers beneath golden breastplates. Each wore a wide, curved scimitar on their hip and gripped a halberd in their hand. The street traffic was much thinner here and more richly dressed, but it was still bustling. Yet they gave the guards and the gates a wide berth like water diverting around a boulder in the middle of a river.

The instant Azerick broke from the general populace and stepped toward the gates, two of the guards crossed halberds while the other two leveled theirs at the interloper's chest. One of them called out something in their foreign tongue that Azerick interpreted as "stop, or I will cleave you in half".

Azerick halted about a body's length from the tips of the halberds. "My name is Magus Azerick Giles, Master of the orphans' academy in North Haven. I require an audience with Vila Mushadan."

"Vila Mushadan?" one guard asked.

"Yes, I need to see Vila Mushadan," Azerick repeated, gesticulating to himself and then toward the palace.

The guards conversed, shifting their gaze between Azerick and his staff. Deciding that the Valerian was not some common rabble, one of the guards called up to another on the wall who promptly disappeared. Azerick assumed that he had gone to fetch someone with the authority to make the decision to allow him inside, so he stood patiently while the two guards stood with halberds leveled and unwavering.

Azerick estimated he had been waiting about twenty minutes before he heard someone drawing the heavy bolt from the postern door. Azerick nearly dropped his staff in surprise when he saw Bran step through wearing a uniform similar to the guards standing watch over the gates. He was a little taller, much heavier, and significantly tanner than when he had last seen him some six years ago.

Bran's eyes flashed over him without a hint of recognition. "You are the Valerian?" Bran asked.

Azerick recovered from his shock and answered, "Yes, I am. I need to speak with the vila."

"Is His Greatness expecting you?" Bran asked.

Azerick could not help but grin. "Depending on what has been said about me, there is a good possibility. He has recently acquired possession of some people close to me. I am here to make a bid to have them returned."

Bran appeared to consider Azerick's request before calling out something to the guards. The two nearest the sorcerer snapped their weapons back to the ready with a single loud clack of their wooden hafts striking the stone street. Bran then motioned for Azerick to follow him through the small gate.

Neither of them spoke until they were at least a score of yards beyond the gates and the nearest guards. Azerick was about to say something but Bran beat him to it.

"Nice to see that someone is important enough to bring you running to this city," Bran said, breaking the awkward silence.

"So you did recognize me!"

"Of course I did." Azerick watched Bran's jaw tighten. "You were my best friend."

Were. That single past tense word hit him with the force of a punch.

"Bran, I'm sorry. I could not have gone then. It was just not possible for me. If I had known where you were, I would have come for you when I had the strength and means to actually be useful."

Bran looked up at the bright blue sky and let out a breath. "I know. It's what I have been telling myself for years."

Azerick looked at his feet as they walked. "Did you ever find Andrea?"

The sound of Andrea's name being spoken instantly brought a smile to Bran's lips just as it always did. "Yeah. We both live in the palace. We're married—sort of. The vila lets us be together. She tends to him when he is in his throne room, serving wine or food."

"You look well."

Bran gave a noncommittal twitch of his shoulders. "It's not freedom, but it's not a bad life."

"Did you never think of escaping with Andrea?"

"I did, at first. Then I looked out beyond the gates and saw a city whose only difference from the one I left was that I did not speak the language. It came down to choosing whether to return to the streets and face starvation, or stay locked up in a palace where I get to eat every day. In the end, it wasn't really a very hard choice."

Azerick considered what his friend was saying. "So this vila, he is not an evil man?"

Bran shrugged again. "He is a man of power, and as such takes what he thinks is his right. Is he sadistic? I don't think so, but he will severely punish those who offend or disobey him. The half-elf boy said you would be coming. He said you would kill Mushadan."

Azerick inclined his head. "So Wolf is here as well. How is he?"

Bran stopped and faced Azerick. "He is not well. Not well at all. The vila keeps him close at hand as a curiosity, but some creatures simply cannot survive captivity no matter how grand their cage. The vila has a private menagerie. He spent a fortune recreating a habitat for these bright crested birds from Lazuul, but even the ones that survived the trip soon died in their pens. I think the half-elf is like that. He had a wolf with him too, but we had to kill it. Maybe if we hadn't he would have the will to live, but without him he has nothing."

Azerick's heart broke hearing of Ghost's fate and what effect that would have had upon Wolf. Ghost was like a permanent part of Wolf; like an inseparable appendage. He swallowed his sorrow and focused on what he could still affect.

"What of the girl and the dragon?" he asked in a tense voice.

"Azerick, you need to understand. When the vila takes on a new slave, especially ones that are close to him and have strength or power, they are broken. I said he was not sadistic, but he demands complete and unquestionable obedience. To achieve that, he breaks them. He breaks their spirit and trains them to do exactly as he commands without hesitation. How far his trainers have to go and what they do depends on the strength and will of the one they are breaking."

Azerick's stomach churned. Both Ellyssa and Sandy were creatures of very strong will, and both would resist as long as they could, but they were both young. Had they already been broken? Could he fix them if they had? His anger raged and it took all his will not to lash out at the magnificent palace just ahead of them with all his might and fury.

"Bran, I am going to kill your vila. You need to know this as an absolute certainty. I am not the boy you once knew, and I am far more than even most of those who know me realize. Will you choose freedom if the vila is dead? Are there others that will choose freedom if given the chance?"

Bran shook his head. "I don't know, Azerick. We have all been trained to obey him without question. You are asking us to rise up against him."

Azerick despised himself for what he was about to do, but he had no choice. He needed to get through to Bran. Calling upon Klaraxis's demonic power of compulsion, Azerick laced his words with it so that Bran would listen and understand. He refused to force his friend to do what he wanted him to, but he needed to get past Mushadan's brainwashing and training.

"I am far from alone, Bran. I have several thousand people inside the city right now, waiting for me to kill Vila Mushadan. When I do, they will take the palace and another man will take the vila's place. He is a decent and honorable man who will treat everyone as human beings and not as animals. I am not asking you or your people to fight, only that you do not raise a weapon against him. This is a big city and I do not know its internal politics or what will happen after the vila is dead. However, there is one absolute certainty. Vila Mushadan is enjoying the last few moments of his life before he dies. When that happens, I need you to tell everyone not to resist. Just put down your weapons and stay out of the way."

Bran shuddered as Azerick's demonic-laced words washed over him. "All right, Azerick. I'll see what I can do."

The two Valerians reached the grand doors of the main palace entrance. Bran handed Azerick off to another guard to show him to the vila while he went to carry out the sorcerer's instructions. The palace was built on a scale Azerick had only seen at the Academy, not just the Magus Academy, but all three branches combined, and was laid out upon grounds that would nearly accommodate the entire city of North Haven.

Such splendor was lost upon the sorcerer as his anger continued to roil within him. All he saw was the endless miles of marble that constituted the prison in which his dearest friends and family were being held against their will. Klaraxis, the demon that Azerick held eternally in check, fed upon Azerick's anger and demanded that he release him to inflict suffering such as only he could conceive and exact.

As he expected, his escort bade him to wait in an anteroom for the vila's summons. Men like the vila would never permit anyone an immediate audience. To do so would imply that the vila was of a lower status. By making Azerick wait, he was sending a clear message that he was the undisputed ruler here and that Azerick was the one being graced with the luxury of meeting him.

Azerick gripped the black gem in his pocket and sent General Baneford a quick message to ensure his people were in place. When Azerick was permitted entry to see Mushadan, he would send him the order to move. It would be nearly two hours before he sent that order.

It took longer than Azerick had expected, but eventually Mushadan's curiosity overcame his desire to show his visitor exactly how little he thought of him or his message. A man in black and purple robes entered the antechamber and gestured for Azerick to follow.

Azerick strode down the center of the enormous room, crossed over the small bridge splitting the pool of water, and looked up at the man reclining upon a sofa atop a high dais. He flicked his eyes around the room and took in every detail. At least twenty men and women stood within the room wearing the same black and plum robes. Azerick recognized them as Mushadan's pet wizards and possibly a sorcerer or two as well, from what he was able to garner from their auras.

They were equally spaced along the walls to each side of where Azerick stood. Three stood upon the dais that occupied the entire rear of the chamber. A man stood to Mushadan's left while a woman stood to his right, and next to her was Ellyssa. Azerick took note of the gold chains running from the gold choker around her neck to the gold bracelets on her wrists.

He saw that they all wore these same accoutrements except that the woman also wore a ring with a tiny chain attached to her bracelet. When the vila raised his hand to plop a strawberry into his mouth, Azerick saw that he wore rings on every finger of both hands and each of them were attached to identical bracelets.

Wrapped around the left end of the sofa was Sandy. She too wore a golden collar, but larger and sporting spikes not just around the outside, but the inside as well. These would certainly dig painfully into her scales when someone jerked the stout chain attached to it. For now, the end of the chain simply hung from a peg on the end of the sofa.

He saw that her scales bore several scuffs and scratches and she was even missing a few in several places as if she had been fighting. There were cuts and bruises evident on the skin beneath those missing scales.

Standing miserably on the left corner of the platform was Wolf. He too was chained, but his looked of more ordinary make and were used simply to keep him from running off. Azerick imagined that the half-elf had tried to escape repeatedly no matter the threat of punishment. His was a spirit that would simply not be constrained. He looked gaunt and beaten down. The weight of Ghost's death showed in his hollow eyes and hopeless face.

Azerick studied Ellyssa's downturned face and saw dark, sunken eyes that shone without a hint of the fiery spark they once held. A brief, sorrow-laden glimpse was all she gave him as a sign of recognition. She too showed visible signs of abuse by way of bruises and scrapes on her face and hands. She also looked as though she had not eaten or slept in days. The fact that Azerick was able to keep from lashing out and destroying the vila this very instant was a miracle worthy of the gods.

Azerick made a small bow and introduced himself with masterfully feigned civility. "Vila Mushadan, I am Azerick Giles, Master of the orphans' academy in North Haven. I come to bid you release the three who stand upon your dais."

The woman studied Azerick for a moment and then leaned down and whispered something to Mushadan.

"What do you offer me for their freedom?" the vila asked in slightly accented Valerian.

"I have wealth. Name your price and you shall have it."

Mushadan laughed heartily. "Surely you do not think you have so much riches you could tempt me?" he asked with a wave indicating the wealth of his palace. "No, but perhaps you do have something more valuable to me and my goals."

"What is it, Vila? If it is mine to give, you shall have it," Azerick swore.

"My chain mistress says you are a sorcerer of extraordinary power. Your girl is strong, but a pale shadow of yourself. I would hate to lose the dragon, but she is young and it will be years before she is truly useful as more than a curiosity, and the half-elf is nearly dead already. What I want is you, sorcerer."

"If I agree to become yours, you will allow the three of them to go free and return to Valeria?"

"Azerick, no!" Ellyssa shouted.

Misha made a small gesture with the hand upon which the ring resided and Ellyssa fell to the ground, writhing in apparent agony for several seconds. When the chain mistress ceased punishing the girl for her interruption, Vila Mushadan continued.

"Become mine, help me seize the throne, and they shall go free. You have my word as vila."

Azerick gazed into the man's eyes and knew it for the lie that it was. He then looked around the vast hall at the score of spellcasters the vila had at his command and knew there was little recourse but to accept his offer.

"Very well, I accept. I give you my word that I shall be yours to command if you free my family."

Mushadan sat up and clapped his hands loudly one time. "Sorcerer Azerick, I have no need for your word. All I need is for you to wear this lovely trinket."

One of the robed figures walked forth bearing a set of golden chains and bracelets upon a silk pillow. Azerick looked at the set of chains upon the pad then up into Ellyssa's face, streaked with twin rivers of tears streaming down her cheeks. He looked at the mage bearing the devices and nodded once.

Another wizard took up the choker and bracelets and affixed them in place upon Azerick's body. He immediately felt his ever-present connection to the Source severed. He reached out for it, willing it to return to his body, but felt nothing. The two wizards then stepped away and returned to their places near the wall.

"Tell me, sorcerer, why would you willingly walk into the viper's nest where only a fool would think he could come out unbitten?"

Azerick slowly turned his head as he spoke, directing his words to everyone standing within the hall. "Because I believe everyone has the right to freedom and dignity. A creature once enslaved me in a very similar manner to this, and I know the pain it causes to one's soul. I will never allow anyone, especially those I care about, to suffer as I did. Mushadan, that creature who enslaved me made a mistake, and for one instant, his control over me wavered. In that mere instant, I brutally slew him with my bare hands. You too will make a mistake one day, and when you do, I pray that those men and women you have enslaved and mistreated will rise up against you as I did against my master."

Mushadan clapped his hands and laughed. "A very good speech, sorcerer. But I am sure you have already noticed that your magic is lost to you. You shall only use it when and how I choose. You are spirited. I shall enjoy watching your breaking." The vila looked at Sandy and Ellyssa and gave a dramatic sigh. "Alas, but I must tell you that I have no intention of honoring our agreement. Why would I give up a talented wizard and my very own dragon for you when I can have you all? I hope you are not too disappointed in me."

Azerick smiled as he looked down at the golden bracelets on his wrists and shook his head. "Not really, Vila. I did not intend to honor my word either. Men such as you do not warrant such consideration."

"Ah, but as you can see only one of us shall reap the rewards of our duplicity."

"On that note, we are certainly in agreement."

The vila looked down at Azerick with a quizzical smile. "So you say. Why then do you still smile?"

Azerick looked up, his intense hazel-green eyes now blazing red with demonic fury. "Because you still think it is you." *Klaraxis, time to come out and play.*

Klaraxis, demon prince of the fifth circle of the abyss, second only to the dark goddess herself, leapt to the forefront of Azerick's consciousness. Reaching deep for his abyssal power, he sent tendrils of decaying magic against the shackles that bound him. Near-invisible strands of black energy slithered through the air like shadows creeping across the floor and along the walls and reached out for the golden chains that bound the wizards and dragon. When they touched the magical devices, they blackened and decayed, crumbling into useless dust in the blink of an eye.

For just a moment, the freed slaves looked at the vila and then at one another. In that instant, every man and woman there faced a fork in the paths of their destiny and warred within themselves for the correct one to choose.

Vila Mushadan raised a trembling, terrified hand and pointed at Azerick. "KILL H—!"

Mushadan never got the chance to finish his command as Sandy, swift as a leopard, pounced with a savage snarl and clamped her powerful maw upon the vila where his shoulder and neck met. Although he was a large man, Sandy slung him around like a furious child with a doll. With a toss of her powerful neck, she flung Mushadan's lifeless body off the dais to land with a great, bloody splash into the pool of the fountain below.

At the moment of their master's death, every man and woman there made their choice. Each of them chose to fight for their own reasons, whether it was for freedom or the sense of loyalty the vila had forced into them, they chose.

Klaraxis was only an instant slower to react than Sandy was. Summoning some of his most horrific power, he lashed out with both hands toward the two wizards standing atop the dais who were too slow in recovering from the shock of seeing Mushadan savaged and killed. Dark, magma-like strands wreathed with black flames flashed out and wrapped around Misha and the other wizard's waists like twin whips. The demon poured dark power into those strands and jerked, burning and cutting clean through the two bodies and sending the four halves flying in different directions.

Lightning, fire, and arcane bursts of power flashed across the room as the mages battled for freedom and misguided loyalty. Although the numbers were nearly even, the power shift was far from it. While wards deflected much of the power of those hurled spells, none could stand against the devastating power the demon lord unleashed. Azerick was only just able to control Klaraxis enough to prevent him from indiscriminately killing everyone in the room. He jerked at the demon's mental leash with all his will, keeping the demon pointed at those who fought against him.

Wolf snapped out of his depression and waded into the pool after the wolf's head sword buckled around Mushadan's waist. He turned the vila over to undo the buckle and saw a wizard raise a hand and point it at him, ready to strike him down. A black blur shot out from behind a column where a young mute serving boy had just been hiding and leapt upon the mage's back and tore into him. No one had really noticed that the boy had joined the serving staff a few weeks ago just as no one was likely to take note that he was gone.

Wolf ripped the sword belt from around the corpse and slogged through the water to where Ghost was ending the wizard's life. The half-elf practically leapt upon Ghost's back as he wrapped the wolf in a fierce hug.

"I thought you were dead, you big jerk!" Wolf sobbed as he buried his face in the thick black fur. "You have so much explaining to do when this over!" Ghost simply looked up at his friend with a big doggy grin.

Still standing upon the dais, Ellyssa lashed out in fury at those who foolishly tried to strike back at Azerick, pouring her grief, shame, and anger into every spell. The battle was as furious as it was short-lived. A few of the wizards loyal to the vila realized they had chosen the wrong path, reversed their decision, and chose to take cover and not continue fighting.

Devlin ran into the room just as Azerick fought to rein Klaraxis back in and the final exchanging of magic attacks ceased. Just over a dozen mages stood back, their hands up to defend themselves should the demon turn on them, despite knowing that such a gesture was futile.

One of the wizards, a woman, recognized the sorcerer as he entered and stood just behind and to Azerick's left. "Prince Devlin!"

Every Sumaran in the room knelt out of pure reflex. Devlin looked at the aftermath of the magic battle and the vila's floating body. He then directed his words to those who were kneeling.

"Go tell everyone that I have come to return this city to my brother, King Yusuf. Tell them to lay down their arms and not to resist the invaders. They are under my command and will not harm them or the citizens as long as they do not oppose them. Go, spread my command!"

The wizards, highest amongst the slaves and who often spoke with the vila's voice, raced out of the hall to do as Devlin commanded. Azerick nodded to his mentor then turned his eyes upon Ellyssa still standing atop the raised platform.

"Do you see now why I tell you the things I do? Do you understand the lesson I have tried so hard to teach you and that you have refused to learn? There are people fighting and dying right now for me because they know how important you are to me. Many of them came and risked their lives because you are important to them. Do you see now how everything you do can affect those who care about you? What you do, you never do alone as long as someone cares about you. You are never alone, and the consequences of your actions are never limited to yourself because the people who love you will never let you suffer them alone."

Ellyssa nodded, shuddering as her sobbing wracked her whole body. "Azerick, I'm so sor—"

She never got to finish her apology. A wizard, thought dead, raised a quavering arm at Azerick's back, and with her last ounce of strength, unleashed an awful silvery lance of pure power. Unprepared for the strike, it cut through his wards and defenses, burned through flesh and bone, and erupted out of his chest, shattering a section of marble in the far wall near the ceiling.

Devlin and Ellyssa were slightly faster than Sandy. Both casters struck at the prone mage with powerful spells. Sandy launched herself from the top of the dais with a single thrust of her powerful legs and wings, landed atop the woman's destroyed body, and savaged it until it was barely recognizable as ever having been human.

"Azerick!" Ellyssa screamed in anguished horror as she sprinted down the steps.

Azerick dropped to his knees and grinned with bemused wonder at the gaping, smoking hole in his chest before falling heavily onto his face. The only sound in the room was Ellyssa's sobbing and the clatter of his staff as it struck the marble floor.

Ellyssa slid to a kneeling stop and lifted Azerick's head upon her lap. "No! We have to do something!"

Devlin could only shake his head as he looked down at the weeping girl then at the dragon and the half-elf boy who walked toward them in stunned silence.

"We brought a cleric with us. Perhaps there is something he can do," the sorcerer told her.

Ellyssa looked up hopefully. "Brother Thomas is here? We have to get to him! Now!"

"Of course. Let us see if we can reach him."

Devlin knew his lie for it what it was. He did not know much about priestly power, but he knew that Azerick was beyond anything even the greatest of them could offer.

With Bran and Mushadan's wizards spreading the word to cease fighting, the battling in the streets wound down, with only sporadic outbursts of violence lasting beyond the first few hours after the fighting had erupted.

Devlin stayed in Bakhtaran long enough to help General Baneford create a treaty with his brother allowing the Valerian to assume the title of vila.

Brother Thomas wrapped Azerick's body in linen and used his magic to keep the body from going foul during the long voyage north. It was a somber time for everyone. Almost every man and woman who sailed with Azerick looked upon him as a friend. Azerick had saved many of them from a life of abject misery and poverty. He had saved their city from siege and the king they admired from usurpers. He was an icon of the kingdom, and now he was gone.

Worried that no one had seen Ellyssa for days, Allister went into the tiny cabin of the ship where she was holed up. He found her sitting on the small bunk, clutching Azerick's staff as if she feared someone might try to take it from her. Her eyes, already sallow and haunted from her breaking, now looked skeletal from days of not eating. Allister saw the untouched plates of food upon the small table and sighed.

"He loved you very much, you know. He would have given his life a thousand times to keep you safe and considered it a bargain well paid. I don't think he would want to see you give up and waste away like this. He wouldn't want you to punish yourself."

Ellyssa looked up with her sunken, red-rimmed eyes. "I hate you," she whispered.

"What's that, dear?"

"I hate you," she said more clearly. "It's the last thing I said to him. When he told me I couldn't go listen to the bard sing, I told him that I hated him. He died thinking that I hated him!"

Fresh sobs wracked her body as Allister held her tightly. "Oh, my dear, he knew you loved him. He looked upon you as his own daughter, and he knew you were just angry and hurting."

"I loved him so much, and I was so awful! I wish he had left me there! I wish I was dead instead. He did good things for people. All I ever did was cause trouble and think about myself! He deserved to live, not me."

"To him, leaving you there would have been worse than dying. Azerick lost many people he cared about, but he persevered. It helped make him strong. What he would want you to do now is to be strong too. If you want to honor him, if you truly want to show that you have finally learned what he taught you, then show him you can be strong. Did I ever tell you about how he and I first met? Talk about troublesome. Compared to him, you're an amateur."

Nearly three weeks later, a grim procession marched up the road toward the school. Miranda raced through the gates, an excited smile upon her face as she saw Ellyssa and Sandy. She cast her eyes about, stretched onto her tiptoes to look over the heads of those in the front of the procession, and looked for Azerick within the group. Her smile slowly faded as she took in the despondency etched upon everyone's face. When she saw the linen-wrapped body upon the bed of the wagon, her hands flew first to her face and then to the slightly swollen mound of her stomach.

"No," she muttered, shaking her head in denial.

Rusty tried to put a supporting arm around her but she angrily threw it off. "No!"

Miranda looked from the wagon to Ellyssa, and in that brief glance, a thousand words were spoken, a thousand accusations were hurled, and a thousand silent apologies begging for forgiveness were returned. Miranda turned and ran back through the gates, weeping a widow's mournful wail.

Ellyssa wanted nothing other than to crumble to the ground and let death take her then and there, but she stood resolute. She would be like Azerick. She would not break, she would learn everything she could, and she would hunt down and kill everyone responsible. The people of Valeria lived in fear of these slavers, but soon, she would give them something to fear. She would make it her sole purpose in life until their entire dastardly trade was nothing but a memory wrapped in the terror she would bring them all.

EPILOGUE

Klaraxis felt his spirit plummeting back toward the abyss the instant Azerick died. He raged and cursed the foolish mortal for failing to keep his host body alive. Klaraxis had hoped for several more years of inflicting pain and death upon the mortal realm. Souls sent to the abyss by his hand went straight to the abyssal kingdom he ruled. Those souls sustained him, fed him, and increased his power. Once again, he would have to rely on those sent to him from followers, those begging for his favor within the mortal world, or those allotted to him by his dark queen.

He felt his spirit form return to the body he had been forced to leave behind. Somewhere within his vault chamber, he heard the voice of the pathetic demon he had left to tend to his physical form.

"Oh look, him so pretty," Skulk cooed. "Does the big blattazuu's butt want to give Skulk a kiss? Yes he does."

Klaraxis opened his eyes just in time to see Skulk's bright red posterior descending toward his face. The little fire demog let out a strangled croak as Klaraxis's massive onyx hand snaked up and encircled his neck.

The demon lord leapt from the stone plinth upon which his body rested and slammed Skulk into the wall. Klaraxis's red eyes blazed with barely constrained fury as they bored into Skulk's wide, terrified yellow orbs. The demon lord unconsciously wiped the back of his hand across his mouth and saw a bright red waxy streak upon his ebony flesh.

"Did you put lip paint on me, you vile little vermin?" Klaraxis screamed in unbridled rage. "How long have you been abusing my body?"

Skulk croaked out, "Never, my great and beloved prince."

Klaraxis twisted Skulk around and discovered a perfect imprint of his lips upon Skulk's left butt cheek.

"Ack, once, my great and awful master."

"Skunk," Klaraxis grated in a tense but controlled voice, "the tortures I will inflict upon you shall be spoken in hushed, terrified whispers for all eternity."

I don't know, I think the color is rather fetching on you, Azerick spoke from within Klaraxis's mind.

Skulk fell to the floor, slipping from Klaraxis's stunned grip.

"No. NO!" The demon lord flew into a fit, thrashing around the room, knocking many objects from their shelves, and pounding himself in the head with his fists as if he could physically dislodge the interloper. "This is my body! You cannot possess me! You are dead, little sorcerer, dead!"

Yet here I am. You yourself told me that our spirits were irrevocably entwined. It appears you were correct. It also appears that although we have exchanged bodies, our roles shall remain the same. Now, get back in your cage, demon.

"NO!" Klaraxis shouted in a drawn-out scream of denial as Azerick once again forced him into that mental cage of nothingness that resided within his indomitable psyche.

Using the prince of lies' demonic power, Azerick shifted into the form of his own image. Azerick looked around the devastated treasure room with his hands on his hips.

"Well…crap," Azerick sighed, then strode from the room.

Far removed in what could only be described as the abyss's opposite realm, four gods stood in conference discussing the fate of the mortals and the future of their own existence.

"It appears Jarvin has survived his tempering," Sharrellan, goddess of death, said.

Solarian nodded. "He has become what his people desperately needed. As long as he can hold his tempering, the mortals may yet stay united long enough to face our great enemy. What of the sorcerer? He did not come to me so I must surmise that you have him?"

"I do indeed."

"And is he whole?"

Sharrellan smiled. "Klaraxis was still weak when he returned from his little vacation and the sorcerer was able to dominate him. Whether he can continue to do so is largely up to him. If he is careless or rash, as he has shown a great propensity to be, Klaraxis may yet regain control."

Serron, god of the seas, was relaxing in an enormous silvery pool and spoke. "We have taken a great risk sacrificing the sorcerer's body and gambling that he will be able to control the demon."

"It was necessary, as we all know. Despite his talent, he had no chance of facing what is to come as he was," Solarian answered. "The question now is will Lissandra be able to return him physically to the mortal realm?"

"She has done it once before," Sharrellan replied with a shrug.

"With someone of her own blood, and still it nearly killed her. To do it again will almost certainly accomplish exactly that," Ellanee said remorsefully. "Even knowing so, she will try. She knows as well as we that it must be done."

"To lose the last living guardian is a terrible thing. I pray it is worth it," Solarian said.

"It is. With the sorcerer in control of the demon's body, he and his offspring shall provide a weapon even greater than Lissandra to be used against the Scions," Sharrellan said. "Assuming of course that he has the strength to use it without Klaraxis gaining control. Azerick will find it far more challenging to keep the demon at bay within his own form. If he fails, we will have to find an alternative."

Solarian looked sternly at his dark counterpart. "Sharrellan, we all know you are capable of great treachery. Particularly when self-preservation is at stake. The Scions know this as well and will certainly seek to use you against us."

The goddess of darkness, lies, and deceit waved a hand dismissively. "I am not stupid. I know perfectly well that if I betray any of you, all that would mean is that I will be the last of us four to die.

The Scions will never allow us to exist, no matter what promises are made."

"Good. Then let us stand united and pray the races do as well so that we might have a chance of defeating our ancient enemy."

Far away, deep within the bowels of the fourth circle of the abyss, a shade watched with detachment as the demon overseer cruelly lashed the insubstantial forms of his fellow shades. The shades gathered beneath the massive ziggurat that belonged to the demonic master of the fourth ring, channeling their energy into its black walls, which acted as a sort of silo from which the lord of this part of the abyss could draw additional power when he needed it.

"What are you?" the overseer demanded with a crack of his whip.

"I am scum. I am nothing," the shade wailed mournfully.

None of the shades remembered who they once were, where they came from, or why they were even here. They knew only their own pain and tortured existence and to feed their energy into the black walls of their eternal prison.

Down the line, the demon continued abusing the shades, reminding them of what they were—nothing. They were nothing beyond a source of food and power for the demonic denizens of the abyss.

The shade watched the demon torment another not far from him. That shade was weaker than the others were. It was too weak or too lost in its own misery to answer. The overseer thrust his hand into the shadowy substance of the weak shade's form and consumed it. The shade found its voice then and wailed a hollow lament as the demon drew in its pitiful life force.

He was next. The shade felt more than heard a short but deep thrumming reverberate through his being. It was difficult for the shade to force his attention into a coherent thought. It was familiar. He knew it had something to do with what he once was and he clawed at the wispy memory with all his pathetic will. Then a single word entered his feeble mind. Sorcerer.

The shade realized the overseer was screaming at him. "What are you?"

Sorcerer, the shade thought and struggled to speak. "I am…"

"What are you, you worthless piece of filth?" the demon shouted again.

The shade tore at his foggy memory and grasped at another smoky strand of recognition. He looked down at the spectral appendage of his arm, used his will to extend and join the wispy tendrils that were his fingers into a curved, shadowy blade. Looking into the overseer's eyes, the shade thrust the ghostly blade into the demon's heart and pulled its life force into him hungrily.

"I am…the Rook! And I have a contract to fulfill."

Deep within the black shroud of the shade's spectral face, two faint pinpoints of blue light appeared like twin stars peeking through a cloud-covered night sky. The Rook was weak. He needed more power. He looked down at his spectral blade and then at the hundreds of shades milling aimlessly about the chamber and knew at once where to get it.

"I am coming for you, sorcerer."

To be continued in:
THE SORCERER'S ABYSS
Book Six of The Sorcerer's Path

FROM THE AUTHOR

I hope you enjoyed this tale and will try my other works. Feel free to look me up on Facebook! You can also check me out on my website http://brockdeskins.com/ where I write serial fiction, free for your enjoyment, and answer questions!

Author page:
https://www.amazon.com/Brock-Deskins/e/B005M6VQ1O

Facebook:
https://www.facebook.com/brocksbooks/

Twitter:
@brockdeskins

PLEASE <u>REVIEW</u> MY BOOKS (Especially if you liked it). Customer reviews are the primary means of enticing others to purchase them. I am dependent upon the sales of my books to earn a living that will allow me to continue writing stories that I hope bring you some measure of entertainment. Thank you for your support.

OTHER BOOKS BY BROCK E. DESKINS

The Sorcerer's Path is an epic fantasy series.

The Sorcerer's Ascension: Torn from a life of comfort and luxury, his family destroyed by political intrigues and aspirations, a young boy must quickly grow into a man before the deadly streets of Southport devour him. Follow Azerick through a page-turning adventure that pits him against thieves, thugs, murderers, and men of power that will stop at nothing to achieve their goals.

Azerick must fight just to survive, but for him survival is not enough. A hunger to avenge the wrongs committed against him burns deep within. But that is not all that lies within the young man. There is a power waiting to be unleashed that may be the key to achieving the justice and security he seeks--if it does not destroy him first.

The Sorcerer's Torment: Azerick flees The Academy but quickly falls prey to powerful beings that use his skills and power for their own amusement. What these creatures do not understand is the power of the young sorcerer's will and the lengths he will go to for vengeance. Despite becoming a prisoner, Azerick finds his first true love, but can he keep it?

The Sorcerer's Legacy: Azerick has found himself a home and tries to settle down. He takes on an apprentice and tries to put all the death and desire for vengeance behind him. But when the Rook finds him, Azerick is once again pulled back into Ulric's schemes. Knowing that all he has worked toward and everyone close to him is in danger as long as these schemes are ongoing; Azerick decides to put an end to it, once and for all.

The Sorcerer's Vengeance: After narrowly avoiding being killed in his own bed by the land's most feared assassin, Azerick leaves his school behind to find out who sent him and to put an end to the threat once and for all. Azerick's search will take him to the very pits of the abyss and back to unleash hellish fury upon those that threaten him.

The Sorcerer's Scourge: With the siege broken and Ulric dead, Azerick can finally relax, study his magic, and run his school in peace. Unfortunately, Jarvin's reign is far from uncontested and the true usurper decides to make his move. Jarvin escapes with help from an unlikely source—a vampire named Landrin who still clings tenaciously to his own humanity. While Azerick and a large force from North Haven race to save the king in exile, evil forces are preparing to unleash a nightmare upon the kingdom that may well destroy them all.

The Sorcerer's Abyss: Now the master of the Fifth Circle of the abyss, Azerick is challenged by another demon lord for supremacy. Azerick must face this threat as well as his innermost demons, all the while searching for a way to escape his hellish prison.

Ellyssa fears she is going insane as she plagued by nightmares of her capture and enslavement. Deciding the key to saving herself lies in the total destruction of the object of her fears, she embarks on a crusade to find and kill the slaver, Captain Jake, and eradicate the slave trade.

Ellyssa's nightmares and battles spill out onto the streets of North Haven and gains the attention of The Academy. Fearing Azerick's school is turning out rogue wizards, The Academy decides to hunt down and destroy the rogue and place the school within their control.

The Sorcerer's Return: Azerick has come back from the abyss in order to try to unite all the races against the return of the old gods who seek to destroy them and subjugate the few they allow to survive a brutal purging. However, fighting ancient gods may be the least of his troubles as he battles to save a fractured kingdom, a brilliant son traveling a dark path, and the splintered soul of his own humanity.

The Sorcerer's Destiny: Brutally purged of his demonic influence, Azerick continues the struggle of uniting the kingdom to face the coming of the Scions, ancient gods banished by the mortal races during the Great Revolution two thousand years ago. The fallen gods' prison is crumbling, and Azerick is powerless to stop them from breaking free and enacting their cataclysmic vengeance upon the world.

The humans must ally with the other races in a final battle against impossible odds while their entire world crumbles to the ground and is trod beneath the feet of an unstoppable foe. How can they set aside their distrust of each other when they fear the very person trying to save them?

Rise of the Order: Banished to the abyss after helping defeat the Scions and saving the world from eternal darkness, Azerick languishes in perpetual misery as Lord of the Fifth Circle. The denizens of his hellish realm view him as a usurper and outsider. The chaotic creatures form an alliance with one goal in mind: destroy Azerick Giles, but Sharrellan stands in their way.

A powerful spell tears through the demonic planes, and when the dust settles, the dark goddess is nowhere to be found. It is up to Azerick to return her to her seat of power, but he has a price: return him to his mortal form and send him home.

Back home, a vast empire is on a crusade to conquer the world, and it has set its sights on Valeria. Their goal is to unite the world under a single banner, eradicate the spawn infestation unleashed by the Scions, and replace the gods who they feel have forsaken them with their mystical rulers.

Can Azerick save the dark goddess from the clutches of her demonic subjects and become mortal once again? Will he have the power to protect his people from The Order if he does?

Descent Into Chaos: The Order has arrived in force, and the fate of Valeria, and perhaps all the world, is poised to come under their iron-fisted control. Azerick and Daebian are forced to flee Southport and make a contentious alliance when King Miles capitulates to the invaders. Reduced to insurgent warfare, Azerick and his allies attempt to battle The Order's vastly superior forces in a series of hit and run strikes, but the enemy legions may not be his biggest threat.

Princess Sylvian Attar, daughter to The Order's godlike emperor and empress, has taken a personal interest in Azerick. Herself a powerful sorceress, Sylvian hunts Azerick in hopes of removing Valeria's legendary hero from the battlefield thus sapping her enemies' will to fight. Azerick decides there is but one course of action he can take against this unstoppable foe. It was time to inject a little chaos into The Order.

Brooklyn Shadows is a modern-day vampire tale. Full of action and snarky dialogue, Brooklyn Shadows is an enjoyable read for anyone who enjoys the supernatural underworld and butt-kicking vampires.

Shrouds of Darkness (Brooklyn Shadows Book 1) Leo Malone has been a vampire for the better part of the twentieth century. Once a prominent Sherriff (vampire cop), he now earns his living as a private eye and occasional bodyguard for anyone that requires some serious protection. Leo is hired by the daughter of a mob accountant who has gone missing.

The fact that her father is also a werewolf has Leo following a trail of grisly murders that will lead him through a web of intrigue and conspiracy involving his fellow vampires and the local werewolves that make New York their home, all the while trying to keep one particularly determined cop off his back and himself out of jail. Leo is not some pretty-boy vampire that all the girls ogle over, but a hard-eyed, remorseless killing machine who does not take crap from anyone.

Blood Conspiracy (Brooklyn Shadows Book 2): While dealing with the aftermath of the failed vampire council coup, Leo discovers that the modified Cure has fallen into the hands of a black ops government project designed to create vampiric super soldiers. When the inevitable happens, the off-book Homeland Security operation forcefully enlists Leo to help them resolve the situation. Worse yet, he has to work not only with an antagonistic werewolf named Meat, he is reunited with his hated creator, Lesile.

Primacy of Darkness (Brooklyn Shadows Book 3): Jack the Ripper, sadistic madman of old London, once thought long dead, has returned to New York in an effort to quench his thirst for blood and mayhem. When the city's vampire enclave finds itself insufficient to deal with a madman of Jack's caliber, Vincent, the enclave head, enlists Leo Malone to put the maniac down before he reveals the existence of vampires as he throws the city into the throes of chaos and terror. Leo soon finds that Jack is not the only monster with which he must contend. A ghost from his past has also seemingly crawled from its grave and seeks to put an end to him and the rest of his kind.

The Transcended Chronicles is the story of an outlandish young man as he goes from being a troublesome youth to one of the kingdom's greatest secret agents. Blessed (or cursed) with an amazing ability to both fight and abuse his body with every conceivable vice known to man, Garran Holt is either the kingdom's greatest hero or its biggest embarrassment.

The Miscreant (The Transcended Chronicles Book 1): Garran Holt is a troubled young man. Unable to tolerate his self-destructive ways, his mother sells him into indentured servitude as part of a work crew building King Remiel's new trade road. When mercenaries sent to disrupt the road's construction attack his work camp, Garran discovers an inner power capable of turning him into a warrior of unparalleled ability. When the leader of his work crew recognizes Garran as being one of the transcended (a fighter able to slip into the swifter currents of time), he is trained as an agent, one of the kingdom's elite spies. Crude, abrasive, and deeply committed to destroying himself with drugs, alcohol, and debauchery, Garran might be the kingdom's only hope against falling to The Guild, the powerful trade cartel bent on becoming the true and undisputed power in the land.

The Agent (The Transcended Chronicles Book 2): The Guild rules the kingdom through their puppet monarch, and Garran must race to save the last living heir to the throne before the powerful syndicate's assassins complete their extermination of anyone who could oppose them. Garran and Prince Adam Altena struggle to find allies in hopes of rescuing Adam's sister, who was forced to marry the usurper in order to prevent even the thought of rebellion, and raise an army capable of defeating The Guild. With The Guild now in control of Anatolia's powerful army as well as their legion of mercenaries, their future is grim. How can a disreputable agent and a deposed prince convince their neighboring rulers to oppose The Guild, an organization that has had them cowed for decades?

Empire of Masks is an exciting and explosive new series that takes place in the world of Hedon and takes you across the land of Eidolan where ships sail through the skies and men and women wage war with magic, swords, muskets, and cannons.

<u>**Highlords of Phaer**</u> **(Book one of Empire of Masks):** Born a slave, descended of kings, Jareen Velarius just wants to provide the best life he can for his family, but Eidolan is a realm that challenges even the most stalwart of souls. Caught between his masters and those brave or foolish enough to strike against them, Jareen struggles to reconcile his role as a dutiful slave with that of a man who desires to be free. His goal: to return his people to a life stolen by the highlords more than a millennium ago.

Auberon Victore, sorcerer, alchemist, son of a powerful overlord, and Jareen's master, creates an alchemic compound he is certain will change the world; he just does not know how. Jareen sees it for the weapon that could break the sorcerers' iron grasp wrapped around the necks of every lowborn in the empire. It will change the world, but not in the way his master desires.

Across the Tempest Sea, a mighty storm has raged for a thousand years, keeping a terrible, long-forgotten enemy at bay, an enemy whose cruelty knows no bounds. Only the perpetual storm and their fear of the sorcerer highlords keep the Necrophages from returning to Eidolan and cloaking the empire in death and darkness. But the tempest is waning, and the dissidents' freedom may well come at the cost of their total destruction.

<u>**Nightbird**</u>: The Great Revolution ended the highlords' tyranny two hundred years ago, but the legacy of that epic war, and that of the principal architects' descendants, lives on. With the highlords' death and their taking magic, as it was once known, to their graves, Eidolan

fell into a time of darkness and its cities lived in isolation. However, some people, dubbed arcanists, discovered a new form of magic and the airships returned to the skies, rejoining the cities in trade as well as conspiracy, but a new darkness, more dreadful and deadly than any they faced before, is coming.

Kiera is a fifteen-year-old nightbird, one of many who flit about after dark, stealing whatever they can find in order to survive. She lives on a derelict airship in the poorest part of the city with Wesley, a young man who plies his trade as an escort to wealthy older women, and his little brother Russel, an autistic savant who communicates only through sign but who could secretly be the most powerful techno-arcanist the empire has ever known. Deep in debt to the underlord Nimat, Kiera dives into evermore dangerous schemes that put her at the heart of a secret war that could spell the destruction of not just the city, but the very empire.

Kiera is caught in the center of several factions on the brink of war. When she can no longer tell friend from enemy, there is only one side she can trust—her own.

Mourningbird: A creature of darkness lurks in the shadows of Velaroth, wearing the skin of its victims, and grips the city in terror. Dorian, a Necrophage bent on sowing chaos and paving the way for his people's invasion, has declared war on the humans of Eidolan, and there appears to be no one capable of stopping him.

Kiera's world is shattered by those who hold power, and she is forced to seek an ally. The nightbird is coming into power of her own, but can she stay alive long enough to seize it? Russel's behavior has taken a turn for the worse, and his actions have drawn the attention of those who would use his amazing talents for their own gain…and everyone else's loss.

The battle for Velaroth, and perhaps the world, has begun. Who will win? Who will live to mourn the dead? Will there be anything left for the victor to claim as their prize?

Standalone books

<u>The Portal</u> is a fun and exciting story of some less than popular teenagers that accidentally open a portal to a mystical land during one of their role-playing games. Drew, a dour and anti-establishment teenager, is pulled through and captured by evil creatures lying in wait on the other side. Now it is up to his friends and older brother to rescue him, but who will rescue Drew's captors from him?

<u>Amelia (Battle for Ardentia)</u>: Amelia is a precocious, ten-year-old girl with a powerful imagination. In her alter-ego guise of a demi-goddess warrior princess, Amelia fights against a powerful demonic sorcerer named Romut and his horde of monsters in a never ending series of battles to protect the people of her imaginary world. However, the true battle strikes home when Amelia is diagnosed with a brain tumor. Now Amelia must fight not just the evil living in her imagination, but for her very life.

ABOUT THE AUTHOR

Brock Deskins was born in a small town located in rural Oregon. At age twenty, he joined the army and served as an M1A1 tank crewman, dental specialist, and computer analyst. While in the military, he became an accomplished traveler, husband, and father of three wonderful children. His military career completed, attended college to brush up on his skills as a computer analyst and gain new skills as a writer. Brock received his degree in computer networking and is now devoting his full time and limited attention span to writing.

BIBLIOGRAPHY

THE SORCERER'S PATH
The Sorcerer's Ascension
The Sorcerer's Torment
The Sorcerer's Legacy
The Sorcerer's Vengeance
The Sorcerer's Scourge
The Sorcerer's Abyss
The Sorcerer's Return

The Sorcerer's Destiny
Rise of the Order
Descent Into Chaos

BROOKLYN SHADOWS
Shrouds of Darkness
Blood Conspiracy

THE TRANSCENDED CHRONICLES
The Miscreant
The Agent

EMPIRE OF MASKS
Highlords of Phaer
Nightbird
Mourningbird

OTHER BOOKS BY BROCK E. DESKINS
The Portal
Amelia: Battle for Ardentia

Curious about other Crossroad Press books? Stop by our website:
http://crossroadpress.com
We offer quality writing
in digital, audio, and print formats.

Subscribe to our newsletter on the website homepage and receive a
free eBook.